The Leaf Slide

A novel by

Tony Hunt

Max Wordsworth
the reluctant
Lakeland Detective

For Wendy – who made everything possible

This book is a work of fiction

The Amazon Endure typeface was designed by 2K/DENMARK in 2025.

Template id: ST-414D415A-25-A01

Printed in The United States

ISBN: 9798284747025

One

They had parked their car as near to the caves as possible, turning left over Pelter Bridge from the main road and then almost immediately making a right turn. Driving past some workers' cottages on the left, they had carried on to the gate that normally would have prevented them from getting any nearer to Rydal Water.

The gate had been forced open, its padlock sheared, but both men realised they would still have to walk the rest of the way: their pool car would have wrecked its suspension if they tried to drive any further.

While passing the cottages, all of which appeared to be occupied, Max had noticed the Range Rovers and assorted large new SUVs parked outside the front doors of those workers' cottages. Workers? Maybe once upon a time, but not any longer. Workers around here couldn't afford to buy properties like these. They would all be holiday lets now; perfect for middle-class metropolitan families enjoying the simple life for a few days.

It was a beautiful Lakeland morning, if a little early for Max's taste. The call from the duty officer had woken him at 0615, and although it could have been midday, so bright was the morning sun, Max's body knew that it had been robbed of at least one hour's much-needed sleep.

'Why didn't you tell me to wear my boots?' snapped Max at no-one in particular as he slipped on some moss beneath his feet.

He had been heard: 'I did tell you, sir. I sent you a text.'

'If we were all as clever as you, Debesh, the world would be a much happier place. How much further?'

'The path is a bit steep here, but the caves are just round that bend.' DS Datta was in solicitous mode as he realised his boss was having some difficulty keeping his feet; his ordinary outdoor shoes no match for the loose shingle that covered the path up to Rydal caves.

That shingle, plus the moss-covered boulders that they both had to negotiate was the cause of Max Wordsworth's annoyance. Debesh didn't want to annoy the DCI more than he had to, because an irascible Wordsworth wasn't pleasant company.

Rounding the bend at the top of a steep incline, the two men came across the first signs of the incident. The area had already been taped off, and various official-looking people, some in white overalls, their slow movements lending an ethereal presence to the atmosphere like clouds that had lost their way, were attending to their duties.

An elderly lady with a dog was sitting on a rock a few yards away and was being looked after by a female police officer.

'DS Datta and DCI Wordsworth.' Debesh flashed his warrant card and continued, 'What do you have for us?'

'Good morning, sir. WPC Melling. This is the lady who discovered the body.'

Max and Debesh looked towards their witness who was nervously petting an elderly Labrador bitch and looking quizzically towards the two men. The tin foil survival blanket covering her frail body along with her nervous body language were both signalling a recently experienced trauma.

'I didn't exactly 'discover' the body, officer. It's hanging there for anyone to see. I must have been the first person to come across it, that's all.'

She was still in shock, her eyes searching for comfort and maybe for affirmation from the three police officers, but her hunched demeanour and passive body language suggested that she had been deeply affected.

Max was the first to engage, 'I'm DI Wordsworth - Max. And you are?'

'Marjorie, Marjorie Bath.'

'Pleased to meet you, Mrs Bath.'

'It's 'Miss'. I'm not married.'

'I apologise - Miss Bath. May I call you Marjorie?'

'If you insist.'

'I don't insist. I simply thought ...'

'I would prefer Miss Bath if it's all the same to you.'

'Certainly madam, forgive me. Tell me, Miss Bath, when did you come across the body?'

'She wasn't dead when I arrived! I tried to get to her - I did try!'

Max and Debesh looked into the anguished eyes of the tiny lady who had stood up and was now moving towards them. She was shivering; obviously very cold. Max noticed that her plaid skirt, woven on a Scottish island and peculiar to ladies of a certain age, was damp around the hem.

'I think that we should get you to somewhere warmer than here, madam. PC Melling, please arrange to have Miss Bath taken to where she can get a cup of tea.'

She knew you were on your way and asked to stay until your arrival, sir.'

'Well, we've arrived. Now please arrange for her to go somewhere warmer, and make sure that she gets something to drink.'

'I'd rather stay here, officer.' For a very insignificant looking little lady, this one had some fire in her belly.

'Maybe you would, Miss Bath, and I would prefer it too. However, you look to be in shock, and I am concerned that you might get hypothermia if you stay here. Do you live far away?'

'No, I live round the back of Grasmere. It's only about a mile away if I go by the Terrace.'

Wordsworth knew she was referring to Loughrigg Terrace, a very popular path round the back of Rydal and Grasmere.

'Where is your vehicle, Constable?'

'It's at the Glen Rothay, sir. Just down there.' The officer pointed towards the main road at the other side of the lake and the small hotel where she had parked her patrol car.

'OK. I want you to walk Miss Bath down to your car and then take her straight home.'

Turning to the subject of their conversation Max said, 'I think you should get changed and into something warm and dry, Miss Bath. DS Datta and I will come to see you later today. Is that all right with you?'

'I wanted you to know that I tried to help the girl, but I couldn't get to her. I felt so helpless. I shouted, but nobody was anywhere near.'

'This must have all come as a terrible shock, and I will ask you about every last detail. But we don't want you ending up with pneumonia, do we?' Max smiled, and his smile was rewarded.

'Yes, officer. I do feel slightly shaky. And I'm starting to feel chilly too.'

'WPC Melling. Off you go. Make sure Miss Bath gets home, and if she will allow you to, make her a cup of tea before you leave.'

'I did try to help her as much as I could - I honestly did try, officer.'

'I know you did, Miss Bath. I know you did.'

'And you will come to my house?'

'Yes, madam. DS Datta and I will come to see you as soon as we finish our preliminary enquiries here.'

'Good. Thank you. I'll appreciate that. I'm still a little confused now. It's all been such a shock...'

'You've been very strong,' Max wasn't very good at this stuff. 'Lacking empathy' had appeared on more than one of his appraisals, and he was aware of this. This was an opportunity, and he wanted to take it. Sadly, Miss Bath immediately blew his best intentions out of the water.

'May I ask one question, Detective Inspector?'

'Of course, you may, Miss Bath.'

'Your name. 'Wordsworth', are you related in any way to...?'

'William? No, madam, I'm not. At least as far as I know. And I might as well tell you something else too. I have no interest either in him or his poetry. I dislike coming here for that reason too because people always ask, and to be quite honest with you...'

'It was only a polite question, officer.'

'It was madam. And I apologise - again. I hope to see you later. DS Datta We need to get on now. WPC Melling, see Miss Bath to her home now. Radio in when she is settled.'

'Yes sir.'

The two detectives moved on up the hill to their original objective, the caves overlooking Rydal Water. Debesh was still exercised about Max and the tetchy way he'd responded to Miss Bath's last question.

'That was a bit strong, sir. She was only being polite.'

'It gets on my tits, Debesh. They're obsessed about it up here.'

'There aren't that many people with your surname, sir. I mean, we're right in the middle of all that - everybody's bound to ask, aren't they?'

'And that's why I hate working in the Lakes. Give me the back streets of Preston any time.'

Debesh wasn't going to give up on this. He'd worked with DI Wordsworth some years ago and had experienced this kind of response to the question before. 'If I wasn't talking to my boss at this moment, I'd be telling him to get over it.'

'You are talking to your boss, DS Datta - and I am over it. Can we now get some work done?'

The two men had bickered their way past the first of the Rydal caves and were now up to the one which was to become the focus of their attention.

Another uniformed police officer, this time male, gestured towards the sight that had so shocked Miss Bath when she had chanced upon it.

A climber's rope was hanging from the top of the sheer cliff face which stretched for ten yards or more above the cave's opening. The rope was attached to the ankles of young female, and she was hanging upside down, her nightdress failing entirely to conceal her long, tanned legs. The body was dangling over a pool of water at the entrance to the cave, her head and shoulders lost under the surface.

'That's what disturbed her so much.' Debesh now understood why Miss Bath was so upset. 'She was alive.'

'And she couldn't get near,' Max added. This little old lady out walking her dog had come across the flailing body of a girl, suspended in such a way that only her head and shoulders were covered by the water.

Alive when strung up there, what had been her death throes - her trying and eventually failing to keep her head above the water - had been the agonising vision that Miss Bath was going to have playing itself over and over every day for the rest of her life.

DS Datta was the first to comment: 'She must have watched her die. No wonder she's in shock.'

Max acknowledged his partner's observation, 'We'll get an exact picture later when we go and see her. But look at the scene, Debesh. Is there anything that surprises you?'

'Apart from the body of a young woman swaying over a pool of water, you mean?'

'Smart arse! Look carefully. See anything? Tell me what you see.'

Debesh looked at the body. Two of the forensics team, the giveaway being their white coveralls, were at the top of the ten-metre cliff.

At that moment, they released the rope holding the girl, and the body slid slowly into the arms of two other men who'd managed to get close by immersing themselves in the freezing waters. Max noticed that the girl's mouth and ankles had been taped, as had her hands.

'Wet suits - good call!' Debesh's observation, 'We don't want our guys getting hypothermia too.'

'Well spotted, Debesh - but have you noticed anything else?'

'Not sure what you mean, sir.'

Max took a step forward, looked to see that the recovery of the body was complete, and then turned his attention to the men at the top of the cliff and called out, 'What was that rope attached to?'

'Pitons, sir!' One of the forensics men was coiling the rope while his colleague prepared a large, white evidence bag to contain it. 'Fixed to pitons. There are five or six of them up at the back here. They've been drilled in. This patch of cliff is used for abseiling practice - these pitons are a permanent feature.'

Max addressed his junior colleague once again, 'So, DS Datta, what do you deduce from that information?'

'Prior knowledge, sir. Somebody knew those pitons were there.'

'Exactly. Anything else?'

'Not sure.' Datta looked around. Nothing sprang to mind, 'I'm struggling now - this is a bit rarefied for me, sir, nosebleed.'

Max smiled, 'I hope not. Think it through. What else can we deduce? Do the Sherlock Holmes thing; look at everything and glean as much as quickly as you can.'

'Sherlock...? Oh, I see what you mean.' And he did. Debesh was young but experienced. He knew that the first few hours of any investigation could provide the most significant results.

'It was planned, sir. Somebody was here before; they must have either scouted it out as a location or they were already familiar with it. You would have to measure it up - to get it right, I mean - and you would have to know about the pitons.'

'You said 'they'?'

'Yes, sir, they. I suppose one person could do the measuring and then throw her over the cliff. But how would one person get the body here - she was alive, remember? So, getting her here - probably by using the same route that we did, would need at least two people.'

Max wasn't so sure. 'There's that gate, near where we are parked. They could have brought a 4x4.'

'We parked behind Forensics. I looked at that gate, sir. I'd thought of driving them up here myself. A tractor could make it, I suppose. A quad bike would do it - an ordinary 4x4 would struggle. But I don't think the gate has been opened recently; the padlock on it hadn't been touched for ages. Forensics had to lug their kit up here the last part of the way.'

Debesh looked down at Max's scuffed shoes and gave him a wry smile, 'They won't be lugging it back. Perk of the job, the body, all the kit - and most of the Forensics team - they're going back to Kendal in luxury. Mountain Rescue have whistled up a helicopter for them.'

Lucky for some, thought Max. But he didn't want any distractions now; he was keen to capture as many insights as possible. 'OK, let's go with your theory for a moment. If you're right, and if they did leave a car at the gate, it means that they must have carried the girl, probably struggling - and the rope - up to here. Then they would lower her carefully down to the exact position where she would have to fight to keep her head above water.'

'The rope could have been placed here in advance, sir. And one person could have tied her to it and chucked her over - if it had all been carefully measured - sir.'

'Are you rubbishing your own theory, Sergeant?'

'No, sir - keeping the idea of a single perp in mind too - devil's advocate.'

'I'm a man, Debesh. I can only think of one thing at a time. Did Helen never tell you that? So, oblige me.'

'Sir. She was a young girl, and probably quite fit. She would be struggling, desperate to keep her head above the water, and it would have taken a long time before she was too exhausted to continue.'

Max and his colleague were reflecting on this gruesome thought as a zip-up black plastic body bag, now containing the remains of the young victim, was stretchered past them to the area where the helicopter would soon be landing.

Her last journey would be to the mortuary. Waiting for her there would be the final indignity of the post-mortem examination.

'I agree that it looks like it was all pre-planned,' Max continued, 'but

I don't think one man could have done it. There had to be at least two people involved.'

Debesh replied, 'You're probably right sir.'

Max looked at his colleague and gave him the long stare, 'It's a good job I don't take you too literally. We'll agree to disagree for now. Keep all options on the table.'

'Yes, sir.'

Max moved to the next matter that was troubling him. 'Something else we do know, though.'

'What's that sir?'

'It's a carefully chosen very public site; a place where she would be found quickly.'

'True.'

'They took one hell of a risk.'

'Of being seen? Yes sir. They did.'

'And the method of killing her was deliberately chosen.'

'Meaning?'

'This is a signal, isn't it?'

'A signal?'

'Yeah. This is for someone's benefit. She's been killed but killed in this very public way for a reason. Do we know who she is yet?'

Debesh shook his head, 'No sir, we don't.'

'As soon as we find out who she is, we should be get a better idea of the motivation behind this crime. We also need to check all CCTV cameras to see if any vehicle was seen approaching this site at around the time...'

'CCTV? Here? That's what I would call wishful thinking, sir. There isn't any. Most of this area doesn't even have a phone signal.'

'Old School policing, then. Get Uniform on the job. I want them to check all possible routes to here. Anything suspicious at all, we'll need to know about it. Also, any walkers other than our Miss Bath? If she was here when the girl died, it means that the people who did this must also have been nearby. I mean, how long would it take for the girl to give up and succumb?'

'I dread to think.'

'It could only have been minutes. Our little old lady might well have seen them. She could even be one of them, for heaven's sake.'

Debesh couldn't allow that line to go much further, 'Sir, that's a bit unreasonable, isn't it?'

'It's unlikely, but not impossible. We need to build a picture, get more evidence. There's a story here, and we're going to find out what it is. There's not all that much more that we can do now. And I've got that bloody hill to slide down - thanks to my wearing the wrong shoes and no helicopter rides being offered to me. Let's go.

'On the way, we'll make some calls, get ourselves organized, and maybe see if we can't use that old police station in Ambleside again as a base. Is it still operational?'

'I think so, sir.' Debesh paused and considered what his boss had just said before he ventured, 'To be honest, sir, that surprises me.'

'And why would that be, I wonder?'

Debesh was straight back at him. 'Ambleside police station, sir - because of the last time we worked there. The time that we - you - got it so wrong with that couple from the charity shop.'

They had almost reached the car; Max's feet were sore, and he had twisted his ankle once or twice, but he felt he had to begin to exorcise this ghost.

'If I was going to treat this lightly, I'd remind you that we both got commended because of that case - and I received a promotion.' But he wasn't going to treat it lightly; it had to be brought out into the open and dealt with.

The last time they were teamed up, he and Debesh had worked on another murder case in the little village of Ambleside, only a couple of miles from where they were now standing. The old police station to which Max had referred was in that village.

It was there that they'd brought a double murderer to justice. A local man had been tried and convicted of killing two people and he'd been sentenced to spend the rest of his life in prison (as he was over seventy years old at the time, that was a reasonable bet).

Max and Debesh (DI and DC at the time) were congratulated and rewarded: Max to the senior management team of the force with the rank of DCI, Debesh, too young for immediate promotion was commended and fast-tracked towards the rank of DS; all because of the success of that case.

Except that the convicted man was completely innocent. He'd been set up by his wife, and Max and his team had fallen for it. After a very acrimonious appeal case, the innocent man was freed. He'd then successfully sued the police force and had been awarded an embarrassingly large amount of compensation.

His former wife, now the main suspect in that case, had disappeared. Nobody truly knew where she was, but rumour had it that she was cruising around the South China sea with a new man.

So, it was with some surprise, and no little sense of trepidation that Max had accepted this latest assignment and, although he certainly wouldn't say it, he was delighted to be partnering Debesh again.

'The last time we worked together, you said you intended to transfer up here. How's that worked out?'

'Pretty well, sir. I love it. Helen and I have a small flat on the outskirts of Kendal.'

'Is she still working?' Helen had met the young man who was now her husband on the previous case. She had been the admin assistant and Debesh had completely fallen for her.

'She'll be starting back soon. She took her maternity leave, and then decided she wanted to be a full-time mum for a little longer.' Debesh smiled, 'The DS salary helps, so I should be thanking you.'

'No, you deserve it. I'm glad it came through. Maternity leave, you said? You're a dad? How old is ...?'

'Ellie? She's almost three now.'

'Good God! It's been longer than I thought.'

'Nearly five years, sir. How have you been?'

Max thought about this before answering. 'All in all, it's been OK. The promotion was a mixed blessing. Committees, paperwork - I bloody hate paperwork - but I've been involved with some interesting cases since the last time I was here...'

'This one is very unusual,' Debesh didn't mean to interrupt, but simply got his timing wrong, 'Murders don't happen here; I mean, they do happen, but there've only been about four or five in the last forty years or so.'

'You've fitted in here, haven't you?' Max smiled.

'Yes sir, I don't ever want to move. We love it and it's where we want Ellie to grow up.'

'It's got you Debesh, I can tell. I only wish I felt the same.'

What Max had said was true, the Lakes had 'got' Debesh; his life had changed completely.

He'd fallen head over heels in love with Helen during that first case. After it was over, Debesh had no intention of returning to Preston and Shilpa, his long-term girlfriend. He'd immediately dumped her, no guilt, he simply had to do it and had quickly moved to Kendal to be near his new love and his new life.

There was a huge family fallout after Debesh made that decision. Shilpa was not simply a girlfriend, but a young woman who Debesh's parents had chosen for him - the daughter of close family friends.

If asked directly, they would probably have denied that this was to be an arranged marriage, but their disappointment and anger when Debesh left Preston and moved to Kendal to be near Helen was all too real - all communication stopped.

Helen and Debesh were married, and their wedding was the last time they'd seen Max. Ellie, their first child, had come along eighteen months later.

The emergence of a grandchild into the family had gone a long way towards mending the bridges between Debesh and his family, and his mum and dad had even been up to Kendal to visit their son and his new family on a few occasions.

Max didn't have such a success story to relate. 'I wish I could say I've achieved half of what you have, Debesh. I'm in the same house - but now I'm single.'

'I thought that you ...'

'She moved out.'

'Oh, I'm sorry, sir.'

'Nothing to be sorry about. It's the job. It eats you up if you're not careful - and obviously I wasn't careful, was I?'

'I don't ...'

'I know. It's OK. But don't let me go down in flames without reason. Take heed, young man. You've a wife, a child and a life. Don't throw them away like I have.'

'No, sir. I won't.'

'I should now ask you to swear an oath and write that promise in blood, but back in the day I would have happily made such a promise. And look what happened to me. Come on, let's find a desk and see what information we've got to go on. Then we'll pop round to Grasmere to see Miss Bath. She should have warmed up by now.'

'OK sir. Do you think that we can use the Ambleside station as a base?'

'No idea. We'll check it out on our way back from Grasmere. But it would be convenient, wouldn't it?'

Two

It's Manchester airport a little after 0730; my Emirates overnight flight from Dubai lands punctually for a change, and I win the baggage carousel lottery for the first time in almost forever. Straight through immigration courtesy of the E gates working properly, I retrieve my car from the multi-storey car park and set off up the motorway, getting home in time to see the kids shooting out of the house and towards our woods.

'Hello Dad!' I say to nobody, certainly not to catch the attention of my children who are out of sight by now - sadly, not out of earshot. Shouting and yelling, making suggestions, rubbishing suggestions, and enjoying themselves like any kids should during their half-term holiday.

'They do love you, I promise.' That's Meg who's sneaked up from behind and put her arms around me. 'And I'm pleased to see you back, even if they aren't.' She smiles as she allows me to turn towards her and fold her into me. I love coming home.

'It would be good if they noticed me once, though. How long have I been away? Ten days?'

'Poor pet.' She holds me tight for a moment. 'They're secure. They love you - they don't need to go through the ritual when they've more important things to do. You'll get your cuddles later when they're ready. Oh, that might not be tonight. They plan to sleep out.'

'Where?'

'Up the hill; near the tunnel. They've made a leaf slide to help them get their stuff up there. Come on, let's get your things in the wash. We'll have a coffee - and maybe later we can wander up to see what this adventure is all about.'

As we go through the more mundane activity of emptying my suitcase, collecting all the washing that needs doing, she explains how yesterday the kids made a leaf slide at the far end of the garden.

Meg kisses me and thanks me for her present - perfume, Issy Miyake. She was quite miffed last time I went away as I forgot to get her anything. There was a reason, but I couldn't explain it to her. I promised that next time - and here we are, and she's mollified. No, more than that, she's happy.

She brings me up to speed, 'They made their leaf slide yesterday, and it kept them busy until I called them in at about ten o'clock. You would have thought they would be tired, but no, they were all up again this morning, raring to go.'

Where they have chosen to build this leaf slide is way past the lawn at the back of the house in an area under the trees that must have about fifty years of accumulated leaves, twigs and assorted undergrowth. We never go there; nobody does. The reason we don't is because normally that whole area is a quagmire, and it's best left alone.

The recent unusually dry spell of summer weather has brought with it some unintended consequences, one of which is that the sun has managed to penetrate this area, drying the leaves to a depth of about six inches.

It's still damp below there, but for the first time in the whole of the ten years we've been living at the house, there's a carpet of crisp, dry leaves and twigs, and evidently, it's deep enough for one of our plastic snow sledges to come zooming down from the tunnel when pushed or pulled by an enthusiastic child.

After our coffee, and my unpacking duties completed, we decide to stroll over to the kids - the Mohammed to the mountain principle. We don't see them at first, but the noise points us in the obvious direction, and the dog adds to the clues that we pick up with his over-excited barking.

'Dad. Look at me!' It's not quite a blur, but if Joe had hit either of us as he came zooming past, he would have knocked us over.

'You be careful - I don't want you hurting yourself or me.'

'Look, Dad - it's so cool. It's our leaf slide. I wish the leaves were dry like this all the time, Dad. We can take our things up to the tent, and we can slide down to get more stuff.'

'Dad!' Another one, this time, one of the girls, Bella, 'Dad - can we go in the tunnel?'

I have to put a block on that. 'No!' I say, probably a little too loudly. 'You must stay away from the tunnel. It's not safe - it's dangerous to go into it. Do you understand me? All of you? Do you understand?'

A chorus of disapproval from all three of them, and in that special passive-aggressive, grumpy way that all kids have off to perfection. Don't you just love them?

Looking around, Meg and I decide we're simply not wanted. We say goodbye for the general benefit of anyone who might be interested, receiving nothing in reply, and walk back towards the house. As we take in the view of the lake, it says again - if it ever it needed saying - this house is my idea of absolute perfection. Every moment like this justifies the risks I take to make living here possible.

For the first time in my life, I've become happily aware of the way the seasons operate. In our garden we see it unfolding – nothing to do with me, just Nature doing its thing.

January brings the snowdrops I'd never noticed before but now yearn to see each year. Then we have the daffodils following on. Our garden has so many you can't count: the kids tried once but gave up when their numbers got into the thousands. Their yellow presence among the green is soon replaced by the emergence of the bluebells, again carpeting everywhere which, along with the flowering of the rhododendrons and azalea, means that we have a riot of colour to wake up to as we look out of our bedroom window.

Later in the year come the apples and the damson trees – when they deign to make an offering. Then it's the Rowan berries that light up for us before the woodland around us turns into its myriad shades of brown and gold. Autumn has arrived. And are you aware of how many shades of green there are? Coming to live in this magical place has given me a grounding I never had and that, coupled with the domesticity that Meg provides, creates the virtuous circle that I've striven for all my life.

Living here has made me appreciate the tiniest shifts - the mellowing of the grass, the appearance of new shoots, and the way the air seems to hold its breath before a storm. I find myself marking time by these natural signposts, each season unfurling its unique palette and rhythm. Summer afternoons are thick with the drone of bees and the laughter of our children, while autumn unfurls its smoky golds and russets, the woods thickly carpeted in leaves. Even the rain, which can be relentless, brings a hush that blankets the house and a gloss to the old stonework - a kind of quiet reassurance that this place is rooted solidly in its landscape.

We watch as the kids are weave themselves into this tapestry with the same persistent energy as the wildlife that scurries through the undergrowth. Their new game, their leaf slide, their tent among the trees – this is how kids should play – not hunched over tiny screens for hours and hours each day. Meg and I watch them with the quiet pride of gardeners witnessing the flourishing of a well-tended plot – as well as worrying ourselves silly.

And yes, we do have a tunnel, our very own tunnel. It was meticulously crafted in the same style as the Lakeland dry stone walls - those walls you can see winding their way mile after mile over the Cumbrian Fells. Take a closer look at them; these walls have stood for centuries all built entirely without mortar.

They used the same method in 1804 when they built our house, and it's still standing, its impressive presence 'commanding the view of the lake' as the estate agent's blurb said over two hundred years ago.

In a previous era, obviously one of abundant cheap labour, our tunnel was built to make it easier for the estate employees to get to work on time - not having to climb over the hill - saving, oh, I don't know, two minutes out of their twelve-hour day. No, really. It's not a tunnel through a hill of any consequence, in fact it's probably quicker to walk over the hill than through the tunnel.

So, it defies any logic; maybe an early experiment in job creation, possibly keeping the local bad lads out of trouble. More likely, it was a folly, some chap with more money than sense and a few spare labourers hanging around decided, 'I know what. We'll have a tunnel there. What larks!'

I own that tunnel now; it's part of our own woodland. Frank Blain, man of property! And nobody is more surprised than me - apart from Meg, that is. She's yet to be fully convinced that we're truly wealthy.

I have always left the tunnel alone and completely untouched as it no longer serves any purpose. It stretches under a hilly area of woodland and is probably about forty yards long.

The narrow pathway through it is two foot deep in mud and slime - nobody has used it for decades. I've thought of reinstating it, maybe making it into a garden feature, but it serves my purpose much better if that whole area is left completely alone.

All the old footpaths behind the house are overgrown; nobody uses them anymore. There's a road that allows our neighbours to drive to their cottages further up the valley, and walkers use it to get to Silver Howe, but no-one has a need to traipse through the tunnel. If anyone does come to my house for whatever reason, they use the drive as you would expect. In fact, if they were to come to the house via the tunnel, I'd be highly suspicious of them.

There's a muddy track around the back of the house; it's rarely used, and only by me as I lock the gate with a big padlock which makes it difficult for anyone else to go down there. There are lots of fallen trees there as nobody has done any kind of forestry stuff for years. Sometimes I take a bloke with me. He's local, Polish, and strong as an ox. I've a very old small tractor up there too with a digger attachment on the back.

Wojtek adapted the digger thing as a crane to move the larger logs, and he uses his chainsaw to fill a trailer with them. He then brings the logs back to the house where he stacks them. I pay him in cash, normally fifty quid, sometimes more. It's an arrangement that suits us both.

We've now stacked up enough wood to last for at least one generation, but Meg likes to see me being a countryman - I've got the Barbours, the Hunter wellies and everything. Even after all this time I am sure she thinks that I am a suburbanite at heart, and my living out here in the country miles from anywhere is some kind of unnatural act. She's entirely wrong for all sorts of reasons: I love it here.

The kids are on half term holiday from school and have staked their claim to the area a few yards above the tunnel. They've spent the last couple days making it their own. They even camped out there last night - pitched the tent themselves - the whole thing. Came back to the house to get something to eat and to use the bathroom - waking Meg up in the process. They also took Nip with them to act as a lookout.

Back at the house, I want to make a couple of calls, and I'm sure that Meg will want to take advantage of the children's absence to try to bring some kind of order to their bedrooms.

'Are you OK, Frank? I don't like you having to fly overnight. It's too tiring.'

'I'm fine. A little stiff, but not in a good way. You should have come with me.'

'Stupid person! And what about the three musketeers? Who would look after them?'

'Good point. We are having a slow waltz here - she never comes with me, but we both dance along. She couldn't accompany me for many reasons - and those reasons were nothing to do with her responsibilities to the children.

She looks pensive for a moment, but then she smiles and says, 'Also, you are a bit slow on the uptake.'

'Why?'

'Really, Frank? Why? Do I need to spell it out? With the children camping over there, you know that means the house is empty?' And she looks at me, her eyes catching mine. 'Maybe I can help your stiffness in a more interesting way?'

She can - and she does.

***

The kids' second sleep-out was a great success - as was our sleep-in. Later than we expected, the children all trooped back for breakfast, Nip the dog included. After stuffing their faces, they've now decided to go back to their tents. This time they are taking food and more blankets as they were cold last night, and books. Books!

They've also taken a couple of spades with them as they want to 'improve' their camp site; they've said that they are going to set up home there for a while. Their only complaint? Joe says that they can't get Wi-Fi up there; I don't know whether to laugh or cry.

To get their stuff up to the camp site, they've devised a transport system that allows them to enjoy lugging everything up to the steepest part of the garden.

That enjoyment is simply deferred gratification; coming from the knowledge that having off-loaded their burdens, they then get to speed back down to the lawn using their newly developed leaf slide.

While part of me thinks this is a great idea - peace and quiet at home, not having to continually moan at them about their bickering and their constant noise, another part of me is concerned for a different, entirely separate reason.

I don't want them to find the bodies.

It's entirely my fault, idiot that I am, but I never expected them to want to play there. I know that yes, they are kids, and I also know that kids love trees and mud. But it's perverse that they have chosen to play there in that part of the garden. We've over four acres, for heaven's sake!

There are so many other places, all much more suitable for camping out, and without the risk of their finding - or Nip finding - one or more of the bodies that I've buried there.

In my defence, they would have to dig quite deeply to find anything. I did anticipate that problem because badgers, foxes and God knows whatever else inhabit this whole area.

I dug deeply; when I say, 'I dug', I mean I used my little old tractor with its digger attachment. It was all part of the logging mission that Wojtek, my Polish guy, helped me with, but I gave him a couple of days off, so I commandeered the tractor and the trailer for this other purpose. And up until now, I thought I'd successfully achieved my objective.

It may well turn out to be fine - nothing to worry about, but with kids you never know. What if they decided to dig their own tunnel? I mean, the motivation for that is looking at them directly, isn't it? We've already got one tunnel, so conceptually, the model and the suggestion are staring them in the face. This is troubling, and part of me wants to put a brake on their adventures straight away.

There are four bodies buried not very far from the area that the children have colonised. Long story, short: I shouldn't have taken that job on. It was far too close to home, but when I decided it was better to disappear them completely rather than wait for them to be found in some random way, I decided to use that patch of land at the back of the house.

This happened just over a year ago, and everything worked out very well for my client and I received a large bonus. The client said that not only was it a clean job with no mess, but the complete disappearance of that whole family without any trace added, in his words, a 'piquant' quality. It's good to be appreciated, isn't it?

Funnily enough, I've a contact in a meat processing factory over near Maryport, and I immediately thought he was the solution. Ha! So many checks, so much Health and Safety - it stopped the Sweeny Todd option in its tracks. But here on my own land in the wooded part: nobody, absolutely nobody going there - ever - except me and my Polish bloke chopping wood in a perfectly legitimate way. And then along come my bloody kids. Honestly, it makes you despair; that damned leaf slide is troubling me.

There are three of them, the kids - one of each as I like to say when I'm being parental. Our oldest boy is Joe - he's Meg's from a previous relationship. Joe is eleven, about to start secondary school, and Meg and I are currently debating whether we should be sending him away to board or not.

I'm all for it: getting the little sod out of the way would be my preference, but Meg is worried that he might feel rejected because Joe is her son, not mine. Although I quite like him, the public-school idea holds many attractions for me, not least that I would be seeing much less of him and not hearing his incessant whining quite so often.

Is it other people's kids, I wonder? The twins whine too, probably even more than Joe - and in stereo. I don't find it that difficult to deal with. At least, not as difficult. I'm happier telling the twins to shut up and go away than I am telling Joe the same thing in the same way. And I'm happier cuddling it better with the twins too; I'm never comfortable doing that with Joe.

Chloe and Bella are the twins - eight years old, going on eighteen. Currently day girls at a local private school, and we intend that they will also be going away as boarders.

But not to the same school. This is Meg the mum for you; I think it's healthy, and I won't be raising any objections. You know how twins are often dressed in the same clothes, do the same things and are always together?

Right from the time they were born, and I'm now beginning to see the thinking behind this, Meg's always insisted on treating our girls as two separate individuals.

And I reckon she's right; they do have entirely different personalities. Our plan: 'plan' sounds too grand - our thoughts - are that they'll both go away to school, but to separate schools.

If it does work out, all three of our kids will be away at school for most of the year - I would consider that to be a result. Yay! Back of the net! Exactly what I'm looking for.

But what about now, what to do about the kids and this sudden desire to create their very own refugee camp right next to my own guilty secret? I could try to deflect their plans by bribing them, taking them to Blackpool or maybe shopping in Kendal or Keswick. Retail therapy always works for Meg, and they are her kids.

So, I try that approach: I go back up to where the three of them are hauling what appears to be tons of equipment, 'How about a trip out? Do you fancy Blackpool? There's a new ride on the Pleasure Beach; it's supposed to be amazing.'

'I bet it's not as amazing as this!' This is Bella - now on the sledge, funnelling her way through the leaves. 'It can't be as fast or as exciting as this!'

And maybe she's right: they have come up with a brilliantly inventive idea. It's hugely dangerous, of course - rocks, logs, pointy sticks and branches everywhere. And Bella has just come down the hill at the speed of a downhill Olympic skier - or is that me being paranoid?

I admit defeat. I'll wait for them to give up on the idea and keep my fingers crossed they won't uncover anything too unpleasant.

Yes, doing nothing is the option, and that's what I'll do. I'll manage the mess if I must, and if I can, I'll find a way of encouraging the kids to find a better location for their tent. In the meantime, I've had a couple of email messages come through that suddenly, are more in need of my attention.

'You lot! Daddy's got to look at his emails now. I don't want to have to take any of you to the hospital, so be careful. And Joe - that means you too!'

17

'It's OK, Dad. We're stopping now. We need to make the fire to cook our meal.'

'You can't make a fire there, you dopey people! Everything is bone dry. Think! That's why you've got a leaf slide, isn't it?'

'Oh – Yeah.' Joe is the first to cotton on.

'Any cooking has got to be done down by the house and away from the woods.' I see the beginnings of a plan here. 'Tell you what - we'll have a barbecue.'

We have this huge, brand-new barbecue next to the house: Icelandic rocks, gas bottles, enough equipment to allow us to cater for a regiment - and it won't set the area on fire when we use it. 'And you guys can get to choose what we eat. Put everything away safe for now, and we'll get off to Booth's.'

'Can we come back to the tents tonight?' Chloe, this time - the plaintive one, the one whose every utterance is a whine.

'Possibly. We'll see how well fed you are, and whether you might prefer to watch a film - we can get some popcorn while we are out shopping.'

I know that I'm throwing the kitchen sink at this, but I've found that it's the only technique that works. And Chloe takes the bait.

'Popcorn, Yay!' The chant is taken up by her sister, and Joe turns to me with all the gravitas that an eleven-year-old can muster and says, 'We'd better get off to Booth's, then.'

Three

In a small apartment in a village about fifty miles outside of Zagreb, Croatia, a mother receiving her weekly Zoom call from her daughter wasn't quite sure what she'd just witnessed.

As if she'd switched channels on her TV, she'd suddenly seen her daughter, one moment explaining why she was working at a camp site and living in a static caravan - she wouldn't say where - the next moment being violently assaulted by two men.

The first sign was the girl responding to a knock on the door, moving towards the door and opening it. Then the mother saw her daughter's facial and vocal expressions alter into a terrified response as two men burst in. In a matter of moments she was attacked, trussed up with black tape, and dragged out of her caravan.

Much of the activity happened beyond the view of the camera, but having completed the job of tying up their captive, both men looked into the computer screen and gave a 'thumbs up' before they bundled the girl out of the door.

Her mother had now been staring blankly into the screen for almost twenty minutes. There had been no movement since the attack. She knew that she had to do something: Janko needed to know about this. She looked for and found the special mobile phone, the one she only had to use in an emergency, and she pressed the speed dial button.

A few moments later, the call was answered. 'Ma, I said to use this in an emergency. I am busy now.' Suppressing the annoyance of his mother calling him, especially now, Janko looked at the small, beautifully rounded little arse of one of the new batch of Chinese girls recently arrived in Dubai.

The eight girls were destined for the local meat market and beyond into Qatar and Bahrain, but Janko and his men always liked to try out some of the merchandise first before it was sold on. The girl was kneeling on the huge leather sofa, that perky little arse up in the air, her hands behind her arched back exactly where Janko had placed them when the phone had disturbed his concentration. She was frozen in her fear, too terrified to move, sobbing and squealing from the moment she had been brought in from the holding pen.

Had she dared to lift her head a little, she would have seen the panoramic view of Dubai's Palm development at Jumeirah. She was on the top floor, the twenty eighth of the Arjan building, a curious brown pair of towers, one let as offices, one as a hotel.

Looking at the development, Gotham City comes to mind, maybe with Superman soaring away from the over-designed towers. Dubai has some of the most wonderful modern architecture in the world; sadly, despite its fantastic position, the Arjan doesn't quite make the grade. Inside however, the building's design is magnificent. The rooms, the open spaces, the corridors all designed to impress, and in that they succeed.

Here it was that Janko's twenty-odd room condominium doubled as his office and sometime warehouse. When the building's owner, a guy who'd built the huge penthouse condo for himself and his family decided not to move into it, Janko had negotiated a special deal on the huge apartment.

This had been his base for some months now: it was one of his four locations in Dubai, and here he sometimes kept girls, sometimes weapons.

It was the eight girls today. And there was cash too, today a total of almost one point eight million dollars in various currencies and denominations - most of them large, all being carefully counted, and even more carefully looked after by Kranti, a little Indian gentleman whose sole job was to look after the piles of cash that arrived at all hours of the day and night.

His mother's insistent voice again: 'Christina has been taken.' Her words were softly spoken, but they were holding back powerful feelings that Janko knew were surfacing. His mother was trying but failing to remain calm.

'Taken? Who has taken her? Where was she taken from? She's with you, isn't she?'

'No, Janko, she's not - she wasn't here. She left.'

'Where did she go?' This was confusing. His sister should have been at home. If she'd been taken from his village, there'd be hell to pay.

'I don't know where she is. She wouldn't tell me. She was in a caravan, that's all I know.'

'She should have stayed with you - I told you to keep her at home.' There was no point in his being angry with her now. That would wait until later. 'How do you know she was taken?'

'I watched it all happen. She was on Zoom to me. She often calls me, and we were chatting. Two men - and a woman too - came into the caravan and attacked her. They burst in - she wasn't expecting them - and they tied her up, Janko. They used tape. She fought them, but they were too strong. I watched it - I watched it happen, and I couldn't do anything about it.'

'Where is she? Where did this take place?' He was frustrated now. The view over the Palm was wasted on that girl. Head down, she was weeping uncontrollably but dared not make any attempt to cover her modesty.

He took a kick at the little arse that was still presenting itself to him. The girl squealed and tried to bury herself into the huge leather sofa on which she had been so beautifully positioned a few minutes ago. Janko wasn't interested now. It was true: men - the one thing at a time thing. Maybe he'd return to her later, but certainly not now.

He called sharply towards the next room, 'Ferenc. Come in here.' Then to his mother, 'Let me sort out some things. Give me a moment and we'll work out what to do. You were right to call me,

Mum, you did the right thing.'

The huge, muscled form of Ferenc, Janko's assistant, lumbered into the room. Ferenc was his utility man, bodyguard, pimp, enforcer and today Janko was pleased he'd someone around simply to get rid of the girl.

'Get her out of here - and don't damage the goods.' He gestured towards the tiny figure of the girl.

'Right, boss.' He moved towards the girl and picked her up, putting her under his right arm, carrying her like a small parcel. He turned, 'A blow job, that would be OK, though?'

'Dickhead. I've got my fucking mother on the end of this fucking phone! Sorry Ma. I forgot. Give me a moment.' Then he muted his phone and looked at Ferenc, 'I don't fucking care what you do, OK? Just fuck off! Now!'

The sixteen-year-old Chinese girl, the girl with the truly beautiful little arse, round and tight, had said goodbye to her family only a few days ago. She'd been lucky enough to obtain a job as a hotel maid in Dubai, and that meant she could begin to remit some money back home very soon.

The friendly Chinese agent had been so comforting to her parents as he assured them that all would be well. He would personally take care of her, he said. They had nothing to worry about.

For their part, they had handed over fifteen thousand Yuan, about fifteen hundred pounds - all their savings and some additional money they'd had to borrow – to ensure the chance of a good position for their daughter.

On her arrival in Dubai, she and her seven companions had been given their passports and visa information to go through immigration and had them immediately taken back once they had been stamped.

Shepherded into the minibus that was waiting for them, they'd been quickly driven to a dirty apartment in Bur Dubai, and it was there that she became aware that all was not what it seemed. This was not a hotel, and she was not going to be working as a maid.

Once inside the flat, they were put into a dormitory. A room the size of a normal double bedroom had twelve sleeping areas, some beds, some bunks, and some mats on the floor.

Suddenly their freedom was restricted, and they were escorted to the bathroom one by one. Their food was placed in their room, and the empty bowls removed shortly afterwards.

Their friendly agent had disappeared and had been replaced by a group of scowling men and women who had suddenly become their jailers.

A few days later had found her being brought, again with her now equally frightened companions, to Janko's condo where the private elevator had taken them to his apartment. They were then herded into one of the many spare bedrooms that Janko kept for such occasions.

A short while ago, the huge man who now had her under his arm had come into the bedroom and gestured to her. She was taken to a bathroom where she had been allowed to take a shower and wash her hair. She was given a silk dressing gown to wear, her other clothes were taken from her, and instead of returning to the dormitory as she expected, she was taken up a flight of marble stairs and into the largest living room she had ever seen.

She immediately understood what was going to happen. Another man, obviously a boss, not Chinese, but white with a very strong growth of beard on his face, had come towards her. He had a glass of something in one hand and a mobile phone in the other.

Retaining his glass in his hand, he put the mobile in his pocket and smiled at her - not the smile of a friend, a different kind of smile, one which troubled her and made her even more afraid, if that was possible.

He moved towards her, lifting and moving the dressing gown from her shoulders and exposing her breasts. Her instinctive response was to cover herself up. She immediately received a sharp slap across the face, and when her eyes opened after the shock, and she saw the face of her attacker, the smile had gone.

This time he did not seek to remove the garment, but simply gestured to her, and for the first time ever in her life she became naked in front of a man. Mortified with embarrassment, she was thankful that she had recently spent some time in the bathroom - otherwise her humiliation would have been complete.

The man put down his glass, tossed his phone on to a nearby chair and came towards her. He reached out, his hand stretching to the back of her head, gently teasing the tresses of her hair, then moving down over her shoulders. He cupped her breasts in both hands and then squeezed her nipples so that she felt some pain and flinched.

The man smiled. Taking her by the hand, he led her towards the massive sofa that dominated the room, a sofa big enough for maybe ten people to sit comfortably. The naked young girl was turned and pushed so that she knelt on it. The man's hands moved to her hips, lifting and placing her so that she was on her hands and knees. Taking both her arms, he moved them behind her back, causing her to drop her head further into the giant sofa and presenting the most intimate part of her body towards him.

At that moment a telephone rang; the man became occupied with something - shouting - and ultimately moving away from her. She did not, dared not move, but slowly, very slowly she sought comfort in the huge cushions that covered the sofa, burrowing her hands and arms, and then her head, out of sight.

Moments later, a huge arm latched itself around her, and the man who'd brought her into this vast room carried her naked and now sobbing, away from his very angry boss and into smaller adjoining room.

Far from being over, her ordeal was about to begin. This man, the big one, didn't have his enjoyment of her interrupted by anything, and some twenty minutes later she was returned to her dormitory, minus the silk dressing gown and having been fully initiated into the world of violent sex.

She was more distressed than she could ever have believed, now knowing for certain that her dreams of working in one of the beautiful hotels of Dubai had been replaced by an entirely different scenario. She moved towards her bed space, curled herself up as tightly as she could and quietly cried herself to sleep.

Four

The framed photo, right next to the massive flat screen television that dominated the room, was of four young girls – seventeen, maybe eighteen years old. The girls were all dressed in ball gowns; Christina looked particularly elegant. The photo had been taken hours before the high school prom, the summer before last.

Rosa, Christina's mother, looked at it at it, reflecting as she did so that that was her last happy memory. So much had changed in those two years, and now that Christina had left, the void and the emptiness of her world was emphasised every time she looked at that photo.

Yet, she left it in full view, right next to the TV that occupied most of her waking hours. The photo was an open sore that she picked at, regularly reminding herself - there was nobody else to remind - that she was now entirely alone.

Her son, Janko, five years older than his sister, was long gone. Whatever he was doing wasn't clear to her, but he evidently was making a lot of money. One thing was certain: it wouldn't be legal.

Janko had been a dreadful student at school. All the way through his teenage years, he'd fought with his teachers, with his fellow students and with anyone else who came near him. On leaving school at sixteen, Rosa knew he'd first gone to Zagreb almost immediately, but after that? No idea - but now, it seemed, he was living in some luxury.

How had this happened? Rosa hadn't dared question the occasional substantial amounts of money that had come her way, mostly in dollar bills, but occasionally in euros. The money was welcome, no matter where it had come from as it had made her life so much easier. She now was living in a small but new apartment bought because of this generosity.

Another tangible benefit was that when Christina left home, Rosa was kept in touch with her daughter thanks to the computer she'd bought with Janko's money. She quickly learned how to use Zoom and could see and chat to her daughter quite regularly, although Christina controlled all contact and never said where she was Zooming from.

Pride of place in Rosa's apartment now was the giant plasma TV that took up almost the whole wall of the sitting room in her small flat.

One day, out of the blue, Janko had arrived at their village in a huge, black Mercedes G Wagon. His driver had got out first - Janko with a driver! - and out of the back had come this massive package. Janko's driver, a powerful looking man with an angry face had installed the giant TV, and as quickly as they had arrived, Janko and his driver were gone.

In one way, Rosa was immediately the envy of the village, but in another way - well, there were those who wondered how that ignorant, loutish young man had obtained such spectacular wealth in such a short time.

The TV was a mixed blessing. Yes, it did bring Rosa into contact with people in the village who wanted to see a special event, or a football match played out almost in life size, but she and everybody else was uncomfortable about where all this money might have come from. She didn't dare ask, but the inherent sense of guilt in her Catholic upbringing made it very difficult for her to enjoy her new-found wealth.

She felt particularly guilty about receiving the large sums of money that arrived in the post because they were almost forced on her. She'd always thought of herself as a good woman, and money that had come from dubious business practices didn't fit with the way that she saw either herself, or the way her children should be living.

Both her children were lost to her, and now Christina was in danger. Something terrible had happened. A big TV, even a computer was of no help to her at all. She'd called Janko, and although she had spoken to him, and he had said that he would get back to her, she'd heard nothing since.

Rosa didn't know this, but Janko knew even less than his mother. What had happened to Christina - if anything at all had happened, was a complete mystery. Firstly, he'd been surprised that she wasn't at home with their mother. He had never even considered that she might want to be anywhere else. Her role was to live near Zagreb, marry a local boy and have kids. Why would she want to do anything else?

Disconnecting the call, Janko immediately wondered what he could do from Dubai. He'd no information to go on, no idea what had happened or where it had happened. He could call his European contacts, but the real puzzle was if Christina had been taken, who would have done it, and why?

He didn't dare contemplate this; maybe he was better off not thinking about it. His worry was that if he allowed his thoughts to surface, they might overwhelm him. Keeping a tight control of his business was difficult enough. He could do without becoming paranoid too.

However, he had to consider what might have happened. His money-making activities had involved him taking some huge risks, and more than one of his clients had been burned when a transaction had failed to work out as planned.

There had been some recent issues over a delivery of girls that had troubled him. He had received an upfront payment from some Arab guys for ten girls from North Korea.

He'd bust his balls trying to get what they wanted, but they'd been very unhappy with the quality of the stock. He told them - what did they expect if they were buying girls who lived on grass? But no, they'd asked for their money back.

Janko supposed it could be them. He'd told them to fuck off and

Ferenc had busted the nose of their main negotiator: no amicable settlement had yet been reached.

The problem was that yes, this was something nasty, but it wasn't particularly special. People had been bribed, even hurt and on a couple of occasions recently, people had been shot. Each of these was enough to warrant someone looking for revenge.

But what had happened to Christina? All he had to go on was his mother's version of events, and that came from her watching something on Zoom. It could be she'd confused herself with a movie she was watching. She might have been drunk and made the whole thing up.

There were a thousand possible explanations, and until he knew exactly what had happened, Janko decided that rather than beat himself up about it, he would wait for something more tangible to appear.

In the meantime, he'd see if that little Chinese girl with the lovely round arse was going to live up to his expectations. And, if Ferenc had made too much of a mess of her, there were one or two others who could serve his purpose equally well.

Five

'Well, this is a pleasant surprise.' Max and Debesh had pulled into the disused Ambleside police station more in hope than in expectation. The same offices had provided them with a base some years ago, and Max had known that even then, this small outpost of the police empire had been marked for closure. It was to be sold, probably to become yet another holiday home in a village already riddled with them.

But the sale evidently had not happened, and Max's remark was echoed by Debesh, 'Yeah, they must have decided to hang on to it. If we have a choice, I'd rather work from here than from Windermere.'

'Let's go in and see what we can find. Is it operational, do you know?'

'I'll call Control and find out, sir.'

'No, Debesh, don't do that. Remember, 'it's better to travel hopefully than to arrive.'

'Sir?'

The 'Noddy' principle.'

The two police officers got out of the car simultaneously, Debesh still thinking about the last part of their conversation.

'The Noddy Principle?'

'Yes, although that's not strictly true - not literally true. The guy who wrote 'Treasure Island'?'

'Robert Louis Stevenson?'

'Yes, he said it, but I prefer to think of Noddy.'

'Thanks for that, sir. It's much clearer now, thank you.'

The men were walking into the open door of the Ambleside station, 'I'll explain later - now let's see if there are any signs of life. Hello! Anyone there?'

Looking around the tiny reception area of the police station, it was obvious that it had been recently decorated. Three or four new chairs, two large desks and what appeared to be a couple of computer terminals, all suggesting that far from being mothballed, the station was up and running.

'What the hell are you doing here?' Debesh's outburst initially surprised his boss, but when he looked towards the doorway and saw what had caused it, he understood.

Helen, Max's former admin assistant but more importantly, the woman who was now Debesh's wife, was standing with two coffee cups in her hands and a self-satisfied smile on her face.

'Gotcha!' It was Max's remark, and Debesh turned towards him, completely bemused.

'You knew?'

'Of course, I knew. I asked for her straight away. As soon as I set off this morning, the first thing that I did was call Control and ask them to open up this place.'

'But it looks as if it's all set up.'

'And it is. It's due to open as a community station next month. I advanced it a little, that's all. Another thing I did, as soon as I knew that you were going to be working with me, was to get in touch with Helen.'

Debesh turned to his wife, 'You never said a thing. Don't you think that you could have let me know?'

'And spoil this? I don't think so.'

'You never said a word. I thought that you wanted to be a mum for a while longer.'

'I think you wanted to think that, and anyway, I didn't know this was going to happen, did I? I had no idea that you'd be working with Max again, but you knew I was ready to come back to work. I love Ellie to bits, but I was starting to climb the walls. I like my work too much, Debesh.'

'Time out.' It was time for Max to intervene. 'Helen called me a few weeks ago. We had a chat because she was thinking of returning to work.'

'You knew that love. I did tell you - and we did talk about it.'

'Yes, but you never told me that you had contacted anyone - contacted Max. I had no idea you were serious about it.'

'Well, I was! And I want you to be too.'

Max was loving this. 'And it was too good an opportunity to waste. The look on your face, Debesh - priceless!'

Debesh could see how much his boss was enjoying the situation - a little too much possibly. His face had cracked up into a real smile - a very rare occurrence, and obviously Helen had been in on the whole thing too.

'So, I hope you don't mind?' This was Helen, looking at her husband and smiling in that captivating, winsome way that had so floored him five years ago - standing in the same doorway as on that first occasion.

'I want to get back to work. Ellie loves nursery and I'm only going to be doing part-time until she starts school.'

Max interrupted, 'And I wanted a laugh. It's not too much to ask, is it? Frankly, the way this case is likely to go, laughs are going to be on the thin side. So, I was gathering rosebuds.'

'Gathering rosebuds. Is this another Noddy reference?' Debesh looked at his wife and his boss, both of whom seemed to be echoing the same look of amused detachment. 'Am I in the right job? This is all too much for me.'

'Noddy was of the same opinion as Robert Louis Stevenson. When I was a kid, my mum insisted on reading Enid Blyton to me - as well as Peter Bleeding Rabbit. The only thing I remember about Noddy is that he was a great fan of anticipation. It was always better to look forward to something than to experience its reality. We had a collection of all twenty-four books, or was it two hundred and twenty-four? Seemed a lot, anyway. And I hated them.'

'You're not much of a fan of literature, Lake District and otherwise - and anyway, what has this to do with my wife coming back to work...?'

'Absolutely nothing and thank you for your perceptive comment. It's simple, Debesh. But I was very much anticipating this moment - that's the 'Noddy' principle at work. And your response has exceeded my wildest expectations - thank you.'

Debesh had had enough, 'That hasn't answered my question.'

Max realised that any amusement left in the situation was rapidly draining away, 'Helen was the perfect addition to the team last time round, and apart from one mistake, marrying you - that was a joke, by the way.'

That didn't go down very well either and Max tried to retrieve, 'Apart from that one mistake, she made a huge contribution to the project...'

'Which was a catastrophic failure if I may remind you...?' Debesh had quickly got his own dig in.

'Which wasn't as successful as it might have been, true. But none of that was Helen's fault. She gathered all the material perfectly, and she was detailed and painstaking throughout. It was me who ballsed it up, not her - or you. I made the wrong decision, but all the evidence was beautifully presented.'

Max permitted himself a wry smile. Helen had been brilliant at pulling all the evidence together; the filing, both electronic and manual was exemplary, as were her organisational skills.

In the end, Max had simply gone for the wrong suspect - but had secured a conviction: he wasn't the only person who messed up. The CPS had also agreed with his conclusions.

'And if it's OK with you guys - with both of you,' Max continued, 'I'd like to set up shop here with you two as my team. What do you think?'

'It certainly is OK with me,' Helen was the first to reply. 'It's exactly what I want - and I would be happy to work alongside the man I love.' That winning smile again - it had Max going, God knows what it was doing to Debesh.

'Debesh?'

'I think I should stop digging. Congratulations, darling. You've obviously been watching too many reality TV shows. I'm looking around for the cameras now.'

'So, we're agreed?' Max needed the commitment of both parties if this was to work, and their chorus of 'Yes Sir!' sealed the deal.

'Excellent! Sort us out some workspace and I'll make the coffee. We need to start.'

Debesh and Helen sat, facing each other across the larger of the two desks and each looking a little warily at the other until their gentle smiles softened the situation. Max interrupted the reverie, 'Helen, we've just come from talking to the first person to see the victim.'

Debesh, picking up on the change of pace and referring to his notes continued, 'Miss Marjorie Bath - very insistent on the 'Miss', out walking her dog very early this morning. Comes across a young girl suspended over the pool at Rydal Caves, her head and shoulders below the water line.'

'This was at about 0500,' added Max.

'A little later, sir. Between 0510 and 0530. The rope suspending her above the pool was attached to pitons above the cave itself. These pitons are used by local climbing organisations for abseiling practice.'

Helen's first contribution: 'They knew about the pitons.'

'We think so,' added Max. 'The other important factor is this: it appears that the victim was still alive when Miss Bath came across her. She says she tried to help the girl but couldn't get near enough to save her. When we met her - she'd been waiting to see us - her clothes, specifically her skirt and boots, were wet - consistent with the statement she gave us.'

'How old is this Miss Bath?' Helen was thinking of what she might have done in the circumstances. Her immediate thought had been that she wouldn't try to get into the pool but would have tried to lift the girl higher. That would have involved her climbing up to the pitons and attempting to haul up the rope and the girl attached to it above the water.

'Late sixties at least, typical of the little old ladies you frequently see on the fells - she's tiny, and probably quite frail.' Helen realised that her idea of rescuing the girl by hauling her to safety would have been impossible.

'She must have watched the girl die.' Even though she had not seen the incident herself, Helen was deeply troubled by this thought.

'Yes, exactly that: she did watch her die. When we first met her, she was in shock. I had a female PC drive her home immediately. The WPC was worried about her and asked a doctor to come and see her too. Debesh and I had said that we would pop around later to see her. We did, and we came here straight from her house.'

Debesh added, 'She was calmer when we went to visit her, but the incident was still raw. It's not going to go away, is it? She'll be thinking about it for a long time.'

Helen asked, 'Did the doctor prescribe her anything?'

Debesh was the first to answer. 'Yes, what she called a 'mild sedative'. It wasn't an easy meeting; Miss Bath has an aversion to doctors. She didn't want to have anything to do with her, but our WPC insisted.'

'Helen pursued this line, 'And what do you think? Is she traumatised?'

Max replied, 'She may well be. I would. And even if she doesn't think so now, these things have a habit of creeping up on you unawares. Helen, you might follow this up. Please call her and maybe call the health centre and get their take on the situation if you can.'

'Data protection, sir. They're not going to tell me anything if I do call them.'

'Nothing medical, true. But showing natural empathy? As long as we have logged our concern - we did involve the doctor in the first place.'

Helen made a note to call the health centre. Max was right, checking up on someone they'd referred to the doctor wasn't a breach of data security, it was an act of kindness. But before she made that call, there was something else bothering her.

'Sir. May I ask a question?'

'Of course.'

'If Miss Bath saw the girl while she was alive, it could only have been minutes after she was strung up over the pool.'

'Yes.'

'Any other witnesses?'

'Not so far,' Max replied. 'And this should be next on your list. Uniform has been doing house-to-house and Traffic has been trying to see if we can get a glimpse of whoever it was that carried out this crime. I'll arrange for them to report to you.'

'Thanks sir.' Helen was already up and running, 'I'll also check up to see if there is any CCTV for us to look at.'

'Good luck with that,' Debesh whispered to his wife. She was into gear now, and the professional manner that quite frankly he found so very sexy, was beginning to return. Even now, there wasn't very much left of Helen that he could describe as being mumsy, and this was only day one of her return to the workplace

Debesh couldn't help but wonder if this was going to turn out to be a good idea. He'd rather got used to the pipe and slippers welcome he received on his return home each evening (although he didn't smoke a pipe and didn't have any slippers). It was the whole family thing, her being there, that he loved so much - something he had craved all his life.

All that was now about to change: Debesh knew how strong his wife was, but also how assertive he could be when pushed. Would these two wills combine into the powerful machine that such synergy could produce, or would the new dynamic set them in opposition to each other and destroy everything?

Five years ago, their first meeting in this very building had produced the most powerful and rewarding relationship that Debesh had ever known. Could it survive being tweaked in this way?

Six

I've been up to Aberdeen for a couple of days, three altogether if you count the travelling, staying in a beautiful hotel near Oldmeldrum.

I was working with two of my client companies. They were proposing to merge, mainly because of the recent downturn of the offshore oil industry and the sudden loss of revenue they now anticipated. My role was to make this happen without too much fallout.

I've worked with these companies for a few years now and I know them well. Each provides a specific type of safety-related service to oil rigs, not only in the North Sea, but in oilfields all over the world. Bringing the two together under one roof would give economies of scale, major savings in overheads, and would also provide opportunities for the new company's range of products to be sold as a package, rather than as discrete services.

I'd been engaged to facilitate the discussions allowing us to draw up an action plan for the implementation of the merger. Lots of politics, conflicts of interest, noses put out of joint and general negativity. Right up my street.

This is my day job: management consultancy. Frank Blain Associates - although there are no associates. I've called my business FBA for many years and if I might blow my own trumpet, it's work I do well.

More importantly, it's the work that Meg, my family, also my accountants - and the tax man - all think of as my main source of income. I'm happy they continue to think that way, so I keep a full diary of my engagements in the UK and overseas. All fees that I earn for this work go into my UK bank accounts and I pay tax like any other upright British citizen.

In fact, I pay more tax than I need to because as you know, my house is quite large, and I and the family live rather well. To justify our expensive lifestyle - big house, holidays, school fees and all the rest, I enhance my consultancy's turnover with fees that I earn in my other line of business.

These fees are paid via the two agencies that employ me, one in the US Virgin Islands and the other in Dubai. They too maintain an entirely legitimate business presence in these countries, and apart from the occasions when I ask to be paid in cash, I raise an invoice from FBA which is always paid immediately on receipt.

I could hide this money offshore and pay nothing in tax, but I truly value my home life and feel that the sacrifice is worthwhile. I know of businesses locally that effectively keep two sets of books, and hide their cash away, using it to fund expensive vacations or in one case, a vast holiday home in Thailand.

I'm happier to show anyone in the UK who cares, the local council, journalists, HMRC - anybody at all, that my consultancy's income justifies my expenditure, and that any money I spend or invest is entirely legitimate. My financial credibility is underwritten by the local firm of accountants - I don't employ the 'big four' and I don't keep my UK money in an offshore shell company.

All this means that I live an entirely normal family life, and I love it.

And that brings me to the issue that has started to trouble me. I was contacted a couple of days ago on my pay-as-you go phone, a number only used by my agents, and even then, only for my wet work.

I answered the call - I was in my hotel room at the time. Only two people have access to this number. One is Archana, my Indian agent based in Dubai; the other is Stephanie, an American woman who works out of the British Virgin Islands.

It was neither of them.

'You ought to keep a closer eye on your people.' It was a man's voice, not English, but speaking English.

'Who are you?'

'I'm not Stephanie, that's for sure,' came the reply, and I frantically tried to picture what was going on. Who was phoning me, and what had Stephanie to do with it?

'Stephanie doesn't even want to be Stephanie any longer. She surprised me; it took a lot longer than we had intended for her to give us this number.'

'Put me on to her - I want to speak to her.'

'Sorry, Frank. There's not much left to speak to, now. And she probably couldn't speak even if she wanted. My men had to be quite severe with her.'

'If you've hurt her...!'

'You'll do what?'

'I will find you.'

'Stop talking, big man. Try listening. I've left a signal for you. You will see it when you get home.'

My mind was racing - when I get home. Had he been to my home?

'When you get home, Frank, you will find your wife and your lovely children waiting for you. They've missed you, and they all want you back. The signal I'm sending is one I've also sent to Janko Stanovnic - but I want you to see it too.'

'I don't know any Janko Stanovnic.'

'You do, Frank. You do. The message is for you, as well as for him. The coincidence was too good to miss. When you get home, you'll find out. And Stephanie sends her love. It was almost the last thing she said. Sorry, but you won't be seeing her again. That was a pity; she was a pleasant lady.'

He closed the call. I sat for a moment or two, trying to work out what had happened to Stephanie. I tried her mobile number and as it rang out, I realised the threat behind what I had heard. He'd talked of my family, my kids. I called home immediately, and Meg answered.

'Hi Meg. Everything all right?'

'Yes, darling. Why?'

'The kids are with you now?'

'They are all upstairs. It's raining outside, and they are all on their tablets.'

'I hope you check who they are talking to - and what they are doing.'

'Of course, I do. Every week - no secrets, no passwords.'

The domestic pattern reasserted itself. My wife and my family were safe, and I could think again of what might have happened to Stephanie in the BVI. I would have to chase that up, but for the moment I knew that my kids were all right.

Meg reminded me that we were still engaged in a conversation, 'I check through each tablet every few days,' Meg continued, 'That's the deal and they seem to be sticking to it.'

We'd recently been pestered into agreeing that our kids should each have a tablet computer. It was at the end of some long kid-type negotiation, and they always win out, don't they? They have that stamina that allows them to go on and on persisting, pulling at the thread until eventually, your resistance unravels.

So, defeated, I'd recently picked up three cheap tablets at Schiphol and brought them home. For about five minutes I was the king of the dads, but that soon waned, of course. Tablets, not iPads. But even if they had been top-of-the-range iPads, that same law of diminishing returns would have applied.

I wasn't so much concerned about what the kids were doing with their tablets as I was relieved to know they were still around and doing something - anything at all. In my world, doom is visited upon sometimes unsuspecting families with immense speed.

My worry was that somebody had information about us and was therefore potentially in a very strong position, a position that was a threat to us.

And they'd got this information via Stephanie. I put that troubling thought to the back of my mind while pursuing domesticity with Meg.

'Anything else of interest I should know about?'

'No, I don't think so. When are you coming home?'

'I'll be back tomorrow night, probably late. Aberdeen is a long drive.'

'I'll stay up.'

'No need - I'll wake you when I get back.' I gave myself the luxury of reflecting on how much I enjoyed waking Meg up at times like these - and how much she enjoyed being woken up. There is always something special about those moments.

'I'll stay awake - so that I can hide when you come home.' She giggled, and almost as an afterthought said, 'Frank, did you hear about the murder at Rydal?'

She wasn't doing it deliberately, but the way that slipped out as if she were gossiping about some imagined infidelity or half-truth that she had been told about by a neighbour, pointed out to me how out of sync I am with this whole domestic bliss arrangement.

Murders, when they do occur, don't happen in the world of Meg. These are concepts that are entirely foreign, and I can't blame her for thinking like that. In fact, in some ways I'm delighted I've shielded her from stuff that happens on the wilder fringes of my life.

But because of that phone call, I was tuned in and waiting for any sign that should concern me, and this one came through loud and clear.

'There was a murder?'

'Yes, it's been on the news. Didn't you see it? A young girl was hung up by her ankles over a pool at Rydal caves. The police have closed off the area, but everybody who drives past can see that something horrible has happened there. There are police cars and those tent things.'

'Who was it?'

'No idea. I don't think the police know, either. Or if they do, they're not saying anything.'

Rydal is only a few miles from where I have my house. He mentioned a signal – this has to be it. This is far too close, I'm thinking to myself. And naturally, my mind is now racing. I've no idea why I should be sent a signal, and I don't want to think too deeply about that - not now, anyway. I need to get back home and work things out.

'I'll come home as soon as I can. I don't want you worrying.'

'I'm not worrying, Frank. It's nothing to do with us, is it?'

And long may that absolute expression of innocence envelop my family. It's what I have been working for, the understandings that make life - and relationships - worthwhile. It's unfortunate that I must constantly tread through a morass of filth - holding my family aloft to keep them from drowning.

Seven

'Her name's Christina Stanovnic. Twenty-two years old, Croatian. Recently started working on a caravan site at Skelwith Bend and she was living there - staff accommodation. It's a caravan and she was sharing it with another eastern European girl, possibly Romanian.'

'How do we know about her?'

'Uniform, sir. There was a report of an incident. Someone heard screaming and called 999. Uniform turned up but by then both girls were gone. This is the victim's passport.'

'Thanks, Debesh. It's a beginning.' Max Wordsworth took the passport as it was handed to him and he opened it, glancing at the photo of a pretty young woman with a captivating smile. Some people can smile at a camera, and it works: this girl was one of those. Max was not, his passport photo criminalised him.

'The Romanian girl? Was she there?'

'Don't think so. I'm not sure. She's not there now, the site manager says she wasn't around yesterday, and he didn't see her last night. Oh, the site manager had only met her once. He thinks she was visiting – she wasn't employed by them.'

'Coincidence? Is she a witness?'

'Possibly. The caravan is a mess; there's obviously been some violent activity taking place. I took these photos.' Debesh switched on his phone and flicked through it. Half a dozen images clearly showed that there had been a struggle inside the girl's caravan.

'Have you called in Forensics?'

'Yes, sir, but they're not there yet. They seem to have a lot on their plate. I've stationed a WPC to keep people away until they arrive.'

'Thanks, Debesh. If this murder was a signal for somebody, it would help us if we knew who that somebody is.' Max was aware of the possibility that this case was opening up to be something more than a local matter; it might soon be taken out of his hands.

'Helen, fire up your computer and do some searching for me.'

'Certainly sir, what are we looking for?'

'Interesting question. Let's start with our victim, Christina Stanovnic from Zagreb. See what you can find about her. Any PNC info - also, get the name of the Romanian girl she was supposed to be sharing with, and see if you can get some contact information on her.'

'While you are doing that, Debesh and I will see what Uniform has found out from their door-to-doors. I want to have something firmly in place, either so that we can proceed as normal or so that the NCA can have a running start at it.'

Helen was up for this: the creative rather than administrative was always her preference. True, she was an excellent administrator, and as Max had previously mentioned, her eye for detail and her organising skills were of great value. But Helen knew that where she truly could excel was when she was given her head and allowed to apply her intelligence to a task.

The girl who'd shared the caravan with Christina was more problematic. The police had recovered no documentation relating to her. The site's manager said that she'd only arrived a couple of days ago, and that she was waiting for her boyfriend to arrive before moving on. He assumed she was a friend, and Christina had agreed to let her stay for a few days.

As far as Helen could ascertain, the name she had given was the only clue to her nationality. The name itself, 'Elena Popa', was the female Romanian equivalent of 'Jane Doe', and she found no trace of her in any of her databases.

She immediately moved on to Christina: Google starting her off, and as she cross-referenced a few points with the PNC, Helen began creating a dossier that was much more substantial than she - or anyone else - might have expected, and all for less than twenty minutes' work.

With her focus on Christina, and using the resources of the PNC, she first made a tenuous connection between Christina and one Janko Stanovnic. Soon it firmed up - they were brother and sister, and their mother was Rosa. Rosa lived close to Zagreb in the hometown declared by Christina on her passport, but Helen was interested to note that the whereabouts of the brother were a matter of speculation with Interpol and some other police forces.

Janko was a known criminal: if there was a definite connection between him and the dead girl, that might be a useful area of exploration. Whether or not it would be Max and Debesh or the NCA who would benefit from this information, Helen didn't know, but she went about her activity in her typically diligent way. Whoever was going to use this information would find it perfectly presented.

Eight

On arriving at Skelwith Bend caravan site, Max and Debesh were met by the uniformed WPC who'd originally been called to the scene of a fracas in one of the staff caravans. He directed them to the remote area of the site where the three staff caravans were located, and it was there they met the person who'd originally called 999.

Max stood on the steps of a small caravan no more than twenty yards or so away from where Christina had been abducted: Debesh right behind him.

The caravan's occupant opened the door. He was a nervous, thin faced young man, maybe in his early twenties, and his demeanour was not at all welcoming. Although Max and Debesh were in plain clothes, the man had immediately known they were the police, and he was in defensive mode.

It was also evident from their initial interaction that he was used to having this kind of conversation. No stranger to the workings of the law, then.

Max assumed that the pungent smell of weed from inside the caravan was the reason. He politely asked the man to open a couple of windows and assured him that they were not going to bust him for drugs.

The young man shrugged a grudging acceptance, and although he was reluctant to invite them in, he seemed slightly more disposed to answer their questions regarding the 999 call.

'Your name, sir?'

'Stan, er, Stanley Field.'

'Did you know the girl in that caravan, Stan? Can I call you Stan?' Debesh gestured towards a small, green caravan, now surrounded with tapes and police vehicles.

'No - I saw her once or twice, but she got up early - for work, I guess. She never returned until late, either.'

'Did you ever speak?'

'No - never. She smiled at me once, that's all.'

'Describe her for me, would you?'

'She was tall, slim. Very long legs - she looked OK. Fit.'

'And did you not try to...?'

'To be honest, I'm not here for a holiday, and I don't want people to see me. So, no - I didn't.'

Stan had his own agenda too: 'How do you know it was me who made the call?'

Debesh was happy to explain. 'My Uniform colleague told me. It's easy enough to work out - I mean, you're here, right next to where everything happened.

'Oh. Right.' Then, 'But you're not here to bust me?'

'Not for drugs, no.'

'OK. Sound.' The lad breathed an obvious sigh of relief and immediately lit up a cigarette. 'What do you want to know?'

'Why did you make the call?'

'There was this woman screaming.'

'Did you go to see why she was screaming?'

'What do you mean?' Debesh was bemused by this answer; something did not compute. He tried again, 'When you heard the woman screaming, what did you do?'

'You know what I did. I called 999.'

'So, you didn't do anything. Like try to intervene? Did you see anything?'

'I didn't look. I didn't see a thing, honest. I'm up here for a few days. A mate at home suggested I get away for a while and he knew of this place.' He saw Debesh's eyes flicker, 'Sorry - long story, but where I come from, you don't get involved - if you don't want to get fire-bombed for grassing.'

Debesh glanced at Max and could tell that his older colleague was drawing hard on his already-depleted store of empathy. He wasn't entirely sure how a philosophical debate would take them any further forward, so he moved to keep control of the conversation.

'So, you heard a screaming. What kind of screaming was it? Did someone assault her? Was she screaming from pain?'

The young man who was the object of these questions gave them some thought, 'No, she wasn't punched - or stabbed. I'm sure of that. It was more of a struggle, a fight. I thought it was a flareup, like - you know - the kind of fight that happens between couples, after a few beers?'

'What else did you hear?'

'Not much. I peeked out of the window, but I couldn't see anything.'

'How many people were involved?'

Stan paused, obviously re-thinking what he was going to say, and both police officers could sense a change in the man's demeanour, 'I think there might have been two men - I heard two voices, both men - and hers, of course.' Then a moment of revelation: 'It wasn't a domestic row, was it? She was being taken.'

All cockiness, all bravado disappearing fast, the tattooed, shaven-headed young man whose preconception of the police had caused him to default into passive aggression, realised that he'd witnessed an abduction.

Max spoke for the first time. 'Yes, she was taken, and that's why we are here. You'll have to come to the station so that we can interview you formally as a witness.'

'Tell him Stan!' The words came from the bedroom of the caravan and were followed by the appearance of a young girl, wrapped in a duvet. She was no more than fifteen or sixteen years old, maybe younger, blonde with dark roots, tiny - and looking as if she had just woken up.

'You've got to tell them, Stan. It's not grassing. They weren't nicking stuff. They might have hurt her.'

Stan wasn't convinced and wasn't minded to respond.

'If you don't tell them, I will. What if it was me they'd come for? What would you do then?'

'I'd tell them, of course.'

'Then tell them now.' Looking at the young man, Max could see that Stan was weighing up his options, probably including his future relationship with his girlfriend.

He decided. 'There were two men. They grabbed the girl from her caravan. They'd tied her up with something and one of them was carrying her over his shoulder like a roll of carpet.'

'And there was someone else - the woman.' This from the girl, now on a roll and determined that her man would do his duty by her.

'Shut up, will you?'

'Another woman?' Debesh sat directly opposite the boyfriend, both now at the fold-down table and heads only inches apart. Max lingered at the door; there wasn't much room left for him. The atmosphere had changed, and it was too late for Stan to get away with his redacted version of events. 'We'll start again, shall we?' said Debesh, taking his police-issue notebook from his pocket.

And this time the young man told the real story. A car had pulled up and it was its headlights that had caused Stan and his girlfriend to be aware of something happening.

'To begin with, I thought they'd come for me. I had to get away from Newcastle for a bit, like, and when that car arrived, I was shitting mesel.'

Leanne chipped in, 'We don't have a car, and our lights were out, so we both looked out the window to see what was going on.'

'OK. Thanks. There were two men, and a woman? And you saw all three of them?'

Both Leanne and Stan nodded in agreement and rather sheepishly, admitted that they had been watching the whole thing.

'So, carry on, please. What happened then?' Debesh had his notebook open now and was busily recording what each of these people - now witnesses - had to say.

'It was the girl who went up to the caravan first; the men got out too, but quietly - they didn't slam the car doors. The girl knocked twice and then said something to the lass inside.'

'Did you know this girl?'

'Yeah. She's been here for a couple of days. She'd moved in, I think.'

'What did she say?'

'No idea - she was speaking foreign, but she wanted the girl to let her in.'

'Did the girl inside want to open the door?' Max, this time.

'She opened it straight away. No problem. She'd maybe forgotten her key - sounded something like that.'

'How do you mean?' Debesh, chasing after every nuance of this transaction.

'It was normal talk, like. I've forgotten my key, let us in.'

'Let 'us' in?'

'Naaa, not 'us'. Let me in - let us in, that's what you say, like, isn't it? Sounded like that anyway - only in foreign.'

Max asked, 'Do you know what language they were speaking in?'

'Don't be daft. How would I know?'

Max allowed that one to ride. 'And then?'

'Then it happened.' The young man, again catching his girlfriend's eye, began to describe the scene, but this time as it truly played out.

'The moment the door was unlocked, the two guys forced themselves into the caravan. That's when I heard - when we heard - the screams. After mebbees less than a minute, things were quieter. The girl outside seemed to be acting as a lookout. One of the men put his head out of the door and whispered something. The girl nodded her head and then the second guy, the big one, came out. He was holding the girl in front of him. Her legs were tied together - she was taped up - her legs were taped together. And her mouth - her mouth was taped, and she was screaming and kicking, but you couldn't hear what she was saying.'

'She was helpless, but she was fighting like mad.' Leanne was now into this moment and living it; both Max and Debesh saw in her eyes the realisation that in a scenario not far from her own reality, she might well have been the victim.

Stan continued, 'The big guy hoyed her over his back like a sack of spuds - or a roll of carpet. The girl opened the boot of the car while the little bloke closed the caravan door - he left the lights on, mind.'

'They threw her into the boot!' Leanne's sense of the horror of the incident was evident in her shaking and the way she was clutching at her boyfriend's hand. 'Then they got into the car, the two blokes at the front and the girl in the back seat, and they left.'

'That was it? Anything else to tell us?' Max had gone down the 'bad guy' route during this interview.

'Naa - that's it.' Stan had no more to add.

'What about the car?'

'The car?'

'Yes, its make - did you get its registration number?'

'Na, sorry. I didn't think to look for the number - anyway it was dark.'

Leanne had something to add. 'The girl, not the one they tied up, the other one. She got into the back seat, but she sort of climbed over into the seat.'

'Yea,' Stan had remembered something. 'It was an old - sort of sports car, two doors, big engine, but a small boot. I mean, they had to cram her in there.'

The momentum of the conversation slowed for a while; each participant dealing with their own thoughts relating to their perception of a terrified young girl being forced into the boot of vehicle - a boot too small to fit her into it - further insult to injury.

Max brought the reverie to a conclusion.

'What time was this?' he asked, looking at the girlfriend.

'Round about two - we were dropping off to sleep as they arrived, weren't we, Stan?'

'Yea - about two.'

'And what time was it when you made the call?

'I'm not sure...'

'I'll tell you, shall I? You made your call at 4.29.' Max moved a step forward, his head bent a little because of the low ceiling, 'Two and a half hours after you witnessed a girl being violently abducted, you decided to call the police?'

'I didn't want to get involved.' The body language sheepish and sullen.

'You are involved, pal. Right up to your neck. Two and a half hours. Do you know why we are here?'

'What do you mean?' The man was confused now.

His girlfriend didn't help him much as she said, 'I told you, Stan. I told you not to wait.' And the to the police officers, 'I did tell him to call the police, but he wouldn't.'

'I know - I know.' The Stan character seemed aware, and as far as he could be, he was contrite. But he had his reasons: 'Look, you said you're not gonna bust me, yeah?'

'That was then. This is now.'

'What?'

'I said that I wasn't going to bust you for drugs. And I'm not. But - Perverting the Course of Justice? You've lied to us, and you've sat on vital information for nearly three hours. What do you think?'

All three people in the caravan looked at the sorry figure of Stan – now avoiding all eye contact; his girlfriend rounding on him and although in a similar situation he might have bluffed his way out, there was no fight left in him.

'Sorry.' this to Leanne and then to the police officers, 'I was scared to call you.'

'Scared?'

'Yea, scared. Leanne kept on at me for ages to call - but I couldn't. And look where it's got me.'

'In a damn site better position than the girl you saw being attacked. That's where.' Max had lost patience now. 'We've only now recovered that girl's body. Now I don't know if we could have done anything to save her, but you didn't help, did you?'

'Her body? She's dead?'

'Oh God, Stan! The poor girl!' Leanne dissolved in tears.

'I should have called earlier, I know. But...'

'But what?'

'But I'm on a warrant from you lot - and I'm being chased by some nasty blokes back home.'

'A rock and a hard place,' commented Debesh.

'What?'

'Doesn't matter.'

'But this does matter, sir,' Max interrupted. 'You're going to have to come with us, aren't you?'

'You said you weren't going to bust me.'

'We're not. But you're doing drugs here - you might be supplying.'

'I'm not.'

'And I ought to turn this place over to make sure. But I won't do that. What I will do is this: both of you will come with us to the station and I will have DS Datta take statements from you.

'At the same time, I will have somebody run a check on you. We'll look to see how serious the warrant is - only one, you said?'

'Yeah, just one - overdue fine.'

'So, here's the thing. If what you say is true, and the warrant is for a relatively trivial matter, I'll think of overlooking it. But I want you and your girlfriend to be absolutely straight with me. I want your full cooperation.'

'Fair enough.' The young man and his girlfriend seemed to assent, and Max was sure that, given the right kind of questioning, both witnesses would give him some valuable additional information to work with.

'There's something else.' It was Leanne who had more to say.

'What?'

Stan interrupted, 'No there isn't.'

'Stan, you really are a fuckwit.' His girlfriend looked at him, took his hand in hers and said, 'They'll find out anyway. Do it - give it to him.'

Stan was too young to be getting away with what Max's grandma would have called 'a long look', but he tried it on his girlfriend anyway. It didn't work. Reluctantly, he reached into a cupboard next to where Debesh was sitting, slid the door open and lifted out a laptop computer.

'This was in her caravan. She was using it when those guys attacked her. It was still switched on - Zoom, I think. I saw a woman's face before I closed the lid and took it.'

Nine

Despite contacting dozens of people in Europe and beyond, Janko Stanovnic couldn't establish what had happened to his sister. He'd no reason to disbelieve his mother; as far as he could ascertain through the barriers of time and distance, she was mentally alert and not prone to fantastical thoughts.

She had seen Christina being abducted, so she said, and this was over twenty-four hours ago. His informal, but complex network said that his sister had travelled, possibly to Germany - and that was it.

Janko sat in the bathroom of his penthouse, the wall to ceiling window giving him an uninterrupted view of Dubai's Palm development. What a fantastic success it had been, the Palm fronds and its branches the sought-after apartments and magnificent villas, now fully occupied by many of the world's mega-rich.

One day that might be him enjoying the lifestyle these villas offered. He could relax and enjoy the wealth he was accumulating.

Now, still at the back of his mind, but persistent enough to concern him, was the emerging worry that Christina's disappearance might be connected to him and his businesses.

No proof of any kind had prompted this thinking, but it was there, scratching away at his consciousness; the doubt, the sense of dread, always present in his mind since he began his criminal career, wasn't buried deep any longer. It was starting to worry him. And in its turn that had affected his appetites. Despite the Viagra, he couldn't get it up since he'd heard from his mother.

He looked out to the right, a little further over the sea and away from the bustling success of the Palm. There, his eyes took in a cluster of what appeared to be islands, small and large piles of sand. There were meant to be three hundred of them, laboriously created off the coast, and originally meant to represent the islands of 'The World'.

Designed to outshine even the Palm, the same mega rich people who had bought into the Palm could now go up a league and say that they 'owned' the island of Russia or Germany or India. Sadly, the financial crisis of 2008 had put paid to any further development and most of these islands were now receding into the sea. Only one, Lebanon Island, had been completed.

Recently, Dubai's real estate market had picked up again; The World might possibly be redeveloped and many of those individuals and institutions that had bought into the project, often buying into it off-plan, might recoup some of their investment. However, it was rumoured that the main developer was now twenty-five billion dollars in debt. It would take a lot of island selling to turn that into profit.

The Palm and The World, two huge examples of the yin and yang of free enterprise, were a metaphor for Janko and his own business interests. There he was, king of all he surveyed, at least, king of the more seamy and unsavoury parts that he overlooked from his own huge tower of sand. Maybe it too was beginning to erode?

Ten

'It's gone international, sir.' Max was trying to brief his chief constable on the phone, but the chief was not in a receptive frame of mind. 'The girl is European, we know that. She's originally from Zagreb - Croatia, sir. She was working here.'

'Thanks for the geography lesson, Max. I'm trying to work out how we can hold on to this. I do get pissed off when offcomers start pushing their weight around. What else do you know?'

Obviously, his boss had been in contact with somebody from NCA.

'We think there's a Romanian girl involved and at least two men. We don't know their nationalities.'

 Max assumed that NCA, The National Crime Agency, as its remit required would be wanting to take over the investigation. Exactly how much of it they would own was a matter of concern to Max's boss. Political and logistical reasons would be in the mix, but above all Max reasoned the chief would be thinking of their recent failure to shine in their last murder investigation.

If NCA was to come in and, based on Max and his team's previous errors, they drew negative conclusions about their ability to function, he could see his task force being used simply as 'useful idiots' rather than as the professionals he knew them to be. And that would also be undermining his boss's credibility by proxy - after all, hadn't he promoted them?

'Are you on top of things, Max? There aren't any traps we're going to fall in to when they send up their people?'

'I'm not quite sure how to answer this, sir.' Max was beginning to bristle. 'I wasn't too happy to take this case on in the first place - I'm sure you know why. But now I am here, the team I'm working with is doing its job very well.'

'It's not easy for any of us, least of all you,' his boss replied, fully aware of the nerve he had touched. 'I've every confidence that you can do a great job. That's why I want to keep you involved.'

'Involved? We are involved.'

'I know, but the NCA have passed on this one. It's the Met that's looking after it.'

'The Met, sir?' Max wondered why London's Metropolitan police would be handling such a case.

'Wheels within wheels, Max. There's something else going on, and the Met is interested. That could be good for us. You know how it would be if the NCA did take over. They'll come in and clear everybody out, lay waste to the current investigating team and start from scratch. It might be different with the Met being involved, a more considered approach, and I am hoping to shoot for that.

'And I want you guys to be part of the investigation - my eyes and ears, if you will. That'll mean not having you banished. I am happy to insist on that, but I need to know if you are confident that your approach is working well.'

'I'm obviously biased, but I think, yes, we're doing a good job. We've not wasted any time, and we've got our systems in place.'

'I assumed that, Max, so this is what I'm going to do. I have some clout in these matters, and I'll use it. I'll insist that you and your team remain active participants in the investigation. There's somebody from the Met on their way up to the Lakes now. They'll be in touch soon. I've asked them to stop off here first so I can set them straight before they meet you. The rest will be up to you lot. Good luck.'

A few minutes later, Max was relaying this information to Debesh and Helen.

'Somebody from the Met? That's not what I expected.' Debesh was the first to offer an opinion. 'If this is as international as the chief says, there'll be some reason why the NCA has passed on it.'

'Agreed, and I told the chief the same thing. However, I know he wants us to be involved in the investigation, but he's concerned that we might be so excluded from everything that we end up playing no useful role at all.'

'That would be a waste of all this,' said Debesh, pointing generally around their office.

'He's on our side,' said Max. 'When we first got the call, it was for a murder. The nature of the death and fact that the victim is a foreigner changes everything. It throws our theory of it being a signal into relief, too.'

'On our side? What do you mean, sir? He is our boss, isn't he?'

'He wants to make sure that we aren't excluded from things. He says that he has a say in the way the relationship is to be set up.'

Debesh was dubious, 'Do you think the guy from the Met will start from scratch and chuck us out?'

'No, I think the chief is going to put his foot down on this one.' Max said this with a confidence that possibly belied his real feelings. 'And it'll help him - and us too - if we have all our ducks in a row.'

He turned to Helen, 'To work, then. The girl's computer? How are we getting on with that?'

'It's here, sir.' She pointed to the purple laptop on her desk, decorated with stickers of flowers and two photos, eastern European pop stars, she surmised. 'Nothing special on it. Her contact lists are all to do with an area around Zagreb. I've read some of her emails...'

'You've read them?'

'Google Translate, sir.'

'Oh. OK - Nope. Still no wiser – Joke!'

'I translated a few of her emails using it. She'd sent a few to some friends. Nothing much more.'

'No passwords?'

'No, sir. There's very little on it. She applied directly for this job in the Lakes. The camp site advertised four seasonal positions on the web. There's a bit of correspondence - she's used Google Translate for that as well, but there's relatively little else. Her search history is about places, seasonal jobs here and in Scotland. She's also written to three or four hotels, but they were on the south coast, Bournemouth area mainly. There's nothing I can find yet that is suspicious.'

'The bad lad?' Debesh was hoping that they might find a link.

'That's Janko. We know he's her brother, but they don't communicate. There's nothing on this computer linking her to him. She doesn't even seem to have his email address.'

'Maybe she's taken a view,' Max was wondering if she'd made a conscious decision. 'Brother's a criminal; she's a good girl. Get away and stay out of contact.'

'It looks like that, sir. Could be.' Helen had thought the same way, 'That's what I would do too.'

'Was there a phone?'

Debesh and Helen both looked at their notes. Debesh was first to say that so far, there was no sign of one.

'To sum this lot up, then,' Max continued. 'The girl seems to have come here, maybe to get away from something - perhaps she was simply bored at home, maybe she was frightened of being drawn into criminal activity. She doesn't want to make a completely clean break; she wants to keep in touch with her mum, so she uses Zoom.

'We need to find out more about her mum and her family, including this Janko guy. If she was hiding, she didn't make a very good job of it. Someone knew where she was.'

Debesh interjected, 'These matters will be taken over by the Met. We can't expect to be in on that loop.'

'You are even more pessimistic than me, Debesh. I would have thought that the love of a good woman would provide you with a more optimistic view of life. And on that very point...'

Max was diverted from his train of thought by the buzzing of his mobile, 'And yes, here we are.' He glanced at the interruption, a new text message. 'Our new colleague, Detective Chief Superintendent Melissa Mordaunt.' He emphasised the 'Melissa'. 'Melissa Mordaunt, will be joining us of this afternoon.'

'The officer from the Met?' Debesh asked.

'Yes, that was the chief. He wants us to meet our new colleague at three. And we'll be here, won't we? The chief said that he'd have a word with her about what our role might be. He's said nothing negative - nothing to warn us about her, so I think that we should look forward with optimism to the meeting. In the meantime, while we wait for the input from the from the DCS, let's get back to why we are here. Christina Stanovnic. The big question must be why was she killed - killed like that? And more importantly... well, you know the answer to that. Suggestions?'

Debesh, covering lost ground suggested, 'The caravan site, sir? The people who employed her. They might have further information for us.'

'Has anyone spoken to them yet?'

'No, sir. They weren't at home when Uniform called at their house. The officer left a message, but they've not got back to us so far.'

'So, that's the first on the list. Next?'

Debesh continued, 'We should see if the bad boy, Janko, has any connections in the area.'

'Agreed. That might provide us with a motive - revenge, a warning - maybe frightening off from something. What's the drug scene like now?'

'Rife, I'd say.' Debesh continued, 'It's the county lines thing. Dealers in the big towns and cities extending their range by recruiting kids locally to do their work for them? Well here, right off the M6, near to main roads, Barrow, Whitehaven, Carlisle, we're right in the middle of it. So, the dealers here are different, not necessarily the shaven-headed thug, but that nice boy next door who's got a 'mate' in Liverpool or Manchester. It's very worrying.'

Wordsworth took up on this. 'We'd be crazy not to start with this, then. It's got all the signs.'

'Agreed, sir,' replied Debesh. 'It has. Sadly. That poor girl is a victim of something or other. Stringing her up like that must be a sign.'

'OK, then.' Max had decided. 'Helen, I want you to do some trawling - have a look for those county lines guys, especially any that are operating around here. Try for some names, places and so on.'

'Debesh, I think that a good first base for us would be to get to see what Uniform has garnered in their interviews of the locals - and we'll chase up on the Janko bad boy to see if he has any connection with the area. If not, maybe we can discount him and start to look elsewhere. Let's get to it. And back here for our three o'clock meeting with the DCS - and all the joys that she'll add to the mix.'

Eleven

Despite each of them having a long to-do list of tasks to achieve that day, Helen, Debesh and Max all managed to be back at the Ambleside police station before three that afternoon - the main reason not being an obsession with punctuality, but their wish not to start off on the wrong foot with Detective Chief Superintendent Melissa Mordaunt of the Metropolitan Police. They were all surprised to find that she hadn't arrived.

'Any message, Helen?' Max enquired.

'No, sir. Nothing.'

'And I took special care - I bust a gut to get here on time.' was Debesh's first comment. He moved across to the small kitchen area where he filled the kettle for what he considered to be a well-earned cup of tea. 'I managed to see the owners at the caravan site, but I must have walked five miles around the place before I found them.'

Max and Helen looked at each other, and without responding in any way to his attention seeking, continued to mine their various devices for whatever information they could find: Max searching his messages, Helen her emails.

'Let's not waste the time; we can make sure that we're prepared. So Debesh, make yourself a cuppa, I'll have one too - and you, Helen?' Helen nodded in the affirmative, a brief smile indicating her pleasure at seeing Debesh's slight domestic discomfort.

'So, the owners. Sit down and tell us what you've found,' Max continued.

'It's not a great deal more than we have already.' Debesh was juggling cups and a recalcitrant carton of milk, which he'd managed to spill on the work surface. 'Largely what we know already. They seem to be pleasant people. They'd recruited through an internet agency in the past, but Christina had written to them directly, using the contact page on their website. They'd employed girls, always girls, from eastern Europe before; they said they were much better workers than they could find locally. They liked her. I think they appreciated the initiative she'd shown in contacting them directly. And they said they were right to employ her; she was a good worker.

'One interesting thing, though.' Debesh had wiped the mess he'd made and completed his multi-tasking by bringing three cups of tea over to where Helen and Max were sitting, 'They didn't know she was sharing the caravan with anyone.'

Max perked up. 'They didn't?'

'No, the owners don't live on the site, and they have a site manager who just works days. He said he'd just found out and noted her name. Christina was on call at night when they went back home to Ambleside. They don't rely on the mobile connection there, it's too intermittent, but they have a phone outside the reception cabin and that was put through to her caravan in the evening.

'So, because she was alone on the site, she could have - evidently did have - anyone she wanted staying with her, and unless the owners came to her caravan to check it out, there was no way they could have known who was there.'

'No indications as to how long the second girl had been there?'

'Not from the owners, no,' Debesh continued. But remember, we do know from the Geordie guy, Stan - and his girlfriend. The second girl turned up about a couple of days before the incident.'

Wordsworth toyed with his spoon as he thought through where they were on all this. 'This second girl was obviously sent. There must be some connection. Debesh, did the owners say anything about employing any more people?'

'I asked them that,' Debesh replied, 'and the answer was absolutely not. It's not been a good season, and they were wondering whether they would keep Christina on. They'd originally intended to employ four people, ended up only employing her. They'd recently decided to leave things for a while before deciding because they liked her so much - and she was a good worker.'

'Helen, you checked her out. What was her job? What did she do there?' Max was wondering if she might have met someone on the site. 'Did she have much to do with the customers?'

'Not as part of her job,' was Helen's reply. 'She cleaned the toilet blocks and emptied the rubbish bins, so she might have met some of the customers. But her main responsibilities didn't involve regular contact with them.'

She continued, 'I also checked up on her employment status. All perfectly legal. She was on the books and was registered for tax and NI.'

Max nodded through that and then he asked, 'Have we found out any more about the brother - Janko, isn't it?'

Helen responded: 'There's no record of him working here in the UK. Strange, there's an Interpol tag out on him, they do know of him, but possibly not enough to arrest him. He seems to spend most of his time in the Middle East. I see no obvious connection to here, other than that of his sister.'

'Maybe he's a coincidence,' said Debesh.

'Maybe he is,' replied Max, 'but - there's something to do with the Lakes - or somebody in the Lakes.'

'Sir, I know we think that Christina's death was a signal, a sign of some kind.' Helen intervened. 'But the fact that we've agreed that doesn't mean it's true. There could be an entirely different reason why she was killed in that way.'

'Such as?' Both police officers came out with the same question at the same time.

'I don't know - jealous boyfriend, maybe?'

'OK,' Max was keen to collate whatever information they had so far.

'Helen, will you stick up the stuff we've got so far so that we all can see it? Debesh, you come with me, we'll have a chat with Traffic, and we'll see if there's any CCTV material anywhere.'

He continued, 'Oh, and see if you can find the missing Chief Superintendent Mordaunt. I don't want to have to send out Mountain Rescue.'

There was a smile playing on his lips as he said this, and as he turned to leave the room, he almost collided with a tall, slim woman who at that moment had walked in the door. The smile vanished as he regained his balance and tried to fashion a smile of welcome but failed. A face contorted by a rictus of embarrassment was Chief Superintendent Mordaunt's first impression of the man standing in front of her.

'DCI Wordsworth?'

'Yes ma'am.'

'I'm sorry I'm late. No excuses. Yours is a lovely area and I took a little more time than I should have coming here.'

The superintendent immediately added to Max's sense of discomfort when she said, 'The door was open. Are you always so lax with your security?'

The door had a keycode, but Max had left the door on the latch when he saw Helen driving into the parking area.

'My fault, ma'am,' Helen quickly interjected. 'I should have set it, but I was carrying an armful of stuff. It won't happen again.'

'I'm sure it won't,' This chief super evidently was one for the detail. 'Formal introductions: I'm Chief Superintendent Melissa Mordaunt. You will be DCI Wordsworth?'

'Yes, ma'am.' Max had regained his composure; it was about to be lost again when the chief super continued, 'Any relation to William?'

Debesh watched his boss as his reply came through politely gritted teeth. 'No, ma'am. No relation whatsoever.'

'Pity,' came the reply. 'I love his poetry - the early stuff obviously. He became boring as he got older, like most men, but some of those Dove Cottage poems are magical.'

Max, Debesh - and Helen, but from a different viewpoint entirely, had the opportunity to form their first impression of the confident woman who stood in front of them, and whose handshake was as firm as her eye contact.

Strong, but not in a masculine sense. The chief super was tall and slim, yes, but she carried herself in such a way that she 'flowed' as she walked. Lithe, easy, relaxed. However, her eyes were not relaxed as she surveyed the room. Those eyes, and their steely gaze, were weapons, and she knew it.

Helen too was immediately impressed. All of the above, yes, but she was aware of the sensitivity that underpinned each of her movements, and her glances, this way and that - to Debesh, to Max - and back to Debesh again.

What was all that about, said Helen - the wife - to herself? But Helen the administrator for this team felt that the person she was looking at had more than a strong stare. What it was, she wasn't yet sure, but Helen's immediate reaction to this new person on the scene was, she had to say it to herself, positive. She would trust this woman - implicitly.

'Tell me about the girl.' The chief super's request startled all three of them from their various reveries.

Max was first to respond, 'What would you like to know?'

'All of it, but not all of it now. Please carry on with what you are doing, and I'll bring myself up to speed.'

Helen busied herself clearing a space on the white board on the far wall while Debesh readied the flip chart that he had brought up from Kendal earlier in the day.

Max picked up a marker pen, stood to his right of the flip chart (as he had remembered from his last presentation skills course - right-handed writers, right side of the board as you face your audience) and he began to sketch a flow-chart of what they thought they knew so far.

A few minutes later, with what turned out to be somewhat desultory additions from Helen and Debesh - not their fault; they simply hadn't much more to contribute, the flow chart, such as it was, was complete.

'Not a lot to go on so far, ma'am. One dead girl and a lot of supposition.'

'Expand a little on the supposition, please.'

'Yes, ma'am, but it's based only on what we have gleaned so far, and that isn't much. The victim, Christina Stanovnic, Croatian, seems to have been murdered in such a way as to send a signal to - someone, but we're not sure who. We know she has a brother, Janko - he's a known criminal with a bit of a reputation, but he doesn't work in Cumbria - or even in the UK. So, you can see that it's a long shot. All this may be nothing to do with him at all.'

'It mightn't even be a signal, ma'am.' Debesh was chipping in. 'Could be someone with a twisted sense of humour.'

'And you might be right,' Max had intervened a little too loudly here and he moderated the volume as he continued. 'But our thoughts so far tend towards the signal theory - and if that's so, it's probably drugs related. There's always been a big drugs issue here, but recently, with the development of county lines, it seems to be getting worse.'

'It's the same everywhere.' The chief super made her first real contribution. 'So, it's not surprising.'

'Many people choose to live up here in the Lakes because they think it's different.' Debesh volunteered his opinion, but it was politely ignored as Max also decided to chime in keeping what he thought was the initiative.

'But it's not different. We've a huge drugs problem here. Big time. A subculture that's always been there. The underworld ...'

The chief super intervened again, 'But it's not the underworld, is it? It's now mainstream. It certainly is in London. Is it the same up here?'

Max answered, 'It's huge here, but most people aren't aware - or they pretend otherwise. From time to time its name changes and the subculture itself mutates. But if it doesn't affect us personally, the euphemistic way that we refer to it keeps us safe from having to confront it.

'I spend most of my time working around Preston and Blackpool. Big conurbations - lots of crime. But even there, the average middle-class resident of a suburban crescent on a pleasant estate knows nothing of the post code wars taking place beneath their noses - but their children may well have to be very careful in choosing the way they go to school each day.'

'We don't have post code wars here - yet.' Helen was thinking about this - wearing two hats again, this one, the professional one and the other the hat of Mum. 'We know that drug dealers aren't the shifty, bullet-headed thugs of our imagination, although, of course, some of them might well be.'

Debesh was remembering a recent event where he had had to arrest a very presentable, perfectly ordinary young boy from very close to where they lived.

Now that they were parents, he and Helen were beginning to wonder if they would ever have to protect their own children from this insidious evil, and how they would do it.

And Max too was right. He was stating the obvious, Helen knew, but he was also pointing out how difficult everything to do with the illegal drugs scene had become. It was impossible to police - and of course, so tempting to so many kids - especially those who knew they could never compete in any conventional sense.

Helen didn't feel constrained in the same way that Debesh did. 'Nowadays, most drugs transactions are simple matter-of-fact purchases, probably not as shaming as buying a packet of cigarettes.'

'So, it's our own fault?' asked Max.

'Probably – yes.' Helen was quick to reply. 'You can't smoke in any public place - disgusting habit. Now we 'tut-tut' smokers in the same way that we might 'tut-tut' a drunk lying in the gutter. But for many perfectly respectable people, a few 'lines of coke', a spliff or two at the weekend, some 'E's at the festival' - keeping me awake, you know - perfectly acceptable pastimes, and enjoyed by people living in the more genteel of our residential areas. That's where the market is - the county lines wouldn't exist if people like us weren't fuelling it.'

'And what are you going to do about it?' Melissa Mordaunt was looking intensely at Helen. 'What do you propose we do?'

'Me?' Helen aware of her feeble response.

'Yes. You?'

Helen tried to counter, 'We're talking about two separate things here. I'm a parent, and I also work for the police. Which do you think I should ...? We do what we can do, don't we?' Still those eyes would not let go. 'I suppose so, yes.'

'And what is that?' This had become a private conversation between the two women, although Melissa was now smiling.

Max broke the spell. 'What we can do is find out who murdered our victim, and why.'

The DCS turned her gaze on to Max, and he experienced what Helen was recovering from.

'Well DCI Wordsworth, what are your plans? What do you propose we do?'

'Rather hoping to hear from you, ma'am. You've been sent up here. We're expecting a steer from you.'

DCS Mordaunt interrupted him. 'I know. And that may well be necessary. However, your boss has asked me to keep you involved. I'd prefer to work that way to begin with. After all, you're the local experts. Is that all right with you? If not, I'll arrange to take over the whole case from tomorrow.'

'Not at all, ma'am. We were hoping for that - keeping the case.' Max looked at his colleagues. 'That's right, isn't it?'

Both Helen and Debesh nodded, simultaneously expressing their agreement. Mordaunt continued, 'I'm not sure what will happen if this truly is international. Obviously, the Met will want to head up any investigation that involves Interpol. But for now, I think it would be a waste of resources spending valuable time bringing a team from the Met up here and getting them up to speed. Let's carry on and see where we go.'

Max asked, 'Why is it the Met that's running things, ma'am and not NCA?'

'As soon as I know, I'll get back to you on that one,' came what Max thought was a somewhat cryptic reply.

As the DCS began to remove her coat and look for somewhere to hang it, the Ambleside team, each in their own way, a surreptitious glance at their colleagues, or by a sly smile, acknowledged the small victory that this decision had given them. They were going to keep the case.

Twelve

It's been a troubling few days at home with the family; a new experience I don't think I've had before. Normally I chill out straight away. Whatever I have been up to on my travels can usually be put in the box - something borderline psychopathic there, I don't doubt. But as Rod Steiger once memorably said in 'No Way to Treat a Lady' - 'That doesn't make you a bad person.'

Yes, I know. It does make you a bad person, killing people. I do know that, but I had it locked in the box, tight and secure - it goes with the job. However, that phone call about my BVI agent, Stephanie has changed everything.

Nothing I do now gets her out of my mind. She's constantly there. Everything, every interaction with my kids, with Meg, with people in the village - it's all background noise. I'm aware of it, I'm making contact, interacting, but I'm not part of it. I'm not engaged - I can't be. Stephanie is always screaming.

I go on the internet to find out more - it's all true, what that guy on the phone said. I won't give any details here because even I am shuddering at what was done to her. You can look it up for yourselves on YouTube, I imagine - or it'll soon be on one of those obscure TV documentary channels.

It's very graphic. Headlines now in the Virgin Islands - and a mention of it on BBC World Service. She was young, only about thirty-one or two. She was divorced or separated, I'm not sure which, but she lived alone. She had pets: I mention the pets because whoever did what they did to Stephanie started with her dog, a friendly, gentle sheepdog that was always with her.

The rest - what happened when they started on her is simply too gruesome - I'm saying 'they' - I've no idea how many, but the details are all over the media when I look it up. On the TV, a guy is standing outside her apartment building, telling us all as much as he dares, using words like 'mutilated' and 'torture' - on daytime TV. And this is all because of me.

It explains why my mind has been elsewhere. I can't stop thinking of her. But I can't tell the family that, can I?

My kids have been loving and kind; still competing to see who can win at extracting the most of everything from me, but as I said, quite loving with it, and a big change from their usual approach towards me.

Meg has been so solicitous, so full of love - our physical relationship as strong as ever, probably stronger than when we first met. Physically I'm strong, I can still do that, thank God, but now even in our most intimate moments, I'm elsewhere - re-running that movie in my head.

I wasn't there, I don't even know what Stephanie's place looks like, but still, I'm watching as these unknown people destroy first her dog and then slowly, ever so slowly, they take Stephanie to pieces -

butchering her. All because she wouldn't give them the information about me that they wanted.

I've got to work this out. I need to know who is after me. The caller mentioned a Janko Stanov... something - Stanovnic? He said I know him. I bloody don't. And Stephanie died because of that.

Meg interrupts my reverie, 'We're going to the Spa. You want to come for a swim as well?'

'Sounds like a great idea, although I'll give the swim a miss. I'll drive, and I'll have a beer while you and the kids enjoy yourselves.'

Meg gives me one of her looks. 'So, I'm babysitting while you ...'

'We've spent a fortune on swimming lessons - those kids are more like fish than than...'

'They're your kids.'

'Amphibians, that's what they are. Throwbacks. Not quite human, a fair imitation, I grant you...'

She's laughing at this thought, not for long though, as she's worked out that I'm going to be down in the clubhouse while the children run amok in the pool.

I reassure her, 'Tell you what. I'll get a beer and I'll sit on the balcony. You go in the steam room, the sauna, have a massage - maybe all three. Knock yourself out. Between me and the super-efficient pool people, we'll keep an eye on the - little alligators.'

She gives up on me, but we are both still laughing. It's tacitly agreed that I'll be keeping watch from the balcony while she goes and does whatever she wants to do.

And so it was that with my pint of Hawkshead Gold, a craft beer I'd only recently come across at the club, and a packet of sweet chilli flavoured crisps, I prepared to keep a weather eye over my children. Meg had helped them get changed and she was off to wherever she wanted to be, somewhere she could get some pampering.

The kids were already in the pool by the time I walked from the clubhouse bar and up to the balcony. One of the waiters had stopped me as he saw I was leaving the bar with a glass in my hand, and he politely mentioned that I couldn't take a glass into the pool area.

I should have known that - and by the time he'd swapped my pint glass for its plastic equivalent, the kids were in the pool and, as seems to happen with all kids when they go swimming, they were all shouting and screaming their heads off as they attempted to drown each other.

When Joe was four or five, we used to come here most Sundays when I wasn't working. I was in the pool with him on one of these occasions when he said that he needed to have a pee. He asked if he could do it in the pool - good of him to ask, I thought, but as a caring parent I said that he couldn't, that he'd have to get out of the pool to do it.

He did. He got out of the pool, turned, and before I could stop him, he'd peed back into the water. He's quite logical, our Joe.

As I sit down on the balcony with my plastic glass of beer and my packet of crisps, I cast my eye over the pool, scanning to see my kids and check that they are all OK, or at least, they are all there.

And they are. Chloe and Bella now bickering at each other as usual, Joe a little distance off from them but part of the group - Joe tends not to get involved in the 'twinnie politics' as Meg and I like to call them. But he was there: suddenly he's practising his surface dive and coming up between the two girls, laughing as he adjusts the new set of goggles he'd obviously manage to extract from his mother as she signed them all in at the reception desk. It's a good idea, that. Having highly priced swimming stuff close at hand so that kids' pester power can work its charm.

Meg obviously doesn't trust me as I see she's her put her head around the door of the pool to check. She sees that they are all still alive and then, clocking me, gives me a little wave.

She's seen me; knows I am on duty, and she returns to whatever it is that she's doing. The door she's opened leads to the sauna and steam room areas, so the chances are that she's going back to something hot and relaxing.

I've brought my iPad, and I'm connected to the club's WIFI to pick up on any emails. Home for a few days now and nobody has contacted me. The stress I've felt has all been internal - guilt driven, obviously, and that telephone call didn't help. I'm no further forward with that, either. It's as if I've been an observer to Stephanie's death and seen a report of it in passing on the telly, not the cause of it.

The 'Messenger' icon on my phone attracts my attention. Strange for many reasons, not least because I don't often use Messenger. I open it up and there is a message, timed two minutes ago, 'Has it happened?'

Has what happened? I'm looking at the children - they are fine, if extremely loud. Meg is in the sauna or the steam room.

Then the scream, long and heart-rending; I know whose scream it is, and I drop the iPad and quickly make my way towards the sauna area of the club. I push past two of the lycra clad pool attendants who've also heard the scream, leaving them in my wake.

When I get to her, Meg is lying on the floor by the door to the sauna. She is in spasm - arching her back and screaming with pain.

I get down beside her, 'Meg, it's me. What's happened, love?' To the two munchkins who've followed me from the pool, who've no idea what to do, I yell, 'Call the fucking police - and an ambulance. Don't just stand there!'

That gets them moving; in that moment or two Meg has lost

consciousness, and I see what's happened. Her hand and arm, from the palm to the elbow have been severely burned. 'Get some cold water, now!'

The slower of the two attendants, even slower than his colleague who at least has moved towards a phone, opens the door to the sauna, reaches in and produces the wooden pail of cold water that they splash on the whatsit to make the steam.

And of course, that's it. She's burned herself badly on the sauna thing - the heat source in the corner. That's clear. I can try to make her comfortable while we wait for the ambulance.

And the manager has arrived. He's a very tall, genial chap with horn-rimmed glasses. He normally wears a professional smile, but not now. Worried about the litigation ahead of him, I expect.

What the fuck am I saying to myself? The message - the fucking Messenger message. What did it say? 'Has it happened?' That's the message, and yes, it has fucking happened. I ask one of the attendants, 'Do you know if anyone saw anything?' No reply.

With the manager being there, they are waiting for him to answer, I suppose. Not their place - and anyway, they were out in the pool area. I assume that there are attendants there and of course I'm worrying about my kids now. This is not good - not good at all.

The manager suggests something: 'Maybe she slipped and fell against the stove.'

'Hasn't it got a guard?' My immediate response. The manager is quick to reply - potential liability does that to people, and I know exactly what he's thinking. He says, 'Yes, sir. Of course. It's a wire mesh. It should be impossible for anyone to come into direct contact with the stove.'

A young man in a tracksuit kneels next to us. He puts a doctor's medical case on the floor and begins to open it. 'Hi,' he says, 'I'm a doctor. It's OK - I've brought my bag from the car. Let me look at her, please. I'm a member.'

I'm reluctant, very reluctant - suspicious of everybody and of everything, but Richard the manager evidently knows the guy and says it's OK and that he's a member of the club, although I've never seen him before.

'The ambulance will be along in a few minutes,' Richard adds helpfully. The doctor nods and says, 'She's fainted with the pain. Pouring cold water over the wound has helped. I'll stay with her until the paramedics come to be sure. Her burns look quite serious, so there might be some slight scarring, but she'll recover.'

Meg was coming back, and as soon as she opened her eyes, she was immediately aware of the pain. 'My arm. He held it against the stove!'

'Who did?' I'm certain that all three of us asked that question simultaneously. Meg is crying now. She's aware of the pain. 'A man -

in ordinary clothes, not a swimming costume. He rushed into the sauna, grabbed me, and forced my arm on to ...'

She stops. My mind is whirring. As I think of asking the question, the doctor is there before me. 'Any CCTV?'

Richard replies. 'Yes, we've CCTV.'

'Does it cover the sauna?'

'Not inside, but all entrances and exits. We should see the person who did it, no problem.'

I'm in two minds. It's obviously a police job, but I'd dearly like to have a run at the guy first. I ask, 'Have you called the police?' Richard says that he hasn't but will do now. I continue, 'OK. While you call them, let me have a look at the CCTV.'

I see Meg look at me sort of doe eyed, worried - I understand immediately: 'I'm not going anywhere until the paramedics come, love, but this man's a doctor, and if I can get a sight of the man who's hurt you, we can get a better idea of what's happened.' Turning to Richard, I say, 'Where do you keep the CCTV?'

'I can put it up here if you like,' he says, pointing to a big flat-screen TV on the wall outside the sauna. 'You won't have to leave your wife. Shall I do that?'

'Please - as quickly as you can. And thanks.' See, I can be polite when I choose.

'Two minutes,' he replies, and he shoots off to his office - or to wherever they keep the CCTV.

Meg has calmed down a little. The doctor hasn't covered up the wound; he's letting the air get to it. I can see the burned area - most of her forearm, and she's in a lot of pain, but she's not screaming now, not even wincing. The doctor sees that I'm processing the situation, and he mentions that he'll give her something to reduce the immediate pain.

The ambulance arrives. I don't see it, but two paramedics come trundling down from the bar area, each carrying a big green bag, and the doctor, having introduced himself, and showing no inclination to retire from the situation, begins the kind of technical conversation that needs to happen, but which allows me to zone out.

I am about to hurry up Richard the manager when I remember the kids. The kids. They are still in the pool - at least, I hope they are.

'I'll be back in a minute,' I say to nobody in particular, and I rush back to the pool, through the door and into the steamy, chlorine smelling atmosphere where I can see that my kids are still busily occupied trying to drown each other, shouting the odds at being splashed, and generally having a great time.

I look to see if any of the attendants is paying attention to them, and one is. A young girl, maybe late teens early twenties, with a long ponytail of blonde hair is keeping an eye on my kids - probably because they are so noisy.

My entrance, or at least my clothing catches her eye. 'Sorry, I'm not swimming. Those three are my kids. Could you keep an eye on them for a few minutes? I've something that I need to do urgently. Thanks.'

I don't wait for a reply. St Augustine says something about presumption, but I've no time to discuss anything with him. I need to see if I can lay eyes on the scrote who's done this to Meg.

Back at the sauna, the paramedics have decided they don't need to cart Meg off to hospital, but they recommend that she goes to our local health centre where a nurse can make sure she'll receive the right kind of care - that's some relief to me. Meg's not as badly hurt as I thought.

One of the pool attendants motions to me look at the screen. Richard's put up the CCTV and we all see the figure of a man. By the way he walks, he seems to be youngish and fit. His head isn't covered, but he looks away from two cameras as he makes his way down the corridor.

He turns into the sauna and steam room area. There we see him look around, open the door to the sauna and a few seconds later he comes back out, exiting the way he came.

'Do you know who that man is?' I ask the young, bearded lad who seems to be most attentive.

'No, That's the first time I've seen him.'

'Didn't he sign in?' I know that everyone signs in. And if he did, there'll be the reception CCTV for me to look at.

'Don't think so,' the lad continues, probably completely unaware of how he is now pissing me off. It's not his fault, but this is a club; they must check who comes in. 'I've been on the desk for the last hour. And I didn't leave - I was doing the charts.'

Me neither. I assumed that he means something to do with the measurements they are taking all the time, pool *pH* and so on, but if he saw nobody, that doesn't help me much.

The kids – again. The thought explodes in my mind. I've been so concerned about Meg and then that guy on the CCTV that I've forgotten I've left them alone in the pool. Yes, they are with that pretty, blonde lass, but she won't know what's been going on.

I'm on my way back to them; no time to wait. I snap at the boy - 'You record all of this, don't you?' As he begins to nod a yes, I follow up with, 'Look at all the CCTV you have. Collect any images of that guy.' I then add the word, 'please'. Well, it's not his fault, and I'm not yet in complete psycho mode.

The boy thinks I am - in complete psycho mood, that is - and it's not so much a beard that he has, come to think of it. Bum fluff. He's a boy, maybe eighteen or nineteen, and my actions? My manner? He looks at me nervously; something about my body language has disturbed him.

'I'll be back in a few minutes,' I say. 'I'm going to get my kids. Do me a favour and get me a copy of anything relating to that man on the video. There's fifty quid in it for you if you do.'

His eyes light up at that, only a little, but enough. I set off down the corridor towards the kids. I'm going to get them out, get them dressed, collect Meg and take her home. Yes, I'll take her to the health centre if I must, but I know she doesn't like a fuss, and it would be so much easier if we could all get home, so I could have a few minutes to reflect on what's happening.

Time for reflection is immediately over. Messenger buzzes on my phone. I open it. It says, 'That was your last reminder. Fix Janko Stanovnic.'

That name again. I don't know who this person is - and I am to fix him?

As I return to reception with the children in tow I am certainly in the mood to 'fix' somebody. My demeanour obviously disturbs my young friend with the beard. He's standing at the reception desk holding a small flash drive and obviously wishing he was somewhere else - anywhere else, rather than here.

I smile at him; I think that troubles him even more, but I thank him for his efficiency and give him the reward that I'd promised. He's still not happy, but the money works its magic - it always does, doesn't it?

I've now got my three shopaholic monsters with me - it's amazing how quickly they can get their hands on the kind of expensive crap the club keeps for its less discerning members.

Suddenly more aerodynamic goggles become a 'must buy' for Chloe – she just seen Joe's new ones; Bella and Joe want ludicrously expensive swimming costumes as obviously, the ones they have now are so embarrassing for them to be seen in. Of course, Chloe agrees.

I capitulate. I've much more important things to do - and quickly. My Meg is languishing somewhere down the corridor, waiting for me. I hurry up the kids, telling them that we've got to get to their mother quickly, as she has had an accident.

You know what? I would have expected at least one of them to show some concern. Joe affects to, but he's much keener on choosing which of the new Speedos he's fumbling with best suits his skin tone, or whatever.

No, the little dears hardly acknowledge this. It's one of those moments that a cynical old bastard like me files away for future reference. There will be Karma somewhere further down the line.

But not now. 'Right, you lot,' I say, 'Choosing time is over. No more. Chloe, you can have both if you choose them now.' She wavers. 'This minute!'

Neither of the others needs prompting and they all line up as the boy on reception, the one who has already trousered fifty quid from me, rings up another eighty-odd pounds for his employers, and I suppose, for his bonus. He's had a good day, although you couldn't tell by looking at him.

The children greet their mother by showing her the various swimming paraphernalia they have acquired. Her response is to mention that they must have caught their daddy in a very good mood. She could not be more mistaken.

Meg appears to be bearing up. Whatever painkillers the doctor gave her seem to be working; she's much more settled now.

She waits until we are in the car, the kids comparing their relative retail victories over me, when she says, 'Who was it?'

'I don't know.' It's an honest answer, but we both know it's entirely inadequate.

'That man came straight for me. It wasn't an accident.'

So that's out as a possible smokescreen - no point in my trying to go down that route. Meg continues, 'He was smiling as he did it, too.'

'Would you recognise him again?'

'Of course, I'd recognise him again.'

I've seen the video, and I hope that if my little bearded friend has done his work properly, I've got a flash drive with me that's got images of him on it as well.

He made no attempt to hide his face. I'm drawing the conclusion from this that he isn't 'known', but overwhelmingly I'm now convinced that he won't be around here anymore to be discovered. He'll have been spirited away, beyond the grasp of our police and probably our security agencies.

This pulls me up, and I only half hear Meg's protestations. I hear she's annoyed; she's hurt, angry and a whole lot more, but now it's white noise to me. I'm thinking.

This is a set up. He's someone who won't be recognised, and who doesn't worry if he is recorded. At the first level, most of us will think of someone simply without a criminal record. And if you do think that, please continue to live your life in blissful ignorance.

Sadly, bitter and twisted cynic that I am, I cleave to a different world view. That of a one off, an innocent if you will, but also a disposable, imported single-use weapon. In my waters I know what's gone on - and I wish that I could unthink it.

Mine's a murky life - coming up for air only when I can be refreshed and cleansed by Meg and the Lakes itself, and with the experience I have from that seamy, aberrant twilight world where I am forced to operate, I conclude we've just experienced the equivalent of a suicide bomber.

That young man has been seduced into thinking that a world of riches and luxury awaits him - if he only performs this one, simple task. Not the 'seventy-two virgins' kind of promise, not the martyr's death kind of promise.

I imagine that he, like many others, would have run a mile if the word death, especially his death, had been mentioned at all. No, his reward was to be entirely temporal; a house for his mum, a flashy sports car, money so that he could indulge himself in any way he wished.

My world view knows that won't happen. Spirited away somewhere, maybe even out of the country by now, my bet was that this young man, the bastard who had sought out and attacked my wife, that man was an innocent.

His reward wouldn't be the promised riches of his imagination. The private jet waiting for him wasn't the first step on his journey to indulgence, it was a convenient way of getting him into the air so that he could be thrown out of an aircraft without disturbing any other passengers.

That's entirely fanciful, of course, but it's what I would have done had he worked for me. I've no real idea what's happened.

He might already be in a ditch somewhere, simply shot in the head or clubbed to death five minutes away from the Spa. Whatever his demise, I know the reason why he didn't bother hiding his face was that he's been told it didn't matter; he was going to be looked after.

Meg now says that she doesn't feel so good, and that we'd better go to the health centre after all. I'm to have those three screaming monkeys having at each other for a long time yet before I can get them to bed and start to think about Janko Stanovnic. If I am to 'fix' him, I need to know who he is.

And I need to know who is sending me messages. The only thing that I do know is that Stephanie had my Messenger address - along with Archana in Dubai. Nobody else.

Thirteen

'It's where?' Janko Stanovnic was standing in the middle of London St Pancras station, looking bemusedly at a statue of the poet, John Betjeman. He'd left the Eurostar platform assuming that his next train would be upstairs, and he'd gone straight up the escalator hoping to catch it.

'You'll have to walk to another station. It's called Euston - you could catch the Tube.'

'The what?'

He was Facetiming his Paris contact, the young man who'd met him from his flight at Charles de Gaulle airport and taken him to the Eurostar terminal at the Gare du Nord. 'It's the Metro - you take that to Euston station - or you can walk.'

'How far is it?'

'Not far. Five to ten minutes walking.'

'I'll walk.'

'There's a parcel waiting for you in Left Luggage too.'

'You remembered? That's a surprise.'

'It's everything you requested, sir.'

'You better be right.'

His plan was for him to get to the Lake District and find out what had happened to Christina, nothing else. He'd taken the big decision, more of a knee-jerk reaction than an informed choice, but he'd wound down his immediate Dubai activity, leaving it in the not-so-capable hands of Ferenc and his accountant, Kranti. Promises had been made, but Janko was certain he wouldn't return.

He'd decided to fly to Paris and take the Eurostar into London, not wanting to risk being recognised at airport immigration as a person of interest.

However, the passport and immigration check was quite as rigorous on Eurostar as anywhere else, but they had nodded him through. His Croatian passport meant that he didn't need a visa, and he was pleasantly surprised not to be stopped. Maybe next time he'd simply fly straight in - although he hoped there wouldn't be a next time.

Now he was in London, he wanted to get up to the north of the country immediately and check out what had happened to Christina. Then he would decide what, if anything, happened next.

His Paris contact was right; the walk to Euston station took him a little under ten minutes. He kept his head down, his brain working hard at trying to make sense of everything.

This was his first visit to London, first to the UK, but he was no tourist. He ignored the British Library building completely but was strangely aware of the nose-to-tail traffic that came towards him as he walked - exactly like the Sheikh Zayed road, but here a new experience for him, as it was always too damned hot to walk anywhere in Dubai.

He'd drawn down on a business connection, someone in his line of work who'd agreed to provide him with some items he felt were necessary while he was in the UK.

As he didn't know what to expect when he eventually arrived at the place where Christina had been murdered, he needed a weapon to protect himself and some money to use as and when he needed it.

A package was waiting for him at Euston, and once he had opened it and checked its contents, he felt somewhat more secure, even if he had no idea what he was going to do when he arrived at his destination.

But there was no weapon. Money that he'd asked for, yes. A large packet of white powder that was one of his currencies of choice, yes, but no weapon.

He got on to Facetime. His Paris contact answered.

'You said everything would be there for me to pick up at Euston. Where's the fucking gun?'

His contact was confused. 'I was told that everything would be there, sir.'

'Well, it's not, is it?' Janko was angry and about to start swearing again, taking his anger out on someone he'd never met before and who was in a different country anyway.

He had to leave the conversation as it was. Maybe he'd pick up on it later. He'd have to let his anger stew a little longer.

What else could he do? He hadn't flown halfway around the world because of Christina's death Because of his love for her. Her death had been an insult to him - a deliberate attack.

He'd never much cared for Christina. Not entirely accurate, it wasn't that he hadn't cared, it was more that he hadn't noticed her. She was a kid, someone of no importance or value to him; she was always there, hanging around at home, watching, observing him, but rarely saying anything.

She was there as he developed his 'look': the stance, the posture, the technique of dealing with every attempt at communication, friendly or not, as it it presented a threat. He perfected the long stare of defiance and the dismissive shrug of contempt by practising them on his mother, and of course, on his little sister.

As he cultivated his 'inner chimp', or in his case, his inner gorilla, he'd practise by constantly demeaning his mother - and when she was at work or out of the house, he'd turn his attention to Christina.

Janko doubted that either his mother or his sister missed him. Why would they? In the couple of years before he'd upped and left, he'd made their lives a misery. The implied threat in his every action, his every response no matter how conciliatory or friendly their approach, meant that they were both nervous and constantly on edge.

He knew they were both relieved when he left home, the permanent sense of dread lifted from them; from then on perhaps only acknowledging his relevance at all as the odd envelope of cash or some undreamed of luxury came their way. That didn't bother him; he knew he had created the person he now was, and that person did not 'do' families.

When his mother called him and told him that Christina had been abducted, his initial response was to do nothing, to let it go. But when the news came through on YouTube, and he saw how she'd been murdered - strung up in public view, with the world's media happily showing all that they could to millions of prurient viewers, it took no time at all for him to conclude that this was a signal meant for him. And that he needed to respond.

His plan, such as it was, involved him finding out who had murdered his sister, extracting all the information he would need for his next steps from whoever this person was - naturally in as painful and lingering a way as possible, and then, if he could find him, dispatching the head guy as a bonus.

Its only merit was that it was a simple plan, a perfect 'KISS' (keep it simple, stupid), but there were other reasons that had precipitated this course of action. In a way Janko's journey to England was more of a displacement activity than a mission.

The incident with Christina was all he'd needed to make this decision, and once he'd made it, he moved quickly. He had to get away from Dubai, and he knew it. Truth be told, things were not going too well for him.

Nothing he couldn't handle, he'd told himself, but his Saudi clients were causing trouble, and the kind of difficulty they might cause him had been emphasised when he recalled the incident of a Saudi citizen going into one of his country's embassies and apparently being chopped up into little pieces by a doctor with a bone saw.

If they could do that to one of their own people, reasoned Janko, then they might think of doing something even more creative with him. Those North Korean girls he'd sold them - he referred to them as the 'grass eaters', hadn't proved to be a satisfactory purchase. Two of them had died and at least three more had a variety of unsavoury illnesses that made them completely unfit for purpose.

Now he regretted what had been his next move. Rather than simply lance the boil immediately and replace the sick girls with another bunch of higher quality merchandise, Janko's response had been immediate, but completely devoid of any forethought. In a testosterone-driven tirade, he'd simply told his Saudi clients to fuck off.

And of course, that didn't work. They hadn't fucked off. In fact, their threats - all made in that creepy, understated 'keep your enemies closer' mode had decided Janko to move on.

It was his own fault; he'd created the toxic atmosphere, and his people sensed it. He saw it in the way they now looked at him, so he would move on while he could. His luck had held so far, and he had amassed a huge amount of money - all of it in cash; he could set up business somewhere else where he wouldn't have a bunch of angry Arabs - he couldn't get that bone saw out of his mind - chasing after him.

And he reasoned, he could always return later, or not. He might decide to go to Hong Kong or maybe Macau. It was so easy to set up business anywhere if you had the capital, and he had piles of the stuff.

Winding down his business in Dubai so that he could get away to Europe was simplicity itself. All the cash that he'd built up went into over forty newly opened bank accounts - thanks to DIFC, Dubai's international financial centre.

He and Kranti, his little Indian accountant, had spent a couple of days moving boxes and briefcases of one thousand-euro bills, one hundred-dollar notes and large and small denominations of a dozen other currencies.

His arsenal of weapons - they wouldn't be used again - was taken out to sea by boat and dumped. He oversaw this process personally: he couldn't take the risk and leave them in the Arjan building; someone might get ideas.

The only things that he proposed to leave were his debts. His twenty-room apartment overlooking the Palm development, gone - the guy could whistle for what he was owed. His cars, his other properties, all leased in the same way. He would simply walk away. Their owners would have to take the hit.

Islamic banking forbids loans bearing interest, so lenders have found creative ways of making a profit. In Janko's case, for each of his acquisitions, the properties and cars that he leased, he'd signed a set of post-dated cheques.

They were set to kick in each month for the length of the lease. So far, he had paid these cheques on the nail, not out of any particular wish to please, but because it's a criminal offence in the UAE to bounce a cheque, and he had heard a little too much about the living conditions in Dubai's prisons. Now, when he left, these cheques would be so much litter.

And it wasn't as if this was going to be unexpected. After the great financial meltdown of 2008, thousands of expats lost their jobs in Dubai, and most of them had written a similar set of post-dated cheques for the cars they could no longer afford.

The rumour was that in January 2009, over twenty thousand cars and other vehicles had been left at the airport when their owners decided not to risk becoming entangled in Dubai's legal processes. A few years later, Janko was leaving the debts on three or four rented properties and half a dozen cars. He would simply be adding to what was already a very long list.

Now in the UK, and with Dubai left far behind him, he hoped that when he understood what had happened to his sister, he could firm up his actions for his immediate future.

The short walk from St Pancras completed, Janko bought a ticket for his journey from Euston. He went first class, wondering when he saw how much it was costing him, if he'd just bought a private carriage for himself.

He saw from the display signs on the concourse that his train was ready for boarding and that people were moving towards it, racing to get to their seats.

Once in his seat on what was a very crowded train, he settled himself down and tried to think about why he'd found himself on this journey. It was his pride, nothing else. Was that enough? Janko, being Janko concluded that yes, it was.

Fourteen

'I'm in a pretty little hotel overlooking Windermere, but I think I'd prefer somewhere else, somewhere that's a little less formal and a bit quieter?' The upward inflection of the last part of the sentence was for the benefit of Melissa Mordaunt's mother, who'd rung up to see how her daughter was doing.

'We stayed in the Lakes for our honeymoon - only a day or two. We always said that we'd go back one day.'

'Can you remember where?'

'Long time ago. A guest house, somewhere near Keswick, I think. But we drove through Ambleside on our way up there. It's beautiful where you are.'

'It is. I like it. I'm staying on to work with the local team here. See how we get on. So, I thought that I'd find somewhere to stay that suits me better.'

'What's wrong with where you are now? It looks lovely - on the internet. It'd be perfect for me.'

'You're right. It is lovely and very expensive - and I know I'm not paying for it; that's not the point. No, it's not me. I'm not comfortable. I can't relax; I hate getting dressed up in the evening so I can go down for dinner. I want to slob around or go walking.'

'You can do that from there. Nobody will mind.'

'I'm looking for somewhere more secluded. Somewhere in one of the valleys and away from the town. It mightn't be necessary. If I finish up here quickly, I won't have to worry, will I?'

'No, I suppose not.'

'And anyway, Mum, what about you? How are you?' Melissa's dad had passed away only a few months ago, and they both were still coming to terms with his loss and the lifestyle changes that it brought about.

Melissa had thought long and hard before deciding to come up to the Lakes - she could have dispatched someone else, but this job was too important for her to let it go. Nevertheless, she was concerned that her mother might still need her.

'I'm fine, darling. Thanks. Better than I thought I would be. I'm keeping busy, that's the answer. No use in my moping about. Don't you worry, I'm ok.'

The conversation continued in the same desultory fashion for a few more minutes. Melissa was an only child; her job as she now saw it was to comfort her mother in any way she could.

Despite this, the reality of her working life had involved her developing the persona of a hard-driven winner, someone who had risen through the ranks of the police force without allowing anything to get in her way - domestic or professional. Nowadays, you crossed

Melissa Mordaunt in work mode at your peril.

She was in her element as a DCS. Her skills as an investigator recognised, her ability to develop ideas and see them through was evident ever since she had first joined the Met as a graduate trainee fifteen years ago.

In some quarters, she was already being seen as a potential Chief, or even Met Commissioner, and Melissa herself was aware of how she was regarded in the force.

She wanted this case to be successful. It mattered primarily because the victim was young and female, but also because it was throwing up the kinds of problem that she seemed uniquely capable of resolving.

She had a knack - the ability to forge a simple result out of an infinite number of increasingly complex factors, and this was becoming her trademark, so adept at it she seemed to be.

Although it was true she had those skills, she hadn't been posted to the Lakes on a whim. The Met had an additional interest in this case, and it was one which she had been asked not to divulge. It might not come to anything, but it could be huge and if it did explode, there would be massive repercussions throughout the UK.

Now settled in her hotel, she looked around her room. Her laptop lay open in front of her, her mobile next to it and the sheaf of assorted papers that she'd been looking through were scattered on her bed. 'That's it,' she said to herself, 'I've got to get out.'

'You know what, mum? I'm going for a walk. I'll call you later, there's lots I've got to think through, and I can't do that here 'cos I'm surrounded by too much - stuff. You take care of yourself and let me know, yeah?'

'Let you know what? What's the matter?'

'Mum, if you want to talk to me, give me a call. I know I'm busy but I'm here at the end of the line if you want me and want to chat about anything.'

Her sudden decision to go for a walk and terminate the call with her mother had been caused by another thought. As she was speaking to her mother, she'd asked a question: would any of her male colleagues have done this - have this kind of conversation?

Was this because she was female, and therefore, naturally more empathetic? Was it because she was shoving her male colleagues into convenient stereotypes? She thought she knew the answer. DCI Wordsworth was a definite no, but she was not so sure about Debesh; he seemed quite sensitive in his own way.

Thinking like this had disturbed her so much that she had to get out, get some fresh air - and soon, very soon, find another a place to stay in which she might relax at the end of a day's work.

Fifteen

That recent experience at the spa has concentrated my mind. Meg is still wearing a bandage covering the burn mark on her arm. The burn itself is less serious than we feared; however, the way it was inflicted and the fact that somebody not only knows where I am but was prepared to take such a risk, has forced me to think of doing some intensive research.

I also owe an apology to my kids. I was annoyed with them when Meg was attacked because they seemed to be much more interested in ransacking the little shop at the spa reception than finding out what had happened to their mum.

I got that completely wrong: on reflection, it seems much more likely they were displacing their real feelings, those of shock, fear - maybe guilt - focusing their minds on stuff that they could control.

They knew that their pester power was a skill they could use; they didn't have to think anything through; it came naturally to them. Hammering my credit card was a much better option than having to confront a rather stark reality.

And so, it proved as when they got home, their genuine concern was there for me to see - they want to care for their mother, want to protect her as well as they can by doing everything possible to help around the house. I hadn't anticipated this turnaround, and I feel ashamed for having misread their behaviours so spectacularly.

I leave them proving me wrong on so many levels and go down to my office. I look out over the lake and give myself a few minutes to think things through.

I log in and start to mine the riches of the internet. I now know the person I'm looking for, and it's up to me to make sure that I catch up with him and if possible, get a few steps ahead. I need to find who this man is and then find out what he wants with me.

And I find him very quickly. Knowing his name leads me straight to the man himself. Google also tells me that Janko Stanovnic is a very unpopular man. He's annoyed many people other than me.

I look at what Mr Google has to say about him. As far as I can tell, he's somebody I already ought to know. Obviously a bad boy; I'm surprised that we haven't connected. He runs the kind of gang I've often had to deal with. Based in Dubai, he's mostly in prostitution - and trafficking, and he also has a reputation for supplying Class A drugs throughout the whole of the Middle East.

That's why we haven't come into contact. Most of my work over the last two or three years has been in South-east Asia, in Australia and the US. I've often been in Dubai, occasionally stopping off to discuss projects with Archana who's lived there for many years, but I've had no work to speak of in that region for ages.

What the hell does this mean? Somebody, somebody who is quite exercised by this Stanovnic guy feels it's so important that he threatens me and my family.

Why didn't he just offer me a fee? I don't take kindly to being threatened, and unlike most people, when I have been threatened in the past, I've done something about it.

This person who is chasing me, threatening my family in order that I do something on his behalf, must know that. He must feel sufficiently confident that he can handle me - get me to comply. Equally, whatever it is he wants me to do must be very important for him to want to take the risk.

I hear a little bit of noise from upstairs; the children are doing their thing and as a result, Meg is cheered up no end. That part is easy. My next step is a different proposition - and I'm still looking.

I've found enough information to know that this guy, Stanovnic, could well be a threat - certainly to other people involved in the same kind of low-life activity. Rats in a sack. What I don't yet understand is why I've been involved, and why I have been threatened in this way?

Sixteen

'The Met seems happy to have us run with it for a little longer.' Max was reading from the email that had popped up on his screen.

'Your DCS Mordaunt's been on your case. That's OK, isn't it - having her on your side?' Debesh was in a sunny mood; he and Helen had enjoyed their weekend. Nothing had been said about that baby elephant in the room - her keeping her husband in the dark as she negotiated her return to work.

'Cheeky sod. She's not *my* DCS, but thanks all the same; she'll have had a word, I guess. And what that means is that we've got to show some progress. So, what do we have?'

Helen had booted up her computer and linked it to a small projector. The resulting image on the office wall used the timeline on a Gantt chart to indicate the progress the team had made.

'We know who the victim is, we know how and when she died. We've an idea - from the statement given at the caravan site - that this was a planned event. There were two men and a woman - we believe the woman could be the same nationality as the victim, Croatian, so maybe the two men were Croatian too.

'We might be wrong here as her name could be Romanian; we don't know whether 'Elena Popa', the name she gave the caravan site owners was genuine. So, we are still assuming the Croatian link, but cautiously.'

Helen turned to her two colleagues, 'That's all we have. We need more detail - a motive, for example.'

No-one had yet said it, but there was a collective feeling in the room that things had come to a standstill.

Over the weekend, Max, Debesh and Helen in their own ways had quietly enjoyed their weekend - particularly the young married couple who, by fully immersing themselves in the joys of playing with their daughter Ellie, managed without too much effort to find some diversion, at least temporarily.

But at some time during the weekend, each of them had turned their minds more than once to their case, and where it was going.

Monday morning, and Max decided that they needed to change the emphasis: 'Debesh, you and I are going to be doing some more old-fashioned police work - it helped us locate Christina, didn't it? Let's see what we can find.

'Helen, you'll stay here. If you get any info, shoot it over to us immediately. I'll catch up with the DCS sometime today, assuming she's still around. When she comes into the office, get her to do some trawling with her own contacts to see if they can throw up anything of value.'

'Right, sir.' Helen's assertive tone belied her own true state of mind. She felt they'd already come to a dead end, not their fault, but possibly a sign of failure to the cold eyes of some decision maker behind a desk in the Met.

With Max and Debesh out of the office and left to her own devices, Helen got on with doing what she did best: organising.

She spent twenty minutes logging all the latest information, prioritising it as she went along - Max was sure to want some of this information soon - and delivered in a timely way.

Next, she spent a few minutes looking at the timeline they had managed to construct. Helen, like everyone else, could see what had happened; she could see where and when, but the 'why' was still a mystery.

And yes, the logic of the case was that someone was sending a signal, that the death of that unfortunate young girl was a deliberate gesture; now they needed to find out for whom that gesture was meant.

'Morning, Helen.' DCS Mordaunt was around, it would seem. 'Any developments?'

'Worryingly, no, ma'am. Max and Debesh are making some local enquiries now - they've just left - shall I call them?'

'No, it's fine. They know what they're doing. There's a big story here, and I think it's working on more than one layer. You are the local experts - our guys in the Met couldn't do anything better. But I'd like to use this time with you. We can do some useful stuff while they are away.' Melissa Mordaunt offloaded her rucksack on to the desk and from it she pulled out her iPad.

'I've got some ideas that we can start with. I did a bit of follow-up work on the Stanovnic family and want to build that into some of our assumptions.'

Helen was interested, 'What have you been looking at?'

'We're missing the information on the people who took Christina, the woman Elena Popa, wasn't it?'

Melissa continued: 'Elena Popa - if that's her name, arrived at the caravan site a couple of days before the murder. Where did she come from? Did anyone see her? There were also two men, the men who carried out the murder. Were they the initiators of this, or were they carrying out orders - orders of the person we should really be looking for?'

Helen offered a way forward. 'I've put up this timeline; it may help.' She projected the image from her computer once again. 'Christina was Janko's sister. We don't know if he operates in the UK and Europe, but we do know that he's a nasty piece of work and has business interests in the Middle East and elsewhere. The message will have been for him, don't you think?'

'If it was a message - and it wasn't the result of something happening closer to home.' Melissa wasn't so sure about the international connection.

'Max and Debesh are making local enquiries now. They may come up with something.'

'And so might we.' Melissa was determined to make her presence felt in this investigation. There was much to be done, and she felt that they were now lagging behind.

'Helen, get on the phone to everyone who might have encountered this group of three. Check for CCTV, check where the men might have been staying while the Elena girl was in the caravan, check service stations, cafes - anywhere they might have been seen.'

'Right. but aren't we duplicating Max and ...?'

'We aren't duplicating anything or anyone yet, are we? We've nothing to duplicate. We need information, details, something to go on. Let's get it. If Max and Debesh get stuff ahead of us, then fine. But now, we've nothing to a grab hold of.'

'I'll start with the village.' Helen was ready to contribute wherever she could. 'They may all have done some shopping locally.'

'The rope.'

'Yes, of course, the rope. They must have got that from somewhere. Almost every shop in this village - and almost everywhere else - sells climbing stuff.'

'We know the rope was new.'

'Yes, it was. I'll start by tracing that if I can.'

'Great,' Melissa responded quickly. 'You'll know better than I the shops they might have used. So, I'll check for any CCTV sightings of the three suspects while you look to see who sold them the rope. Give me the connection to the server.'

She pulled out her laptop from her knapsack, placed it next to her iPad on her desk and soon the connection was made to the Met's secure browser. When it was up and running, the DCS turned to her new assistant and smiled, saying 'And it would be fun if we got a step ahead of the guys at the same time, wouldn't it?'

Seventeen

Max and Debesh had been talking to the residents of Rydal, at least, as many of them that they could find.

The difficulty they experienced was one they probably should have anticipated. Their first stop was a small group of cottages between Pelter Bridge, less than a mile out of Ambleside and overlooking Rydal Water itself. There were a few people about, but none had been here last week when Max had been called out to view the crime scene. Then, he and Debesh had both noticed the number of high-end vehicles, Mercs and Land Rovers, parked outside the cottages. These cottages were all holiday lets. The then residents had been interviewed on the day by local police, but nothing had turned up. Nobody had seen anything.

Now, those non-seeing people had returned to their own homes and another group of holidaymakers had taken over - some of them more than interested in the fact that a murder had taken place the week before.

'There's nothing here, sir. New people now. Shall we move on?'

'No-one here of interest, you're right. Have you tried over the road?'

'I'm sure they've been spoken to, sir. Last week.'

'The locals?'

'No locals here, sir. All holiday lets.'

'Over the road, Debesh. Over the main road. There's at least a couple of households on the way up to Rydal Mount.'

Before Debesh could respond, Max was back in the car. 'We'll pop over there and have a look-see. Come on.'

Those of you who are familiar with the Lakes will know that Rydal Water is among the most beautiful of them. It's a tiny gem, surrounded by easily accessible paths that offer the casual walker a stunning array of views.

And it wasn't surprising, therefore, that, wishing to make a statement, the caves - visible to all who walk and drive through the vale - had been chosen by a couple of sadists as the ideal place to end the life of an innocent young woman.

Max had taken the left turning over Pelter Bridge and back on to the main road. A few moments later he was turning right into the lane that led up to Rydal Mount, the poet Wordsworth's home for many years.

Debesh was surprised - given his boss's antipathy towards his namesake. 'Dodging a bullet here, sir? Do you want me to do anything?'

Max smiled: 'Needs must, lad. Locals live in some of these cottages. It's worth a try. We'll start here. Four or five houses here are lived in permanently. We'll take alternate ones, then maybe go back to the main road because there are a couple there too.'

Once out of the car, the two police officers looked at an ivy-covered cottage with a small, well-tended garden. 'I'll start here,' said Max.

As he opened the gate of the pretty cottage next to the little church front door opened, and a small, elderly man greeted them and called out to Max.

'Yes, can I help you?'

Debesh decided to take charge. He didn't want any difficulties with names and introductions. He turned back to join Max and said, 'Hello, sir. Sorry to bother you. We're from the police. I'm DS Datta and this is my colleague - my inspector.'

The old gentleman seemed amenable. He looked at the warrant card that Debesh - and only Debesh - had proffered and said, 'What can I do to help you? Is this about that murder?'

'Yes, sir, it is. We're asking people if they have seen anything that could help us.'

The man looked at them both. 'I spoke to your young girl last week.'

'Have the police already been to see you?'

'Yes, a girl in uniform. Very pleasant, she was.'

Max intervened: 'What could you tell her?'

'Not much. I didn't see anything that day, and I told her so. My wife and I were asleep. It wasn't until the morning when you lot arrived, and that helicopter started buzzing around that we noticed that something was going on. It's a right bad do. That kind of thing doesn't happen here. We're very quiet - apart from the coaches and the tourists, that is.'

Max was concerned that the man was about to get astride his hobby horse and was wondering how he could best end the conversation. However, he had suddenly taken a different tack. 'There was something, though.'

'Did you mention it to our WPC?'

'No. It hadn't occurred to me then - when she came around to see us. It may be nothing, but we were going to give you a call today.'

'What do you want to say?' Debesh wanted to hold on to the initiative; he didn't want his boss becoming angry or frustrated if the 'W' word came up.

'It wasn't something that happened on the night that girl ...' The old man's face told the story; both Debesh and Max could see that although personally, he had seen nothing, certainly not seen the girl herself, he was troubled. There was something he wanted to say.

Max said - in a gentle manner, rather catching Debesh by surprise, said. 'It's all right, sir. This event has touched a lot of people. It must have been a great shock. Would you like us to come back later?

'No. Not at all.' The old man had taken a deep breath and straightened himself up. 'I was twenty-two years in the Border Regiment. I've seen more than this, lad, let me tell you. No, I want to help. My wife agrees. A few minutes ago, she said I should call you. And she was right. I'm pleased you're here. Now, it might be something of nothing...'

'It might,' again the bedside manner was a little surprising, but there was no doubt that Max was working as hard as his patience would allow him. 'Why don't you say what you wanted to say and let us work out its relevance?'

'Yes, that's the best way. I'm sorry, I'm a bit nervous about this whole thing. It was last Wednesday, about 11 o'clock. I was listening to the news, so that's why I know. There were two men.'

'Two men. Where?' Debesh had got to that question first.

'Just here. Right outside the house. Near to where you've parked.'

Max listening to this was a little puzzled, 'But this must happen all the time. There are always cars parked all the way from here up to Rydal Mount. What was so special about these men?'

This man must have been in his late 70's, and maybe as a soldier he'd seen a lot, but his eyes now gave him away. He wiped away a tear. 'I was going to call you, today. I've been puzzling about this for a while, trying to put my finger on exactly what troubled me - and it started with the car.

'You know that old Jaguar XJS - the two-seater with the huge bonnet? We mostly see them on rallies now that come to the Lakes every now and again, but this one, this one was strange. Dirty brown, faded paintwork, I'm sure that there were bits dropping of it. It was a wreck of a car. It should have been in a scrap yard. Then these two men got out of it.

'They were maybe forty-odd years old, both white, but deeply tanned: foreign tan, not the kind of tan we get on holiday, but like you get living in the sun, in a Mediterranean country for example. I thought that they might be Maltese - or Cypriot. Only because I served there.' He was reminiscing but soon stopped himself.

'I didn't recognise their language. I think I would have if they'd been Maltese or were speaking Turkish or Greek. But I heard them talking as they left the car and started to walk down the hill. They both had suits and ties, and I thought that maybe they were going to the hotel, but then they crossed the road and began to go over the little bridge that leads up to the walks on the other side of Rydal.'

'Why did you follow them?' Debesh wondered.

'It wasn't right   there was something odd about them, strange, dressed like that, and getting out of that car. So, when they crossed the road, I wandered down to see where they were going. Their behaviour was - wrong. It seemed wrong.'

'Wrong?' Debesh again.

'Their clothes. They weren't going to the hotel; they were going up to the fell. When you're out walking, especially walking the hills, you have to dress for it, don't you - the right walking shoes or boots? Ordinary shoes are no good, no grip, see? As I say, these men were dressed in suits and both were wearing slip-on shoes, you know, those ones with tassels on them? I thought to myself, they can't go walking up the hill in those shoes, but they did.'

The mention of inappropriate footwear for walking up to the cave had Debesh glancing towards his boss: the person who, a few days ago, had ruined his own pair of totally inappropriate shoes on that very same walk up to the cave.

The old man continued, 'These two men weren't kitted out for walking. That, and their car made me notice what they were doing. I watched them. They walked across the road over the little bridge in front of the hotel and then made their way up towards the cave, the cave where you found that poor young lass. Over the weekend, when it came on the news, I made the connection. They were checking out the site. It was part of their planning, wasn't it?'

Max took a moment before replying. Then he said, 'You could be right, sir.' He then went on, 'You say the two men were wearing suits?'

'Yes.'

'Were they smart suits?'

His witness laughed. 'Smart? No, not at all. They were both wearing - I don't know exactly how to put it. The suits were - greasy? No, not so much greasy, they were dirty, though, worn - shiny because of the wear.

'I was in East Germany one time - way back, long before the wall came down. Those two men looked exactly like you'd find in an office over there, like civil servants - having to look smart.'

Max knew exactly what the old man meant. 'My granddad was a civil servant. He had this one suit he always wore. Even at the weekend, he'd wear the same suit; except without a tie and he'd have his collar outside of his suit jacket - that meant the weekend, or he was on holiday.'

However, these two men innocently reminiscing had an unintended consequence, sparking dark and troubling thoughts in the old man's mind. His demeanour had changed, his eyes teared up as he took upon himself the enormity of what he was thinking.

'I could have done something about it, couldn't I?' Both officers could see the man rewinding his actions - seeing if he could have done anything differently, anything that might have saved that young girl. 'If I'd reported them straight away.'

'No sir. You couldn't have had any idea what they were planning. Nobody could.' Debesh wanted to reassure the man. 'What you've told us may well turn out to be very useful. It gives us information to work with; it's information we didn't have before, so thank you. We're grateful and we'll get back to you if we need anything else.'

'One other thing, please,' an afterthought from Max. 'Did you get the registration number of the car, the XJS, wasn't it?'

The old man was crestfallen. 'I didn't, and I've been kicking myself ever since. Old, brown, dirty - even the seats were ripped - it shouldn't have been on the road. But it never occurred to me. I'm sorry because I should have.'

'What you have given us is much more than we had before, sir. We're very grateful. Thank you for everything. We'll get back to you if we think you can assist further.'

The three men shook hands and Max and Debesh decided to continue with their original plan, that of interviewing as many local people as they could, checking that Uniform had gathered all the available information.

That they'd scored a hit with their first interview didn't lead on to any further success. Twenty minutes later, and after talking to only four other residents of the hamlet, they'd added nothing to their store of knowledge.

Making their way back to the car, Max thought of his first visit to the Rydal cave, and the horrific sight of the young woman suspended from the overhang.

'That'll be when they found the pitons. They would have given them the idea of suspending her over the pool in the cave, and they'd have measured up the rope length too. That would have involved a tape measure. Eleven in the morning. Somebody must have seen them, must have seen something.'

He continued, 'So, they didn't just visit the cave, but they'd have had to walk up behind it to get up to the top of the overhang. There's no other way they would have seen the pitons. Surely somebody, some walker ...'

'You'd think so, sir. Two men in suits clambering around the caves. Anyone passing would have thought it odd.'

'We're going to have to do something. It's ludicrous that this should have happened in plain sight. I mean, there are cars driving past Rydal Water every day even at five in the morning. Seeing nothing? I'm getting frustrated by this, and I'm sure that the Met will count this lack of progress as a black mark.'

'I'm not so sure.' Debesh had also been thinking the same thing, but as far as he was concerned, he simply didn't see it the way that his boss did.

'I think we're doing quite well, sir. This additional information, the car, the two guys, there's bound to be something there that we can work with. We'll trawl for CCTV; we'll check the garages and the B&Bs and look at these self-catering firms. I think we'll find these people quite quickly.'

'Debesh, you have restored my faith in human nature. Let us return to the office, seek appropriate permission from your lady wife, and have a celebratory pint of something at the Golden Rule.'

'You know, sir. That's exactly what I was thinking. Not the permission bit - Helen will have gone home by now. She's picking Ellie up today. No permission needed.'

'It will be politic for us to go back,' Max replied. 'We need to park there, and it's at least possible that our new boss the DCS will be about. If she is, we might ask her to come and join us. We'll know by her answer a little bit more about how she's going to work with us.'

'A bit Machiavellian, sir, don't you think? She seems to have been entirely reasonable so far.'

'Yes, Debesh, she has. And frankly, it's a bit worrying. I would have thought she'd have made her move by now. '

'Her move?'

'Yes. There's got to be a power grab sometime and I'm surprised she hasn't worked a little harder at it.' Max had been thinking for some time that DCS Mordaunt had been back-pedalling. Given her reputation, he was expecting a much more aggressive management style, and so far, he'd been surprised by the entirely reasonable way in which this woman seemed to be working.

'I think you've got it wrong, sir.'

'How so?'

'I think this is her style. MBO - managing by objectives. She's not into micromanaging. I'm hoping it's true - I've no proof yet - but I suspect she's relying on your expertise rather than trying to tell you how to do your job. I think you should be patient with her. She's got a lot to offer.'

'And once again I'm in your debt, Debesh. I want to think you're right. No, don't look at me like that, I do want to think you're right. Let's go and get that pint.'

Eighteen

'So, this is it? Looks a bit quiet. How long have you been here?' Janko's question was delivered to the tattooed young man who'd met him off the train. Nothing like the 'Marhaba', the Dubai airport meet and greet service he'd been used to in Dubai, but adequate.

'Almost two years. I like it. It's quiet. A big change from Zagreb.' Mika, the young man who had met Janko at Oxenholme station worked as a waiter in a Bowness restaurant. He'd been quietly serving his customers when his boss had given him the keys to his car and ordered him to pick up an 'important guy' from the train.

'You like quiet?' Janko's mind could not compute such a thought. Living on his nerves and even now, after a train journey of only three hours, frustrated and looking for action, any action so that his body could get back up to speed again.

He lit the cigarette that he'd been craving for so long and looked around. The station seemed to be in the middle of nowhere. 'Where is everybody?'

'This is it. This is everybody.' The young waiter was trying to crack a joke but wasn't sure how to deal with this man. They were at the mainline station where the spur to Kendal and ultimately Windermere connects the Lake District to the rest of the world. This was not to Janko's liking and he was further angered when the young man directed him towards a dirty-looking old Ford Focus.

'This your car?' Janko, more by way of conversation than interest.

'No, it's my boss's. Sorry. It's shit, I know, but it will get us to where you want to go.'

'This is a joke, yeah?'

'What do you mean?' The boy was confused. He'd left work early, got in his boss's car and driven down to Oxenholme station to meet this man.

'What's with the piece of shit car?'

'It's his car - all he can afford, I guess. I don't have one.'

'Where's the car I ordered?'

'Ordered? What car? I was asked to pick you up, sir. I've been at work all day. There isn't any other.'

Mika turned to look at his passenger as if to offer further explanation. He stopped: the man was livid. He felt that at any moment he would attack him; it was if he was deciding whether to strike him or not. The sense that he was in danger of being assaulted by someone for whom he was doing a favour was inexplicable. He couldn't work it out. Who was this man and why was he so angry?

Up until now, Janko's first experience of the UK had been pleasant enough. He'd managed to catch the right train; he'd found his seat easily and had time to reflect on the fact that he'd learned more English at school than he thought.

He could read many of the signs, even listen to and understand one or two of the desultory conversations that were taking place around him. The few lessons of English that he could remember from his school days had evidently not been a complete waste of time.

It was true that much of his work in Dubai had to be conducted in English, but the vocabulary he had learned focused mostly around the scatological and violent end of the spectrum.

He had never learned a single word of Arabic - or any of the myriad other languages spoken there, but people like Kranti spoke English and Arabic as well as they did their first languages, so he'd never had to work at it.

Knowing the extent and the limitations of his understanding of English, he'd reasoned that he would face difficulty the moment he tried to check into a hotel or ask for something special in a shop or a restaurant.

Anticipating this, he arranged for one of his people to meet him. This young waiter, Mika, wasn't one of his people and had no idea who he was conveying up from Oxenholme station to the Lakes.

Janko was young - only twenty-eight and probably looked the same as any one of many itinerant eastern Europeans who'd come to the UK seeking employment. His anger at the way he had been treated so disrespectfully, subsided. It wasn't the kid's fault that he'd come to meet him in this filthy old vehicle, but someone was up for a kicking.

The old Ford Focus, having wheezed its way into life, was now making its way on to the Kendal by-pass and ultimately towards the Lakes.

Sitting in the front passenger seat, the rear seats being full of assorted junk, Janko reflected on what he'd left behind. Sure, parts of it were dangerous and risky, and as the two men clattered up the road, Janko remembered a business associate of his in Dubai.

This guy, a Lebanese, had looked after all his transport needs, and very well too. As a side-line, he had thirty-two leased Lexus cars which he operated as a limousine service. These cars were always available for Janko, always pristine and always squeaky clean. That was certainly one aspect of his former life that he missed at this moment.

'Where will you be staying? Do you want me to take you to anywhere special, sir?'

The boy's naive question startled Janko. He hadn't thought - assuming that, rather like in Dubai, there would have been some very special arrangements laid on for him. As this obviously wasn't the case, Janko thought for a moment or two and then said, 'You're the expert. Recommend a good hotel, somewhere special for me, and take me there.'

This request placed Mika in something of a quandary. He was a waiter; his experience of Lake District hotels was purely that of a functionary, not a guest. He'd started in his present job as a kitchen porter, but he'd been promoted to waiter, and then effectively to head waiter within a matter of weeks.

This was not so much because of his amazing talents, although, to be fair, he did have a pleasant smile and naturally polite way of talking to people. No, his rapid rise in the hierarchy of his small boutique hotel was entirely due to the tendency of other members of the hotel's small staff to disappear suddenly, either because they simply hated the place or had found a better position elsewhere.

There were vacancies all over now - the law of unintended consequences had worked its magic in the Lakes, and there were far fewer eastern Europeans working in hospitality than there were before Brexit. Nowadays, good workers could choose from a whole range of jobs - and demand higher pay. This was why Mika had decided to remain.

It wouldn't be a good idea to have Janko stay near his place - Mika decided that the less he saw of this man the better, but where should he suggest?

He'd some small experience of other hotels, but only of staff living quarters when he'd got lucky on a couple of occasions with a chambermaid - and then he'd had to sneak in and out of them through the back doors and past the rubbish bins.

As he reached the Windermere turning where he would drop down to Bowness, he decided that rather than take his passenger anywhere near where he worked, he'd drive on.

A few minutes later, he turned into the Merrywood hotel, a recently refurbished nineteenth-century pile - the very one where he'd had a short tryst with a young commis chef a couple of weeks ago. If what she'd said about it was true, this place would be as good as any.

'If they've any vacancies, I think you'd like this place.'

'Do you know anyone who's stayed here?'

'Yes.' Well, he did. Not strictly speaking as Janko would have taken this answer, but nevertheless, 'I think you'll like it. It's got a very good reputation, but I think it's expensive.'

'OK. Have you a phone?'

'Yes.'

'Book me in for five nights from now. Name of Stanovnic. Do it now. Use your English. If they require a deposit, no problem. Say I'll be there in five minutes, and I'll pay in cash on arrival. Go on.' Janko pointed to the phone that Mika was now holding in his hand. 'The number's on the sign.'

And it was. Mika called the number, and whether or not it was the promise of a cash booking for five nights, the reservation was made immediately.

'Good,' said Janko in receipt of the translated conversation. 'Take me up to the hotel - here's some money for you - and then piss off. Oh, and tell your boss I'll call him.'

'Shall I tell him why?'

'What you will do, my friend, is do what I have told you to do. Now fuck off!'

Mika did exactly as he was told without a second thought. At the bottom of the hotel drive, he stopped for a moment to see how much Janko had given him. Five one-hundred-euro notes. A lot of money - even for a Lake District taxi. But it would take much more than that for him to be involved with that guy ever again.

So concerned was Mika that his next thought - and one that he acted upon that very next day - was that it would be wiser for him to leave the area entirely, pack up and go, thereby obliterating any trace, and any possibility of his ever being contacted again by that man.

He'd seen the look on his boss's face when he'd conveyed Janko's message to him. That was a psycho, if ever there was one - and not for the first time, someone had read Janko's personality correctly.

Nineteen

I'm looking at a message that's popped up on my phone. It says 'He's arrived. It's now up to you'. I'm presuming this is referring to the Stanovnic guy, but Messenger was not that specific, of course. I'm getting used to living in a cryptic crossword. Hardly surprising: whoever's contacting me is keeping our relationship at arm's length.

Nevertheless, even though he, although it could very well be a she, has been quite distant, they've certainly caused me and my family far too much trouble, and whenever I think about what happened at the spa - something I frequently do - not to mention Stephanie in BVI - I know that if ever I do get my hands on this person - well, I've run so many scenarios through my mind, I'm currently spoiled for choice.

Meg is recovering, and the children seem to have their heads stuck in their tablets a little more frequently than they used to, and I'm assuming that's some compensatory action on their part. They don't seem to be particularly empathetic, my kids, but is that kids in general? I suppose it could be.

My anger hasn't subsided, and I've kept it at a high level through all the work I've been doing to find out who this bastard is. That, and my constant checking of my home's security systems takes up a lot of time.

Of course, I do understand why the children are spending so much time in their virtual world: I've put a complete stop to their playing outside in the garden.

This means that the leaf slide and the dens that they recently created with such fervour are out of bounds; they can only play outside on the terrace and the small lawn at the side of the house - and that only when Meg or I am available - and willing - to take a turn at sentry duty.

Meg's accepted my flimsy rationale for this change of heart, hasn't even questioned it. It's all to do with atmosphere - mood. The dynamic of our personal lives has shifted - and the spa incident acted as the precursor to our changed behaviour. We're being more careful and banning the leaf slide is one of the small acts in that process.

I don't like what's happening: I've worked damned hard over the years to build a safe space for my family, and it's all come crashing down.

Now, despite the risk of someone noticing it, I'm routinely carrying a weapon, something that I have never done before in the UK; the alarms and sensors in the house are all working 24/7, and I've decided to have them upgraded.

I've restocked the safe room that I had built some years ago but never felt the need to use. That's down in the cellar and is a long and creepy walk down some rickety stairs, something that I deliberately kept as a deterrent, and seems to have worked.

Meg knows about it but doesn't know that I've brought it back into use, and the kids, so far, are too scared to venture down there.

All this plus the fact that whereas once I enjoyed the serenity of my home, and sleeping was a genuine joy - six, sometimes eight hours - I'm now drifting in and out of sleep all night, finding myself catnapping wherever I can, but waking up to the slightest noise from whatever source.

Come to think of it, my kids' current obsession with their virtual worlds is probably not a bad idea at all. As I said before, Meg keeps an eye on the content of all three of the darlings.

We've not talked about it much, but both of us are aware that someone might try to get to me via one of our children - the internet, grooming, all that stuff. Yet another cross to bear.

Given the shock she's had, Meg's been brilliant, so brilliant that she's almost, I say almost, got me thinking suspicious thoughts. Is she naïve, or is she very much aware of what is going on?

Is she possibly more aware than I wish to think about the kind of work I do, and prepared to accept the reality that some unsavoury stuff is now coming our way?

I mentioned that I was upgrading our security. A few weeks ago, I asked a company in Kendal to come and review our systems at the house, and that's happening now. Exquisite timing if nothing else.

To begin with, Meg carried on as if nothing was happening while two young men re-positioned sensors, directed the new Wi-Fi video cameras and connected everything to a couple of computer monitors in my office, as well as to my safe room downstairs in the cellar. Seeing the monitors in action, her sense of equanimity disappeared.

'Are you recording everything that goes on in this house?'

'Not everything,' I smiled. 'The motion sensors kick in when there's movement. And before you ask,' I went on, 'that doesn't apply to our bedrooms, the kids' rooms and all the bathrooms.' (By the way, I felt I simply had to lie here: the bedrooms and the bathrooms do have security cameras in them, but they are hidden. Needs must.)

'Are you sure all this is necessary?'

'Probably not, but I want to make sure. We don't want another incident, do we?'

'Like at the spa?'

'Yeah, I'm still not sure why that happened - if it was a random idiot, or something that we should be worried about.' Of course, it wasn't a random idiot at all, but I hadn't gone so far as to share my concerns - not yet anyway. 'But I thought that while we were making some changes to the house, it would do no harm to upgrade our security.'

'Mmm. If you're sure.' At that moment I was expecting more of a push back, but Meg was suddenly distracted by the twins suddenly screaming at each other from the other side of the house.

Off she went to broker a peace agreement, so I didn't go into detail about the new internal security doors we were also installing. Ten of them, each costing over four hundred pounds plus fitting - and palm operated, no keys to lose.

I thought she ought to know more about the situation, and why I'm toughening up everything, but there is this softer, more romantic side to me, if you will. Part of me is saying that she ought to know more - not everything, obviously, that wouldn't work but maybe making her aware of a certain level of risk that has jumped up to bite us.

But the reality, at least as I see it, is that by troubling her with this information, I'm going to be even more distracted by her concerns and her worry, right at the very time when I need to concentrate on the imminent situation: fighting a battle on two fronts is a bad idea.

I decide to maintain things as they are. Meg will get her updates as and when necessary, I guess. 'Need to know' is the healthy option.

I decide to see if I can get to know more about the target, Stanovnic, and whoever is the driving force behind the pressure I'm getting.

First things first. I've not used Messenger to try to initiate contact before, and I suppose that part of me thought that if I didn't do anything, the threat would fade away, like a scam email, troubling to begin with, but eventually forgotten.

But now that one of my loved ones has been attacked, I'm feeling quite different, much less chilled than before - and what a stupidly complacent position that was for me to assume. Maybe if I'd been a little more proactive, chased up this guy faster and more firmly, Meg wouldn't be nursing a badly scarred arm.

The message I received said 'He's arrived. It's now up to you'. It seemed to be a good idea now that I reply.

'Who the fuck are you?'

It didn't take long for the reply. 'I could be your salvation, or I could bring disaster to you and those you love. Which is it to be?'

Tricky, that. How to respond? I don't wish to get involved in a pointless slanging match: whoever he is, he's obviously a bit up himself. But I need information and I've nothing to go on. Here's someone who's accessed a phone number only known to two people, Stephanie in the BVI and Archana in Dubai.

'Why do you want me to carry out this task?' My words are carefully chosen. I want to write in the same idiom as the man who is threatening me. I suspect that English is not his first language. Could be wrong; he might have a stick up his arse.

'Stanovnic has created a situation for me. He is to be punished.'

'Punished?'

'Punished and then made to disappear.'

'You mean killed?'

'Precisely.'

'But punished first?

'Precisely.'

'How?'

'You will decide.'

'Why ask me?'

'You came recommended.'

'You could have purchased my services. You obviously know my work.'

'I decided not to contract you because you created difficulty for me in the past. And I chose you for this project because of that. You will do as I ask, or you and your family will pay.'

'You killed Stephanie in BVI?'

'Not personally. She did not wish to divulge the appropriate information; the information demanded of her.'

'Were you the man I spoke to then?'

'Yes,' came the reply. 'We did speak – briefly.'

'Did you kill her?'

'Not personally. I'd quite like to visit your British Virgin Islands, I have some bank accounts there I believe, but on this occasion, I sub-contracted the mission.'

I was feverishly trying to work out where he might be from while he continued. It wasn't native English but was very fluent, maybe the translation? 'They worked for me, that is true, but no longer. That business with your assistant was uncalled for. They enjoyed it too much. I have dispensed with their services, and with them.'

At that point I disconnect; close it down before I start losing my rag. This is the bastard who had Stephanie butchered, and I'm chatting to him as if we're arranging a visit to the theatre.

I recorded this interaction, and I suppose I could find someone who might trace the IP number or whatever. Obviously, that doesn't seem to worry him, so he may well be routing his messages in the same way that I route my bank transactions - making any search too complicated to carry out. I'm not getting much else, apart from a feeling that the isn't British.

There is one other thing - he says that I have 'created difficulty' for him in the past. So, I must know him, or at least, have some connection to him. The tone of his language seems stilted, forced. Maybe he's an old school British mobster, but I doubt it. More likely it's Google Translate that's giving me the sense that he's working in another language.

All I can deduce is that whoever this is has a complicated game plan. My chipping away isn't going to get me any further. He knows a lot more about me than I do about him, and that's not a good place to be in.

What have I learned from this bizarre exchange? At first glance, sod all, but not entirely blank. I've apparently had some dealings with this person in the past, and he seems to want to kill two birds with one stone, linking this Stanovnic guy with my past misdemeanours - whatever they might be.

Push has come to shove. Enough, already.

Twenty

In his elegant, serviced office on one of the upper floors of the Emirates Tower, Hesham el Hashimi, a young Emirati princeling, switched off his computer and looked out the window. The tower blocks that lined the Sheikh Zayed road, the offices, hotels, shops and apartments plus the solid lines of traffic crawling slowly along in both directions, all testifying to the vibrant, almost frenetic, pace of life in Dubai.

That frenetic pace wasn't reflected in the speed of the traffic down below as it crawled along for hour after hour. The recently developed Metro system ran parallel to the road. It was fast and cheap, but people like Hesham would never dream of leaving their cars to use a mass transit service.

The conversation with Blain, such as it was, had gone much as he anticipated; if anything, a little better.

He'd told Blain he was responsible for a crime against Hesham's family. His parents and two of his siblings had disappeared over a year ago, and Hesham now knew that Blain was responsible. After a long and difficult process evidence had been found, and it was definitive. Now was the time for revenge. If all went to plan, Blain would soon be no more, and before his death he would see his own loved ones pay the ultimate price.

But not tonight. In a break from his normal routine, Hesham's driver would be waiting for him downstairs, and he would be joining the thousands of cars, lorries and taxis as they slowly made their way up the Sheikh Zayed road. The two blonde Latvian girls he had ordered were waiting at the Dubai Mall, watching people fully dressed in fashionable winter clothing hurtling down the indoor ski slope - one of the mall's main attractions.

The temperature outside in Dubai was forty-five degrees Celsius, but inside Ski Dubai, the skiers and snowboarders were enjoying a temperature of only 2C - 43 degrees lower.

The two girls weren't skiing, of course, they were enjoying cocktails in the downstairs bar of the hotel while they waited in anticipation for their client, watching the winter sports through a giant plate-glass window.

Far from being suitably attired for a cold winter's afternoon on the ski slopes, they were dressed for an entirely different purpose - a purpose which was obvious to the many men, and women too, who had been watching them during the last hour or so.

Both girls had already received their generous payment; all they had to do now was please their client, and as he was young, attractive and exceedingly wealthy, this wouldn't present much of a challenge. They were looking forward to their evening, upstairs in that special and familiar suite in the Movenpick hotel.

Hesham was one of their favourite clients, and the girls enjoyed the opportunity of working together, so tonight wasn't simply going to be transactional, it would be exciting - for them as well as for him. They received a message. He'd set off and he'd be with them in twenty minutes. His car had the flashing blue and red lights that encouraged other drivers to pull over for fear of what might happen if they didn't. His twenty-minute estimate was probably correct – other drivers might take over an hour or more to travel the same distance.

Twenty-One

'Where's your family from originally, Debesh?' DCS Mordaunt was asking this question as she off loaded her shoulder bag, removing her laptop from it at the same time.

'India. Kolkata, well it was Calcutta then. My dad came to England - to London in the late sixties. When he was settled, he brought my mom and their six kids over.'

'Six! That must have been hard work.'

'You're right and I've no idea how he did it. I came along later. I'm the youngest - by a long way. There are eight of us now.'

'If you don't mind me asking, why England?'

'Not sure. I know he travelled overland - he sort of landed up here. I mean, He spent some time in Russia, and a couple of other countries. I suppose it was the language. He'd studied English at university in India, and once he got here he got a job as a teacher. London was crying out for them then.'

Melissa was logging on now and the conversation seemed to fade while she concentrated on getting online, but then she came back to him.

'Do you know why he left Kolkata in the first place? With six children, he must have had a very good reason.'

'You're right - politics.'

'Politics?'

'At that time in West Bengal, just before Bangladesh was created, the Naxalites - communists - were causing havoc, and my dad didn't think it was safe for the family to stay. There was too much violence - bombs, shootings.'

'But you said he went to Russia.'

'Yeah, he did. Overland from India. Once he'd left, he was determined his children weren't going to become victims. I think he was a socialist - not a communist, exactly. I don't know this for sure, but I think he fell out with them - the Naxalites - felt it safer to leave.'

'Oh, so he was a political refugee?'

'I suppose so, but he never said. He was an old man when I was growing up - I was a surprise to everyone. He didn't talk much about why, but I don't think that's why he came to the UK. All he ever said was that he disagreed with the Naxalites - and their violence.'

Debesh halted in mid flow; the conversation had shifted in its tone. 'May I ask you why you are asking these questions, ma'am?'

'I was thinking about stuff as I drove here.' Melissa had opened her computer and was now online. She continued searching for something while she replied to Debesh.

'It's not you - or your dad - specifically. I was thinking about immigration in general. Why people choose to leave their home - why they go to live in a different country, sometimes having to make the most risky and uncertain types of journey and we're working this case, this murder, with people who've come to this country for a variety of reasons, aren't we?'

'Yes, but why is my back story of interest?'

'Not you particularly, Debesh - you're as British as I am, but if you are an immigrant, an illegal for example, someone who can't work, can't get the permission, or if you are simply someone from overseas who has come here for a proper job, I was wondering if people see this country differently depending on the circumstances that brought them here.'

'I would have thought that was obvious,' Debesh countered. 'If you are a refugee, if you're an illegal, or you're simply strange, it makes all the difference.'

'And the people we're looking for?'

'All the signs are that they are transient, but we're not sure, are we? Both the men who went to measure up the drop at Rydal caves give us an indication. Our witness said they were foreign, and I'll bet they don't work locally. They'll have been brought in.'

'I was thinking that - and I'm sorry for the convoluted way of getting there.' Melissa Mordaunt smiled to herself. They said that women could multi-task better than men. The last few minutes had not exactly born out that theory.

She'd been checking the progress of the team, accessing the central registry, the point where all case information ended up. Wordsworth, Debesh, Helen and Melissa all had made their contributions overnight, and Melissa was scanning them while holding her meandering conversation with Debesh.

She was about to shut down her computer when she saw a late entry.

'They've found the car.'

'The brown Jag?' Debesh opened his laptop too.

'Yes, it's in Bowness. A local patrol noticed it last night. False number plates. That's not far from here, is it?'

'No, ten, maybe fifteen minutes, depending on the traffic. Have they done anything about it?'

'Only what they were told to. They've left it alone - awaiting instructions.'

'They've kept a watch on it all night?'

'A virtual watch, 'Quiet Eye'.'

DCS Mordaunt was referring to the recently introduced Quiet Eye system, now rolled out nationally, enabling the police to keep watch on and monitor suspicious activity without the need of a physical presence.

Although the UK has more CCTV cameras per head that almost any other country in the world, previously it was often more by good luck than good management that officers obtained useful footage when seeking evidence.

This new system changed all that. If the location was suitable and a senior officer would sign it off, officers could now conceal a small wireless video camera at or near the location, and this would feed back to a central control room.

This system allowed for the surveillance of dozens of places of interest at the same time while only requiring the minimum of manpower to keep watch on the array of screens.

Debesh had stood up and was getting ready.

'Where are you going?'

'I'll pop down and see. We need to get a look at the Jag, see if we can find the owner.'

'Give me a moment while I shoot off this email and I'll come with you.' Melissa typed for a few seconds, hit the send button with a flourish, popped her laptop, along with her phone into her shoulder bag saying, 'I've sent a note to Max and Helen. So they don't worry about us.'

'You think they'll worry?' Debesh could see that Helen might have some concern, but not Max. He'd assume everything was fine until he was told otherwise.

'No,' she smiled. 'But it's polite, isn't it? Come on. Let's have a look at that car.'

Their journey to Bowness took less than ten minutes. For a change, traffic was flowing quite freely between Ambleside and Windermere - none of the roadworks that constantly frustrate drivers throughout the year were in operation, and the tourist traffic also was relatively light.

As she passed the hotel where she was currently staying, Melissa mentioned to Debesh that she was thinking of moving out.

'Why ma'am?' Debesh's immediate question. 'Lakeside hotel, beautiful views, great food - we've eaten there twice - loved it.'

'I know. I know. I don't feel comfortable there, that's all. I hate being a guest. I'd like to have my own place, somewhere I can slob about - I feel that I'm on parade there all the time.'

'Maybe you'd be better off self-catering, a cottage or a flat, maybe.'

'Yes, but it's summer and the prices are crazy - you can pay thousands.'

'It's on expenses, isn't it, ma'am?'

'It is - but that's not the point.'

The tone of Melissa's reply to what Debesh had thought a perfectly reasonable comment suggested, quite strongly, that he ought not to go further down that rabbit hole.

Her next comment was more gently spoken; she was aware that she'd overcooked it. 'I'd prefer self-catering, maybe in a cottage,' she continued, 'I've checked all the sites, all the Airbnbs, but they're holiday rentals, and I wouldn't feel comfortable paying all that money.'

Turning right at the roundabout at Cook's Corner, Debesh had an idea. He knew of a place, somewhere that might very well suite his DCS. He'd make a call - later - after whatever dust was going to be thrown up today had settled.

They pulled into Bowness, turning left past the Albert pub to go up the hill. Debesh had chosen this way, rather than going through Windermere, so that he could show his boss the police station where they would have been based, had they not been lucky enough to resurrect their offices in Ambleside.

'I understand why you were so keen to work out of Ambleside,' was her only comment.

As they turned into Queen's Drive, Debesh pulled over. He'd seen the Jaguar, and he pointed it out. There it was, in plain sight, some hundred and fifty or so yards ahead from where they had stopped.

'What now?' Either of them could have asked that question: it was Melissa who had blinked first, but the same words were on Debesh's lips, a millisecond behind.

'Do you want to take a walk past, ma'am? You look much less plod-like than I do.'

Melissa smiled. 'That's the nicest thing anyone has said to me today. Of course. I'll take a turn around the block.'

'If you walk past the car, I'll go round and meet you by the school at the top - the junction of Prince's Road. OK?'

'Yes.'

'And you'll take a photo?'

'That I will. Good idea.' Out from her bag came her phone. She then began walking up towards the car.

Debesh saw what she was doing. Holding her phone as if she were following the mapping system on it to find her way to a particular place, she used her camera surreptitiously, passing the target vehicle while at the same time taking half a dozen shots.

Debesh reversed into a house driveway, pulled back on to Lake Road taking the next right along Prince's Road, allowing him to park up near the school almost at the same time that his colleague arrived.

'Next time, park up here, so that I can walk downhill.'

'Sorry, ma'am. Will do. Good exercise, though. It wasn't that far. Anything interesting?'

'I got the index number.' The DCS flicked through a few photos until she found the one she was looking for. 'PNC confirms the plates are false.'

'Anything in the car?'

'I couldn't see much as I walked by. The windows are filthy - the car's a wreck. Shouldn't be on the road. Look at these tyres.'

The DCS showed Debesh two of her photos, capturing the two nearside tyres of the old Jaguar. Melissa was right, no doubt about that. The tyres were badly worn, certainly illegal. Debesh assumed the other two tyres would be similar.

'We have these in London. Mostly gang cars.'

'Gang cars?'

'Yea. Cars the gang can use. Stolen and then fitted with cloned plates. I'm surprised they're using that old wreck, but that's what it'll be.'

'Anyone can use it?' Debesh was interested.

'Anyone in the gang. There'll be a place where the keys are kept.'

'This'll be the car they used to get our victim to Rydal.' The pieces were coming together. Debesh continued, 'It matches the description given by our witness, the old guy who saw them - and to be fair, there aren't all that many of those cars left running.'

'Could be. We've had Quiet Eye on it since yesterday, haven't we? But so far, it's told us nothing. What do you suggest we do?' The DCS was keeping to her promise of letting the locals make the key decisions.

'I'll have a word with Max,' Debesh continued, 'I think we'll get local Uniform involved with this as well.'

The Jaguar was parked only a few hundred yards from the Windermere police station, so they would be the ideal people to do this. Once there was any movement, they could quickly get Max and his team involved.

On the short drive back to Ambleside, Debesh called his boss to bring him up to date.

Max agreed that this was probably the car. 'Do you think we should take it in and have a Forensics guy look at it? That would probably mean taking it down to Lancaster, maybe Preston.'

Debesh was on speaker phone, so Max was a little surprised when the answer came from Melissa. 'Don't do that, Max. If it's all right with you, I'd like to know who's involved. Let's leave the car in place for a while longer. We'll keep it local.'

'As you wish, ma'am. I'm happy with that. Anything else?'

'Not at this stage.' It was Debesh who continued the conversation. 'If we can link the car to a driver - or even to someone local.'

'I have something for you.' This was Max again, 'Border Force flagged up a name. Janko Stanovnic. We know him. He's the brother of the murdered girl.'

'And?'

'He's in the country. Arrived by Eurostar. He's a Person of Interest.'

Melissa again, 'If he's a person of interest, he should have been questioned on arrival. The dead girl's on the database, and the name's unusual. Why didn't that happen?'

'No idea, ma'am. You might help us here. Could you see if there's any kind of story?' Max was clutching at straws; this might be all they would get today.

'Story?'

'If there's anything to add. I imagine he's come to England because of what's happened to his sister. There can't be any other reason, but I'd like some confirmation, if we can get any. And, as you say, if he is a POI, he should have been detained. Could there be some other game being played.'

'What kind of game?'

'No idea. It seems strange that if he had a red flag against him, he wasn't detained.'

'I'll see what I can do,' replied the DCS. 'I'll make some calls when we get back to Ambleside.'

'Thanks, ma'am. We'll find out who's involved with this car, and we'll move from there. We might be getting somewhere, after all.'

By the time they'd returned to Ambleside and made their way into their offices, Helen had stolen a march on them.

'This car that you've been looking at,' her first words, 'There's no information at all. No owner, no insurance, nothing.'

'Odd,' Melissa's immediate response. 'How has it been living in that road without anyone picking it up? We've ANPR cameras all over the place.'

'Not around here, ma'am. If the car was used frequently, it's likely a patrol would have pulled it over. But what if it was kept off the road - or even, what if it had been parked up there and no-one had picked it up?'

Debesh intervened. 'Helen, find out if there has been any mention of this car, and send a local uniform to knock on a few doors - see if anyone has noticed it for any reason. I'm sure if it was parked up outside my door, I'd want something done about it.'

DI Wordsworth joined the group as he was concluding a mobile phone conversation. 'News?'

'You know about the Jag,' Debesh replied, 'We've had a look at it and now we're seeing if Helen can get Uniform to check it out. How long it's been there, if anyone noticed anything suspicious.'

'Good idea. Helen, you can do that?' Without waiting for her reply, Max continued. 'Now let me move things on a little further. I've been quite busy myself.'

'Tell us more,' Melissa Mordaunt chimed in. She was one of the group now, or so it appeared and quite at ease with the new dynamic.

'The news is not good news. It does move us on a bit, but it's likely to slow us up too.'

'My first is a riddle without any ...'

'Not a joking matter, DS Datta. Two bodies have been recovered - down by the Leven at Greenodd. They fit the description of the men described by our witness in Rydal. If so, that's what going to slow us up.'

DCS Mordaunt, unfamiliar with the area, needed more. 'So, where exactly is this?'

Wordsworth moved to the large wall map that Helen had put up some days ago and which was already proving to be useful. She'd also found a pack of little flags and some pins with coloured heads. These she had used to mark where significant events had occurred, and in her mind, she was already rummaging in the top drawer of her desk for more.

'Greenodd's down here.' Max pointed to a point on the map, way south of Ambleside and a few miles beyond the southern end of Coniston Water. 'The river Leven comes out here - this is the sea, and this,' he said, pointing to a road that came very close to the edge of the water, 'this is the main road between Barrow and the M6.'

Debesh knew what he was getting at. 'The bodies could have been dumped and then the killers, or at least those charged with getting rid of the bodies, would have quickly left the area.'

'Could be. Looks that way.'

Helen wasn't so sure. 'Would it not have been a better idea to take the bodies further away? There'd be less chance of a connection being made.'

'Another possibility - and we're all on a roll here.' The DCS - and probably the others too - noticed the barest hint of sarcasm in Max's tone; too slight to call out perhaps but there, nevertheless.

Melissa broke the spell. 'It's all circumstantial, isn't it? Maybe too soon to impute motive. We have two bodies. First, we need to establish if they are ours. That is, can we connect them to the car, either by DNA or fingerprints? Also, if that is our car, there'll be forensic evidence connecting it to our victim. If all those ducks line up in a row, and I'm reasonably confident that they might, then we'll have moved forward.'

'We will.' Max was the first to reply, and he seemed genuinely heartened by the positive way in which his new boss had summed up things. 'Helen, get in touch, please. Find out where Forensics are with the bodies. We'll need to establish if they are ours before we move forward.

'Debesh, the car. Tell the local lads to leave it until tomorrow morning. If there's nothing new happening, bring it in. We need to know if that is our car, and there'll be stacks of evidence to connect it with those bodies and our victim. That is, if we've got it right.'

Twenty-Two

It's the silence that first attracted me to the Lake District, and to house. Coming home, especially from wet work, I need that sense of tranquillity and the peace that so quickly renews me. But this morning, that very same silence has me awake at four, wrestling continually with my demons, completely unable to sleep, even to doze.

For years when its arisen, I've solved the problem with whisky - my preference, a full bottle of single malt at my bedside wherever I was sleeping. Often a difficult ask in some of the Islamic countries that I found myself, but once so important was it to my wellbeing that I was prepared to take the risk - and a serious risk it often was, so that I could have that liquid comfort blanket when I needed it.

Later, as I have matured, if that's the word, I've tried to reduce the risk of finding myself in a Qatari or Saudi prison cell by replacing whisky with medication. Amitriptyline became my sedative of choice, and for a few years it guaranteed me a good night's sleep wherever I happened to be.

However, I went off the medication route very quickly when once I took a couple of pills and settled down to sleep, only to be woken almost immediately when the job I was on was brought forward by twelve hours. The amitriptyline made me too chilled-out to respond quickly enough when danger hit me, and that stupidity almost had me end my days in a dusty suburb of Riyadh.

That was my Epiphany, and from that moment I foreswore all sedatives. I do still enjoy the whisky - I'm no saint, but I don't drink myself into oblivion anymore and when I am working, I stay sober and medication free.

I'm looking at that bottle now; a sixteen-year-old Lagavulin, a beautiful ultra-smooth Islay malt, and in my opinion, the best of them all. I can't tell you how much I now want to break my self-denying ordinance.

Through the early morning gloom, I pick it out, staring accusingly at me. It's not at my bedside now, but on the dressing table in our bedroom's bay window. Meg, lying perfectly still next to me is spark out. Nothing would wake her, and it would only take a moment for me to get to it, enjoy a mouthful or two, and I'd be off to sleep within minutes.

I do know that four in the morning is the very last time to choose if you want to delve deeply into your worries. I know that. It doesn't stop you though, does it?

It's the kids who've started me off. That bloody leaf slide. They're banned from it, of course, but that hasn't stopped Mr Stupid here and his four am reverie in which my children have been starring.

The reverie started with Joe, the boy, impaling himself on some tree branch as he rocketed past me down the hill. Chloe followed him in my dream, Chloe the barrier buster, the non-compliant twin, running off to the woods with a campfire stove and some sausages, only to find herself on fire and screaming in agony.

That woke me up, obviously, but as I tried to put these fantastical thoughts away, the obvious correlation with that incident with Meg at the spa putting my mind at rest somewhat, I immediately fell into another dream which caused me to sit bolt upright and in need of that stiff whisky.

Someone had taken Bella. I didn't know who had taken her or where she'd been taken. All I could hear were her screams, screams of a kind that that I'd heard before, yes, but only from adults, and then from adults in extreme agony and at the very end of a slow and measured journey to their cruelly painful death.

Of course, those screams have kept me awake at night on many occasions. But these screams I was hearing in my dream were from Bella, not some target, not some job. This was my child and although I could hear her - and she was close by me, nothing got me any closer to her.

Forcing myself awake and out of the dream that has so disturbed me, I get up very quietly, stretch and take in some deep breaths. Bella's screams recede; the dream floats away over the horizon.

I'm sweating cobs and I need to check the kids. I sneak along the corridor to look in on the children. They're all there, each in their own bed and sound asleep, oblivious to the turmoil in my little world.

I come back to our bedroom, look out of the window and over the lake. Everywhere is calm and ordered except in my febrile mind. I see the geese moving about at the lake shoreline, planning their day's activities. I catch sight of a young deer disappearing into the woods and moving peacefully towards where the leaf slide remains abandoned, Dad's grumpiness spoiling his kids' fun.

At least, while I'm in Grasmere, I've something guaranteed to make me feel calm and centred. There she is, my beautiful Meg, peacefully enjoying her dreamless sleep. I move back to the bed, leaving the tempting bottle of Lagavulin where it is, and I loop my arms around the most important person in my life.

But it's not working. My head is still spinning. All that's gone on in the last few days means that relaxation is simply impossible; maybe it's the bandage on Meg, still there, an insistent reminder. There are so many things that I must do.

I set myself a goal: tomorrow I've asked Wojtek, my Polish guy, to come over. He often stays at the house if I ask him to - I need to go and find out exactly what is going on, or maybe, he can do something for me.

Somehow, I need to find out if I'm a target. I'm behaving like this; it must be my inaction producing this heavy burden of guilt. 'By not doing, you do', isn't that what they say? If you choose not to do something, that is what you are doing.

And that's me - choosing not to do, maybe on the assumption that whatever it is, will go away. I've waited too long for that, and I know that it won't go away, and I'm the only person who can make a difference.

And there is something that Wojtek can do for me. He's Polish and that means he has his own network of eastern European contacts that may well have more information for me than I can find on my own.

By eight in the morning, I'm up and about. I've grabbed less than one hour's sleep before Nip the dog and then our kids made their presence felt. Nip is always first; his requests firstly come in a polite growl, as if he's embarrassed to have to trouble us. However, if we then choose to ignore his polite requests, he moves into phase two.

That will involve him scratching madly at one of the doors and increasing the volume of his yelps into fully-grown barks.

That normally works, especially now, considering our expensive new set of doors, and one of us, usually Meg, gets up to say good morning to him and let him out so that he can wander into the woods and do whatever he needs to do.

And should we fail to respond to his final demands, his reward can often be a large unpleasant gift that he leaves for us to clean up. He regrets having to do this, you can see it in his eyes, but in his mind, he has given us ample opportunity to do the correct thing, and this punishment is the logical result of our unreasonable behaviour, not his.

Today, Nip was out in good time, and later, when I get downstairs, he's waiting for me. He knows when I am at home, I love to go out with him, throw a stick or a frisbee and watch him career away after it.

We're out for maybe ten or fifteen minutes, walking around the edges of the garden, checking the fences and gates for - I'm not sure what.

Our security system is up and running and I've a few cameras located in what I would call strategic places around the gardens and up into the woods.

A few weeks ago, I would have been happy enough that the cameras were installed simply for reasons of safety. The one that focuses on the leaf slide for example, and a second now covering the camp site the kids had made, put there so that I could check up on what they were doing.

Suddenly, it's all change. Now those cameras are strategically important and part of a network that ties back to a video array in my office. I also have a second array set up in the safe room we created down in the basement.

Altogether, there are seventeen cameras, all motion-sensitive, and they automatically record any movement on the property -

including, as I can now see for myself, my recent wandering with Nip.

Now, sitting with my freshly made coffee in front of the array, always Lavazza, I check all the cameras, those outside first, and then the others - including those hidden in the bathrooms and bedrooms of the house. I feel slightly ashamed that I've now created a pervert's palace. If I wish, I can watch the most intimate activities of all my family members, and those of any guests who might be staying with us. Were I a jealous husband worrying about his wife playing away, I'd have her bang to rights: I can even record all telephone conversations made anywhere in the house.

The system is set up so that everything feeds back to both my office and the safe room. I alone have access to the codes, but I also have a direct connection to my mobile phone. I'd never previously thought too much about this, but I now know that I can oversee every activity in this house from wherever I am in the world.

It's a tragedy that I didn't have either Stephanie in the BVI or Archana in Dubai wired up in the same way. If things pan out as I hope they will, maybe I'll set a similar system in place at Archana's - sadly it's too late to do anything about Stephanie.

Except avenge her death, I suppose - that would go a long way, and it's early days yet, but I can't help thing that all these weird circumstances are connected.

Wojtek, my Polish guy, roars up the drive on his quad bike. He got my message, and he's arrived bang on time. We've not met for weeks; he's been doing some building work down in Kendal, but he looks fit and well and, as he looks around the garden, he's smiling.

'Hey Boss. Kids enjoying their holidays?'

'Wojtek, Hi. Yeah, I think so. You can't tell, can you? Mostly grunts. How've you been?'

'I'm great, thank you - fantastic.' He's not just smiling, he's beaming. 'Have you won the lottery?'

'I wish.' He smiles. 'That would be good, wouldn't it? No, Frank, maybe. But better - I'm in love.' I think of Wojtek as rather a taciturn man, tough outward appearance, but this is another side, something I've not seen before.

'In love? You?'

'Yes, new woman - not Polish, but seems OK. I've never had English girlfriend.'

'She's English?'

'Yeah. She lives locally - in Ambleside, but she's not local. From down south somewhere. Moved up here when her husband retired, but there's been some funny stuff, and they are divorcing now. She has her own house and everything. Works in ForGiving shop.'

ForGiving is the name of a charity shop in Ambleside; she must be one of the volunteers. 'Lucky you,' I say, 'you look well on it.'

'Yeah. I like her. She's older than me - but I've always liked older women. Do you think that's weird?'

'Me? Why should I think that's weird? It's whatever works for you, I guess.'

'I met her at work - her work - in ForGiving shop. I was looking for some stuff, I wanted a fleece, and she came to help me. We got talking and that was it. When she finished work, we went for a coffee - you know that café across the road, down Church Street? There. I never thought - she's amazing - honestly.'

'I believe you, Wojtek. I do. Congrats - I'm happy for you.'

'You don't look it. Is everything all right with you, Boss?' I can see from his eyes that he's noticed.

I'm tempted to blurt it all out. Everything's definitely not all right with me, and Wojtek has shown empathy, firstly talking about his new girlfriend and now with me. I used to think he didn't understand half of what went on in a conversation, I assumed the language got in the way, but as of this moment, I've immediately revised that opinion. He's interested in people other than himself, and he's sensed something in me.

I do the alpha male thing. 'Yeah, Me? I'm fine. Home for a while now and it's great to be back with the kids. It's all good, but I do want you to do something for me.'

'You've not got through all those logs?'

I smile. 'In the middle of summer? No, we've enough logs for ever. Probably longer.'

'So, what is it?'

'It's delicate. I won't mind if you say no, but if you say yes, you'll take a load off my mind.'

His immediate response, 'If I can help...' I jump in, 'I want you to check someone out for me - discreetly.'

'What do you mean, I don't understand - discreetly?'

'Discreetly - I don't want anyone to know about it. Would that be OK with you?'

'Depends on what it is, I don't want to get into any trouble with police.'

'Of course. I wouldn't ask that of you, anyway.'

'I know.'

'Good. It's not illegal, but I don't want anyone - anyone - to know about it.'

'Why can't you do it?' A fair enough question. I could see that Wojtek was pushing back on this strange request. I've never asked him to do anything like this before, and I can see he's worried.

I'd prefer to have him on my side rather than the opposition's in a bar fight, but that's not proved necessary - yet. And we've never been out to a bar together.

It's been practical tasks that allow him to excel. Once he knows what to do, he gets on with it.

He's brilliant with logs, chopping and stacking them. I'd already gone beyond the logs arena with him when I asked him to do some building work in the house and he helped me create the safe room in the cellar.

That involved our working together in secret. We completed the job when the kids were out at school and Meg would be at one of her classes, or out with friends, so he has conspired with me already.

I press on: 'I can't do it because I haven't got your connections. It's an eastern European thing and you'd be much more likely to find out stuff than I would.'

'What kind of stuff?'

'I'm under a bit of pressure.' I don't want to share too much with Wojtek for obvious reasons, but he could be of great use to me now. I continue: 'There's someone; he's Croatian, I think, and he's around here now - or at least, that's what I'm led to believe.'

'I'm Polish - we're not all the same, you know.'

'Fuck off, Wojtek, I am aware of that. I'm not racist - I don't think you're all the same, you foreigners. Give me some credit.' I'm quite exercised at this because Wojtek has surprised me.

Does he honestly think that? Maybe he does. Well, bollocks to it, to whatever he thinks. He can help me if he chooses to, so I try to get back on track.

'It's that you've got contacts that I don't have. I don't quite know what's going on, but I can tell you this.' I'm now trying to keep as much as I can on a need-to-know basis.

'There's someone who's annoyed me - no, not annoyed, he's angered me because my wife has been affected by this, and one of my overseas colleagues has also been involved.'

'What happened?'

'I don't want to go into detail - yet. First, I need to know one or two things. Then I can decide what to do.'

'And what you want me to do?'

'I'm told there's a guy, his name is Stanovnic, Janko Stanovnic. He's in the area, around here, apparently. If he is, I want to know where. He's Croatian, from the Zagreb area - and I know that's not in Poland.'

Wojtek smiled, enough to indicate that that he'd been winding me up. I decide that he's now on my wavelength, so I press ahead. 'I thought you could maybe ask around and see if anyone has come across him. That's all. Do you think you could do that?'

'No problem, Boss. Then what? You want me to take him out?'

My jaw dropped. 'What the fuck?'

I caught his eye and could see that his smile had now developed into a grin. And he was laughing when he slapped me on the back. 'Your face, Boss. What do they say? Yes, your face is a picture - is that it?'

My feeble reply was, 'I knew you were joking.' He nodded in agreement, but the look in his eye was that of someone a little more circumspect.

'I'll ask around today, and if I hear anything, I'll get back to you. There are some Serbian guys around and I know one or two of them. After all, we are all the same - foreigners.'

He was laughing again getting back on to his quad bike to leave. As he started it up, he waved and shouted, 'I can't stay now, I've some business to attend to in Ambleside.' And as he left, he gave me an old-fashioned wink, setting off, a little too quickly, I thought, back down the hill and I suppose to his love nest - where he would be soon attending to his business and, I hoped, to mine.

Twenty-Three

Janko was on the phone. He'd slept badly and had failed to contact anyone before falling into a troubled sleep. Now though, still feeling groggy - he'd raided the mini bar last night - he had to make some progress. He contacted the man who'd sent Mika the waiter to meet him at Oxenholme station.

'His mobile's switched off. I can't get him. I went round to his room earlier, but there's nothing there. He's gone, I think.'

'Where's he gone?'

'No idea. Really, sir. He's disappeared.'

'Fuck him. Find me someone else - and get me another car - not that pile of shit you sent for me last night. Also, I want a gun.'

'A gun? I can't get you a gun. I've no idea where I'd find one. I work in a hotel. I'm a chef. And I don't have another car - that's the only car I have, sir.'

'I won't be asking you a second time.'

'What can I say? I don't know anyone who has a gun - not here, anyway.'

'Then where?'

'I heard that one of the Polish boys on a building site brought one over from Rotterdam.'

'Get it for me.'

'I don't know if he still has it - or what kind it is.'

'Find out. Offer whatever he wants for it. I'll pay him in cash. And send that pile of shit car around to me now.' Janko disconnected, immediately making another call. 'Yeah, it's me. I'm where Christina...' He stopped for a moment; the image he inadvertently recalled startled him, stopped him for a moment.

'Email me now. Show where she was found and where she was working. Yes, Google Maps will do. It's not far from here and I want to go over her route.'

Another piece of information was offered, and the mug of coffee that he was holding was flung against the wall.

'What? When?'

His source tried to explain. Two men had been found dead. They were connected with Christina's disappearance.

'How connected? Are you there? How were they connected?'

And now yet another messenger understood entirely what it was like to be shot by a man like Janko. The menace in his voice, the unnerving sense of threat in every word. He wanted to get out and away from this conversation immediately.

'I heard that they took her - two guys turned up, wanted one of our cars. I don't even know if it was them, but it seems likely. I don't know anything else. I've sent you that map.'

Janko disconnected, looked at the attachment that was now waiting for him. The route the men had taken was only a few yards away from where he was staying. He called his local contact again: 'Are you ready?'

'Yes, sir. And I've borrowed a better car for you. I'm picking it up now.'

'It's now ten minutes past nine. I want it here by ten. You've hired one or is it one of your own?'

'It's one of ours. It belongs to a friend. BMW - Three series.'

As the phone was peremptorily disconnected, yet another frightened individual began weighing up the consequences of tangling with Janko Stanovnic.

This time, however, the idea of an immediate escape was hampered by the fact that his two children were at school, his wife was out at work and their mortgage payments on the house they had worked so hard to make possible, were ticking over nicely.

But he would extricate himself from this firing line. He couldn't escape completely, so the risk would remain, but that was the last telephone call from Stanovnic that he would accept. He'd arrange for someone else to drive over to his hotel, but his impossible request - obtaining a gun - well, he'd have to spin on that one.

Meanwhile, Janko was pacing his room. He tried two other contacts - nothing. He called the chef again, not for any further information, simply to let fly at him while he waited for the car. No answer.

He left a range of expletives as his message, packed his small bag with his phone, his passport and his cash, and went downstairs to get something to eat and to wait for the next useful idiot who would annoy him.

So far, all the contacts who might have helped Janko, maybe in a minor way, but at least assist him, had opted out. This was par for the course with Janko; his direct approach, as he liked to think of it, had worked very well in Dubai. Here in England, he wasn't making much headway.

Twenty-Four

Debesh and Melissa were at their desks finishing off for the day. Each had come back to the Ambleside office separately, Debesh from Lancaster, where the bodies of the two persons of interest to their investigation had been taken, and Melissa from an afternoon tea date with a senior officer who had asked to meet her privately. He'd requested a venue somewhere other than the office.

Each had decided, for different reasons, to write up a report of their meetings. Debesh was following protocol: he'd seen the bodies, talked to a couple of doctors who'd established the cause of death - not too difficult to work out - one shot to the head and two shots to the body in each case.

Forensic tests on the bullets had defined the type of weapon used, but the information they had didn't tally with any firearms currently on their database.

The murder victims had been restrained with cable ties to their wrists and ankles, and the only obvious conclusion that could be currently drawn was that they'd been executed.

So, Debesh's report on the day was relatively simple and consisted of the few facts that he'd gathered and not much more.

This evidence suggested that these men were the same two who had captured and then killed Christina Stanovnic. Debesh was considering whether he should stop by the cottage in Rydal and ask the witness that Max and he had found there to identify the men, but this had placed him in a quandary.

The quandary being that their witness was an elderly man, and although he'd mentioned to both officers that he'd served as a soldier in the Border Regiment, Debesh was concerned that showing him any of the photos now in his possession would traumatise him.

There was no getting away from the truth of what they showed. The men had been deliberately shot, the photos were disturbing and could not be sanitised.

Debesh knew he might have to ask the Rydal witness to look at these dreadful photos but hoped there was another way of resolving things.

Melissa on the other hand was reasoning with challenges of her own. Her report was more personal. Some factual elements she'd put into the daily log, but she'd decided to record only the gist of the rather confusing conversation she'd just had with her AC. This was the same assistant commissioner who'd suggested she come north and join her current investigation. He'd said that the meeting was to be informal, and that he was passing through the area and would like to meet.

He had chosen where they were to meet, and as they sat down on the sunlit terrace of the Sharrow Bay hotel at the top of Ullswater, it soon became apparent that this was to be more than a friendly chat:

there was a clear agenda that the AC wanted to discuss.

'It's not far from the motorway. I've a meeting with Police Scotland tomorrow.' The AC seemed to want to justify his choice of venue.

'That's fine, sir. I've never been here before, and I enjoyed the drive up the lake. Why the secrecy, though? We could have met in Ambleside.'

The AC was on a mission: 'We want you back in London.'

'You could have called me. I would have said no, but you could have called. There's no need for this...'

'You would have said no?'

'Yes, I think I would.'

'You don't even know what I'm going to say.'

'I expect to return to London, of course, sir. But not yet. The case I'm working on is developing well, and I don't want to let down my colleagues. We're a good team.'

'Your DI Wordsworth? How's he doing?'

'I like him, sir. And I like the way he works. Very collegiate; he likes to discuss everything.'

'I've read reports about him. Seems to be an interesting man - and with an interesting name.'

'It winds him up that people associate him with the poet. He says he hates poetry - and he might - but it does annoy him when people go on about it. Apart from that, I think he's very professional - and I enjoy working with him and his team.'

The afternoon tea arrived; a three-tiered serving platter filled with small sandwiches, cakes and scones and brought out on to the terrace courtesy of a friendly young waitress. The AC took charge of the teapot, poured two cups of tea, and offered a freshly baked scone to his colleague.

'Thank you. Well, this is very mysterious, sir. Can you please tell me what's going on? Are you actually on your way to Scotland? And why choose this place to meet me?'

'You don't like it?'

'I love it - but it's a bit out of the way - for both of us.'

The AC smiled as he also negotiated his way into one of the scones.

'Here? I've often stayed here at Sharrow Bay. I first came as a kid with my family - we didn't stay at the hotel; we rented a caravan near here every summer, and this was our treat on the last night. I always remembered it. So, no mystery there. And yes, I am on my way to a conference in Glasgow - drugs. Is there anything else, recently? I wanted to see you though, and I don't want to intrude on your current work. I'm sure the rumour mill is as pernicious here as it is anywhere else.'

'I'm not sure it is. Most people I meet seem straightforward. I have to say that the more I see of people around here, the more I like them.'

The AC decided to jump right in. 'Melissa, I've been asked to bring you back. And I would like that to happen when I return from Glasgow.'

'Bring me back? Why?'

'There's a very good reason.'

'I'm sure there is, but I'm heavily involved here.'

'Notice the 'would like'. I won't order you; you are too senior for that, and I want you on our side and not feeling resentful. There's a lot going on in London - and further afield, and we feel that you might be wasted up here - as a resource, I mean.'

'You sent me up here for a reason.'

'I know I did. Are your local colleagues aware of the bigger picture? The Syrian issue?'

'I've not mentioned anything other than that which is relevant to their investigations.'

'Good,' the AC replied. 'Let's keep it like that as long as possible.'

'And I'm needed here, sir. Whatever happened is bigger than we maybe thought. Three deaths now...'

'Three?'

'Yes, two men were found murdered not far from the scene of the original crime.'

'How far are you along in the investigation?'

'It's continuing. We're all following up leads and I'm reasonably confident. The thing is sir - and it's the reason why I'm reluctant to leave. I've a feeling that it's going to turn out to be much bigger than we anticipated. There's a definite foreign dimension; then there's the way the girl was murdered, who she is and who she's related to.

'And now these two men and the way they died suggests that there's much more to uncover. I feel I ought to stay here, and if I have any choice in the matter, that would be it. After all, you sent me up here for a purpose.'

'I did - we did. And if what you're saying is true.'

'It is true.'

'I didn't mean it that way.' The AC was in a dilemma. Melissa was right; she ought to remain on the case. He tried another tack.

'Melissa, you made DCS at a ridiculously early age and the trajectory you are on suggests much more for you.'

'The trajectory I'm on?'

'Yeah - sorry about that - too much time in meetings, drowning in management-speak.' The AC smiled at the way those words had come out so easily. 'What I meant to say - in English - is that if you are interested, and I think you are, there are promotion opportunities waiting for you.'

The AC continued, 'Priorities are changing. We've a lot of cases, many of which would benefit greatly from having someone like you lead them. That wouldn't harm your career at all, would it?'

'No. I understand - and thank you, sir. If you order me to return, I will of course comply. If you give me the choice, I'd prefer to stay here and finish off what I've started. I was brought in at a time when the Met decided to leave the investigation with the local police. Seeing them work, and how they work has vindicated that decision. And now, I don't want to let them down. It's as simple as that, sir.'

'How long do you reckon?'

'Piece of string, sir. If it peters out, I'll want to get back to London in a flash. But as I say, there's a lot more here than we first thought, and if that is the case, obviously NCA will have to come in and I'll be well placed to liaise with them.'

'You like it up here, don't you?'

'What's not to like? But I am committed to my work in London. This is only temporary, sir, but I would like to see it through.'

The AC found himself in a cleft stick. It was true that he wanted DCS Mordaunt back to work where he thought she belonged. He was certain that her talent was needed, now more than ever, and in the work to which he felt she was best suited.

His meeting with her however, was because he was on his way to Glasgow and otherwise he might not have wished to press his DCS as firmly as this. There was also some sound logic in her remaining with this case. The Met hadn't released one of its finest officers so that she could enjoy a Lake District holiday. She'd been sent north because of their suspicions of international involvement, and that had begun to materialise.

The fall of the Assad dynasty in Syria had brought some collateral issues that were troubling the security services. The Met had been asked to take any Middle Eastern concerns seriously, and the massive switch of priorities that Janko Stanovnic seemed to have put in place had troubled them.

Their challenge was the drug now known as Captagon; a party drug which had been marketed all over the Middle East. It was used recreationally, but it was also used by fighters, soldiers and anyone else who wanted to be alert and awake for hours on end.

It turns out that the Assad government eventually was deriving much of its revenue from the manufacture and the distribution Captagon, and security services all over the world were now concerned about what would be the future for this lucrative product.

The changing of the guard in the Dubai drugs scene had alerted MI6, and the Met had been carefully tracing any suspicious activity. Stanovnic exemplified such suspicious activity, and after they became aware of what seemed to be going on in Cumbria, a decision was taken to sound out whether Stanovnic might be reorientating his business to take advantage of the new situation.

So far, no such conclusion could be reached, but DCS Mordaunt had been dispatched to keep her eyes open. This might be a much simpler case, and so far, it seemed to be murder - serious and possibly gang related, but not necessarily with an international dimension.

There had been no signs or mention of Captagon so far, and the Assistant Commissioner was happy to play things out a little longer.

'I'll tell you what we'll do. I'll saunter on up to Glasgow, and over the next few days I'll have a rethink. Let's see if the Captagon problem does raise its head and at the same time, I'll see whether our London work is so vital that it needs your kind of strategic input. If it does, I'll bring you back. Otherwise, we'll wait for you to finish this off - but we can't wait for too long. You must understand that.'

Later, and now back in Ambleside, Melissa was struggling with those mixed messages, trying to process them into a status report for her team. She wanted to explain what she was doing and why but didn't want to sow seeds of doubt in the people to whom she had become so attached.

She knew that there were certain matters like the Captagon matter she couldn't divulge because that would have meant her mentioning the security services. But she was also loath to mention that Stanovnic's arrival in the UK was being carefully monitored too. She would have to work out a way of sharing this information at some time but now was not the moment.

'Finished?' It was Debesh, logging off and ready to leave.

'Me? Yes,' she answered. There was nothing left to write that would add value. She'd compromised by simply noting that she'd met her boss as he travelled up to a conference in Glasgow. She'd reported the current status of the investigation to him and that was that.

The arm twisting that he had indulged in she left out of her report. That would or would not happen. Either way, discussing it now would only be a troublesome diversion from the main thrust of what they were doing.

Melissa responded, 'I saw my London boss today - FYI. Nothing else to add. How about you?'

'Those two bodies are ours - could be a gangland killing. Looks like one. I've written it up, so we'll have something to discuss straight away tomorrow morning.'

Debesh then changed tack. 'Have you got a moment? There's something I'd like to show you. Come with me. I'll drive and I'll bring you straight back here. It's no more than a couple of minutes away. OK?'

'A mystery tour, Debesh? I'm intrigued.'

'Something like that. Come on. Prepare to be surprised.' And with a friendly smile, he held open the main door, allowing his colleague to pass by as she organised her laptop, mobile phone and carry bag all at the same time.

The officers got into Debesh's car and pulled out sharp right on to the road. Then, at a mini roundabout only fifty or so yards ahead, they took the left up a steep incline and past the Golden Rule, the pub which was now in danger of becoming their second home.

'I came this way this morning,' commented Melissa. 'I went up to Ullswater to meet my boss.'

'That would have been fun. Enjoyed the Struggle, did you?' The clue was in the title of this road. As it wound its way up to the Kirkstone Pass Inn, it was a challenge to any nervous driver – but evidently not to Melissa Mordaunt.

'There was nobody else on the road and I loved the drive. Steep, though.'

They'd no further time to discuss the drive over Kirkstone. As Melissa was about to elaborate, Debesh announced, 'And here we are.'

Not three hundred yards from their office, he'd stopped next to a chapel on a hill. There were a dozen or so cars, all tightly parked, but he managed to find a space.

'It's ok. Leave your stuff in the car - we'll only be a few minutes.'

Melissa, remembering some of her London experiences, was looking for a way to make her carry bag less conspicuous. The rear seat had kids' toys and a booster seat on it, and she used that as well as she could. Debesh saw what she was doing and smiled.

'Have you seen the lady up there - the one in the chapel? Don't worry, she'll keep an eye on your stuff for you.'

Melissa noticed that the chapel had been converted into apartments - she could see windows with curtains - and she glimpsed the curtain-twitcher at work. Debesh then invited Melissa to follow him as he walked a few steps from his car.

She was slightly surprised when, expecting the chapel to be their destination, Debesh walked past the gate and over the road to an attractive-looking stone house with a dark green door. After a moment or two, a smartly dressed, grey haired woman opened the door and smiled at them both.

'Welcome to Dalton's Mount, she said, 'Your cottage is right at the back, behind here.'

'My cottage?' Melissa was taken aback.

'Come and have a look,' Debesh interjected. The friendly woman came out of her front door, closed it, introduced herself as Jo and led both Melissa and Debesh down a short ginnel to the rear of her property. There Melissa saw the small stone cottage the lady had referred to.

'We call this Marigold Cottage. We let it as a holiday rental. Debesh said that you might be interested in taking it for a while.'

Melissa looked at Debesh, not quite sure of what to say.

'You did say that the Chase hotel was not for you, ma'am. And this is much closer to work - you couldn't be nearer, but it's also more akin to what you said you were looking for.'

The lady added, 'There's only one bedroom, and it is quite small.'

Melissa found herself joining in the conversation for the first time. 'There's only me. I wouldn't require anything larger. But it's the middle of summer. Most of the places I've looked at are ludicrously expensive.'

Debesh intervened. 'Jo and Martin are our friends. They were talking to Helen only a few days ago about taking a break from their holiday rental. They're going abroad for a few weeks and they'd asked us if we fancied staying in the cottage and keeping an eye on their house while they were away.'

'You'd be doing us a favour,' Jo added. 'But only if you'd like to.'

Debesh chimed in, 'It seemed too good an opportunity to throw away. I hope you don't mind, ma'am.'

'Mind? It looks a perfect choice. Thanks, Debesh. Thanks for thinking of me.'

'Maybe you'd like to see inside before you decide?'

'You had me when I saw your garden,' Melissa replied. 'But of course, I'd love to have a look around.'

The three of them filed into the small sitting room, Melissa immediately noticing the French doors leading out on to the small terrace and garden.

'That's where I'll be breakfasting from now on,' she said to herself, and to her new host, 'When would Marigold Cottage be available, Jo?'

'It's available now - whenever you want to move in.'

'And how much is it going to cost me?'

Jo smiled, 'You know that we northerners like to make a profit, but we thought that if you'd be kind enough to keep an eye on the house ...'

'You do know I'm working on a case with Debesh and his boss.'

'Yes.'

'When the case is complete, I'll not be remaining here. What would happen if …?'

Debesh intervened. 'Helen and I have said we'll look after things if you leave early. No problem.'

The rent they agreed on was well within the margins that Melissa allowed herself. Yes, it was on expenses, but she did have a view on that, and one of the reasons why she wanted to move out of the hotel was because she felt that she was spending far too much.

Marigold Cottage would be perfect for her. All she had to square away was the agreement of her London boss. Their earlier conversation had been sufficiently positive for Melissa to feel confident that the next few days, if not weeks, would be spent here in this beautiful Lakeland cottage.

Twenty-Five

'So, do you know the area?' Janko was in the back of a newer car this time, a black BMW Three series, much smaller than his Dubai forms of transport, but a BMW, nevertheless.

'I know little of the area, sir.' His driver had arrived shortly before a quarter to ten. That was earlier than Janko had expected, so he took his time to finish his breakfast before leaving the restaurant and starting his day.

'Your name?'

'Zivko, sir.'

'Croatia?'

'Rijeka, yes.'

'You've travelled around here much?'

'I've only been here since March. I'm working six days. So, I haven't, no.' Zivko, the middle-aged chef, and the third person to encounter Janko since yesterday, and very wary of what he'd already heard about his passenger, was treading as lightly as he could.

'But you can find your way around here?'

'Yes sir.' As an afterthought and delivered with a smile, 'Google Maps.'

'I need to see some places. Are you gonna waste my time?' The joke had not worked as well as the driver intended.

'Sir, I'm a chef, not a tour guide. This is my day off. If I can help you, I will.' The man's reply, polite as it was, did include a put-down that ordinarily would have riled Janko. Maybe it was the man's age, but Janko chose to let it go. If he needed to, he would sort him out, but at this moment, he wasn't sure how many other willing drivers could be dredged up.

His first driver had disappeared, and now his main contact wasn't answering his calls. Janko could sense mounting resistance to him and to his way of dealing with people. He reminded himself that this wasn't Dubai. Things were different here.

'Is this your car?'

'No, sir. I can't afford one of these. It belongs to my boss's friend.'

'Where's your boss? I expected to see him today.'

Although the man did know the answer to this question, he didn't want to give it. He'd drawn the short straw for this job, and he was beginning to see why.

'A family thing, I think. I'm not sure.' And to deflect the direction of the conversation, 'Can you tell me where you wish to go?'

'There's a caravan site. It's called Skelwith Bend. He pronounced the name Skelwith with a hard 'w', which would be a direct giveaway to the ear of any local.

'I can find that.' replied the man as he looked at the name that Janko was showing him and entered it into his phone. 'Yes, about fifteen minutes away from here. Do you want to go there now?'

'There's another place I also want to see,' continued Janko. 'The caves at Rydal Water. How far is that away from here?'

'It's about the same distance. They're both very close. Which do you want to see first?'

'The caravan site. Let's go.' Janko lit a cigarette and sat back as they set off. The car turned right out of the hotel on to the main road and headed north. Skirting the northern tip of Windermere and before reaching the village of Ambleside, they turned left on to the Hawkshead road and meandered down to the main entrance of the caravan site at Skelwith Bend.

Janko's driver had bitten his lip when his passenger lit up his cigarette. He wasn't a smoker, but more importantly neither was the guy who owned the car and had so unwillingly lent it to his boss. He knew that he would be fuming when he returned his car stinking of tobacco.

There was a valet service in Windermere that he might have to resort to after he'd finished dealing with this man. Now, however, he was keen to keep him mollified. This man was an explosion waiting to happen and now he fully understood why nobody wanted to deal with him.

On arrival at the site gates, Janko knew his language skills were not up to what he needed to achieve.

'You'll do the talking for me, OK?'

'My English is not very good, sir.'

'It's better than mine, so do it. I want to see the caravan where my sister Christina lived. Tell them I'm her brother - I've got my passport here if they need ID.' Now they were in the grounds of the site itself and were approaching the wooden building which housed the camp's reception area.

'In you go,' said Janko. 'Make it quick.'

Janko's driver, having rehearsed what he was going to say, walked into the reception area. Behind a counter a young man was there to greet him.

'Good morning, sir. How can I help you?'

'I have a question. My English not good. My - friend's sister, Christina - she works here. My friend wants to see where she lives.'

'Christina? Oh yes, the girl who ...' The young man didn't quite know how to complete the sentence. 'I'll phone my manager. He'll be happy to help you. He knew Christina. I didn't - I only started here yesterday. Will you please take a seat? It'll only take a minute.'

'Yes,' replied the man. He had only understood part of that message, but enough to realise that Janko needed to know what was happening.

'Yes, thank you. I tell my friend.'

Out at the car, Janko's driver updated him. 'He's calling his manager. Is that OK?'

'Yeah. Tell him I want to see where she lived.'

'I've told him. His manager won't be long. He's on his way now.'

And he was. Both men could see the manager cycling down the hill to meet them. He leaned his mountain bike up against the wall of the reception building and came straight to the car.

'You are Christina's brother?'

'Not me, him,' said the driver, pointing to Janko, who he saw was getting out of the car. 'He is brother of Christina. Name Janko.'

'Hello, sir. I am David. I am very sorry about what happened to your sister. I believe she was a lovely girl.'

The fog of the language prevented Janko from fully understanding, but he got the gist.

'I want to see where she lived.'

'Where she lived? Of course. And maybe you would like to take her things away. She left - clothes and so on. Would you like them?'

Janko turned to his colleague for a translation.

'He says that you can see where she lived, and I think he also said that there are clothes that you can take away.'

'Why would I want to do that?' snapped Janko.

'Maybe to remember her?'

'Fuck that. The only thing I want ....'

The manager interrupted the conversation, completely oblivious to its content, although the tone disconcerted him. 'Would you like me to take you to her caravan? You can see her things there - the police have released them, and you can decide if you want to take anything away with you. They'll only go to the charity shop if you don't.'

The last sentence was lost on Janko, but he understood that the man was offering to take him to where Christina had been staying when she was taken.

'To her caravan? Christina? Yes - please.' The most civilised thing that Janko had said since they met, his driver remarked to himself. The manager continued, 'If you get into your car and follow me, I'll take you there.'

The manager's gestures, plus the words 'car' and 'follow' cleared up any potential misunderstanding, and a few minutes later the manager had stopped at a dark green caravan, set with two others in a remote area of the site and well away from the commercial pitches.

'This is where Christina lived.' Janko noticed some blue and white tape by the door, and before he said anything, the manager intervened. 'Don't worry about the tape. The police have finished their work. I'll clear it away for you now.' And he immediately began to do so.

The young manager produced some keys, one of which opened the caravan door. 'I'll leave you to it. Everything laid out on the bed belongs - belonged to your sister. Please feel free to remove whatever you wish.'

Roughly speaking, both men understood what had been said to them and nodded their thanks. The manager, adding that if they required any further assistance, would they kindly pop into reception - all of which was lost on them.

He then smiled the professional smile of all managers, and he was up and off on his bike, readying himself for his next managerial challenge, and leaving Janko to absorb what was set out before him.

She had been abducted from here. Janko looked around. The caravan was very clean, but he remembered she'd always been a tidy girl. He fancied that some of the scratches around the door and possibly that broken cupboard, had been the result of Christina fighting off the men who had taken her, but maybe that was his imagination.

Nevertheless, there was an atmosphere to the place, and it weighed on him. Knowing what had eventually happened to Christina and standing in the very spot where it had all begun, had his heartbeat rising, his already hyper state now wanting to lash out - lash out at everyone and everything. He compromised by punching a hole in the door of the caravan as he left.

'Don't you want to take anything with you, sir?' Zivko had been standing outside, not wishing to intrude and more importantly, keeping completely out of the way of a man who was now simmering, showing signs of becoming completely unhinged.

'Take what? There's fuck-all there. What do I want with her clothes?'

'There might be some - memento you could take. Perhaps a photograph or a piece of jewellery? Something to remember her by?' Zivko was working hard to calm the man down and wasn't sure if this was the way to go. Maybe it would set him off again.

However, Janko was obviously reflecting on what the man had said. Up until that point, his only thoughts were focused on ripping the guts out of whoever was responsible for Christina's death. But this Zivko had a point: 'Er - maybe. Maybe there's something for her mother in there.' And he went back into the caravan.

Looking around, he saw that someone had placed all of Christina's possessions in neat piles on the sofa bed opposite the kitchen area.

Nestled between two of these piles was a small box in which when he opened it, Janko saw some items of Christina's jewellery and a few photos, one or two of them in frames.

His first thought was one of surprise that nobody had stolen the box. He saw a thin gold chain first and picking it up saw that it was attached to a small gold crucifix. He remembered it; Christina had been given that for her first communion. Then he noticed one of the photos in the box showed her wearing it. There were some bangles and a couple of rings, but nothing of any value.

He decided to take the box with him. If he ever were to see his mother again, he'd give it to her. Or maybe he'd post it. So much easier, and he'd not have to deal with the sullen resentful looks and murmurings that always accompanied his visits home.

Leaving the caravan with only the small box of Christina's personal items prompted a response from Zivko.

'Is there nothing there that you'd want to take with you?'

'I've got what I need - and I don't need any of this crap,' gesturing towards where the dead girl's clothes were neatly piled. 'I want to go to where she was found - now.'

'Are you leaving everything there?'

'Yeah. Why?'

I've a wife and two daughters, sir. Would you mind if ...?'

'If you took some of her clothes? Naaa! I don't want them. Be quick. I want to move on. I've seen enough.'

The older man didn't waste a moment. In he went, quickly picking up a couple of the piles of Christina's clothes, and he was back out of the door almost before Janko had returned to the car.

Swiftly, he opened the boot of the BMW and flung them in. He had no idea what he'd taken; he would look more carefully later when he had some time.

'Right,' said Janko. Let's go. I want to see those caves now.'

'Do you want to see the manager before we leave, sir?'

'No. Fuck him!'

'As you wish, sir. Rydal is about fifteen minutes from here - the traffic sometimes slows things up through Ambleside, but ...'

'Shut up and drive. If I want to talk, I'll tell you. Do your fucking job now and get me out of here.'

Outside the reception building, the site manager was waiting for Christina's brother. Out of courtesy he wished to offer his condolences and give her brother his best wishes. He was waiting, professional smile firmly in place, when the BMW, returning from Christina's caravan failed to stop.

Instead, as it passed him, going far faster than the five miles per hour speed limit of the site, the manager was surprised to see Janko in the rear seat of the BMW, very definitely giving him the finger.

That was a gesture not often seen at the Skelwith Bend caravan park, and the young manager returned to his desk in reception deeply offended.

Focusing his mind elsewhere, he began dealing with the more mundane aspects of his work: ordering gas cylinders, arranging for shower blocks to be cleaned and planning for that day's new arrivals. But try as he may, he couldn't get Janko's pointlessly offensive gesture out of his mind.

Later that day, and with the memory of it still rankling, still troubling him, he cycled down to Christina's caravan to clear it out. The accommodation was needed for two new members of staff who would be starting next week.

On entering the caravan, he immediately noticed that the door had been seriously damaged. It was as if someone had punched it. That would have to be fixed, and quickly. Next, he saw that most of Christina's clothing, which had all been set out in neat piles, had been taken.

Two black bin bags were all it took for the last memories of a girl he'd never met to be removed. His employers had remarked on how pleasant and friendly she was, and they'd been deeply affected by her death.

All a complete contrast to the crass and ignorant man who for no reason at all, had recently offended him. This was no grieving brother come to pay his respects and gently move his family into a better understanding of what had happened. This man was on a different mission altogether.

That thought prompted him to call and leave a message at Ambleside police station. The least he could do was let the police know that he had received a visit from Janko, Christina's brother, and that he had not left a very favourable impression. The man was up to something and maybe the police needed to be made aware of it.

Twenty-Six

The short drive from the caravan park to the caves at Rydal water took less than ten minutes. As Zivko followed the route suggested by his phone app - through Ambleside to the A591 north towards Keswick, he imagined that he was tracing the exact journey that Christina had been forced to take prior to her death.

Janko was aware of this too, although he experienced something that Christina didn't - the glorious view on a sunny day defining the reason why the Lakes was loved by so many people. At the same time, he was thinking that she would have made the journey in different circumstances.

He viewed the abduction from a different standpoint than most of us might. His view was that of a professional. He'd been involved in the odd abduction himself, and on more than one occasion had smuggled people, young girls mostly, through borders and checkpoints of various kinds.

When he arrived at Rydal and Zivko had parked their car in the grounds of the Glen Rothay hotel, he looked across the expanse of water and up to where the caves were. They were a long way from anywhere you could park a car, and he - putting on his professional's hat - couldn't understand why Christina's murderers would take such a risk.

They would have had to carry the girl - he doubted that she would have happily walked up the hill with them - for at least five hundred yards, if not more.

'Is this the nearest place to the caves?' he asked Zivko.

'No, I don't think so. Look here, sir,' came the response. Zivko handed his phone to him. 'You can see - over the road is a lane parallel to the main road and nearer to the cave. They probably parked there; it's off the main road and quieter. I brought you here so that you can see the cave better.'

'So, this is not where Christina came?'

'I don't know. How would I know? I thought you wanted me to...'

'Take me to where you think they parked their car.'

'Yes, sir. It's over there. Maybe three hundred metres. Do you want to walk there?'

'Does it look as if I want to walk there?' In truth, it did not, and Janko's eyes said so.

'Then start driving - and stop asking fucking stupid questions.'

The Croatian began to take a view of his passenger: not a very favourable one. He was thinking of what he might do should this dreadful man ask him to drive him again.

His decision made, but obviously not shared, Zivko started the car and took a very difficult left out of the hotel - and drove the couple of hundred metres to Pelter bridge, where he turned right over the bridge and immediately right again.

Janko immediately knew this would have been the road to take. He glanced at Zivko's phone again. Seeing where they now were, he noticed another road, leading to the Hawkshead road, but avoiding the village of Ambleside. It all made a lot more sense to him now.

This is the way he would have come, Janko the professional, were he ever in the situation of wanting to bring a terrified young girl from that caravan to her agonising death in Rydal caves.

'This looks to be as near as we can get. This is where they must have carried her from.' Janko and his driver had come as far along the lane as possible; their further progress now hindered by a locked gate.

'They must have started from here. Park up. I want to walk up to the cave where she was found.'

'I'll stay here,' responded Zivko.

'Fuck off. If I've got to climb up there, you're coming too. I want to know how it was done and then I'm going to find out who did it and cut their fucking heads off. So, come on!'

Zivko was the size and shape of any middle-aged chef who seriously enjoyed his food. That, coupled with his lifelong dislike of exercise of any kind, had created in him a sort of radar that allowed him to seek out and then avoid, any form of physical involvement.

He didn't fancy that walk up to the caves at all. He tried again. 'I'll come as far as the gate, but I can't walk up to the cave. Bad ankle, sir. Sorry.'

That worked. Janko couldn't be bothered to negotiate with the man - he'd knock a couple of hundred euros off the money he'd thought of paying him. That would teach the fat fucker.

'Fine. Stay here and wait for me. I see the path. I'm going up to the caves and I'll have a look around. Make sure you're here when I get back.'

'Certainly, sir. And thank you.'

Not quite sure of the sincerity of that last remark, Janko thought of picking him up on it, but decided not to - the walk up to the cave beckoned.

When he was over the gate and on the path up to the caves, Janko once again tried to think of the situation from a professional perspective. His first thought was that they would have had to tie his sister up. Duct tape rather than cable ties would have been his restraint of choice.

He would also have drugged and carried her, rather than try to get her to walk - one man couldn't do this by himself, so there would have to be at least two on the job.

Arriving at the second cave he immediately saw the small expanse of water where Christina had drowned. Now it was obvious that two men had been involved in the act. Logistically, it would have been impossible for one person - so precise were the tolerances required for the job to have its maximum impact.

Christina had been hung from the top of the cave so that her head and shoulders would, after a few minutes of thrashing about in the water, eventually be overwhelmed by it.

That took preparation and careful measurement. Had it been any victim other than his sister, Janko might have applauded the ingenuity of the idea. Because it was Christina, however, any form of professional acknowledgement was lost in the maelstrom of hate and resentment that was now fuelling Janko's desire for the most extreme form of revenge that his imagination could dream up.

As far as he knew, and this information came from the first chef - the now unobtainable chef - the two men who'd probably abducted Christina were now dead. There wouldn't be much left to extract from them.

This angered Janko even more. Who were they? And more importantly, who had sent them? They weren't prime movers; they were muscle, employed for that job and dispatched soon after.

Although Janko's desire for revenge was fuelled in part by his sister's death, truth be told, he was far angrier because her death and in particular, the way she had been murdered was aimed directly at him. As far as he was concerned, he was the victim in all of this: he was the real target.

Twenty-Seven

It's been a troubling few days for Max Wordsworth. He's come to terms with - no, more than that, he's accepted Melissa Mordaunt as his senior officer and is impressed by her professionalism. Debesh and Helen are also working well. Information is coming in from all over and his colleagues are processing it, but, and it's this that's worrying him, apparently without their needing any input from him.

He asks himself, is this paranoia or old age? Is the job taking more from him than he can give? And he's spent the last ten minutes pondering this, aimlessly stirring his now cold coffee.

This uncomfortable reflection has had him descend into this mood where he is now, and not for the first time, considering his options. Pack it all in? Possibly. He's frequently thought about retirement. But the same question always comes up: if he did retire, what then?

He'd lost more than one good relationship to the demands of his work, so now, if he did retire, what would he do? How would he spend his time? Who would he spend his time with? There was nobody, not one person who could fill his days, be with him - look after him.

He knew he was being a drama queen here: of course, he had friends, many friends both in and out of the force, but it also was true that bridges had been burned on too many important relationships.

'Brilliant way to start the day.' he said out loud. He did a lot of talking to himself but rarely descended into this level of self-pity. This wasn't him. 'Get a grip, man.' he told his other self.

'Get a grip of what, sir?' It was Debesh, arriving early and on the ball as usual. Chirpy, full of ideas, purely positive Debesh.

'Morning Debesh. Erm, I'm looking at our notes over the last few days. Nothing much is happening.' The best he could improvise. 'Losing those men who took Christina. That's held us up.'

'Not for too long, I hope,' Debesh replied. The man's cheerfulness, this seeing the glass half-full didn't help at moments like this, thought Max. He let him continue the riff.

'We've the car and we've got the bodies of the men who we think were in that car with Christina. When Forensics have done their job, we'll have a fuller picture. And on we'll go. And on another note, I think I've sorted something else out for your boss.'

'My boss?'

'Yea, Melissa. DCS Mordaunt, sir.'

'I know who she is.'

'Sorry. I know. I've got her a better place to stay. You know she hates that hotel; she feels uncomfortable there, so I had a bit of a think.'

'And?'

'I had an idea. And she liked it.'

'Your idea - what did you suggest?'

'Up Chapel Hill, sir. Behind the Rule. I've a friend - with a cottage.'

'Good kind of friend to have.'

'Yeah. Anyway, the DCS can have the cottage if she wants it, and I think she's quite keen. Is that OK, sir? Is anything wrong?'

'Not at all, Debesh, not at all. I've brought one of those late-evening, end of days feelings to work. I'm not concentrating. You heard me say I should get a grip - and I should; I was talking to myself.'

'Oh. Right.' Not quite knowing how - or if - to pursue this line, he went on, 'The DCS'll be in soon. Helen's on her way - school run. I think we're all moving forward. It's finding out why Christina was killed in that way that's holding us back. When we have a better idea of that, those end of days feeling, well, they'll vanish, won't they?'

Debesh's own sense of wellbeing was dampened for now, simply by looking at the expression on his boss's face. He'd never seen Max like this before. Angry, certainly; cantankerous as hell from time to time - that was par for the course for any senior police officer but etched on his boss's face for the first time in their nine-year relationship was something that he wished he'd never seen - it was the face of a loser. Max had given up.

'Has something happened, sir? You don't seem to be your normal joyful self.'

'Joyful?'

'Well, you know what I mean.'

Max considered his reply. 'I'd tell you if I knew. I woke up this morning feeling lousy. No, it wasn't the drink, thanks for not asking. I'll tell you what I think it is - you coming in here with that smile on your face has reminded me.'

'Me?'

'Yeah, when we were working here last time? We thought we had everything sewn up, and then - remember what happened?'

'That ForGiving case?'

'That's what's worrying me, yes.'

Debesh considered his answer. 'Sir, we got it wrong, but I thought you were OK about coming back here.'

'I am - I was. Things have stalled a little, but we're up to speed with what we've got. I'm certain that we'll crack this. A little more patience, I guess.'

Helen arrived, smiling as usual. She'd brought in some coffees too. 'Where's the DCS?'

'She's on her way, I believe,' replied Max. 'Don't worry, her coffee won't go to waste. Brilliant idea. I feel better already.'

'Better?' Helen had missed the beat, wanted clarification. Max obliged, 'Felt a bit off, first thing. But you know, it's amazing what a thoughtful cup of proper coffee can do.' And for the first time that morning, Debesh saw a smile on his boss's face.

'Your husband has been exploring a second profession.'

'He has?' Helen didn't quite know how to respond.

'Yes. Estate agent. Would you like to have an estate agent for a husband?'

'If he was called Debesh and was as sexy as the one I already have, I don't see why not.' Helen winked at her husband as she said this and moved towards her desk.

Debesh joined in, 'The hours are better - and you get commission on sales too.'

'Is this latest job a commission one?' asked Max.

'Where is this going?' Helen was confused. Then it twigged. 'Oh, the cottage. I get you now, sir. No, that was a favour. Debesh said that Melissa - DCS Mordaunt - was unhappy in her hotel and was looking around. I mentioned that our friends, Martin and Jo had ...'

'I know the rest,' interrupted Max.

'I don't understand,' said Helen, 'Where's this going?'

'It's me being narky,' replied Max. 'I obviously got out of bed on the - take no notice. It was a kind gesture, Debesh, and if it makes our DCS happier, it'll be good for all of us. Let's crack on. Let me get back up to speed and I'll be happy, I promise.'

Helen and Debesh caught each other's eye. Something wasn't right. Neither of them knew what, nor did they know whether to pursue or leave the line of questioning. Instead, each moved to their desks, firing up their computers in unison and reflecting on what had taken place, both embarrassed for different reasons.

Debesh, because he worried that his boss was allowing that old case to affect his judgement. Helen, because she simply had no idea what, if anything, was going on. The dynamic of the team had changed; she could feel that, but for good or bad, that remained to be seen.

Complicating matters further when she arrived, DCS Mordaunt was in a mood that was - ebullient. Completely the opposite to Max, she was smiley, brisk and obviously very happy.

'Did you hear what your clever DS has done for me, Max?' All this said while she was laying out a series of files on to the largest desk in the room, hers.

'He's found me somewhere to stay where I can slob around whenever I want. I can have my breakfast in my pyjamas - and on a terrace too.'

'We are blessed to have him among us, what can I say?'

'My thoughts exactly, Max! You took the words straight out of my mouth.' Helen had chimed in, but the tone of her response didn't exactly match the content of her contribution.

And Max piled in. 'All right. Stop it - now! I'm sorry. It's my fault. I'm delighted that you are all so pleased with yourselves. Let me inject a note of reality here. This case is going backwards, and at some point, our new friend - you DCS Mordaunt - our new colleague, I should say, is going to have to express this thought to her lords and masters. And what will happen then?' He looked around. Time lapse. Nothing.

'So, allow me to continue - as it seems you won't. This is why I came in here a little less than my normal self.'

'DCI Wordsworth.' Levity stopped - immediately. It wasn't that she spoke loudly or gesticulated in any dramatic way. No, for the first time in her relationship with her new colleagues she exerted her natural authority, that ability she had to draw the attention of others seemingly without effort, and the reason why she was so prized at the Met, and which had occasioned the recent visit of her assistant commissioner.

'We're not going backwards.' They all picked up on the 'we'. 'You've done a great job in collecting all the available information from this area. You've blended well as a team - and you've been very accommodating to an outlier like me. I've every confidence in you - in us - as a team. You should have too. And here's my contribution.' She pointed to the half dozen or so buff folders that she had placed on the desk a few moments before.

'Here is the info that the Met has collected on Janko. He's a naughty boy and could have been picked up on arrival. However, and this information is something I feel that I ought to share with you now: we let him through.'

'What do you mean, ma'am?' It was Debesh who asked the question that was on everyone's lips.

Melissa continued, 'The Met has been aware of Interpol's interest in this man for some time. There's a power struggle going on in the Middle East, what with Assad's fall from grace and so on. There's a massive drugs industry there, run by the Syrians, and now with him gone, there's concern that those drugs might be seeking another market. We wondered if Stanovnic might be coming over here for that reason, so we let him come into Europe.'

'Is that why you've been posted up here?' Max was more than curious.

'It's one of the reasons, yes. But things have moved on now - these murders were not expected, so we have to play catch-up, and quickly.'

Melissa gave each of her colleagues a folder she'd prepared for this moment.

'Each of these folders deals with some different aspect of his work. Girls, drugs, the odd killing. His sister is clean - there's nothing on her at all. In fact, I'm thinking that she came here to keep clear of Janko. She spoke to her mum on Zoom or whatever but always kept her location secret.'

'How did Janko find out?' said Debesh, already flicking through the new information.

'Don't know exactly. We might get lucky, but so far, we've nothing. I think your original theory was right. She's been murdered, but in a way calculated to send a signal to Janko. And he's seen the signal and that's why he's come to England.'

'Where is he now?' Debesh again. 'Is he up here?'

'I'm not a betting person,' interrupted Max, 'but I think he's here in the Lakes. He's come to find out what's going on.'

Debesh had moved to where the DCS had placed the folders. He picked one up.

'Girls. Into and out of Dubai.'

'Yes.' Melissa responded, 'That seems to have been his main work. You'll see from those other files that he was also into drugs.'

'Drugs? In Dubai? Pushing his luck, wasn't he?'

'Probably. I don't know - the files contain pretty much all we have - but it doesn't seem to have worried him. Guns, girls, money, drugs - all part of his business at some point. We're pretty sure t he was involved in the Syrian drugs business too. He was a busy man.'

'Was a busy man?' Max was interested. 'Past tense?'

'Oh yeah. Past tense is right. We don't know why, but - he's liquidated everything in Dubai. He had a big thing going, quite a complex network - obviously keeping a lot of people happy. We were very tempted to pick him up when we knew he was on the move to find out more. But the people upstairs - and MI6 - decided to see what he was up to.'

'What do you mean, ma'am?' This was Helen. Her naive question although not quite so naive, was on Max's lips too.

'Running a business like that in Dubai?' Melissa helped them all out. 'He'd offices, storerooms - cars and people working for him. You can't hide that for too long. He needed to keep a lot of people happy - or maybe one very important person happy. One way or another, especially with drugs. But now, he's on the naughty step. Properties, cars - even utilities; debts everywhere. Leaving a lot of very angry people. And if he has an important protector, that's going to be even worse.'

'Why's that?' Helen was certainly asking questions that both Max and Debesh were interested in.

'It's a question of Face. If Janko has a protector - someone he's paying to grease the wheels, that person - or those people - will now be having to explain to their bosses, to landlords, to lease holders - all those greased wheels, why they're losing so much money because they trusted his recommendations. He'll look weak to the people who matter. And that will matter to him.

'Janko may well have escaped Dubai, but the world is much smaller now. I presume he's taken his money with him, but unless it's in a lorry - and he's driving it - and living in the lorry, he'll be leaving digital signatures. It won't take long.'

Debesh had finished glancing at his file. 'If he's up here, we can find him. NCA or your lot can help, can't they?'

'That's all we have so far,' Melissa replied. 'There's work for us to do. We need to establish if he is here and if so, why?'

'So, let's get started.' Max saw how they - correction 'he' - could get back up and running. 'Check everywhere we can. Is there any way we can get info from locals? People who might know him?'

'Some countries send the police around to hotels every night - collecting registration cards. That would help.'

'Thanks for that, Debesh. Dream on. We don't do that, yet. We can access them, but it'll take forever to swing into action. What we do have in the meantime, is the telephone.' Max was now keen to start. 'Helen, get us a list of all accommodation - hotels, B&B - self-catering, Airbnb - whatever you can. We can split that up and spend the morning doing some more old-fashioned police work.'

Helen looked up from her screen. 'On it, sir.'

Melissa gathered her files and started to look through them more carefully. The first two produced nothing that she and the team didn't know already, and she put them to one side.

The third though, was much more interesting. It was a report that detailed some of NCA's ongoing work; much of it relating to Janko's recent behaviour, adding context if not a specific reason for his sudden arrival in England.

Logging on to the NCA website, she inputted the file reference number and pulled up the complete file. What she was now looking at was all the NCA had on Janko Stanovnic, his connections in the Middle East and his known European associates.

Also, someone had taken the time to attempt to link Janko with various incidents which, while not having enough evidence to make a strong case against him, certainly seemed to have his imprint associated with them.

There were documented records of transactions that had been made to and from UAE bank accounts, payments that had come from Riyadh, from Macao and from Belize.

This man had only been allowed into the UK because the red flags had been removed. And, when cross checking with the information that NCA had retrieved from the UK Border Agency, she saw no red flags there either. She had assumed they would be there but there were none.

Janko was a 'person of interest'. Someone had taken a very significant decision simply in order to see how Janko chose to move. The Met were in on it, but Melissa had none of their strategic thinking to work with.

Hers was a watching brief, and her attachment to the Cumbria investigation was meant to be a cover for her. All that had changed, of course, when matters started to develop their own momentum.

Nevertheless, Stanovnic, it had to be remembered, had taken a great risk in making the journey. There must have been a very strong reason to justify it.

While Melissa was readying the new files, the team was into its 'old fashioned' police work. Each had a list of places where Janko might be staying.

They were using a South Cumbria accommodation list - published by the tourist board, and they were asking hotel receptionists, guest house proprietors and self-catering agencies for information about any European guests who had recently checked in.

'Look here. This is what I've got.' Melissa indicated the flat screen on the wall where she had arranged to direct the information.

'You can see that we've a trail of events. It is Janko Stanovnic. He's definitely left Dubai - and he's left a bunch of creditors too. He's flown to France and then taken the Eurostar to London.

I'm guessing, like everyone else, that he's the guy that the manager at the caravan site mentioned. His behaviour fits the description too.'

'And what do we do when we find him? What then?' Debesh, ever the realist, was rightly wondering what the next step could be. 'I mean, we couldn't arrest him, could we? He's not done anything. And even if we took him in for questioning, what could we ask him? After all, given the circumstances, he's a victim too.'

Max had to intervene, 'Yea, but so are we. He should have been stopped on arrival - or we should have been given more information sooner.' He looked at Melissa as he said this, certain that she knew much more about the situation than she so far had admitted.

'But that's blood under the bridge now. Too late. Now he's here, I don't want him arrested. I do want to know where he is, though. We'll keep an eye on him if we can - let's see what he uncovers. I can't believe he's come all this way to pay his respects.'

'True,' continued Debesh. 'But, if we do find him, we should have an idea about how to deal with him.'

'And so we shall, my boy, so we shall.' Max gestured to his colleagues to pull up a seat at his desk. All three responded, Melissa bringing with her the file that she'd been reading.

'While we are all together, and before anything kicks off, let's have a go at some scenario planning. It would be sensible of us to do a few 'what if's' so that we all understand what we are aiming for. OK?'

And once again, DCS Melissa Mordaunt allowed herself to be impressed by this new, somewhat crumpled colleague. What was his back story, she began to wonder?

Twenty-Eight

I finished my second cup of coffee a moment or two ago, and I've and agreed with Meg what we might do today. A walk in Grizedale Forest is favourite for the two of us, and luckily, we've sold the idea to the kids because there's a play area and they love 'Go Ape'; that's there too - and we've thrown in the promise of a picnic for good measure.

I've had a couple of phone calls to deal with, nothing urgent, and we're about to gather up the kids and Nip when up the drive comes Wojtek on his quad bike.

He's met firstly by Joe, obviously on the lookout for a ride around the house and then Chloe and Bella join in. Chloe leaps on behind Wojtek and grasps him with both arms, imploring him to take off, leaving her siblings in his wake.

Within seconds, there's a full-scale riot happening with the kids all screaming at each other and Nip running round and round the quad bike, barking his head off.

'So much for a quiet trip out,' smiles Meg. 'Wojtek knows how to wind them up.'

And he does. He's joining in now, pretending to move off, revving up the quad and joining in their laughter.

Joe's pulled Chloe off the bike now, and this action starts a fight between the two of them. Obviously, this is an opportunity for Bella, and she takes advantage of it, goading Wojtek now that there is a clear path ahead, into taking off at speed.

A few minutes later, they are all smiles. Wojtek has negotiated with them so that each gets exactly the same turn around the house, and honours even, the kids gather up their stuff, including their rucksacks - each a different colour to avoid misunderstanding - and that's when Meg intervenes.

'Right, you lot. No phones, understood? There's no reception at Grizedale anyway, so let me see them now.'

Out come three phones that the kids reluctantly hand to their mother. This has become our new normal. Whenever we have what we class as a family event, and that includes meals at the table, we do the phone thing.

To begin with, all three of the kids, each in their own passive aggressive way, played up, trying to conceal their devices, arguing the toss each time. But we persevered, and now the system is working. Curiously, they now also accept handing them in at bedtime.

Meg's original reason for this was that there wasn't any point in their having their phones overnight as, conveniently for us, the internet 'went off' at 8pm. Now the phone routine occurs at the same time as they brush their teeth. If everything in life worked as swimmingly.

Wojtek catches my eye. He wants a moment. Meg is bundling the kids into the car, rucksacks and Nip into the boot - we're using the G wagon, plenty of room - and she's just got into the front passenger seat. Perfect timing for Wojtek to interrupt our domestic arrangements.

'I've found him, boss. At least, I know where he's staying.'

'Where's that?'

'Merrywood hotel - on the way to ...'

'I know where it is. What's he doing?'

'He's not there now. He went out. That's how I know about him. A guy I know in Bowness is driving him around, and he's not very happy.'

'Who's not very happy?'

'The guy. My pal. He says he's a cunt. Ignorant, coarse - swears a lot.'

'Did you call him a cunt?'

'I could have used the Polish word - but you wouldn't have understood.'

'Smart arse!'

Wojtek smiles. 'What do you want me to do?'

'You see that I'm a bit tied up now - and I don't want someone you've described so elegantly to spoil my day. Can you find out about him? See what he's doing, why he's here? I'll work on this when I get back but today is a day for the kids.'

Meg peeps the horn - a gentle reminder that she's trapped in a tin box with three wild animals and a stupid dog. This is her call for help. She needs to be rescued and that only can happen when I get into the car and start it up.

'I've got to go now, Wojtek. Can you do this for me? Stay away from him, but find out what he's doing?'

'Sure, boss. You get off. I'll lock up everything and see you later.'

'You're a star, Wojtek.'

'That's what my lady says,' he smiles as he says this. 'And I prefer to hear it coming from her.'

It's days like this that make it all worthwhile. On the odd occasion when the stars seem to align themselves favourably for my family, there's no place - and no group of people anywhere - where I'd rather be.

When my kids are in sync with each other, they are a delight. When they put aside the grasping, avaricious behaviours that aggravate me so much, and they revert to being ordinary children, there's nothing I won't do for them - even to the extent of acceding to their wishes as they dare me to 'Go Ape' with them.

You'll know about Go Ape? It's everywhere now, a series of scary, very challenging walkways, high up in the trees in woodland and forests all over the country. Here it's in Grizedale, only a few miles away from us, twenty minutes or so, near Hawkshead.

Of course, we're all wearing harnesses connected to a safety line above us, and when we have to change safety lines and release our carabiners, there's a staff member there to make sure we do it all safely.

While it's meant to look dangerous, it isn't really, but it is high. If you don't like heights, that certainly adds some extra excitement to the experience.

Our very own scaredy cat this time turns out to be Joe. Strange, he'd been all right last time. The girls, Meg included, took to the ropeways, the bridges and the swings like a bunch of gibbons - their cries of joy and excitement echoing over the forest. Joe, by contrast, clung to my legs, completely crag fast - although he was up a tree and not marooned on a cliff face.

Nothing I could do - no cajoling him, no pointing out that the girls were enjoying themselves by offering to hold his hand - nothing could tempt him to move anywhere.

'I'll take him back down, Meg. We'll wait for you in the car.'

'Are you sure? Joe - don't you want to come and help me, darling?'

Nothing. Joe wasn't having any of it. So, the two of us turned to get back down to ground level, and at that moment, my phone pinged.

This was a surprise. Meg wasn't fibbing to the kids when she said there was no signal in Grizedale; there isn't, normally. But here, right at the top of a very tall pine tree, in the middle of the forest, there was enough of a signal from somewhere to alert me.

It was Wojtek. 'Boss, some guy with a gun.'

'Where?'

'Here at the house. I left the door open - I was bringing stuff in - I'm sorry boss. He's in the hall, walking around, looking for something.'

'Where are you?'

'I'm down in your special room. I went straight there.'

'The Panic room?'

'Yea, I'm watching him on your CCTV.'

'Is he alone?'

'He seems to be. There's a car outside by the gate, but there's nobody else around.'

'He's got a gun?'

'Yea. Not a pistol. Bigger than that.'

My mind was racing as I tried to process this information. Bigger than that? A machine gun? Maybe a Mac 10 or an Uzi? I've used both before and I know how lethal they can be.

'Is it a long gun, a rifle?'

'No, not long like AK - possibly a Scorpion, I'm not sure.'

The Scorpion. Now the weapon of choice for bad lads everywhere. It's replaced the old AK 47 used by terrorists of every hue, jihadists from everywhere, and sundry eastern European thugs who can't get hold of the more modern, more sophisticated weaponry now readily available.

It's a fiendishly powerful weapon, despite its lack of sophistication, and I was relieved that if Wojtek was in the panic room, he would be safe, particularly if he hadn't been seen by the intruder. And if our palm-operated doors did their job, the bad guy couldn't access anywhere else in the house.

'Did the guy see you?'

'No boss. I was going to the quad when I saw the car come up the drive. I went into the house and waited for him to get out of the car. He couldn't open the main gates, so he parked up and waked in through the side gate. When I saw the gun, I came straight down here. I watched him.'

'You did the right thing, Wojtek.'

'No, Boss. I left the door open. That was stupid.'

'Don't worry. You're safe where you are. He can't get through the new doors, and there's no way he can get into the panic room. I'm coming over now. I'll be about twenty minutes.'

'Right, boss. I'll wait.'

'One other thing, Wojtek. Can you use a gun?'

'Of course, I can. Military service - back in Poland.'

'OK. So, in the cupboard to the right of my screens, you'll find some Glocks; there're a couple of Sigs too - ammunition in a box on the shelf below. The code is 0911. I think it's better to be safe, eh?'

'Thanks, boss. I hope I don't have to use it.'

'You won't. Now I need to get back to Grasmere. Call me if anything develops. I'll be there in about twenty minutes.'

I had equipped our panic room so that I could defend myself and my family if I needed to. The handguns I'd put there offered a choice, but knowing now about Wojtek and his military training, I was sure that some of the other options in my gun safe might have been of equal interest to him.

He knew where the room was - nobody else did, not even Meg. As I've said before, I've kept the cellar area deliberately cluttered and unlit to discourage the kids from going down there.

When I was thinking of creating the room, I'd shared my original idea with Wojtek, and he'd helped me with the construction of it and was now using it for its true purpose. He would be safe there, but my chief worry was what the hell was somebody with a gun doing in my house?

It's obviously connected to the conversations I've had on Messenger. But I still can't work out why. The violence against Stephanie in BVI, the attack on Meg at the sauna in our club and now this - an attack on my home, and by extension, on my family, is all the more concerning because I've no idea what's prompted it. Why?

What's going on that's so dangerous to us? I've no clue where I can start to respond. How do I take control of something I can't grasp?

Of course, I'm not naïve. There are many situations that could have prompted someone to have a go at me. I'd like to know which one, that's all. And my very expensive security system is only partly working too.

The weak phone signal here at Go Ape means that I can't see online what is going on in my home. I've had to rely on Wojtek's reporting to me, and while it's a great improvement on our previous arrangements, I want to see the person who's come looking for me. That'll have to wait until I can get to where there is reasonable phone coverage, and to do that, I've got to get my wife and kids down from the trees.

Twenty-Nine

Back in his room at the Merrywood hotel, Janko weighed up his options. It was a stupid idea coming all this way, leaving everything in Dubai, or at least, one half of his brain told him that. The other, more logical part told him that Christina's death, worrying and brutal as it was, had been his reason, his ticket to escape Dubai.

He was simply kidding himself if he were to start thinking about any sacrifices that he'd made by leaving Dubai. Yes, the apartments and cars and of course the cash; all the money that came from his various enterprises, much of that had been given up.

On the other hand, he was still alive - and he'd taken most of his money with him. He'd millions in safe bank accounts all over the world. That was a bonus - even if the information he'd collected so far suggested that someone was on the lookout for him and that his life was now in serious danger.

Coming up to the Lake District was a mistake, a conceit. Yes, he had to escape, that was his reality check, but he'd put himself at even more risk now, perhaps more than he'd felt when he was in Dubai.

Those last few months had been a battle. And there had been consequences. He knew what had started the rot, and he now regretted sending that shipment of North Korean girls to Riyadh.

The Saudi clients had been quite specific in their request - the girls had to be North Korean - but like so many people who think they know exactly what they want but are disappointed when it arrives, that group of under-nourished, gap-toothed peasants hadn't met the standards of his clients' fantasy. Yes, it was buyer's remorse, and not his fault, but he knew that they were holding him responsible for the fiasco.

Even then, weeks before his final flight from Dubai, he knew that mistake was terminal. Liquidating his assets as soon as possible was the only alternative, and to be fair, that part of his scheme had gone surprisingly well.

When contemplating where next he might set up shop, the UK was way down on his list. Money laundering regulations would make large cash purchases difficult. Of course, he'd heard about wealthy Russian and Chinese businessmen buying and selling properties in London for huge sums, but he didn't have the connections for that - yet.

It would have to be South America he concluded, or maybe somewhere in Asia - obviously somewhere he might easily change his identity and live a more anonymous, quiet life.

Quiet life? He reined back his thinking. How could he square this quiet life with the risky journey he was now undertaking, rushing up to the Lake District with all the hazards that entailed without the slightest idea of an objective? What was he going to do now that he had arrived? It was likely that the men he believed had killed his sister had themselves already been eliminated.

There was no local intelligence of value that might further his investigations here. Seeing where his sister had been living, and where she had died had simply frustrated him even more. He was angry and would certainly know what to do should he meet his unknown enemy, but that was the point - unknown. Who the hell was he, or she - or them?

He called Zivko, the unwilling chauffeur who'd given him his tour of Rydal and Skelwith. 'How did you know those two men had been killed?'

'What two men?' Zivko had been woken by the call, and at first, he hadn't connected the voice to the person.

'The two bastards that killed my sister! Who the fuck did you think I meant?'

'The police came asking, talking to all eastern Europeans. They'd used one of our cars. One of the Poles lent the car to him.'

'Give me his fucking number!'

'Who?'

'The Pole, you prick. Give me his number!'

'I don't have it, sir. I was doing a favour on my day off. Somebody asked me to drive you around.'

'Somebody?'

'Yeah, I got a phone call. Asked if I wanted to make some money on my day off.'

'Who was it?'

'He didn't say, sir. He asked me to turn up at your hotel on time, that's all.'

'You must know who he is. What's his fucking name?'

'I don't know, sir. I've no idea. I work fourteen hours a day, six days a week. I meet nobody except the people I work with. I got a phone call; the car was left for me, and I came to meet you. Nothing else.'

Getting nowhere fast, Janko terminated the conversation, throwing his phone on to the bed in frustration. Having angered or frightened everyone who might have been disposed to assist him, he was stuck.

Possibly he'd expected Christina's killer to be waiting for him, maybe twirling his moustache like an old fashioned movie villain, but it was unlikely that the person behind all this, the person he needed to get to, would be anywhere nearby.

What had happened to his sister was a signal to him. If anything, coming to the Lakes as he had, may well have made his adversary's job easier.

He phoned his connection in Paris. He was based in St Cloud and Janko reckoned that Paris would be as good a place as anywhere for him to reset his life. He would stay there for a week or two; there were people he knew who could get him new passports, and if Paris didn't suit him, he could take his time deciding where he would create his next life.

The 'signal' as he had termed Christina's death (seen entirely as a signal to him, nobody else) and meted out to him by some invisible presence was the very way he would work from now on. He'd outsource everything; he could easily afford to have others do the leg work for him. He would employ the right group of contractors and leave it to them to find out who was responsible - and bring him his head on a plate.

No, even better, forget the plate bit. Just get him and bring him; Janko himself would have the opportunity to exercise his creative skills on the complete person. The head alone wouldn't provide the atavistic satisfaction he now craved.

Thirty

Max and Melissa are sitting in the back room of the Golden Rule, the small pub a two-minute walk up the hill from their office at the Ambleside police station. It wasn't a planned event. Each had gone out at about the same time - Max a few moments behind his new boss, and she'd stopped to take a phone call before she got in her car to drive away.

'I'm moving in this weekend, Mother. I'll let you know when I'm settled. No, I'm not proposing anything of the sort. It seems more - suitable for me. I don't like staying in hotels.'

Her laptop bag was perched on the bonnet of her car, and as she turned, maybe emphasising a point to her mother, the bag slipped.

Max was walking past to his vehicle, expecting to nod goodbye as he had done half a dozen times before.

His quick reflexes meant that the bag - and possibly the laptop - were saved for another day. And as Melissa whispered her thanks - at the same time explaining herself to her mother - still on the other end of the phone and as hypersensitive to atmospheres as most mothers are, they both looked at each other and smiled.

An immediate change of plans: Max, replacing the laptop bag on the car gave the universal gesture for 'Would you like a drink?'. Melissa found herself answering in the affirmative, nodding her consent while batting away what had become intrusive questioning from her mother.

A few minutes later, they'd walked up to the Golden Rule, Melissa's mum still concerned about something and obviously on a mission, although Max couldn't tell precisely what. Melissa, in daughter mode, far less assertive than Max had previously experienced.

'Sorry about that, Max,' her first words to him spoken directly. 'My mother still thinks I'm an impressionable teenager - or worse.'

'That's mums for you.'

'It's because I decided to move into the cottage.'

'Maybe she thinks you're moving here permanently.'

'I've probably made worse decisions, but that's not going to happen. She's paranoid. Too much time on her hands.'

They'd reached the bar by now. Max motioned to her to take a seat at a table in the side room. 'What would you like, ma'am?'

'A coke will be fine, thanks. Soon I'll be walking to work, but not yet.'

'Debesh and his magic.'

'Yeah, it's a little further up the hill from here. And I'm grateful. I'm already beginning to feel entirely different now, so much more relaxed. They're a bit up themselves at the hotel - pleasant enough, but it's not me.'

'A Coke and I'll try a pint of Cumbria Way, please.' Max deflected his gaze towards the patient barman. He'd been caught up in what Melissa was saying, even though she wasn't doing much more than chatting.

'I'm surprised. I'd have thought you'd like a touch of luxury. Lake view, excellent restaurant.'

'Ha! I wish. No - in fact, I'm a cheap date. I don't go for all that stuff. Especially when I'm working - my puritan work ethic clicks in. Racked by guilt.'

'Here in Ambleside? You'll be paying a fraction of what it would cost you in that London.'

Melissa clocked the 'that London' remark - although Max had accompanied it with a knowing smile. By now, they were both seated, Melissa on a bench seat, and Max across the table from her. 'True, but I've always been uncomfortable about expenses,' she continued, 'I can't appreciate the experience. The cottage is very comfortable, and the best thing is I get to decide my own mealtimes and I won't have to worry about how I look.'

And as an afterthought, she added, 'I was thinking that once I'm settled in, I could invite you all to come round one evening.'

'Sounds a good idea - after all, you're a local now.'

'Probably not,' came the reply. 'I hear that even if you live here for fifty years, you're not considered local.'

'Off-comer, that's what you'll be called. But don't let that worry you.'

'It won't.' And after a short pause, Melissa continued, 'I've quite a lot going on down in 'that London'.'

It was Max's turn to smile. And he understood why; he'd heard all the gossip about this fast-tracked officer who could soon be in line for the Met's top job.

'Yeah, I know you're busy there, but on an evening like this, up here in the Lakes, aren't you even slightly tempted?'

Her eyes met his directly as she asked, 'Tempted by what?'

Max was caught off guard. 'I was thinking - different lifestyle, fewer people around, if you know where to go, that is.'

'Oh. Of course, there's that,' but said as an afterthought. What else was she thinking of? She continued, but on an entirely different tack and again she caught Max unprepared.

'And you, Max. Would you think of becoming an off comer here?'

Max's response was to trot out his often used, hoary old response to the question he was asked almost every day when up here. 'With my name? Wordsworth? Not a chance.'

'Would that really stop you?'

'I've been carrying that burden all my life.'

'A burden? A little precious, don't you think?'

Max considered how he should answer. 'It's the same question every day. With little variation.'

Melissa pressed on. 'Take it as a badge of pride. Look at it that way and wear it proudly.' And then, 'Don't you think you should get over yourself?' That last question said with a smile, but with more of that disarming, steely eye contact.

The best he could come up with was, 'Maybe you're right.' And this he offered to the altar on which he was willingly sacrificing his self-esteem. For years, and on dozens of occasions, he'd varied his responses to the question with replies that ranged from sarcastic to tart, from angry to offensive, justifying his various outbursts to himself as somehow protecting the person he was. He was a fully rounded adult, wasn't he? He was defined by his own set of skills and his own life experience. He wasn't the inadequate namesake of a long-dead poet,

'So that's a promise?'

'What's a promise?'

'You're going to get over yourself?' He could see in this woman why she was so well respected among her colleagues. She was powerful, yes, and beautiful too. He could drown in those eyes. He forced himself to look away; the only thing he could do to reset himself, but he found it impossible to drag his eyes away from her gaze.

'So, who is Max Wordsworth? Tell me about him.'

'What do you want to know?'

'Whatever you'd like to tell me would be a good start. You're a successful DCI, brought in to troubleshoot difficult cases - even though you don't like working up here. That's all I know.'

'Not much else to tell.'

'Yeah, yeah! Max, I think there's a lot more. Are you married, do you have a partner, what do you do when you're not working? I'm sure you can flesh out things a little more - without divulging any secrets.'

Max could feel himself blushing. This woman was fixing him with those eyes and at the same time, the smile playing around her lips was softening the experience in a gentle, hypnotic way. She was luring a response, dragging from him a wish to tell her everything, to confide in her eyes as she mesmerised him.

What should he say, how should he respond? He decided to go down the CV route. Facts. That was what he would give her. He was comfortable with facts.

'Twenty years in the Force.'

'You're forty-five now.' The immediate response. Facts were important to Melissa too.

'Yea, I joined late. I was twenty-six when I signed up.'

'And what did you do before then.'

'Professional footballer - for about eight years.'

'I didn't see that coming. I'd no idea. Who did you play for?'

'I wasn't famous or anything. I was what you'd call a journeyman midfield player. I stayed up North. I played for Tranmere, Crewe Alex, Stoke - had a trial for Man U, but that didn't work out.'

'But you made a living from it?'

'Yes. It was OK. I bought a house, ran a car - had a wife. All that stuff.'

'Had a wife? Past tense?' Melissa was interested in Max's choice of wording.

'Footballer's wife. She was investing in my future, I guess. A future I never had.'

'Why was that?'

'Injury. Cruciate ligament – my knee. That and a lack of any real talent. They fixed my knee up and I kept playing - but not as a pro. The damage was too severe for clubs to take the risk. My contract came to an end, and when I lost my job, my wife bailed on me. Nice girl, too - she married another footballer as it happens. Same result. Obviously, she couldn't pick a winner.'

Max smiled to himself as he took a sip from his beer. All this was long gone, and it had been a while since he'd thought about Donna and her expensive tastes.

Poor girl, she'd obviously hoped that by marrying a footballer she'd be enjoying the kind of lifestyle that involved huge houses, fast cars - international travel. Not that any of that stuff interested him, but he could see that his career, which at its apex, revolving as it did around his playing for semi-solvent, lower division clubs, could quickly lose its attraction. As it did, and one night she upped and left, went back to her mum's. Max didn't go after her.

'And then came the police?'

'Sort of,' replied Max. 'Before that, the players' union, the PFA, sponsored me to get a degree.'

'Oh, I didn't know they did that.'

'Yea, part time, Business and Sports Science. Most footballers have too much spare time. Golf fills the empty space, but I've always thought golf spoils a good walk. The PFA scheme allowed me to keep playing and study in my spare time. I'd completed my second year when I got injured, and they let me carry on until I graduated.

'So, for year three I became a full-time mature student - and I got a 2-1. I also played non-League football - cash in my boots - for a while. The PFA paid my uni fees, but I still had to earn money for day-to-day stuff.'

'You said you were injured. How could you continue playing?'

'I couldn't pass the medical to get a pro contract, but I was still a useful player. I enjoyed it - being a student, especially when people got to know I was a footballer. Played for the university and won stuff. That helped with the social side of my life too.'

'Women?'

'Yup. I'm amazed how many women go for footballers.'

Melissa smiled. She wasn't surprised at all. Or at least, if all footballers were like the fascinating man sat in front of her. 'Hold that thought,' she told herself as she came back into the real world.

'At the same time,' Max continued, 'I looked round for something steady. I wanted a secure job, but I knew I still needed that adrenalin rush every now and again. I applied to the Force - got accepted straight away. The rest ...'

'Is history,' chimed in Melissa, having rapidly readjusted her earlier perception of this man. Hidden depths. Not unattractive either. Her next question suggested more than simple conversational interest. 'And now, is there someone you go home to?'

Max was aware of the altered tone of the relationship. Now this woman, someone whom he'd been working with for only a short while was herself displaying facets of her personality that he hadn't noticed before.

She was beautiful as well as intelligent, but that was a given and he'd been aware of it from the start. From a professional point of view, having an attractive colleague hadn't troubled him.

He'd long ago learned to separate work and play, and recent scandals which seemed to be erupting everywhere were as powerful a warning to him as they would be to anyone else. Don't go there, keep it professional. Simple.

But this woman. Looking at her now, he was astounded at his insensitivity, his failure to pick up signals, but there again, had there been any? His mind raced through his earlier interactions with Melissa, but no, there was nothing. Not a clue. How had he not seen this?

'I've had a few semi-serious relationships since Donna - my wife. Nothing that lasted. The job kills them off, doesn't it?' He was looking for affirmation - none came. Melissa was waiting.

He continued: 'To be honest, I've not been on a date for a long time. As soon as I'm asked about my work, you get that look. And I'm too old to go out on the pull.'

'Social media? Have you tried that?'

How much should he divulge? He felt that he needed to be straightforward, but he also wanted to retain some shreds of his dignity. Of course, he'd been on social media and yes, on one or two occasions there had been some furtive coupling as a result, but this information he definitely didn't want to share.

Also, those embarrassing Sunday evening Singles Nights in eerily quiet hotels that he rocked up to on a few occasions - disasters, every single one. Twenty odd desperate middle-aged men circling around one or two blowsy women. He shuddered at the thought.

'I went speed dating once.' That seemed to do the trick. Those eyes again - lighting up; complemented by the slightest of smiles, a definite show of interest. Yes, this would do. 'I've lived in Morecambe for a long time - I've a flat there,' he continued. 'One of the hotels ran speed date evenings, so I went along.'

'And how was it?'

'Those five-minute conversations. They last forever - time stands still. I should have prepared more for it, chat up lines, maybe a few anecdotes? It wasn't for me. After two or three attempts and then a look round the room to see what was coming, I gave upon it.'

'You ran away?'

'I suppose so, although it wasn't quite like that. I 'made my excuses and left', as they used to say in the Sunday papers.'

'And you still live in Morecambe?'

'I do. When I split from Donna, I lost the house - well, half of it. We had no kids, so a few months later I bought my flat - I had a small mortgage then, but that's paid off now, and as most of my work is around the Preston, Lancaster area, it's handy. I like Morecambe. My flat looks over the bay and those views - especially in the evenings are...'

Melissa interrupted the reverie: 'And when you are up here?'

'I commute. Forty-five minutes away - on a good day. Easier than travelling into Manchester - I bet it's a shorter commute than yours.'

'You're right. Sometimes mine takes well over an hour - and that's using the Tube. If I drive, it's even longer, and what with congestion charges...'

The conversation had wound its way down, swiftly becoming desultory and stilted; the opposite of what they both had hoped. Max and Melissa were stepping gingerly around not one, but two elephants in the room.

The first was the case itself, so they stayed away from work-related matters to focus on this, their first social conversation.

The second 'elephant' was much more difficult to define. Each was aware that the dynamic had changed: something had happened. Melissa, seeing this man in an entirely different way, wanting to know much more about him, but having no idea how to progress things, or indeed, whether there was anything to progress.

Max, equally aware of the spark between them, but similarly constrained; personal versus professional, and his history of failed relationships weighing heavily against him having another go.

They finished their drinks in polite silence, both feeling uncomfortable with the atmosphere that they'd created. When they left the pub, there was no question of anything further happening, or of the evening being prolonged.

They returned to their separate cars and Max drove down to his flat in Morecambe, ordering a Chinese meal on his phone and picking it up on the way home. Melissa went straight back to her hotel and to a lonely room service snack.

As she sat down to eat, her mother called and she found herself fielding more questions, questions that she either couldn't or didn't want to answer. Later, as a displacement activity, she began packing her things for her move to the cottage, but try as she might to remove it, lodged firmly at the back of her mind was the nagging reminder of a wasted opportunity.

Thirty-One

Wojtek hiding in the house from a man with a gun has spooked me, and we're driving back to Grasmere at speed - the pretext being that yes, I know I'm driving too quickly but I've a Zoom call to make, and the local signal in Hawkshead isn't strong enough to risk using my phone.

Meg has bought that - at least she hasn't pushed back - and I move on to the next phase of this emergency plan: getting back to the house without the family. I try convincing her and the kids that having a pizza at Sarah's, a restaurant in the village, just down the hill from the house, is a great idea.

That's proving to be more difficult: 'Darling, I'm filthy from swinging around on Go Ape. All I want is a hot shower - and there's plenty to eat at home.'

I go for the low blow, 'We don't have any Thunder and Lightning ice cream at home, though, do we?'

That hits the spot. Bella first, then a chorus from the other two in the back of the car. Even Nip joins in the excitement. 'Thunder and Lighting, Thunder and Lightning. Please mum, please mum, please Muuuummmmm!'

That does the job and Meg caves. 'All right, all right! Settle down, all of you. We're going for a pizza.'

'And Thunder and Lightning!'

Before the chant recommences, Meg capitulates again. 'Yes, and Thunder and Lightning - but we can't stay long. We all need to have a bath, me especially, and I want all that done before your bed times. No staying up late tonight, OK?'

The kids agree. They know intuitively that they can work on stretching their bed time a little later. This small victory is all they need - pizza, followed by their favourite ice cream.

The next battle will be waged at the appropriate time - which is not now. What is now, though, is the real possibility that there won't be any bath time for anyone unless I can sort out what's going on up at the house.

Keeping my doubts to myself, and now that we're all agreed, I drop the kids and their mum off at the restaurant. Sarah's has always been one of our favourites, and although the family is not dressed for an evening out, there's nothing out of order in the way they look.

Walkers and hikers are Sarah's main demographic, and the friendly Romanian manageress greets them with a smile, nods to me and finds a table for us.

I head straight back to the car; my mind focused on the task in hand. My handgun is in its secret place under the driving seat. I take it out to check it. I unwrap it from the oilcloth, load it with the full magazine I keep in the same place, and drop it into the side pocket of my car door. I'm as prepared as I can be.

I've also kept Nip with me as I'm not sure what I'm going to find. Nip may turn out to be useful - if giving the intruder a severe licking is required.

I cross the cattle grid; the house is about 100 yards away high on the left. Wojtek's quad bike parked outside the front door is the only vehicle I see. I stop and call his phone, but of course there's no signal, not even his voicemail.

I check to see if there's enough juice in the phone signal to allow me to access my security app, but there isn't. I know it'll all be on the hard drive, and I'll have a record of everything that's happened so far - and of anything that may happen in the near future, but at the very time I truly need to access my technology, it's sadly kaput.

I drive up to the main house, and yes, I'm annoyed by my phone letting me down, but more so by the accumulation of other circumstances - Meg's assault at the spa and now with some bastard invading my house. Enough's enough - confrontation is the only way to resolve this.

I park up next to Wojtek's Quad, retrieve my gun from the side pocket of the car and release its safety. Looking towards the front door and the windows either side gives no clue. I let Nip out from the back of the car and he has a sniff around.

The front door opens with keypad rather than a latch key, and it doesn't seem to have been tampered with. So, my first thought is to walk around the house with Nip to see if the intruder has left any signs. He followed Wojtek in through the front door, that I do know. There's no car at the gates now, but has he parked around the back of the house - and maybe, is he still there?

All the windows have toughened glass in them, and the outside doors are steel lined and embedded in steel frames. As I walk round, I see nothing troubling and there is no vehicle at the back of the house. I'm now assuming he left the house by the same way he came in, and he's driven away.

Another assumption is that all the security work I've done has been worthwhile - I have to trust it. And if that is so, and all the doors leading off the hall are working properly, the guy could still in the hall - there would be nowhere else for him to go.

I return to the front door and carefully key in the combination. Using the steel lined door as a shield, and in case the guy is waiting to welcome me with a burst of machine gun fire, I take the chicken's way out and send Nip in.

I watch my dog as he slowly sniffs his way into the hall; his behaviour not suggesting in any way, apart from the sniffing, that there's anything to worry about.

I take the risk. Leading with my gun, I make a cautious entry. There's a short corridor with my office to the left and the kitchen to the right before we enter what is the most spectacular part of my house; a huge space two storeys high, with a minstrel gallery running around two sides of the hall and all lit by the massive atrium above.

A wide oak staircase turning a full ninety degrees follows the other two walls and completes the scene.

From where I'm standing, I look up to check for any movement on the minstrel gallery. Nothing, and none of the doors to our reception rooms and dining room has been opened either.

I look carefully around, even checking behind the old jukebox that I occasionally wind up for parties and special occasions, and there is nothing there: the man has left.

And I'm now online. My WiFi has kicked in and I can access my system and wind back to get a look at the intruder. Then I remember Wojtek. I call him. 'Wojtek. I'm inside the house, and I don't see anyone.'

'Boss, is that you? Open your cam, pls.'

I open my cam. I see Wojtek now and he looks at me. 'There's nobody here, Wojtek.'

'No, he left a few minutes ago. I was waiting until the coast was empty. I wanted to make sure. Your system works. He tried all the doors, couldn't get in. He poked around a bit and then he left.'

'Was he in a car?'

'Yes, parked at the gates. He went round to the back of house, looked in the chapel and then walked up by tunnel.'

'OK, Wojtek. Come out now. There's nobody here, and I need to go and get the family; they're waiting in the village.'

'Two minutes!'

And up he comes from the cellar. The panic room has done its job. Wojtek is safe, and our metal doors have prevented the intruder from entering any of the rooms leading off the hallway.

'How the fuck did you let him get in?' I was not in an entirely welcoming mood.

'My fault, boss. Sorry. I left the front door open - I kept it open with a bag - I was bringing stuff. Then I saw him and saw the gun. I didn't want to buy a chance, so I went straight downstairs. I watched him from there. I don't think he saw me.'

'Let's have a look.' I opened the door of my office and in we went. It took seconds for me to find the recording of the intrusion.

I didn't recognise the man: I did recognise the gun - hard not to. It was a Scorpion, just as Wojtek had suggested. Slightly unusual to see it carried this way in rural England, but hey, that's globalisation for you.

We watched as the man carefully made his way up and around the back of the house then, noticing the bag propping the front door open, he slowly moved into the house itself. There, he tried each door in turn, finding it impossible to gain entry to any of the other rooms.

Wojtek was right. The man hadn't seen him go down to the cellar - he paid no special attention to the door that led there, but we watched as he tried every door leading off the hallway in sequence.

'I should have a lockdown option. We could have locked him in the hall - maybe gassed him at the same time?'

Wojtek wasn't convinced: 'With that gun, he could easy blast his way out.'

'The doors wouldn't have held out?'

'Yea, possibly. But those windows surrounding the door, boss. They're not bullet proof.'

True. The front door had toughened glass windows surrounding it because I'd balked at the bullet-proof option when I found out how much it would cost.

Vanity. I love the art nouveau oval shape of those windows and I'd decided to keep them, not anticipating either a siege or having to use my home as a prison cell. Big mistake, as it turns out. Lessons learned. If I had a To Do list, I now know what would be heading it.

So, suitably chastened, I rewind the images of our intruder, and both Wojtek and I search for everything we can about him. Male, 30 - 40 years old, no mask, white, big - tough looking, shaven head. He knows how to carry himself and his weapon. Wojtek was right to steer clear of him; this man knew what he was doing.

'Who is he, boss? He's a pro.'

'I wish I knew, mate. There's someone who wants me to do something for him.'

'How do you mean?'

'You know I asked you to see if you could find out anything from your friends?'

'Yes.'

'And did you?'

'I've not had chance. I've been busy - in Ambleside.'

I don't know if he's joking or being serious, I honestly can't tell. 'What the fuck, Wojtek? You see what's going on here - and you're more interested in shagging.'

'It's love, boss, not shagging. Really like her.' And he had been joking because he turned to me and said, 'Some of my contacts left the area. They've disappeared. Strange.'

I was reviewing all the video I had on the armed intruder - and I was aware of the simmering issue down at Sarah's restaurant, so I didn't fully pick up on Wojtek's comment, safe to say, 'So you did ask around?'

'Of course, I did.' Then he hit me with it, and it was worth the listen. 'There's movement. New people arriving, older people leaving all because of this.'

'Why, what's going on?'

'You know that girl died - at Rydal Caves?'

'Yea.'

'It's all to do with that, they think. She was murdered, but they're saying the two guys who did it were also killed and then dumped. Then this other man come here looking for them, and he's such a scary guy that everyone who meets him leaves. Up and gone. They don't work notice, no excuse, no reason.'

'All because of this man?'

'Yea. Not the man who was here, boss. Someone else, I think. Nasty guy. Frightened them so much that they decide to leave. These men, they are like me, they come here to find work. They've all left families behind...'

I interrupt. 'Wait! There's someone else? Where is he - this nasty guy?'

'Fuck knows, boss. And I don't want to find out, do I? And I don't want to leave the Lakes - not when I'm just starting to ...'

'Yea - I know, I know. So, we have two of them?'

'I think so, yes. This one,' Wojtek pointed to the figure on the screen, 'he's different - not like the guy that's frightened everyone. That guy was much younger, and it wasn't his - physical size - is that right? It was his ...'

Wojtek, lost for words. I knew exactly what he was trying to say, and I didn't need any further explanation. Two men, both troublesome in their own way. Maybe acting together, maybe not. I was pondering, thinking it through when Wojtek pointed out the obvious.

'This is all connected, boss, isn't it? It's all connected to you.'

I decide: 'Yes, Wojtek, you're right. There's something going on that involves me, and it's connected to what happened to that girl, but it's connected in a way I don't understand. I've put you in enough danger already. I didn't mean to, I had no idea - I still haven't, but it would be best for you to curl up with that new love of yours and wait for me to get in touch. I don't want you involved in this.'

'I am involved.'

'No, this guy didn't see you.'

'Not him - or maybe him. I mean, this wasn't accident. He - or someone else has been watching the house. They see me; see my quad bike - probably my car too. I'm involved in this, boss. Like you, I don't know much, but I do know that.'

Of course, he's right. He's involved, in the same way that Meg and the kids are, and they're down in the village, only a few hundred yards away.

'The house is too prominent,' he adds.

'Prominent? What you mean?'

'Sorry, it's high on the hill, and it can be easily seen.'

'A sniper ...'

That's what's coursing through my mind. It's a beautiful house and the views are splendid, but you could take up a position at virtually any angle and you'd have a perfect view of anything that's happening.

A good sniper could cover the whole of the house - choose the aspect - with a good enough weapon, and the skill to use it - they could be a thousand yards away, and I couldn't do anything about it.

'It's never crossed my mind, Wojtek. It's obvious when you think of it.'

'It never crossed mine - until now.' Then, 'Do you think he's watching now?'

Again, something that had not fully registered. 'He could well be - it would be strange if he wasn't.'

I'm talking to Wojtek - and to myself - as if we're two old fellas in a pub. The truth is somewhat starker, and I snap out of it.

'Where?'

'Where what? Oh, where do I think?'

'Yea, if you were the sniper, where would you choose to spy on me?'

'Could be anywhere, boss. Anywhere. I'd probably want to watch the front door - and the drive - so I could see anyone coming up here, but that still leaves...'

'Too many options? You're right. I'll assume from now on I'm being watched. You'll have to assume the same.' Almost as an afterthought I say, 'So, think about your new lady.'

'Already have. You mention this before, and this thing now has decided me. Can I stay here for a while? This is the safest spot for me, and I think if I work with you, we'll have a better chance of keeping an eye on each other.'

Will Meg understand? I'm thinking of what I'll be saying to her and the kids. I start to outline my doubts, 'Meg is the ...'

'You're gonna bring her and the kids back here?'

'I have to - they're waiting to come back now.'

'Boss, I don't think that's ...'

'You're right, it isn't. But there's no alternative. I've got to bring them back - for tonight, at least. This place is like a fortress when everything's working, and I'm prepared to trust all the money I've spent on it. I'll go down to get the family - and then you and I will get ready. All right?'

'Sure, boss, if that's what you think.'

'It's exactly what I think. Lock the door, take some time to check out our weapons, and make sure our systems are up and working, cameras, monitors - let's use what we've got. I'll keep you a secret tonight - while I work out what to say to Meg. You'll be OK downstairs, won't you?'

'Yea, I'll be fine - it's comfortable enough down there.'

'So, that's our plan. I'll go down to collect the family, you sort yourself out and - and I'll be in touch, I guess.'

I'm not entirely sure that I'm making the right choices here, but leaving Nip in his basket, I set off down the lane to pick up everyone suddenly aware of how exposed we are from all sides of the house.

As I turn into the main road, I'm strangely reminded of a biblical verse - the curse of a good old Catholic education hitting me - 'A city set on a hill cannot be hid'. Neither can my dream house, evidently.

Thirty-two

That phone call changed everything. On leaving the big house in Grasmere, intending to return as soon as the family came back, the man had driven to a café in Ambleside to grab something to eat before returning to finish off his task.

His phone buzzed. 'No, they weren't at home, sir. I'll go back - if they've returned, I'll finish the job.'

His boss was surprised to hear he'd not yet carried out his mission.

The man explained. 'I got to the house. It's well protected and very secure - but I sneaked in through an open door - a guy was carrying stuff in and had propped it open with a bag.'

'Was he your target?'

'No, he wasn't the target, sir. He was a worker, maybe a servant. But when I got into the house, he'd disappeared. I waited - all the doors and windows are impossible to break in to.'

'Was the rest of his family there?'

'No, sir - as I said, they weren't anywhere to be found. The family was out.'

The man waited. His boss was angry and frustrated, but this wasn't his fault. He'd been ready to do his job; there was no-one about.

'I'll go back in an hour or so. I'll see if I can get to them then.'

And then the change of plan. He was to forget Grasmere and his current target - for now. His boss said that he'd decided to deal with Blain differently. Something else had come up, he said, and the man was given a new task; the implication of its seriousness there in the tone of his boss's voice.

It was a new target and very close to where he now was. A single man, staying at the Merrywood hotel, and only twenty minutes away. The photo he received on his phone during the brief conversation was of a glowering, sallow - skinned man, a lick of dark hair partially obscuring one of his eyes.

This new task turned out to be the easiest job he'd ever done. No sooner had he pulled up at the entrance to the hotel than his target appeared. He was exactly as his boss had described, strolling down the drive towards the main road. He carried a small bag with him, a leather man-bag, slung over his shoulder.

This man's thoughts were elsewhere - mainly his annoyance with the way he felt he'd been treated since he arrived in the UK. He was entitled to more - if it had to be an old car to pick him up, why not a Lincoln Town Car or a classy Merc. The S Class was OK, although he preferred a Maybach. Not some crappy twenty-year old Ford.

He'd order a taxi for the day - fuck these chefs and kitchen porters - if they didn't want to earn some easy money, he'd make his own arrangements. He'd decided to walk down the lane to meet his taxi at the hotel's entrance, rather than allow his pent-up anger to make him do something he'd later regret. This wasn't Dubai, and he was already aware that his man-child antics didn't work too well here.

Nearing the main road Janko glanced around and noticing the parked car he assumed it was the taxi he'd ordered. He moved towards it, not with any sense of urgency, his radar simply wasn't working. He'd decided to sit in the rear seat. And the car was another disappointment, a small Toyota saloon, but at least it looked clean. He opened the rear nearside door and that was it.

The three bullets that went through him, two to the chest and one to the head meant that Janko was dead before he hit the ground. No sound was heard, either from the victim or from the gun that had just taken his life.

Main road or not, it was a happy coincidence of circumstances that no traffic was passing, and as far as the killer could see, there was no CCTV covering the entrance to the drive.

The man placed his gun on the passenger seat, got out of the car and moved round the back to the near side where Janko's body now lay. First, he closed the still-open passenger door and bent over the body. He removed the shoulder bag which had fallen next to it and then got back into his vehicle and drove away, another clean job done.

A few minutes later, Janko's taxi arrived. The driver was the first person to see the body, and as he called 999, sorry as he was to see the body of the murdered man, he was possibly angrier at the loss of a very lucrative day's work. A full day on the meter was what he had been promised, not that he had one, and what was that going to add up to, and now wasn't, was foremost in his mind.

As he made his way south, the customer who had caused the taxi driver's disappointment was also unhappy. It was frustrating that he'd been pulled from the Grasmere contract, and it irked him slightly that he hadn't completed his mission in the way he would have wished.

However, by way of compensation, he was on his way out of the country and back to his beautiful Thai girlfriend, someone who, in a couple of days' time, would soothe away any lingering frustration he might be feeling.

His first stop on the way home was to Lancaster, where in the shadow of the old castle prison, he swapped his car for another equally anonymous saloon. He then drove straight down the M6 and then the M61 to Manchester airport. After parking up, and before he left the car, he investigated the contents of Janko's bag.

Apart from Janko's passport and some papers, there were three items, all of great significance, but two of which he knew he couldn't take with him. The first was a large wad of notes, over twenty thousand euros in total and several hundred GB pounds too.

The money he would happily take to Thailand. The other two items, along with his own weapon, he deposited in the Left Luggage facility in terminal Two.

His own pistol was a beautiful new Glock 43, fitted with an Osprey silencer. He'd used it for the first time when he dealt with Janko and was very impressed. He'd picked it up on arrival and knew he'd have to leave it behind, but nevertheless he regretted having to do so.

There was another weapon in Janko's bag - a rusty, very old revolver. Looking at it, the man wasn't even sure that the thing would work, so old and rusted up it was. How had Janko obtained it - and more to the point why?

The answer was quite mundane; entirely to do with Janko Stanovnic and his foul-mouthed behaviour on his arrival in the Lakes. So much had his brief presence among the catering staff of eastern Europe troubled them that one of the Polish boys, recalling the whereabouts of an ancient pistol lying in the drawer of one of the fine old houses surrounding Windermere, had acquired it without the knowledge or permission of its owner.

It was given as a peace offering, and Janko accepted it, there being nothing else available. A new chapter was now being added to the life story of this ancient handgun.

The weapon itself, a truly venerable Webley Mk 6 revolver, had been brought back to the UK having last seen service on the battlefields of Flanders over a hundred years ago. It had probably lain in the drawer since then, completely forgotten, and its owner long gone.

As a weapon, it was more likely to damage the person who fired it than any intended victim and Janko was well aware of this. However, he'd decided to keep it in case he might have to threaten someone.

The other item that couldn't be taken aboard the plane was a half-kilo or so of white powder. The man knew nothing about drugs himself, and he wasn't sure what kind of drug it was - or how valuable it might turn out to be. So, he hatched a plan.

Instead of leaving the items in Left Luggage until they were found by the periodic sweep that all such facilities employed, he emailed the locker's code to a man he'd worked with in the past. If he was prepared to take the risk, he would benefit from an unexpected bonus.

Still, he was feeling slightly hard done by as he searched through the remainder of the shoulder bag. Yes, he was getting a substantial fee for his efforts, but despite that and the twenty thousand euros that he'd come across completely by chance, the professional in him was disappointed as he'd failed in his primary task. That he'd been almost immediately directed to a new target was scant consolation.

Thirty-Three

It had been a sudden decision, but the right one he thought, given the circumstances. High up in Dubai's Emirates Tower, the young sheikh put down the phone. His latest request involving the shifting of the target had been carried out: Janko Stanovnic was no more.

It was annoying that Stanovnic's presence had muddied the waters: the sheikh's plan had partly succeeded in that he'd got him to wind down his Dubai operation, but the intended coincidence of having another much more important target in the same geographical area had become confusing and frustrating.

Having that girl swinging in the wind at Rydal had been important. It had concentrated Stanovnic's mind better than he had dreamed. As a result, Stanovnic's departure from Dubai had probably opened an important new revenue channel for the young sheikh.

This new channel, Stanovnic's extensive network, wouldn't be for himself of course, but for others who would thereafter be in his debt. Whoever they might be would have to work quickly before the Russians or the Albanians caught sight of what had happened and moved in. But that was an issue for others to resolve. He'd thought about developing the market for Oxycontin and Fentanyl before, but now the chance of enabling Captagon distribution in the region offered immense opportunities - and huge profits.

If it worked, it worked. If not, there were always other options, but the most important point of the current exercise - removing Stanovnic, had been achieved.

But he hadn't fully thought through what he wanted to do with his primary objective, Frank Blain. The big mistake had been to set everything up without a carefully developed plan. The coincidence wasn't a happy one. Had he known how geographically close Blain was to Christina, he'd have thought differently and probably made other choices.

To begin with however, two birds with one stone seemed at least possible, and he let things go, against his better judgement.

Neither had he fully considered the collateral damage that would occur. His man had disposed of the two men who'd acted on his behalf and strung up Christina. He'd also dealt with the young lad who had been tasked with attacking Frank Blain's wife at her leisure club.

But the parallel mission, pointing this same contractor towards Frank Blain had been the wrong choice. Yes, it might have been tolerable had his man done a clean job to begin with, but the outcome would have been unsatisfactory: Blain had vital information that he needed, and with his death that information would have disappeared.

It had taken months of frenetic activity, investigations of all kinds, several painful deaths too, to establish what had happened to the young sheikh's mother and father, one of his younger brothers and his twelve-year-old sister.

But he had found out: Frank Blain was responsible, and Frank Blain would pay. In retrospect, it wouldn't have been satisfactory to have his man simply eliminate Blain. The revenge this young man wanted required more than a simple death.

And convenient as it was that Janko Stanovnic was no more, it wasn't enough but would have to do for now. Blain, his main quarry was still available - now alert to his threat, at least alert to the fact that someone was after him, but that might make things more interesting.

In the back of his mind was the difficult decision he might need to take regarding his contractor. His man was a professional, probably as skilled, if not more skilled than Frank Blain. Should he be more concerned about the information the man now possessed?

True, he had no direct link to the UAE as all transactions were Whatsapped, but he did possess knowledge that could become threatening, were he ever to find out the truth of who his client was - and the billions of dollars, GB pounds and assorted middle eastern currencies that he controlled.

Hesham el Hashimi, a young man of twenty-four who, because of the mysterious and so far, unresolved disappearance of his immediate family, was now in control of the fortunes of one of the region's most important families.

Although he had a group of men on his payroll - his Enforcers, he'd chosen not to use them for this mission. This whole affair was the first challenge in his new role. As a result of the sudden disappearance of his father, his mother and two of his siblings, he'd suddenly found himself running his father's businesses.

Hesham had not wanted to use any of his own people for the Blain project; he'd felt it better to outsource it. And so far, it had seemed that the choice was a good one.

Two Croatian men based in London had been recruited to dispose of the girl. That part of the mission accomplished, they'd then been removed from the scene by a separate contractor, a professional who worked out of Thailand. It was he who had similarly dealt with the young man who had attacked Meg. He'd also been tasked with eliminating Blain: this had proved to be a bridge too far, and Hesham had decided to rethink his plans.

However, he was closer now to finding out what had happened to his family and had withdrawn his man at the right time. Pointing him towards Stanovnic instead had provided an unexpected benefit.

He was now motivated entirely by the sense of duty that he owed to the missing members of his family, and his sense of outrage that anyone could think that they could attack them and get away with it.

He would take time to think through what he was going to do with

Blain. One of his favourite sayings concerned how much better a dish tasted when it was cold. The dish, whose main ingredient would be Frank Blain, could wait a little longer before it was sampled, and the young sheikh knew that by waiting that much longer, the victim would experience much more stress - at no extra cost or risk.

And as for his contractor? He had completed his mission, dealt satisfactorily with the change of target, and had now left the UK. He might follow up on him later, but now he would concentrate on the demise of Frank Blain - and his whole family.

Thirty-Four

'So, that's a surprise. Were there any witnesses?' Debesh was looking at the hastily convened team. His boss scrolling through the messages on his phone, DCI Mordaunt likewise, and Helen, who had driven up from Kendal with her husband, was making coffee for everyone - slightly miffed at the assumption that it now seemed to be her role. Debesh had also annoyed her - he could have put the kettle on. The man was obviously still a work in progress.

'When did this happen?' Max Wordsworth placed his phone on the desk as he waited for an answer.

'About two hours ago, sir. Six-thirty. A taxi driver called it in. Patrol got there within minutes. He was dead when they arrived - two shots to the body, one to the head - again.'

'And at this point, somebody should pop up with the words 'a professional job'. Am I right?'

'It looks that way, sir. It would be fair to assume it, too. Given all that seems to be happening.' Debesh had no doubt. Melissa was of the same opinion. 'You don't think so, Max?'

'I don't want to think so. It all points to it, I know. But the idea of having a professional hitman wandering around eliminating people isn't a prospect to relish.'

'Yeah, I get that. But it's why we're all here, isn't it? And we've got to assume it's connected with the death of the girl.'

'Why assume that? Do we know who the latest victim is yet?'

'No, we don't - but ....'

'Until we do, let's not jump to conclusions, eh?' Something was worrying Max. He couldn't explain. Logically, his colleagues were right, but he wanted to wait until he had better information before bowing to the inevitable. For him, that meant handing the whole investigation over to his very attractive new colleague and her metropolitan pals. 'Very attractive': what was he saying to himself?

The disappointing experience of the drink they'd had together at the Golden Rule and the seeming failure of their relationship to ignite had certainly got Max looking at his colleague in a new light. She was magnificent. But still, she was a colleague - and she was his boss.

He had to tread warily, he knew that, and maybe his perception of the way the case was going was colouring his responses more than he'd ever expected.

He blundered on: 'Helen, call the Merrywood. See what they know about our recent victim. Forensics should be there by now. They may know if the weapon used was the same one that killed the first two men down by Greenodd.'

'On it.' Helen was pleased for the proper police work, rather than the care in the community stuff she seemed to have been landed with.

'Will you want to go to the scene, ma'am?' Max, with what now seemed an unusually formal way of addressing the DCI.

'Yes, I think so. It's not far from my hotel, is it?'

'A few hundred yards.'

'Then I'll be off. Are you coming?' This came as a bit of a surprise to Max, but was welcome, nonetheless.

'I'll follow you and then carry on to Morecambe.'

'Good. See you there.' And gathering up her bag and phone, she nodded goodbye to her colleagues and was out of the door.

'Is it me, or is it hot in here?' Debesh's facetious comment was meant in a light-hearted way, but that didn't seem to be how Max saw it.

'And what do you mean by that, sergeant?'

'Seems a bit tense, don't you think so, sir?'

'Murder number four - enough to make anyone tense, I would have thought. When you've finished, Helen, after you've checked in with the hotel, please take your man home.'

As Max left the station, Debesh and Helen looked at each other. Helen was the first to smile.

'Do you think what I'm thinking?'

'I think I am. But he doesn't seem too happy about it.'

'It adds an extra level of complexity to an already complex situation,' said Helen, reflecting on the difficulties that she had encountered in her own personal and professional relationships.

'Cart. Horse,' was Debesh's attempt at oriental wisdom; completely lost on Helen.

'What do you mean?'

'I - You may be jumping to conclusions.'

'Oh, come on, Debesh. It's obvious, isn't it?'

'No, not to me. But there is a certain frisson, I grant you that.'

'Frisson? Max, he's burning up. Completely smitten. And it's good to see. Come on, we'll stop by on our way home. I've never been to a crime scene before.'

'Call the hotel first. Max is going to want an update to his request.'

'Sorry - I forgot. Too excited. Give me a minute.'

She sat down to make her call. Within a minute, she established that his family name, Stanovnic, was the same as that of the unfortunate first victim, Christina.

She closed the call and turned to her husband. 'It's the same name -

Stanovnic. The victim is the girl's brother - Janko Stanovnic.'

'Bollox! I'll call Max now. He'll want to know straight away. Come on, lock up and let's get off.'

In their car, and on their way to the hotel, Debesh got through to Max and informed him that the latest victim was Janko Stanovnic, Christina's brother. He heard Max swearing and then an immediate apology. 'Sorry, Debesh. I was obviously wrong. You lot were right. I'll see you at the scene.'

They arrived at the Merrywood's drive a few minutes after both Max and Melissa had parked up. Their car added to the line of police cars, the ambulance and the Forensics' van helping to slow down even further the line of cars on the main road between Windermere and Ambleside.

That, plus the inevitable rubbernecking, meant that it was taking vehicles more than ten minutes to snake past the assorted group of official vehicles attending the scene.

The young man's body had now been removed to the ambulance, all photos and measurements taken. Desultory conversations were taking place between the various interested parties, most of which simply filling in time, as there wasn't much else to do.

The body had been found, was on its way to the mortuary, and from now on anything that might happen next wouldn't be determined by hanging around the hotel entrance. People like Max would be making decisions, but from somewhere other than here.

It was Max who brought proceedings, such as they were, to an end. Once his permission had been given, the patrol cars left, following Forensics whose preliminary work had been completed a while ago. The ambulance, there being no other type of vehicle available when the call came in, had already started its journey and Max, his colleagues and their three cars were the last to leave.

'So, we'll have a busy day tomorrow, won't we? See you all tomorrow - nice and early.'

Thirty-five

Janko Stanovnic's demise had been decided on the whim of a petulant young man. It was a decision taken in anger, but one which had been smouldering for months.

It was only a few months since the twenty-four-year-old Hesham El Hashimi, now de facto head of his family, had begun holding court in his new Dubai office.

His newly acquired responsibilities, foisted on him because of the sudden disappearance of his father, his mother and two of his siblings some twelve months previously, now sat lightly on his shoulders, or so he thought.

He was pleasantly surprised by the way he'd handled the enforced transition of power and was now sufficiently confident to deal with a long-standing personal issue.

He was on the speakerphone with his brother Mohammed and listening in to the conversation were two of his staff, both young Emiratis, and both completely in the thrall of their young boss.

Hesham knew exactly what he was doing: the two young men were there, not so much because they could be of any practical value, but because their presence was massaging the ego of their new master. He wanted them to hear how he would deal with his brother, the outcome of which would be an object lesson of what might happen to any of his people who created any difficulty.

'I've told you before, Mohammed. Too many parties, too many drugs - too much alcohol. What kind of behaviour is that?'

Mohammed was spluttering denials as Hesham went on, 'Stop now! I've had you watched, remember? I've video evidence - too much to bother looking at it all. And remember, I'm paying all your bills. When you're locked in some expensive hotel room with how many women? Five, was it? Who pays? You know who pays - I do!

'And let me tell you something. Personally, I don't care how you spend your time - while you are in the US. But you won't behave like that here in Dubai.

'I've got the businesses running well, and I'm not happy to subsidise you and your lifestyle. But you are my brother and although you disgust me, I still love you. I'll continue the arrangement provided you remain in the US.

'If you even think of coming back to Dubai without my agreement, I'll stop all your allowances immediately. You won't be turning left as you board the aircraft. In fact, you won't even get a ticket back to Dubai in Coach.'

'You can't do that, Hesham - I'm your brother - your older brother.'

'Only in years. Not in behaviour. You disgrace us all, Mohammed. You've disgraced the memory of our father and of our whole family. And yes, I can put a halt to everything - all payments to you - and I will.'

This deciding conversation between Mohamed and his younger brother was acrimonious, but timely. Hesham, now working out of Dubai and with his hands on the family's purse strings, simply threatening to cut off Mohammed's enormous allowances, did the job.

Rather than argue any further, the elder brother accepted that the current situation offered much more in the way of immediate gratification.

And, with Mohammed out of the way at least for now, Hesham could spend all the time effort and money it took to find out how and perhaps why his family had disappeared.

To begin with, all he knew was that it had happened during one of his family's regular trips to the UK. They'd been seen in their apartment at the Savoy hotel in central London. Room service staff recalled serving them their evening meal as on this occasion they'd decided not to eat at their normal table in the main dining room. Of itself, this was not unusual; they had made this choice before.

What was unusual was that when the staff returned to the apartment to freshen up the room, the meals were untouched, and the family was nowhere to be seen.

At the start of the investigation, the hotel's CCTV showed that the family had all left their suite together. Cameras followed them down the corridor and outside the hotel to a waiting car, a silver S Class Mercedes.

There was nothing in their demeanour to suggest anything that might be worrying them. In fact, they seemed particularly happy. The hotel's concierge later reported that he'd obtained tickets to a West End show for them, and the assumption was that they were on their way to an evening of entertainment and had chosen either to eat somewhere nearer the theatre or wait until after the show.

But the family didn't return to the hotel, even though all their belongings had been left in their rooms. After a couple of days, the management of the hotel became concerned. Apart from anything else, a large account had been left unsettled, and personal items including cash, valuable jewellery and passports were locked in the room safe. The hotel called in the police.

It was then that a mystery began to unfold. The Mercedes' number plate was false; there were no images of its driver, and traffic cameras had tracked it only as far as Jermyn Street, just off Haymarket.

There, the car had vanished: no other cameras had picked it up, and the police concluded that either the number plates had been changed, or the car itself had been hidden.

Hesham was as perplexed as anyone at the way in which his family had disappeared, but life had to go on and after a short while, it did.

He was quick to understand the scale of the challenges ahead as he was catapulted into heading the business. There was nothing subtle - no induction, he was straight in. Everything seemed to be in meltdown: the businesses were complex and needed constant oversight, something that had not been happening.

His MBA from Dubai's American university could have been useful here; he understood theoretically what he had to do, but he needed to concentrate on the firefighting he'd unexpectedly inherited, so to begin with, many immediate emergencies and deadlines took up much of his time.

He began to realise that he was not as competent managing the situation as he would have wished. Maybe it was simply his lack of experience, after all, he had been thrust into the job without any preparation, maybe he assumed that everyone would see the world in the same way as he did.

Whatever the reason, it began to be apparent, not just to Hesham, but more importantly to those who reported to him, that he was going to find it very difficult to handle his new role.

The first signs were in the changes to his own behaviour. He was losing his temper more frequently, and he very rarely listened to what his colleagues had to say. Rather, he'd listen to a sentence or two then cut them off with some offensive remark and tell them what they should be doing, and how they had failed him.

The result of this was that his people began to tell him only what he wanted to hear and not what he needed to hear. The business began to develop issues that a competent CEO could have handled, but which began to press heavily on Hesham's inadequacy.

Consequently, having to work constantly in emergency mode meant he took longer than expected before he was fully immersed in the mechanics of the business.

Everything seemed to be going wrong at once, although it wasn't all Hesham's fault. His father couldn't or wouldn't delegate anything to his highly paid managers, and it was months before Hesham began to feel he was making some progress. He'd had to sack many of the older managers, but when he did that, he found replacing them created even more problems.

And at the back of his mind was always his missing family. They couldn't have completely vanished, but he knew it was wishful thinking to believe that somehow, they might return. He also believed that the police, both in London and in Dubai, had been seriously remiss in their actions - or as he saw it, in their lack of action.

An entire family just can't go missing; something must have happened to them, so Hesham decided to find out what.

As he now had access to almost unlimited resources, he handed over the search for his family to one of the USA's most successful - and most expensive - detective agencies.

The agency had thrown its men and women into the task - to find out what had happened in central London that night. Hesham waited - and waited.

Dig long and hard enough, you come up with results; it's the expense of the process that is so inhibiting. Hesham had put no limit on his budget, and he demanded results, not excuses.

And his chosen agents did not disappoint. When they did report back, it wasn't with the full story. Even they couldn't establish that, but the information they did come up spurred Hesham on to bring together Janko Stanovnic and the man whom he now knew was guilty of his family's murder.

It wasn't too difficult for Hesham to follow on from where the American investigators had come to a halt. His moral compass was different from that of the agency - and his ethical code worked in a way that demanded outcomes whatever collateral damage might occur.

The result he eventually obtained pointed directly to Frank Blain, and it was quite easy for the US company to establish that Blain operated through two of his own agents, one in The US Virgin Islands, and one in Dubai.

Hesham chose the US Virgin Islands as his starting point. Things were already happening in Dubai, and he didn't want to stir up a hornets' nest. So, it fell to Frank Blain's quiet and unassuming friend Stephanie, the woman who looked after his finances, to be visited by two of Hesham's more imaginative colleagues.

Their creativity eventually made it necessary for Stephanie to divulge where Frank had his home. She also found herself volunteering information about his family, including the names of his wife, his children, and even the name of his dog. What she did not give was any information about his finances, his bank accounts, or his present whereabouts.

However, in almost her final breath, and as her life was finally ebbing away, Hesham's colleagues managed to extract the access code to one of her computers. Here they found a list of Frank Blain's contracts stretching back over more than ten years. Included in that list was Hesham's family, the logistics of the process as well as the date and time of their demise.

They found a contact address - Frank's address on MS Messenger, and by using this address Hesham began his mission to destroy the man who had murdered his family. He also intended that Blain would pay dearly for the chaos he had caused the family businesses when his father disappeared without any planning for his succession having taken place.

On the positive side, the law of unintended consequences also kicked in to Hesham's advantage. As part of their research, his American detective agency had looked hard at many of his organisation's business transactions - those Hesham was happy to let them see.

They discovered it was Janko Stanovnic who'd been responsible for providing a group of North Korean girls to one of his Saudi clients. The 'girls' had been totally unfit for the purpose his clients had in mind. He'd sold them in advance to them as being a tantalising, epicurean dish for jaded palates.

Instead, no amount of dressing them up could disguise their wretched skinniness. Slim is attractive, skinny not so, particularly when added to an overall sense of misery expressed through dull and defeated eyes. Naturally, his clients had demanded not only a refund, but serious compensation too.

Hesham lost a lot of money on this deal, but more importantly, his reputation with his Saudi clientele took a serious beating.

It was the reputation, much more than the loss of the money, that had spurred him into the complicated actions that had culminated in the deaths of so many people: Stanovnic's sister, Christina, thrashing around on the end of a rope and slowly drowning in a rock pool in Rydal, and of five other people - the two men who abducted and then strung up Christina, along with their female accomplice, the young man who had been commissioned to damage Frank Blain's wife at the spa and now of course, Stanovnic himself.

That final assassination, the sudden choice to direct the hitman away from Frank Blain and on to Janko, had been an act of petulance that Hesham had immediately regretted. The timing was wrong, as his overwhelming need for revenge wasn't remotely satisfied.

Hesham wanted Stanovnic to experience more pain and much more humiliation before he departed this world. But despite the power he now wielded, he was still a young, impetuous man, and he'd let his anger get the better of him.

However, with Stanovnic out of the way, many of the Croatian's various business interests were brought under Hesham's overall control, as well as the newly acquired understanding of how and why his family had disappeared. Hesham still had the only target that truly mattered there for the taking.

His complete focus from now on would be Frank Blain. Until that issue was resolved, everything else would take second place. Blain himself, because of the incidents that Hesham had already initiated, would obviously be aware that someone was coming for him. Hesham was happy to allow this tension to build yet more before he struck, but when he did strike, the result would be decisive and absolute.

Thirty-Six

I'm running around like that chicken, seeing threats everywhere. I was freaked out when I heard about Stephanie but now, having someone invade my house - and the associated implied threat to my family - is completely new. It's wound me up and I can't quite keep control of the level of anger it's induced.

I got the family home safely, reminding Meg and the kids about the palm prints and the safety codes now applying to the different parts of the house. I couldn't sweeten the pill as much as I would have liked.

'What's going on Frank? Why are you so tense?' Meg's got this meter - some kind of internal sensor that reads me right every time. On most occasions I go with it, rather like it, but now at a time when I need to disguise my feelings, she's hitting the nail once again - and it hurts. I hate lying to her.

'I'm not tense. I'm tired, darling. I've not been sleeping well - too many things on my plate - and the kids have been manic ever since I got home. Sorry!'

'So, it's the kids' fault, is it?' She's got a look on her, a look that I can't fully work out. Is she playing with me, or is she more worried than she's letting on?

'No, it's me. All me, Meg. I'm too much up myself with some of the stuff - difficult clients. I'll work it out.'

'What's the matter? Can't you tell me?'

In all the years that we've been together, this issue has come up time after time. No, I can't tell her - obviously. I can shade the truth, elide certain elements, but the façade must stay firm. Honestly, if she knew when I did for a living, I doubt that she would stay with me. I know I wouldn't.

Obviously, the murky part of what I do is always there just below the surface. It's now come close to home. I've tried to fix the hardware side of the threat with the electronics, the security systems, the safe room, and the CCTV system. That side seems to have worked well given Wojtek's recent experience, but I can't get rid of the feeling that the edifice of normality that I've spent so much time creating seems about to come tumbling down around my head.

I try to settle myself down - and reassure Meg. 'I'm a bit hyped up because I didn't close my last job properly. I'm concerned that I might have to go back.'

And here's the lie, 'Let's have a quiet night in. I'll be fine tomorrow. We'll get the kids off to sleep early; I'll open a bottle; snuggle up on the sofa - and who knows?'

Meg smiles: it's not a full-on happy, genuine smile. There's something knowing about it, but as I've said, she reads me too well.

However, a small win and it's enough to be going on with.

Tomorrow, I'll get myself into gear and work towards gaining better control of things. The last few days have been too stressful for us all. Obviously, I never wanted any my work to come back here and disturb us. Home life is important, isn't it? What's the point? What's the point of anything if you have no safe place in your life?

This morning, I took a risk. Meg and the kids have gone shopping, and I let them. Yes, I know - but a rock and a hard place? It's allowed Wojtek and me to check out our defences. I'd also arranged the delivery of some food and domestic items from the supermarket, and Wojtek has been stripping down our weapons and testing everything.

I've no idea if we're going to be attacked, but I'm assuming that the guy who made his way into the house hasn't gone away and may well return. If he does, it'll be a different reception he'll receive.

I'm still balancing home life with real life, and Meg has been remarkably accepting - either that or I have been remarkably clever in keeping her away from things. Personally, that I doubt. Her radar is always on, so I'm sure she's aware that something's amiss, but she's waiting to have something substantial to hit me with.

But I'm not hanging about waiting for something to happen. What happened to Stephanie, what happened to Meg at the spa has got me juiced.

I call Archana in Dubai. She's been my agent for over ten years, and I can tell by the way she answers the phone to me that she's already worried.

'I was about to call you, Frank.'

'Why?'

'You'll think me stupid; I know. But I got this feeling...'

I'm straight in. 'Feeling, premonition, whatever. You're right. Something's happening. There's someone after me - and I think you might be a target too.'

'How?'

'They got to Stephanie. I don't know how they did, but she gave them information about me - and I imagine about you too.'

'Who's 'they'?'

'I can't tell you that - it's not that I don't want to, I honestly don't know. Somebody's after me; a couple of things have happened, and I didn't want to worry you, so I've not bothered you before...'

'What happened to Stephanie?' I can hear the urgency in Archana's voice. As it should be, but worrying, nonetheless.

I ask her, 'Have you heard of a Janko Stanovnic?'

'Stanovnic? Of course, I have. Everybody has. He's a mobster here in Dubai.'

So, I'm right. The connection has to be Dubai, and I'm starting to piece things together.

'Stanovnic's based in Dubai?'

'Yea,' Archana seems to know a lot about him. 'He's into drugs and I think he brings girls into Dubai as well. Why do you ask?'

'Have you ever had anything to do with him?' Things are coming together, and I'm beginning to understand what's going on. I've not done much in that part of the world, but I do recall there was a UAE connection with a job I did a few months ago.

I get back into the groove with Archana. 'I'm thinking it's connected to a recent contract, a few months ago. Do you remember that family?'

'They were from Riyadh.'

'Did they have a Dubai connection?'

'Possibly. There's always a connection. I can find out, though. Wait. I'll check.'

Archana keeps records of everything, but she keeps those records at arm's length from me. I'm pretty sure this job originated with her.

She gets back to me straight away. 'Yes, Frank. Dubai, well, mostly in Abu Dhabi. It's a huge family. I've a spreadsheet on my screen and I'm looking at it now. Our contract was for one of the family. He was from Riyadh but based in Dubai.'

'Name?'

'The family name is el Hashimi. There are lots of them. Our contract was for their main man, the father. That's why the fee was so high.'

I remember this now. I remember being surprised at the fee Archana obtained. The client had been curiously satisfied that the wife and two of his younger children had disappeared too.

'Archie, you must leave Dubai. Get out now. Go back home to Pune until all this is over. I'm worried for your safety.'

'I can't leave Dubai now, Frank. Too much going on.'

'If I'm right, and I think I am,' I reply quickly, 'the family knows who carried out the contract. Stephanie was killed because of this, and it's likely she's mentioned you.'

'I don't think Stephanie never knew my name.'

'Archie!' I'm getting frustrated now. 'We don't know how much they know. They knew enough to get to BVI and Stephanie. Chances are they can find you - after all, you're on their doorstep - and I don't know how much influence the family has...'

'Lots.' Archana's tone is changing. 'Lots. They are one of the big Emirati families; they can find out anything.'

'So, they'll know about you. Drop everything and go. Go to Pune, stay with your mom, and keep quiet until I can get a handle on this.'

'But if I stay here, I can perhaps get some useful information...'

She's a terrier - refusing to let go.

'No. You must leave. Get away now - please. Don't fly direct to Pune, either. Take a route that's difficult to check. Maybe drive over to Oman and fly out from Muscat.'

'You've got me worried now, Frank.'

'About bloody time. Let me know when you get to Pune. I'll send some extra to your account now - you've no excuses. It's time to go.'

'OK. I can work from Pune. What about the office, what about the apartment?'

'Leave everything. Take your computer, that's all.'

'I can't fly from Muscat.'

'Why?'

'I'd be an unaccompanied female. They won't let me board the aircraft - and I probably wouldn't get past passport control into Oman.'

I hadn't thought about that, but I remembered she'd had that experience when once she needed to get to Bahrain. They wouldn't let her board a flight without her husband's or father's permission. And she was stuck - had to drive back to Dubai spitting feathers.

'So, take a flight from Dubai, but to Mumbai - not directly to Pune. Don't even book the Pune segment here - wait until you get to Mumbai. And move out of your apartment now, straight away. Take a hotel room and leave everything as it is. I'll look after the details. When I know you're safe, I'll get in touch with the building's concierge.'

'But the office?'

'Don't worry about that - or anything else. Get yourself out of your flat now. Book a room at the Capitol and I'll call you. OK?'

When we end the call, I think that I've convinced her - I hope I have. The hotel I know very well. It's discreet, not far from the airport and isn't in a popular area of Dubai. Times change, and nowhere faster than in Dubai. Amazing modern hotels have sprung up everywhere, leaving those hotels that are ten years old, or even more ancient, lost in their wake. The Capitol would be fine.

I know Archana won't leave any incriminating evidence behind. Long ago, she'd migrated everything to the Cloud. No shredding of papers or anything as old school as that, but I know her, and she'll want to make sure that the office is squeaky clean before she leaves it.

That office has been the front for all our work, and it's been very successful. She runs her travel business from there, booking flights, accommodation and so on for conferences and their delegates.

And to be fair, she makes a good living out of it. I'm a minor shareholder and I've invested, yet another way of finding a perfectly legitimate way to offset some of the fees I receive. And today, when she does leave, she'll leave behind all the signs of a successful travel agency and nothing else. Her behaviour will be no different from the many occasions in the past when she's taken a break for a vacation or a business trip.

If things work out, we can retrieve our 'new normal'. She'll want to get back to Dubai, re-opening her business as soon as she can. But that's in the future - way ahead. I'm not sure if I've convinced here of the seriousness of the situation, but I am trying.

 Archana's own apartment is on a higher floor of the same building as her office. She lives alone, no partner, and I expect her to be as thorough about sanitising her apartment too. However, knowing how detail-conscious a person she is, I'm concerned that she'll spend a little too long before leaving her building to go to the Capitol.

And even then, she might not be safe; it might already be too late. If all this mess is driven from the UAE, she's in the worst possible place. And if the bad lads have any government connections, Archana might not be safe at any hotel as all registrations are recorded and centralised.

So, now I'm thinking I might well have to make a trip to Dubai. If the boil is there, that's where it'll have to be lanced. Too much has happened for me to sit and wait for the next surprise to come my way.

Thirty-Seven

Max coming up from Morecambe and Debesh driving from Kendal had arranged to meet at the site of last night's crime scene. Most of the blue and white tape had been removed, but the small area of the site had, in that time-honoured fashion, been detailed by a chalk outline of where the victim had fallen. The two men walked together.

'That won't be attracting much custom,' observed Debesh.

'You can let the hotel know they can clean it up - Forensics has finished. And it'll attract interest - rubberneckers, not customers. This road is notoriously slow at times, so it'll be sensible to hose that outline down if only to stop an RTA.'

'This wasn't random, was it?' Debesh was trying to work out how Stanovnic's body had been found in such an open spot, and right by the side of a very busy A road.

Max knew he had a point. 'It wasn't random, Debesh. It was deliberate. I'm concerned about where it happened too - so risky. The killer was lucky. Stanovnic was walking down to meet a taxi. Maybe he mistook the killer's car - it was the driver who called the shooting in. Stanovnic was the target, so it'll help when we find out who the driver is, what he saw and where he is now.'

'I'll get on to that straight away, sir.'

'Yes. Let's get to Ambleside and start collecting evidence. You focus on the taxi driver, I'll chase up Stanovnic's movements and see if any CCTV - anywhere - can give us an idea of what the hell is happening.'

'Did we get the victim's phone?'

'Don't think so. I'll check with Forensics. There was no personal information on the body. Nothing.'

'The killer took it?'

'Maybe he did, Debesh. Maybe he did.' And on that sombre note, Max and Debesh made their separate ways to Ambleside. A new challenge involved unravelling the reasons why a brother and sister should have been drawn to this beautiful area of Cumbria only to have their lives brought to such a violent end. Neither was confident they could resolve it.

And on top of this melancholy, Max was still rewinding that empty and pointless evening at The Golden Rule. What had gone wrong? All the signs of mutual interest were there, both parties had begun their conversation with smiles and positive intent, but the way it had all unravelled, and so quickly, had Max re-visiting every aspect in the hope that he might find some key to releasing the potential he still believed was there.

For the first time in a long while, Max had met someone who'd completely captured his attention. Melissa wasn't popping up in the back of his mind from time to time: she was now centre stage and all pervasive. He was seeing everything, filtering everything through his perception of her.

All-encompassing through this was, Max also knew that professionally, he should be thinking differently. He had a case to solve, and Melissa was a both colleague and his superior officer.

'Get a grip, man!' he told himself as his vehicle turned into the Ambleside police station.

Thirty-Eight

Melissa Mordaunt experienced a different kind of nervousness as she too made her way to Ambleside. Previously, any nerves she felt were a result of her excitement at something new. This nervousness made her lively, sensitive to nuance and she enjoyed feeling that way.

Today was different. That bloody man! Time and time again she'd kept the professional and the personal separate. There'd been opportunities galore - she was a very attractive woman and she knew it, but her insistence on not allowing herself to be drawn into personal relationships at work was something she took pride in.

But Max Wordsworth? What was she doing? What was she thinking? He was a middle-aged, angry man with an interesting back story, but he was nothing exceptional. His career had plateaued; his own personal relationships had all gone pear shaped. Why was she so interested in him?

And that toe-curling experience in the pub should have put an end to any further speculation. Almost as observers, they'd watched two clumsy strangers, both of whom should have known better as they trampled over any potential, any positive next steps.

Before that session in the pub, Melissa had been aware of Max, even aware that he might have something valuable to offer. She'd happily gone for a drink with him, not with any great expectation, but with an open mind and a preparedness to engage, something which she'd never thought of doing before with a professional colleague. Maybe it was the Lakes?

So, it was with a different sense of nervousness playing around her eyes that Melissa entered the station. The team was already present, and Debesh immediately offered her a coffee. Melissa saw Helen clock the gesture, a knowing smile on her face as she focused on her computer.

Max and Debesh had come from the scene of last night's shooting.

'We stopped off to see if there was anything else we could pick up.' Max's opening words to Melissa.

'And was there?' The backhand cross court reply landed straight back.

'We're chasing up on the taxi driver now. The victim, it was Stanovnic, had ordered a taxi and evidently walked down the hotel drive to meet it. He must have mistaken the killer's car for his taxi.'

'Did the taxi driver see the incident?'

'Don't think so. We're not sure. He phoned it in but left before the police arrived.'

Melissa wasn't happy at this. 'Leaving the scene of a crime? Do you know anything about him. We need a statement.'

Max bridled. 'I'm aware of that, ma'am. Uniform are tracing him now.'

Helen spoke up. 'They've found him. Traced his phone. He's local and he's reporting to Windermere police station as I speak.'

It had not gone unnoticed that, once again, there was a certain something in the air. Max and Melissa, once again, the protagonists.

Helen decided to break the ice. 'Debesh, should we go to Windermere so you can have a chat with the taxi driver?' Hardly subtle but well meant.

Debesh, walking on eggshells, asked his boss. 'Would that be OK, sir?'

'If the DCS has no objection?'

'That is correct. The DCS has no objection.'

'Then it's agreed.' The dance had slowed to the tempo of a Pavane. 'DS Datta and our administrative assistant will now leave for Windermere to obtain a statement from the taxi driver.' Max continued, 'In their absence, The DCS and I will examine where we are now and look to the future of this investigation.'

Debesh and Helen couldn't get out of the building fast enough. Debesh was the first to speak. 'What's going on?'

'Lovers' tiff.' Helen's response was not what Debesh had expected.

'That's daft - they're not - are they?'

'I wouldn't be surprised. That's sexual tension. You could cut it with a knife. Don't you remember?'

Starting the car, Debesh glanced over to his wife. That smile was there again. The smile that laid him out whenever she used it in these situations. Yes, he said to himself, I remember.

'Let's go and see what this taxi driver has to say.' Thoughts about Max and the DCS swirling around, but too deep for him to contemplate never mind hazard an answer. 'We've a couple of murders to deal with, and I'd rather concentrate there.'

Meanwhile, now alone at the Ambleside station, Max and Melissa sat at their respective desks. Each was pretending to work on some vital information relating to the case, but each separately trying to think of an opening gambit, their mutual embarrassment being reflected in the passive aggression that had characterised their first remarks of the day.

The atmosphere had developed to such an extent that two perfectly articulate, well-educated and grown-up adults were now behaving like moody teenagers. Each knew it, and they both wanted to break down the barrier that had appeared between them.

Max made the first attempt to ease things. 'I owe you an apology.'

'For what?'

'For last night. I don't know what happened. I'm sorry.'

Melissa was unmoved. Her sense of hurt - or annoyance - was evidently deeper. 'You've nothing to apologise for. Now, what do you propose we do with this case? This is a fourth murder, and so far, we're nowhere.'

Cards were on the table. Max was happy to follow this more circuitous route. At least they were talking.

'We'll see what the taxi driver has to say. There's some ANPR information come in that's worth looking at, and somebody has to talk to the press at some time this morning.'

'You can do that.'

'That's what I was thinking. Unless you...?'

'No. I'll work on the Interpol stuff. We've got some useful info on Janko Stanovnic. Nasty piece of work. He's come over here because of the death of his sister, but I want to know why he felt it necessary to come in the first place. And by the way, I owe you an apology too.' She looked up, and for the first time that morning, their eyes met. 'I have no idea what happened last night. It went flat.'

'Chalk it up to experience?'

'Or give it another go - if you feel?'

'If that's OK with you?'

Max smiled. 'I would love that.'

'In that case, let's get back to catching murderers.' Her professional hat firmly in place, Melissa wanted to get things moving. 'We're not going to find someone local's been doing this, are we?'

Max agreed. 'No, the victims are all foreign. The two men who were dumped near Ulverston were eastern European - possibly Croatian like our two victims here. It's likely that whoever killed them is long gone. We need to gather all the evidence, so that at some point the NCA or Interpol will move with it. But we don't know for sure...'

'That the killer has gone?' Melissa was surprised at Max's assertion.

Max tried to flesh out his thinking. 'There's something else. There has to be. It may be that all that the killer wanted - or whoever employed them wanted - was to get Janko over here and do away with him. But it seems too elaborate - all the organising and so on. I'm thinking there's more to it, and I know it's frustrating, but I'm sure there's a local connection.'

'Why?'

'Because the murder of that young girl was so gruesome. It was a display - a message for someone. Yes, it could have been for Janko, but given all the thought that's gone into it - I mean, four deaths, and bringing him all the way over from Dubai? No, there's something here we don't yet understand.'

Melissa was inclined to agree. 'You may be right. Let's see what the taxi driver has to tell us. I'll start looking for some ANPR information

- there must be some somewhere, and you?'

'Me? I'm going to look at all we've collected so far. I want to make sure we've not missed anything.'

'Just a thought.' Melissa was already scrolling through her computer, and the 'just a thought' was evidence of her multi-tasking, the way she was keeping all her plates spinning at the same time. 'Do we know of anyone in the area with strong connections either to eastern Europe or the Middle East? If there is another strand to this that we're missing, we might pick it up by looking a little more widely.'

'It's worth thinking about.'

Melissa continued, 'What if the events of the last few days weren't the end of something, but the beginning of something larger?'

'Larger?' Max wasn't quite sure of where this was going.

'What if the death of the young woman was the beginning, not the end? We've agreed that the way she died was carefully planned, the men who killed her were themselves disposed of - and then her brother? It's all too neat. It's not over, is it? There's something else going on.'

It was obvious, and it was a lingering thought, but for each of them a different kind of threat now presented itself.

For Max, it was inevitable that after the Met, the NCA would come in trampling their heavy boots over all the work he and his team had done. For Melissa, it was slightly different. Yes, she'd considered that any escalation would completely alter the focus of the investigation and possibly a new form of command would take over.

But that was no longer uppermost in her mind. It was both frustrating and annoying that her mind was focused on whether or not she would still be around to get to know more about this fascinating man, a man who was now taking up far too much of her thinking time for her comfort.

Thirty-Nine

For Hesham El-Hashemi, the young Emirati whose anger had got the better of him, life had now become more complicated. His recent impulsiveness, and his knee-jerk decision to have Stanovnic removed from the scene, meant that he now had to rethink what he was going to do about Frank Blain, the man responsible for the death of his parents and siblings.

He'd been stupidly reactive, and he knew it. Even as he was giving his order, he knew it was the wrong thing to do. Nevertheless, he'd gone ahead. By redirecting his man away from Frank Blain and towards Stanovnic, he'd achieved an instant result but had blown the practicality of the whole mission. Frank Blain was still walking around but now he'd be aware that someone was looking for him.

The young sheikh had also hoped that by now he would have useful information from his enquiries in the Virgin Islands. As the unpleasant death of that young woman had made headlines all over the world, it was likely that Blain had also joined the dots.

However, when his men reported back on their interaction with Stephanie in the BVI, he'd been disappointed by the results of their interrogation. The young woman had provided very little: she was either very brave or simply didn't have access to the details that Hesham needed. Despite their best efforts, his men had reported that she wasn't forthcoming, even with the vigorous encouragement their activities had given her.

Small consolation: in total, he'd discovered the name, address and contact details of his principal, Blain. Nothing more. But that would have to be enough as he was determined now to move to the next stage.

His impulsive behaviour suddenly involved a certain amount of reinvention as the killing of Janko Stanovnic, although offering some quiet satisfaction, had been a foolish choice. It made his present objectives much more difficult than otherwise they should have been.

He decided to do what he normally did in these circumstances - shout at somebody. Most of the planning for this mission was in the hands of Abdul, his semi - trusted lieutenant. So, he became the beneficiary of this angry young man's pent-up frustration.

'Bring me four of our Enforcers - they'll need to be good English speakers, so that will limit our choice, but I want them here in my office within the next hour. They're going to the UK - don't tell them that yet - I'll give them all the information they'll need when I give them their orders. Do that now - off you go.'

Much as he would have liked to, Abdul knew he couldn't comply and was extremely uncomfortable - as he knew exactly what was going to happen.

The signs that his young master found stressful situations difficult to manage were already hoisting red flags with those used to the previous, more professional ways of handling challenges, methods such as those used by Hesham's father. The old man might have been inefficient with his administration, but Abdul reflected that at least he'd always been polite.

'Sir, I can't find four men within an hour. It's nearly midnight.'

'Fifty-nine minutes left. Start moving. If they are not here within an hour, you and I will have some serious talking to do.'

These words were delivered gently, quite unusually for someone who, when he was very angry, tended to the more violent end of the spectrum. But Abdul new that the ultra-peaceful way in which the message was delivered underlined the seriousness of the demand. He'd better make things happen, otherwise there would be consequences.

'While they are on their way, organise the transport. I'll fly them to Schiphol in my aircraft, and from there they'll take different flights to different airports in the UK. When you have their names, sort that out too. You can arrange the further flights, car hire and accommodation. I want them in separate hotels too.'

'Will they need to hire cars, sir?'

'Of course. The UAE has an arrangement, doesn't it? But a good point - check they have valid driving licences. We'll also need our supplier to provide them with weapons. What would be the best way to do that?'

Again, Abdul made a positive contribution. They already had a contact in the UK, so at least for this part of the looming logistical problem, he had an answer. 'Probably at their hotels, sir. They wouldn't have to carry any weapons until the last moment. Or perhaps at a single drop-off point - reducing the number of transactions would be safer for us. I can arrange that.'

'And again - well done. See, Abdul, when you're pressed, you work very well. So, get to work - I need four men here in my office - fifty-five minutes from now.'

A few minutes later, Abdul was pleasantly surprised; he'd only to phone six people before he'd acquired his team. All were members of the group known as the Enforcers. The clue to their work was in their title: these men were used by the organisation when business affairs visited the dark side. This happened sufficiently often for the company to keep a stable of ex-military Emiratis, many from good, respectable families, but men who'd enjoyed the taste of military action and missed that taste once they returned to the relative boredom of civilian life.

Hesham currently retained twenty-five men in this group. They worked mostly in teams of three or four and they were all very well paid. Their only duty was to do exactly what was required of them. Hesham's father had created the group, and when his son first took over the businesses, it seemed to Hesham that it was probably the only setup in the whole organisation that worked properly.

Abdul's first two calls went straight to voicemail - the men weren't on call, and it was the middle of the night. Four others did answer, and no threat was needed to encourage all four, coincidentally all ambitious youngish men, to grab their UAE passports and their driving licences as requested and make their way immediately to the Emirates Tower office.

Ten minutes after Hesham had made his demand, Abdul reported success. Nobody was more surprised than Hesham at this outcome as by now he'd expected to be throwing telephones and sundry office items at his subordinate, expressing the full force of his anger in the normal way. He was mildly surprised to hear himself say, 'Well done, Abdul. A pleasant surprise.'

'Thank you, sir. The men will be here soon.'

'Good, in the meantime let's get started. I want my aircraft fuelled and ready to go tomorrow morning. I'll fly them to Schiphol and then each man will take a separate flight - use KLM – two to Manchester, the other two to Glasgow and Newcastle upon Tyne. There, they'll each pick up a hire car.'

'And when they arrive, where will they stay?'

'I don't want them staying together. The region where they will be working is in the north of England - the Lake District. Find letting agencies which can hire out an apartment or a house for each of them. Don't use the same agency. Maybe we'll start with Airbnb and then see if you can find some alternatives. You might have to use hotels but try to avoid that.'

'How will I pay for this, sir?' The enormity of this project beginning to dawn; Abdul was already seeing problems - problems that would land on his head if he didn't navigate things carefully.

'It can't trace back to me, obviously. When they arrive, get their private bank details and put fifty thousand dirhams into each of their accounts. Use one of our offshore accounts for all of this. Can you do this?'

'I'll try, sir.'

'You'll try?' The eyes were flashing, and Abdul immediately had doubts that he would get to the end of the transaction unscathed. 'What's the problem?'

'You want this done now - so that the men can fly tomorrow?'

'You know I do.'

'There are things I can do, sir. I can transfer the money to your men's accounts, and I can book the flights from Schiphol - and possibly the car hire too - although for traceability, it might be better for the men to hire their cars on arrival. But do they have to travel tomorrow? I'm concerned that we won't get the right kind of permission.'

'Permission? You don't need permission to fly to the UK. I've done it many times.'

'Things have changed, sir. There are new rules and I'm sure they'll apply to us. I need to check it out.'

The bit between his teeth, Abdul continued: 'This will also affect how we book the accommodation, and I'm also must check whether they can hire the car with a UAE driving licence - I'm thinking they may need an international driving permit, I'm not sure about that. And sir, there may be a problem with visas.'

'What do you mean?'

'Let me look it up.' Abdul opened his laptop while he continued, 'Everything is changing, sir. It's not like it used to be. UAE nationals could get into the UK without a visa, but now, I don't think that's possible. Let me check, sir, but if do they require one, we can't get it tonight.'

Both men knew that strictly speaking, making impossible arrangements after midnight in a country thousands of miles away, and with a four-hour time difference, was not in Abdul's job description - and wouldn't have been even if he had a job description. However, Hesham's world view, and that of so many men like him, was entitlement - and it was the job of the little people in his life to service it.

'Get on with it. Let me know when the men arrive. I'll brief them before I go to bed.'

'If I run into difficulty, can I call you?' At this point, Abdul felt he was taking his life in his hands. 'There may well be some matters that I can't resolve. I am concerned that you might fly these men to Schiphol, but they'll be prevented from travelling any further.'

'Why is that?' Abdul realised his boss was being deliberately obtuse here. This was not entitlement speaking. This was stupidity.

'Sir, as I've said, there is only so much I can do. I can make the bookings for the hotels, or Airbnb accommodation, if you prefer that. I can also make preliminary bookings for hire cars - although it might be better as I've said, to do that directly at the airport on arrival. All of these I can do sir. But I can't get over visa requirements. Please have a look at this.'

Abdul had scrolled to a page. He lifted it for his boss to see. 'This is our ministry for foreign affairs.'

Hesham was reluctant but agreed to look at the page on Abdul's iPad, gesturing to his assistant that he place it on his desk before him. There, he saw his point.

The page clearly set out that there was indeed a new visa arrangement, Electronic Travel Authorisation, known as ETA. This now applied to everyone, even to the employees of an overly entitled young sheikh from Dubai.

It had to be obvious even to Hesham that Abdul was right, and it was Abdul's duty to point out any potential difficulties in the plan. It was a non-starter; that was now apparent.

For most people, a simple apology would now follow, and then a change of plan. However, people like Hesham, who feel their position in life gives them special privileges, find it difficult when they are in the wrong. Climbing down, changing a decision, admitting that what you want to have happen can't happen, these behaviours all require humility.

Humility is empathetic. It is a warm characteristic, a characteristic which allows someone to change their mind, make a different decision without feeling uncomfortable about it - and most importantly, without losing face. It is also perceived as strength by those who experience magnanimity from those holding power.

This concept was completely foreign to Hesham. To him, such behaviour was unforgivable weakness. His response in these circumstances was to be aggressive. Clinging to his position while trying not to concede was a difficult task, but he did his best.

Obviously, the men couldn't travel tomorrow, obviously they wouldn't be going beyond Schiphol and to the UK without the required ETA. Hesham still wanted to turn this round to Abdul: somebody had to be blamed.

'Make sure those men are waiting for me when I return. We'll make our plans then. In the meantime, find out all you need to about these ETAs, and have that information ready for me. I don't want any more mistakes, is that understood?'

Even if he had wanted to argue this point, and he didn't, Abdul wouldn't have known where to start. They both knew that to bring those men to his office in the middle of the night was a stupid idea. It would inconvenience everybody including Hesham and it would achieve nothing. It was simply Hesham's attempt to maintain some credibility.

So, rather than argue with his boss, Abdul accepted his orders; said that he would do all he could to make the necessary arrangements. He also confirmed that he would have the four men waiting for Hesham on his return.

What he didn't say and was very careful not to imply, was that his boss's insistence was yet another very worrying sign of weakness, an indicator that perhaps this young man might not be the right person to run the complex business he'd so recently inherited.

Maybe it was time for Abdul to consider his situation and perhaps think of working for another, more competent boss.

No such signals were apparent to Hesham as he brought the conversation to a close. 'Bring the men here. Have them wait outside. I have plans. They can wait for my return.'

The sheer pointlessness of bringing four men to the office during the middle of the night was more evidence that Hesham wasn't up to the job he'd taken on. Despite his apparent confidence, he obviously felt the need to prove himself through these micro-aggressions.

And the plans that Hesham had alluded to? The reason why he would now, at one o'clock in the morning leave four men kicking their heels in his office until he returned? It was yet another example of his outrageous sense of privilege.

Hesham couldn't deal with his plans immediately because of one overriding reason - sex. Before deciding to have Stanovnic killed, and thereby throwing everything into confusion, he'd arranged to meet an extraordinarily beautiful Somali girl, a girl whom he'd first seen in one of the hotels near Jumeirah Beach the previous day. This exquisite creature's role was simply to stand in the hotel lobby, smile and look beautiful, something that she achieved with little effort, but to Hesham - and probably to many other men - it was a great waste of her time. She was made for better things, and Hesham had made it his business to see if he could find out what her true talents were.

In his new role of running his father's organisation, one of the first and to him unexpected perks of the job, turned out to be his sudden access to women.

His family's reputation went before him as he had yet to prove anything at all in his own right. However, the reflected glory of his father, a man whose reputation had been passed on to him, meant that certain dreams and wishes could magically be made to happen.

It was as if a private service had been opened for him, a service that offered a variety of immediate options. The most obvious was that girls and boys of all nationalities were available - should he want them.

And of course, he did. A word to a certain deputy manager earlier in the evening from one of his underlings, and this girl had been despatched to wait for him in his apartment at the Emirates Towers hotel, and Hesham had been preoccupied with the potential of this encounter all day.

Now he was miffed that suddenly other matters had taken precedence. However, the temptation was too great - he couldn't put off meeting the girl any longer.

It took two elevator rides, one down and one up, plus the short walk between the towers, and in less than fifteen minutes he'd made his way up to his apartment on the forty-second floor. On arriving, one of his Filipina maids greeted him, and he checked with her as to whether his guest was waiting. Of course, she was.

Stepping into his grand living room with its floor to ceiling windows looking out over the always busy Sheikh Zayed Road, his sense of anticipation increasing with every step, he noticed that the glass door was open on to his wide balcony. There she was - the vision he'd carried all day. She was tall - at least a head taller than he was, possibly embarrassing in some situations, but not this one. After all, she was there to be worshipped. Haughty, elegant, still, but above all, astonishingly beautiful.

She turned to face him and her eyes caught his directly. Not the slightest attempt to avert her gaze, noted Hesham. Other girls in this situation would be passive, modest, non-confrontational. Not her - not this creature. She was annoyed, and Hesham saw she made no attempt to pretend otherwise. Annoyed yes, but certainly worth the effort.

On the short journey from his office, Hesham had thought about how he would handle this moment. At one level, it was purely transactional. He would buy her, have her, enjoy her and then discard her. Simple.

He'd done this dozens of times before, and the women who were brought to him - he never went searching - all understood their side of the bargain. It was in their interest to comply - for many reasons. Transactionally of course, but there were other ramifications too. If they didn't comply, might there be repercussions? And for whom?

In at least one incident, one where a girl had refused Hesham's approaches, the girl in question, an attractive young Chinese housemaid had been immediately returned to her lodgings and then to a much more precarious future.

The person who had pimped her to Hesham, a young, ambitious junior manager in one of the many five-star hotels of the area, didn't dare to be seen to offend. The girl's refusal might well affect him more than it did her, so he had to be seen to respond assertively - and so he did.

The recalcitrant young housemaid, not startling, but pretty enough to attract attention, had found herself suddenly removed from the relative safety of her luxurious five-star hotel, an environment where she had been deliberately chosen to enhance its general ambience.

In many middle eastern countries, room service and housekeeping duties are normally carried out exclusively by male employees. Here in the UAE, many hotels now regularly employed Filipina and Chinese women in these roles. Because she was very pretty, she'd occasionally added some value to the hotel's offer and to her own bank account. She'd previously offered extra services to the occasional foreign traveller who found himself alone and kicking his heels in his expensive bedroom.

However, when she met Hesham, the girl was repulsed by him, had refused his advances and fled back to her hotel and to her own room. As a result of this rebellious behaviour, she very soon found herself fighting for sleeping space in a crowded dormitory in Bur Dubai, and within a few hours of arriving there, the consequences of spurning Hesham began to play out.

Her new role was to service an entirely different sort of clientele. These were mostly itinerant construction workers, but sometimes the very kitchen porters, waiters and commis chefs that she'd spurned so easily in the recent past.

This action also served another purpose, of course. It was a direct and completely unsubtle warning to her immediate colleagues, and through their informal grapevine, to those in similar situations in other hotels.

The girl who now stood before Hesham was fully aware of many incidents that had happened in the past to girls who had proved to be difficult to people like him.

However, such a situation was not new to her. Her extraordinary beauty had become apparent from the age of twelve, and from then on she needed to defend herself.

And she had succeeded - there was a quality to her that came not from her physical strength, but simply from her character. She was a strong woman and so far, despite many potentially dangerous situations, that inner strength had protected her.

Hesham's first glance at the creature now standing tall, erect and confident before him confirmed what had been his first impression on seeing her for the first time.

This girl was made for balconies such as his, for looking magnificent in expensive sitting rooms, and for lying elegantly in huge ornate beds - exactly like the bed waiting for this moment, here and now.

This girl was an investment: Hesham wouldn't force himself on her. He wanted to enjoy her and was prepared to work at the task - even though over in the other Emirates Tower, four of his mercenaries had been ordered to report to him.

Surprisingly, it was the girl who initiated the conversation. 'Why have you brought me here, sir?' Her question was polite, her Arabic slightly off-key. Hesham heard the resentment in it. She did not want to be here.

'I think you know.'

'I don't. Tell me.' There was the suggestion of a smile in the piercing eyes of this stunning creature, but only a suggestion.

'Your name?'

'My name is Amina. You don't even know my name, yet you command that I come to you.'

'I saw you in the Burj Al Arab. You took my breath away and I had to see you.'

'Thank you for your compliment. I was told to accept your invitation. I did not choose this meeting.'

'I know. Forgive my behaviour, Amina. I did not know what else to do. I am grateful that you accepted my invitation.'

'Sir, I did not accept your invitation. I repeat, I was told to obey.'

In other circumstances, Hesham might have allowed his temper to get the better of him. He'd already exhausted much of his patience in his frustrating conversation with Abdul, so had he been the observer, rather than the principal mover in the next sequence of events, he might have surprised himself.

'Let me try to ease your concern.' Hesham moved towards the girl but stopped at an ornate desk that was nearer to him. He opened a drawer and took out a small, beautifully lacquered box.

The young woman could see the box contained a thick wad of bank notes, more money in one place than she had ever seen in her life. Hesham slowly counted out ten notes, replacing the rest and returning the box to the desk drawer.

'Here. Please take this. Ten thousand dirhams. Take it as a sign of my good faith. It is for you, whether you are prepared to be interested in me or not.' He placed the money on the desk for the girl to take.

This was unusual behaviour on Hesham's part. The transactional part not so, he was always happy to pay for anything that needed payment. But to offer a choice? This was different, and it caught the girl unawares.

Hesham noticed the change in her demeanour. 'You will give me this money - even if I ...?'

'Even if you decide not to stay, yes. You are beautiful - too beautiful to - I want to enjoy your beauty, not force you into anything. Yes, Amina, the money is yours. And if you wish to leave, feel free to do so.'

'I do wish to leave. And thank you for the offer, although I won't accept your gift.' The girl glanced at the money laid out before her. It was more than a full year's salary, and she was greatly tempted. She could read in the demeanour of the man who had brought her here that he was desperate to have her. How desperate, might he be, though?

This might be the opportunity. She hadn't planned for it nor had assumed anything, but maybe such an idea had been whirling somewhere in her imagination. She'd never gambled before, never placed a bet and this was possibly the greatest wager she might ever make - if she dared make it.

Her heart was racing, but outwardly, she remained calm and smiled politely. 'Would you please arrange a taxi for me? I will be happy to pay for it.'

'You have a family, Amina?'

'I do sir. Back home in Somalia.'

'Do you remit money to them?'

'Yes, sir. Every month.'

'So, take the money. Please. Send it on to your family. It will make a great difference to their lives.'

The girl looked at Hesham - and then again at the money laid there on the coffee table. Ten thousand dirhams, money that truly would make a huge difference to her family back in the village. This was the chance that she - and her family - had been waiting for.

This exceptionally beautiful girl had made her way to Dubai solely to capitalise, to find a way of monetising her beauty. All this had been done at a great cost. From the beginning of her adolescence, it was apparent that she would become a truly beautiful woman.

Even so, she'd successfully managed to escape the clutches of various elders in the village and had avoided the usual fate of so many of the other girls in her village, the disastrously early forced marriage.

Hesham had not been the first man to experience the steeliness in her: she intimidated men. And although she could have been raped or somehow abused like so many of the girls back home, she had stayed safe, even escaping the horrific, still prevalent ritual of genital mutilation - another example of the power that she could wield.

On one occasion, she had promised herself to the imam - a promise that was never kept, but which had saved her from having her body despoiled in the name of religion. She had escaped from so much, and so successfully. If she was going to play this last hand as she wished, she at least had the experience of being a natural winner to back up her choices.

Dubai had allowed her to free herself from the more primitive overtures of her village men, but now in Dubai her beauty attracted a different kind of interest. Men like Hesham in his elegant apartment on the Sheikh Zayed Road wanted her, and he as were many others, was prepared to lavish money on her. If she played this correctly, her ambition might well be rewarded.

'Sir, I'm grateful for the offer, and more grateful for the fact that you've not tried to embarrass me. I wasn't happy to be brought here, but I see that you might be a gentleman.'

'Of course, I'm a gentleman.'

'On another occasion, sir, maybe we could meet?'

A chink in the armour. Hesham had almost given up and now suddenly this girl was smiling, catching his eye in a much more friendly way. Maybe an approach worth developing? Perhaps beyond a simple commercial deal; something more attached to it.

He was kidding himself. This was fantasy. The girl was here because of his power - not out of choice. She probably loathed him, but had seen an opportunity to take advantage, and on her terms.

He knew it, but his other brain - the Greeks would explain it as Man being chained to an idiot - Freud would blame it on the Id - whatever it was, this power was now making the decisions; logic playing no part.

'You'd be happy to meet me again?' Hesham was surprised to hear himself say this being led by someone who, although astoundingly beautiful, was after all only a servant. But, completely mesmerised as he was, he could see nothing but the opportunity as it was opening to him. He continued.

'Yes, I would be delighted. In fact, it would suit me much better to rearrange our meeting for another time as I have many pressing matters to deal with now. Allow me to arrange to have you taken back to the hotel. Will you promise me that we can meet again?'

The girl smiled and for the first time, her smile was warm and welcoming. 'If you wish to see me again, sir, we can meet. Although I can't guarantee that I will meet your expectations.' And again, that smile adding value and promise to the possibility.

'And the money?'

'I won't take it but thank you for the offer.'

'Take it as a token of my good faith. Because that is what it is. If I do see you again, I hope to convince you of my sincerity.'

'I believe you are sincere, sir. As am I.'

'So, take the money.' The ludicrous nature of the situation now becoming ever more apparent, Hesham was now frustrated - and not only because this girl was holding out on him.

She looked directly at him once again; those deep, dark eyes knowingly aware of his vulnerability. He was smitten and she knew it. Surprised as she was that the man had not attempted even to touch her, she was gambling at a high stakes table and this was her moment.

'Maybe if I?' He stopped mid-sentence: 'I'm busy now. I must go but let me do this.' He moved back to the desk, opened the drawer again, took out the box and began, once again, to count out one-thousand-dirham notes.

He added to the pile that was already on the desk. 'Here. Fifty thousand dirhams. That shows my sincerity, doesn't it? It shows I want to see you again, and it shows my good faith. The money is there. Take it - let it make a difference to your family. My car will take you back to the hotel, and if you will allow me, I'll contact you soon.'

The girl held her nerve. Still unable to grasp the enormity of what was happening, but aware that she must retain her composure, she allowed her eyes to offer the signal that Hesham so craved for, but at the same time, without offering anything tangible at all.

'Thank you, sir. You are very kind.'

Hesham handed the money to her, bowed to his goddess, and left the room. He had to get back to the office. Four men were waiting for him, and he had much to do - even though it was the middle of the night. He'd been too distracted already and had to get on with the main purpose of his evening. He no longer cared that he'd made himself look stupid in front of her. He would have her - whatever the cost. The money itself was an irrelevance.

And so it was that the beautiful and now very surprised young Somali girl arrived back at her hotel, chauffeur driven there in Hesham's Mercedes Maybach saloon, and with fifty thousand dirhams in her handbag.

She arrived at the hotel as a queen might arrive. The door to the Maybach gracefully opened by one of the concierge staff, a tall Indian ex-soldier whose towering presence impressed the many guests who arrived in such luxury. He was surprised when he saw that he was opening the car door to one of his own fellow workers, but he allowed the fantasy to continue.

'Welcome to the Burj Al Arab, madam. I do hope that you enjoy your stay.'

'Thank you, I shall.' She smiled as she swayed through the lobby, the very picture of a wealthy, confident woman, catching the immediate attention of every man within twenty yards of her.

She continued walking past reception and through the long corridor that led back to the real world of the hotel staff quarters. She continued out to the back of the hotel where she opened the door to the compound outside.

The change of mood was immediate. The staff sleeping accommodation was located there; this was where she truly belonged. Looking around, she was aware that fate had now allowed her to make a massive change to her future. Once inside, she glanced around her tiny room. Apart from the bed, some hangers for her uniform and a cabinet for her clothes, there was nothing else, no ornaments, no pictures on the wall.

She'd only been at the Burj for five weeks. Although she had this tiny room to herself, she shared a bathroom with five other girls. She ate in a canteen, and she earned a little under one thousand dirhams a month. Four hundred dirhams paid for her accommodation and food, and she'd agreed to remit another four hundred back to her family in Somalia. This meant that she had two hundred dirhams a month for herself.

Yes, it was a two hundred dirhams a month improvement on the post she had recently left, but not kind of income she had expected when she came to follow her dream, and neither was it something she was prepared to accept.

Coming to the Burj, however, had given her an extra advantage, one which now offered a great opportunity to her given her new circumstances - the one tangible benefit and the true reason why she'd agreed to the move. The Burj was a magnificent hotel, seven stars! But her role wasn't any different from the one she already had at the Grosvenor House, a few minutes away.

She was to smile at the guests, that was all. However, as part of the proposed new deal to get her to change her job, during the interview she'd suggested that she might retain possession of her passport - and with that, the ability to come and go from Dubai as she pleased.

The hopeful young hotel HR manager, completely in Amina's thrall, and now also having his own agenda - seeing a different kind of opportunity presenting itself to him, had agreed. It was a very unusual arrangement; most employers held on to the passports of their workers, and he desperately hoped that his own boss wouldn't find out about it.

Once settled back in her room, and fully aware that it was still the middle of the night, the girl called a Dubai number, and this call determined her next steps and her immediate future.

Yet another importunate and wealthy young man had recently made her an offer. Similar to Hesham's approach, his had not been pushy or demanding, as he had too decided to play the long game. This girl was truly worth his investing some time in the hope of a significant payback.

Upon first hearing his somewhat fantastical offer of private jets, exotic islands and unimaginable luxury, she had readily but politely dismissed it. She hadn't thought about the offer since, but suddenly her new circumstances decided for her. She would accept his offer - and fly with him to the Maldives.

This young man was another wealthy boy from yet another wealthy family, and he'd been politely but persistently importunate since her arrival in Dubai. Her call woke him up while he was in the middle of a dream, coincidentally a dream involving a beautiful and so-willing Somali girl.

Her only condition was that he should immediately save her. She had to flee - she was frightened for her life - and she believed and trusted in his sincerity.

The young man needed no further incentive. He couldn't agree quickly enough. He arranged to send a car to the Burj to pick her up and he guaranteed that her safety would be his sole priority.

He immediately opened his laptop and arranged their flights. Money talks, and a request for first-class service always requires - and receives an immediate response. Within fifteen minutes, the boy had confirmed his commitment to Amina.

Now she had nothing to lose. Apparently, she would be flying to the Maldives courtesy of her young man, and now she had time and space to decide her next steps. In one evening, she had transformed her life chances - and those of her family back home.

With fifty thousand dirhams in her handbag and her escape from Dubai to an ocean island with a man who would look after her, the opportunities of a new life for her had opened up. A new life where all choices made would be hers. She was determined to enjoy every moment of it.

Forty

The two-elevator journey back to his office gave Hesham time to ponder. Had he really given fifty thousand dirhams to that girl? What was he thinking of?

The amount itself didn't matter to him, it was only money, but if he'd been asked about this before he'd met the goddess, his plan of action would have been completely different. Instead, completely mesmerised by her, he'd allowed himself to be taken for an idiot - and he'd enjoyed the experience.

In mitigation, she was amazingly beautiful; those eyes were still burning into him, and he told himself she was worth the risk. Deferred gratification meant that he would be reaping the benefit of his investment soon - wouldn't he?

Abdul wasn't going to be so lucky. Hesham's physical frustration remained; he'd so much wanted to have that girl. He was sorely tempted to call her back but decided that he'd keep the pact he'd made with himself. Instead, he'd enjoy a compensatory Nuru massage when the evening's business was over.

The four members of the Enforcer group, still kicking their heels in another room, would also be in his line of fire. This had better go well. Abdul was waiting nervously for him. The powerful young men whom he had called were standing together, looking for all the world as if they'd been called to the headmaster's study.

'Well? Is everything arranged?'

'Yes, sir. Mostly - I think' replied Abdul. 'We have flights, cars and four hotels booked. I've also booked Airbnb accommodation, but I'm waiting for confirmation - it's the process, sir; it needs to follow the process.'

Running out of words wasn't a good sign and Abdul knew it. However, with ninety percent of the tasks completed, he was hopeful that his boss wouldn't fly into one of his rages.

'So, they can fly tomorrow?'

'No, sir. They can't fly.'

'Why?'

'Sir, the ETA will take at least three days to come through. We can apply for it now; it's an app, and I've already downloaded it. But the website says it would take a minimum of three days for it to be granted.'

'We can apply for it online?'

'Yes, sir. It's attached electronically to the passport. The men all have valid passports. All they need is a photo - we can take that now - and pay a small fee. It's simple enough but it could take up to three days to come through. You might,' Abdul suggested as a way of softening this pill, 'you might have more influence than I.'

Hesham considered his options. The men had reported for duty; Abdul had already made most of the arrangements. It would be more secure for him to proceed with the plan, remove his team from Dubai and keep them isolated until the ETA came through. And yes, he might speed up the process: he did have influence.

'Have you filed a flight plan for the trip to Schiphol?'

'I was waiting for your agreement.'

'You have it. Do that now. The men will leave tomorrow. Find a hotel in Amsterdam where they can stay until they're ready to travel to the UK. Do they require a visa to stay in Amsterdam?'

'I'm not sure. I can look now, sir.' Once again, the laptop provided an immediate answer, this time to see what the visa requirements of the Schengen countries were. The news was not good. 'It looks to be very complicated, sir. There is a Schengen visa. We'd have to apply for it. The website says there are problems with delays: currently three weeks to three months.'

Hesham was losing patience. 'We can't leave them for a few days in Amsterdam?'

'No, sir. I'm sorry, sir. They would have to be in transit to avoid the need for the visa. We can fly them to Amsterdam, but they'd have to remain within the airport.'

'Change of plan. Forget my plane. Forget Schiphol. Four flights from four separate airlines from Dubai and Abu Dhabi. Take them to three or maybe four separate UK airports. You can do that?'

'I can, sir. But we will still have to wait for the ETAs to come through.'

'We'll use the time wisely. I have a contact at the ministry - we were at school together in Switzerland and I think he could speed things up. In the meantime, you'll take these men to my apartments - the Jewels 2 at the Marina. No phones, no internet and no communication with anyone - the door will remain closed, and you'll station security outside.

'You'll also stay with them to prepare them for their mission. Also fix their bank accounts, their passports and this ETA nonsense. If you can, try to get a house for them to stay in the UK, rather than hotels. You'll have more time to do that now, but not three days. I'm not waiting that long for the ETAs to come through. You will get this right, won't you?'

'I will sir. The extra time will help.' This was a massive project that would require hours, maybe days to get it right. And it had to be deniable too. Better to nod this through than raise objection. If it fell, it fell. Abdul had to make sure that it didn't fall, or if it did, it didn't fall on him.

Hesham was on a roll now, still hyped up because of his frustrating interaction with Amina. 'I'll make my objectives very clear to the team, and if any man can't accept them, you'll have time to replace him - and deal with the consequences that will apply to his family.'

Hesham didn't need to say any more. Abdul knew exactly what would happen to any man who declined to follow the orders of this young man, a man who wielded enormous power, but so far a power that didn't sit naturally with him.

Abdul habitually did whatever he was asked rather than risk the potential consequences of disobeying. These men would probably do likewise, but he wondered how truly inspirational such an approach was - managing people through fear.

His former boss, Hesham's father, could never be called a 'good' man, but he was as honest in his dealings as he could be. He seemed to treat his people with respect; he was always polite, even when he was dealing with the more squalid elements of his business. But Hesham, this young, totally inexperienced princeling who'd unexpectedly taken the reins of the whole organisation, was turning out to be different. His management style, coupled with his inconsistencies and those frequent rages, de-motivated and angered the very people he had to rely on; every decision he made was beginning to create resentment.

Time would tell if the approach worked. The Enforcer team were soldiers; they were used to military discipline and would follow orders. But how far would they go to please a superior who seemed to devalue them with every word he uttered?

'What else do you need?' Abdul's brief reverie was interrupted.

'Nothing, sir. I understand what you require. I'll start making the arrangements tomorrow morning. In the meantime, I'll organise secure transport to the Marina. Is there anything else?'

'No. You may go. Send the men in.'

'Yes, sir. Thank you, sir.' Abdul left the room feeling relieved. He could go ahead and make the arrangements, and he hadn't been screamed at when Hesham's original plan had collapsed so quickly.

In the lobby of Hesham's offices, the men were waiting for their orders, wondering why they had answered an emergency call but had been left standing for so long.

Abdul didn't help. Worried as he might have been by Hesham's management style, he still felt obliged to take advantage of his slight authority. He was important, he was Hesham's assistant: he too had influence. The last few minutes had been stressful and unpleasant for him.

'The sheikh is now ready. When you enter, salute and remain standing unless you are asked to sit. Say nothing unless you are required to answer a specific question. When the sheikh has finished with you, a car will be waiting downstairs. Go directly to it. And oh, give me your phones now.'

This last request took the men by surprise. 'You will be allowed to contact your families later today. Until then, and from now on, the sheikh has demanded that you contact nobody until you have completed the mission. You have been carefully selected: you will not let us down.'

Four tall, tough, powerful-looking men, each a former soldier with combat experience, two of them as mercenaries in chaotic and violent arenas, held their own opinions of what they might like to do with this ineffectual little man and his pompous sense of superiority. Nevertheless, they reluctantly handed Adul their phones.

'Please go in. The sheikh will see you now.'

Despite feeling like naughty schoolboys, all four remembered that above all, they were soldiers. Hesham was their commander and as Abdul had requested, they marched in to see their boss, stood to attention, and saluted. After saluting, they looked towards Hesham, waiting to be offered a chair.

That offer never came. They were to stand throughout the whole of the briefing as Hesham explained precisely what they were to do.

First, he pulled up a photo on his computer and projected it to the large TV screen on the wall. 'In a few days' time you will go on a mission. This man is Frank Blain, and he is a British citizen. He is your target, and I want him terminated - and most importantly, you will also terminate his whole family.'

In his own way, each man responded to that last sentence differently, but their faces expressed a similar level of surprise and doubt. Hesham picked up on this immediately: 'I have my reasons.'

He didn't go into details: he made no mention of the revenge he sought, and the compensation he needed for the loss of his own parents and his siblings. His motivation was not their concern.

The next photo the four men saw was of Blain with his wife and his family. 'You don't need to know the reasons, other than that they are genuine and necessary. I promised myself that Blain would live to regret his actions, and before he died, he would see the most important people in his life die in front of him.' Hesham was quite explicit.

'Blain must see his family as they die, all of them. Nothing less will do. And for your own safety, you must know that I've already attempted to have him eliminated and failed. So, he will be on his guard, and he is as skilled and professional as you. You will be challenged and will be called on to use experience and your skills to achieve the outcome that I require.'

He looked at his four men, each of them coming to terms with the enormity of the task they'd been given. 'Can you do this?'

'Where is this mission, sir?'

'The detail in good time. Somewhere in the UK. That's all you need to know. This is what will happen. Until we can obtain the ETAs for your travel, the new visas that are now required, you'll stay at one of my apartments. When you leave for the UK, you will fly separately, and each of you will land at a different airport in the UK. On arrival, you will hire a car and drive to a rendezvous. My assistant is booking accommodation for you now - we're waiting confirmation as I speak. Abdul tells me you all have valid passports and valid UAE driving licences, so you'll hire your cars at the airport without difficulty. You all speak good English. Is that correct?'

All four men nodded in agreement.

'Have any of you been to the UK before?'

The youngest of the men volunteered an answer. 'Yes sir. I have. A six-week training course for battle tanks at Bovington.'

'That's in the south of England, isn't it?'

'Yes sir.'

Hesham continued. 'When you arrive, Abdul will send you the location of your accommodation. You will meet each other, scope your target and decide upon your action plan. You are the professionals, and I leave it to you to decide your tactics. My only requirement is the one I have already mentioned: it is not negotiable. You'll only succeed if you achieve the objectives exactly as defined by me. I'll consider anything else a failure and there will be consequences. Success, however, will be well rewarded.'

Hesham thought about asking if the men had any questions but left it for a moment as it was apparent they were thinking it all through. Although each of these men was experienced in warfare and had practised dark arts if not on behalf of Hesham, certainly for his father, seeing that photograph of Blain and his family had troubled them. These men weren't psychopaths; they were professional soldiers and what they were being asked to do troubled them.

Hesham couldn't wait any longer. His original plan to start this project immediately had left him feeling both angry and frustrated; he wanted this meeting to end.

'Are there any questions?'

The youngest member of the group was the first to speak. 'Sir, it's the children. I'm uncomfortable about that, sir.'

'What about you three?' Hesham could feel his temper rising. He looked at the others. They were now standing like three naughty boys, eyes fixed firmly on the floor, hands clasped behind their backs.

'Well?'

The oldest of the four answered. 'I'm a father, sir. It's difficult.'

'What is difficult? Obeying orders is difficult? Who are you to tell me it's difficult? I'll tell you who you are. You're men whose lives, whose families and whose future relies entirely on me and my good will towards you. Do you understand? Where does your choice come into that?'

'It doesn't, sir. I will do as you ask.'

Hesham fixed his eyes on the two men who hadn't yet said anything. 'And you?'

'It's a job, sir. No problem,' said the first.

'And you?' Hesham looked at the last of the four. 'I will follow your orders, sir.'

Hesham had been ready to fly into one of his rages and was about to dismiss all four men, have their livelihoods taken away from them immediately and blacklist them from any further work in the Emirates. The 'no problem' erased those thoughts for the moment.

'That's exactly what I wanted to hear. I didn't bring you here to be friendly and understanding. I brought you here because I need to have a task completed, and I employ you to complete such tasks.'

The men, the decision already taken for them, glanced quickly at each other. Each was a father and because of this had immediately recoiled at the thought of what they were being asked to do. All had extensive experience of working in war-torn regions as mercenaries, one in Yemen, the others in both Syria and in Iraq. Each of them had seen horrific scenes of death as well as the collateral damage caused to civilians, but none had ever been required to deliberately target and kill children.

As enforcers for Hesham's father and now for him, they were sometimes required to perform actions they considered distasteful, but these actions, punishment beatings, home invasions and the like were part of the compact, part of the agreement they'd made. That agreement had so far allowed them all to live comfortably. They earned good salaries, much more every month than they could have earned in any kind of conventional employment. On top of their salaries each had his house, rent paid, as well as free education and health care for his family. Financially, they wanted for nothing.

In return, they were required to perform unsavoury and sometimes violent tasks. That was the downside. And for at least two of the men tasked with this project, it questioned for the first time whether they could keep to their side of the bargain.

Forty-one

'I suppose it was inevitable.' Debesh was the first to respond. The email was the first he saw at the top of the short list of items he intended to deal with immediately. This slowed him down. Helen had started to make the coffee - as nobody else seemed to be offering. Max and Melissa, having arrived at the Ambleside station simultaneously, were catching up on a couple of things.

'What was that, Debesh?' Melissa had half heard. 'What's inevitable?'

'They're winding us down.' The collective deep breath that they all had been waiting to make began to take hold. Everyone stopped and immediately tuned in to Debesh.

Not a word. Max and Melissa had stopped their conversation. What they were saying to each other could wait - although it couldn't. There was more going on between them than mere chatter, but a trump card had now been played, and for that moment, even their clumsy bridge-building project would have to wait.

'When?' Max was the first to request some supplementary information.

Debesh read from his monitor, 'Because Stanovnic has been removed from the scene, there's nothing more to pursue that can't be done by local CID.'

'That's you and me?' Max was now looking directly at Debesh.

'And Helen, I guess. She's local too. And there are reports, stats, lots of stuff that'll need to be cleared up.' Debesh was clutching at straws, holding the conversation aloft while its relevance to them all slowly sank in. Melissa would be leaving. That was all any of this meant. The original team itself would have to stay together, tying up loose ends.

But not Melissa. She was now redundant and would soon be returning to her own desk in London, the best part of 300 miles away. She was far too important to continue working in the Lake District now that things were settling down. With Stanovnic dead, there was no longer an international dimension to this case; the expensive asset that was Melissa Mordaunt would be deployed elsewhere.

Each member of the team absorbed this revelation quietly, and in their own way. The person most seriously affected was Max. Although he'd told himself that he'd given up any romantic aspirations after that disastrous evening in the Golden Rule, part of him still held out some hope, and that recent attempt to reboot things had perhaps offered a new opportunity. This woman was out of his league, granted, but God loves a trier, doesn't he?

He looked around the room. It was evident the others were coming to terms with this new information, and they would draw their own conclusions, as he had. What he did know, and was sure of, was that neither Helen nor Debesh was experiencing the same gut-wrenching sense of panic that he was now trying to deal with. What would he do if he lost her?

Melissa had recently come to dominate his waking life and many of his dreams. Whatever ideas he had in his mind were now filtered by his asking what would she think about it? Did she care? Most importantly, did she care about him?

Obviously, his colleagues wouldn't be thinking in this way, and he assumed that were he to admit this to them, it would come as a surprise. But surprise or not, this was Max, and now he was completely overwhelmed by the thought that he might be losing Melissa. He knew, despite all evidence to the contrary, despite that car crash evening in the Rule, that somehow, he had to keep her in his life.

As so often before, Melissa brought matters back to the here and now.

'I'm not so sure about that. I don't see myself leaving any time soon. There's still too much that we haven't found out about this whole business. These murders, all four of them, happened here in the Lakes. Why they happened here, and who is involved in them has yet to be established.

'We still don't know who's driving this. Even if I were overseeing this investigation from afar, I'd feel there was good reason for it to continue until we have a better understanding, not least so that we could pass on some kind of informed opinion.'

Melissa's words didn't matter as much as what Max interpreted as the sub-text of those words. She meant something more than the words themselves. There was a chance, possibly a hope that things might continue a little longer. And if his interpretation of that subtext was correct, she was right: there was still a lot left to understand.

There was very little violent crime in this area. There had been a murder in the village a couple of years ago, the first in almost living memory. It was domestic, a mental health matter which had been quickly resolved. Before that, you'd have to go back about forty years to the last murder, and that was such a surprising event that it still shocked new members of the community when they found out about it.

But four violent deaths in such a short time? This was new; nothing like this had ever happened before. It was huge and it needed to be resolved. Max and his team simply had to continue the investigation.

Bringing on a new group of people to start from the beginning was, as they had discussed previously, unlikely to produce any great insights. No, they had to continue, this was not finished. It was worth fighting for and Max was pleased to hear the way Melissa was thinking.

She continued: 'It's not going to happen. I won't endorse it. They've not thought it through. We need to get to the bottom of this issue: too many people have been affected, and we still don't know why. I think it's entirely possible that there are others in the area, people we don't know about, who may be under threat. So, until we do know what is caused this, my suggestion will be that we carry on.'

Music to Max's ears. The more objective side of his mind erred on the side of logic. The accountants at police HQ would already be playing with the abacus, fiddling with the spreadsheets, and coming up with inevitable conclusion that money could be saved by changing the way they were doing things.

After all, the project had already re-opened the defunct Ambleside police station, had already involved co-opting a very expensive member of the Metropolitan police to the team, and these factors alone would have some bean counter in his little office in Preston salivating over the savings that could be made, were they to disband the team immediately.

However, beyond the objective lay the simple transactional side. Max considered the real reason why they were here. It was the people that mattered, their skills and professionalism that would bring the case to a close.

The emotional side of his brain was thinking of the intellectual property the team had collected, of the understandings that they'd created between themselves, the valuable local knowledge and the leads that had been generated. There was far too much to throw away, so he was delighted both professionally and personally that Melissa seemed so keen to maintain the status quo.

Forty-two

Over two million passengers pass through UK airports each day, so it was no surprise that the arrival of four young Emiratis at three different UK airports passed without incident. Their luggage had excited no interest when it was checked, and their passports hadn't flagged up any worries.

The four men, all members of Hesham's Enforcer team, had flown in from Schiphol Airport within about three hours of each other. One had arrived at Glasgow, two at Manchester, and one had a slightly delayed flight, arriving in Newcastle about ninety minutes late. Each man had then chosen a car hire firm and arranged onward transport there and then - avoiding, as far as possible, any potential traceability.

Hesham had been quite specific with his next set of instructions. The first message that each man received as he opened his phone was the reminder that he was not to use the hire car satnav under any circumstances. They would use Google Maps on their own telephones to find their way.

Only one of the four had been to the UK before. He'd once driven a tank over the range at Bovington in Hampshire. Each initially found coming to terms with driving on the left-hand side of the road was a challenge but quickly managed to adapt. And the drive to their hotels gave them time to reflect on the mission ahead.

The primary objective, the first command that they'd received, was that the entire family of their target was to be eliminated. Only one of the team had accepted this unconditionally.

The other three were deeply conflicted, but their understanding of the potential consequences to them and their families should they refuse to carry out their orders had weighed heavily. Each man had recently become a parent, and one was the father of two girls.

Hesham had made his point very clearly, perhaps too clearly. He'd underlined the nature of their relationship and how they owed every aspect of their lives to him. Their whole lives, their houses, their families, the education and healthcare of those whom they loved, each of these separate obligations they had to Hesham was now lined up against this monstrous demand.

It was true that all four men had killed before, and all had carried out various unsavoury tasks as part of their pact with Hesham's father, and recently for Hesham himself. But to murder a family with the sole intention of traumatising the father prior to his own death?

The youngest member of the team who himself was the father of two young girls knew this demand might turn out to be well beyond his capability. He carried the thought at the front of his mind for the whole of the drive from Glasgow to his hotel, a Travelodge in Kendal.

Otherwise, it was an uneventful drive for each man: motorway in the main, apart from the drive from Newcastle, and not much traffic either. The idea of using Airbnb had not worked out: Hesham wasn't prepared to provide the security information that Airbnb required, so instead, four separate hotels, each between ten and forty miles away from Grasmere had taken a booking, each for a single guest and each for three nights.

On arrival at their respective hotels, each man checked his WhatsApp group. The first rendezvous was where they would pick up their weapons.

The weapons transfer took place in a small car park and recycling centre on the outskirts of the village of Ambleside. A British ex-soldier with a useful side hustle providing weapons to a select clientele had previously been used by Hesham's father and was only too happy to strike up an arrangement with the new head man.

It was he who had chosen the location, primarily because it had no CCTV coverage. Moreover, although it was close to the main road, there was a bend in the lane approaching it meaning that any car arriving to use the tip would be seen before its headlights illuminated anything that might be going on in the car park. The recycling skips at the far end of the car park also allowed for vehicles driving up, stopping for a few minutes and then moving on, their tasks completed.

On four separate occasions in this special hour, a different small saloon car pulled up next to the Transit van in the car park. Its young driver opened a sliding door, and a transaction took place.

After exchanging a code word, weapons were taken from the Transit and loaded into the boot of each of the cars. The total selection included four assault rifles, four handguns, twelve hand grenades, two boxes of ammunition and two boxes of ammunition for each man.

The driver of the fourth vehicle was surprised when in addition to his expected cache of weapons, he was also handed two Starstreak hand-held missiles.

Abdul had added the two missiles as part of the deal. He'd seen them on the Zoom call with the supplier and insisted they were thrown in as a bonus. He knew Hesham would approve of such an action as they hadn't cost anything, and the Enforcers who were all military men, would know how to make best use of them.

Starstreak was a hand-held surface to surface weapon designed to take out tanks and similar heavy military vehicles. Its black-market value had plummeted recently mainly because of YouTube videos of the Ukrainian army and its successful use of drones. It appeared that a well flown drone could create as much damage to a tank as the infinitely more expensive missile system. Abdul, working on the principle that a little extra wouldn't do any harm, had decided that they would complement the already substantial arsenal that he'd acquired.

And he was right. The enforcer who picked these weapons up,

coincidentally the same man who'd expressed no qualms whatsoever about eliminating both the target and his family, was pleased to see them as he loaded them into his vehicle. He was already wondering how these missiles might be used, and he seriously wanted to be the person to use them.

Forty-Three

Archie may be in trouble. It looks like she's been detained at the airport. I can't contact her: her phone goes straight to voicemail.

The plan was for her to get out of Dubai for her own safety. Stephanie in BVI had already been the victim of a grotesque series of events, and I was desperate that the same didn't happen to Archana.

I avoided having to explain too much, but I'd convinced her that it would be sensible for her to fly home to India and do so from Oman - hoping that would keep her away from prying eyes. That plan was binned when we realised that as a single female she wouldn't have been allowed to fly from Muscat.

So, we'd decided to risk it and have her fly straight from Dubai to Mumbai. We'd planned that once there she would buy another ticket to take her on to her hometown of Pune. I was aware that if they wanted to, those same prying eyes would easily track her journey, and maybe Archana knew that too - there are few secret spaces in our new digital universe.

I'm assuming that it's more than over-zealous border officials; the coincidence is too great. I'm seriously worried that the bad guys have got her now. She was sufficiently alert to switch on her phone as she presented her documents, and I've a recording of the whole detention process - and very polite it was too - until they try to remove the phone from her. I've just listened to it again.

'Is something the matter with my ticket?'

'No Madam. I need to check something. Please wait here.'

About thirty seconds later. 'Hello. Can you tell me what's happening? Who are you?' This question is addressed to another voice - someone new has appeared on the scene.

'There is an issue with your passport, and we need to resolve it. Please come with us.'

'Where are you taking me?'

'The other passengers need to check in, so we'll go to a quiet place and resolve this matter.'

She now gives a running commentary, asking questions about where she's being taken and why she's being held. The answers, such as they are contrived and non-committal. Almost a mantra, a script being parroted - 'administrative detail', 'needs resolving', but of course she would be free to leave in good time to catch her flight to Mumbai.

Obviously, that didn't happen. I hear her footsteps as she walks from the concourse into a quiet area; the bustle of thousands of travellers disappearing from the sound landscape as if someone has clicked their fingers.

And there the atmosphere changes: a switch is thrown, and

everything is more charged. I hear first a request, then a more insistent demand that she hand over her phone. I hear her protesting, Archana exercising her rights, but then the phone goes silent.

I'm thinking about this, and I have to say that it's almost a first for me as I have no idea what to do now. As the guy said more than once it may well be an administrative matter. But if it were, I would've heard from Archana by now. What concerns me is that the people who have her may not be the employees of passport control; they could simply be Airport Security, but they also could be truly troublesome. They might be the same people who killed Stephanie in such a brutal way.

If they are, what can I do to protect Archana? The simple, most immediate answer is nothing at all. It may well be that the authorities have officially detained her, but as I know she is so careful, and will have made sure that everything was in order before going to the airport, I can't believe there is a genuine reason behind her being detained.

On the other hand, does that mean that somehow there is a connection between the officials of passport control and the truly worrying people who are causing me so much grief?

I can't accept that. Not the UAE, not Dubai. Of course, there are so many countries where officials can be bought, and where people can be disappeared, but not the UAE. There must be an explanation, and I have to find out what it is. I need to know what's happened to Archana, as I suspect it will be connected to my present local difficulties.

As Archana was my only remaining conduit of information, I'm now goosed. I've always avoided taking any work in the UAE because of how well the country is run. And as I've never wanted to compromise Archana, our business has always been entirely legitimate; any organising she has done for me has always been layered and carefully hidden.

Not that I have a choice, but I'll leave it for a day or two and hope that Archana will contact me. If she doesn't, I'll have to go to plan B - whatever that is.

On the Blain domestic front, however, life isn't all bad news. Last night Meg agreed it might be a good idea if the kids were to go away to school, rather than continue locally as day pupils.

I thought she might have changed her mind because of the recent events at the leisure club, but no. And it's nothing to do with the lazy parenting either. The main reason behind Meg's thinking is how she wants us to handle the twins, Chloe and Bella. As I've said before, she's very keen to make sure that they grow up as independent individuals, and not continually treated as a pair, as two peas from the same pod.

She's always dressed them differently and where possible she's encouraged them to take up different interests. Bella plays the flute, Chloe rides horses - and she's tried to get them to develop different friendship groups too.

So, this new initiative would see each of the girls board at a different school, to be educated and socialised as individuals rather than always being seen as twins. Of course, the additional benefit, to me anyway, is that Joe would be going away too.

There's a little part of me that is now singing and dancing. I love my kids, at least I think I do, but I'm seriously inclined to the belief that I'd love them more if I saw a little less of them.

With Joe in particular, I've noticed I'm becoming more and more short with him, less prepared to listen to his constant excuses, and to be fair, the twins do a lot of whining too. This may just be me, but because Joe's not mine, he came as a package with Meg, I've always had a slightly distant relationship with him. I've worked at it because I love Meg so much, but as he's getting bigger and louder every day, I'm becoming more and more frustrated by him.

Of course, everything that's going on at the moment is heightening the atmosphere, and it could be I'm looking for excuses, but I'm pretty sure that it would help in so many ways if the children were to go away to school.

What can I say? It's obvious I'm not a natural father, and I struggle with the need to control my anger and frustration. It's also becoming evident that as I seem to be bringing more of the consequences of my work nearer to my family, it's impossible to strike the kind of work life balance that I've fantasised about since I was a child.

Who am I kidding? What kind of work life balance is possible for a man in my line of work? I've got away with it for too long, enjoying the luxury of what I've been happy to call domestic bliss while in reality, shamefully deceiving those whom I'm supposed to love.

I've never believed in Karma; I've always been more comfortable telling myself that the choices you make are your own responsibility and nobody else's. The consequences of those choices are yours to suck up and deal with; they're not the actions of some malevolent third party.

I get a call from Wojtek, my Polish guy. 'What's happening, Boss?'

'It's possible something in Dubai's going off that's connected with us. Would you be around to help me keep an eye on the House?'

'And the family?'

See what I mean? A shit sense of priorities. Obviously, the family first, then the house. I owe them so much more than ever I seem to give.

'Of course, the family,' I say - just missing the beat - again, 'Could you help keep an eye on them for me?'

'You want me to stay at the house, boss?'

Complicated, this one. Yes, I'd want him to stay, but I'd rather the family didn't know.

'To be honest, Wojtek, I don't know what I want. I've got a problem with somebody who works for me in Dubai, and that visit to the house may be connected. I don't want to make things into an emergency - I'd rather the family stayed at home - the security measures we've got here are better than we'd find anywhere else.'

'Is that guy worrying you again?'

'It's not him, no - I've not seen him. But I think he's part of the same problem.'

Wojtek is brilliant. He seems to know exactly what the right thing is to say. 'If you need me there, I'll come.' He laughs, 'I could do with the rest.'

'Too much loving?'

'She's a wonderful woman - and that's all I'm going to say. You could tell Meg I've got some work to do on the house, and I could sleep in the safe room and keep an eye on things with the CCTV.'

That clinches it for me. 'Great! I hope it doesn't get nasty; We'll know in a couple of days. Maybe you'll have to work harder with your lady for a little longer - I bet you wish you were fifteen again.'

'I am fifteen again, boss. You don't want to know, but...'

'You're right, Wojtek, I don't want to know. But thanks anyway.'

We meander to the close. Wojtek will move into the house - surreptitiously if possible - if the vibes from Dubai work out in the way I fear they might. We leave the conversation, both of us laughing, both of us pretending that banter was the real substance of what's just gone on. Of course, it's not. It's nowhere near.

There's a strengthening current that's forcing every move and every thought towards a vortex that neither of us can navigate or control. That's what we should be talking about, but we can't find the words.

My next steps, however, are outlined in bold within five minutes of my call with Wojtek.

A call from Archie: 'I think I got away with it - I say, I think.' She sounds scared, not surprising, considering what she's just said, but unusual in that she normally manages to retain control of her feelings, even in difficult circumstances. 'I'm at Rima's. Oh God, do you think they're listening?'

'Hold your horses, lady!' Yet another completely stupid culturally inappropriate response. 'I thought you'd been detained. I was worried for you.'

'Keep worrying - it's not going away. Rima says I can stay for a while.'

Rima is Archana's oldest friend in Dubai. She's a Lebanese girl, a successful Dubai businesswoman, and someone who would do anything to help a friend - providing, as in circumstances that Archana seems to be outlining - her altruism isn't going to get her into trouble.

Here, I suspect it might do, especially if someone is listening and has clocked Rima's name.

Too late now. I have to push on. 'Maybe no more names, eh? Tell me what's happened. And as an afterthought, I add, 'Drop this call and WhatsApp me.'

And she does. 'Sorry! I should have done that before. I was panicking.'

WhatsApp prides itself on its security. I decide to bet the farm on it. If UAE security has been listening in, it's likely they may have enough information to chase after Rima, but that would take some time. Meanwhile, I decided that Archana - and now possibly Rima - are both in need of some long-distance TLC.

We connect in WhatsApp and Archana continues, 'I bought my ticket to Mumbai, as we agreed.'

'OK. Which passport did you use?'

'My Emirati one. I thought that if there's a risk involved, I'd be better holding on to my Indian passport.'

Archana has dual nationality. Her travel business was the reason she also has the UAE passport. It won a 'Success in Dubai' award two years ago, and part of the prize was a government invitation for her to become one of the few expats, other than fabulously wealthy individuals, to be granted UAE citizenship.

'They took me to one of their back rooms, and I waited for ages. A young man came to see me. He asked about my Emirati passport. I don't think he was certain what he was looking for. My name had been flagged, but they weren't sure why. He kept trying to contact somebody - or some department. Got through on a couple of occasions, but he didn't get the answers he was looking for.

'It was bizarre. Seems somebody wanted to keep me, but there was no reason for them to do so. I've heard all sorts of stories, and I expected to be locked up until they sorted things out. I think he became exasperated.

'After his last phone call, he looked at me and said he'd no idea why I was being held, and that I could go. I got into a taxi straight away and went to Rima's. That's the only place I could think of going.'

'And with one bound she was free.'

'Sorry? What was that?'

'Just a saying - my sense of relief has me saying stupid things. You've been very lucky, my dear. Probably a computer glitch.'

'You think so?'

'I hope so. Let's think positively.'

The bottom line of this, something I truly don't want her to realise, is that if they are on to her, there's no immediate or obvious exit for her to take.

Some time ago, one of Sheikh Mohammed's daughters tried to escape from Dubai. He's the ruler of Dubai and the girl made careful plans to leave in a fast motorboat. Special Forces caught up with her and dragged her back home. So, if one of Dubai's princesses, with presumably infinite resources can't get away from the place, we're going to have to be very careful.

And I decide what to do. It's probably a stupid decision, but I'm good at making those and I've no choice. I say, 'You'll have to take a chance and try again. Use your Indian passport, not your Emirati one, and fly to Mumbai.'

'You think that will work?'

'Honestly, I don't know. I've thought of so many alternatives, but the main problem could be that if you don't have an exit stamp from Dubai, you may have even bigger issues when you land in India.'

I'm not entirely sure how true this is, but knowing just how labyrinthine Indian officialdom can be, I think she'll be better off taking the risk and bricking it.

I could possibly get her out of the country by hiding her in a car, driving over to Oman and attempting to fly her out of Muscat, but the anomaly would still be there - yet another barrier to surmount. Or am I completely over-thinking this? And would it be a sensible choice for me to fly to Dubai with all this going on at home?

And then the immediate challenge is resolved. 'Ah. Yes, I suppose you're right.' Archana's acquiescence surprises me a little, but our minds are in sync. 'I'd rather be held by the authorities in Dubai than by any of Stanovnic's crooks - and it may not happen anyway.'

I am relieved. 'Good. WhatsApp me when you show your passport. I'll keep my fingers crossed for you.'

We close the conversation. I'm sure that I haven't set her mind at rest, but maybe she'll feel better knowing I'm thinking of her.

She won't. Feel better, that is. How could she? Both she and her friend Rima will be desperate for this to end. Something, anything to relieve the stress.

And at times like this, friendship is likely to be tested. Rima has nothing to do either with me or with Archana's business. But she's now implicated, so the sooner Archana gets out of Dubai the better for us all.

If it goes tits up, what should I do? Will I fly over there to rescue the maiden? There is a simple answer to that, and sometimes I hate the person I've become.

Forty-four

'He's a young man, sir. Late twenties, I would say.' The Kendal based PC was reporting to Debesh. 'My sergeant asked me to contact you, or specifically, your DCS, she's the SIO up from the Met, isn't she?'

'DCS Mordaunt? Yes, she is. Why is this of interest to us - or her?

'I'm not sure, sir. Maybe because he's foreign? And because of what we found in his car.'

The conversation hadn't got off to a good start, but as it limped along Debesh began to see that there might be some relevance here.

'Foreign?'

'Yes, sir. He has a UAE passport. He's in hospital in Kendal now and they'll take him into custody in Lancaster or Preston when he's discharged. He's been arrested under the Terrorism Act, and we've officers there waiting to question him, but my boss thought your DCS might want to see him.'

'What happened?'

'He stayed at the Travelodge in Kendal last night and when he drove out of the car park, he must have been in a bit of a hurry. He turned right - and drove straight into the oncoming traffic - which happened to be a bin lorry. It's all on CCTV. They drive on the right in Dubai, don't they?'

'They do in most countries. Is he hurt?'

'He was knocked out. They think it's concussion from the airbags, maybe superficial, but they need to make sure.'

'Why is he of interest to us? And why is he under arrest?'

'The weapons, sir.'

'Weapons?'

'Yes, sir. An assault rifle, a handgun, ammunition and three grenades. In the boot of his car.'

'What?' Debesh immediately saw why this might indeed be of interest both to him and the team. So many boxes ticked, so many new worries to think about.

'Anything else for us? Does he speak English?'

'No to the first question. And to the second, if he does, he's not admitting it.'

Debesh was keen to see the man: apart from anything else he was alive. Everyone else they'd come across was way past communicating with anyone.

'We certainly want to talk to him, so thanks for the call. Let us know when he's released from hospital. Our SIO will want a crack at him before anybody else has a go.'

'That's fine by us. I'll be in touch.' Debesh sensed that the PC was relieved by this conversation. Terrorism, weapons and Middle Eastern suspects all bunched together were probably above the pay grade of most rural police officers. Beyond anything that Debesh had experienced too, but here he was, accepting what might be an enormous responsibility on behalf of his team.

There was no alternative as there had to be a connection with the ongoing investigation - nothing tangible yet, but it was obvious in that gut-feeling way that old school coppers often talked about. Even in a world of 24-hour tech, there was still a place for intuitive decision making, and Debesh knew, he simply knew this man was connected with their cases.

He WhatsApped his colleagues, and over the next few minutes he received acknowledgement from everyone except Melissa. Only Max called back, the other two evidently happy to wait until they got to Ambleside.

'He's obviously one for us, isn't he?' Max's first comment.

'Yea, I thought so. Too much of a coincidence. And even if he's not, he's worth

talking to because of where he's from.'

'A lone wolf?'

'A bit melodramatic?'

'You're right - I watch too much telly.'

'Cop TV?'

'Yea, I know. Crazy. All part of my sad life - late night meals for one and too much booze. However, we need to know who this chap is and why he's here. When can we question him?'

'As soon as the hospital lets him go. He's secure now - under armed guard - bit of a step change for Kendal hospital. They'll want him out of the way.'

'I'm not surprised.' Max imagined the consternation at WGH, the hospital in Kendal which served South Lakeland. Granted, there was the occasional prisoner who might spend some time there handcuffed to a bed with a PC stationed outside his - or her - private room. But that kind of occurrence was more frequent in towns like Lancaster and Preston where various prisons and YOIs were located.

Max couldn't think of any situation at WGH where armed officers had been required to attend, and he was as sure as Debesh that Kendal would quickly want to offload this particular patient.

'I'll call in at Kendal nick and wait for him to be released - save a journey up to Ambleside. Call DCI Mordaunt and let her know the change of plan.'

'Would that not be better coming from you, sir?' Debesh was aware of what seemed to be a ticklish situation between his two senior officers and didn't want to become embroiled in anything.

'Is the concept of an order alien to you, DS Datta?' The reply surprised Debesh; somebody was very touchy today.

'No sir, sorry sir. I thought that...'

'On this occasion, I'd prefer some action, rather than your thoughts. Just do it. Thank you.' And the call disconnected.

Debesh, slightly miffed, called Helen to tell her to take her time coming up to the Lakes; she was likely to be the only person in attendance at the Ambleside police station today.

'Somebody got out of the wrong side of his bed today - and that somebody wasn't DCI Mordaunt.'

'Debesh! That's inappropriate and unprofessional - even if you're right.'

Debesh could hear her smile, and he concurred, 'Obviously something's going on.' And he segued to the present, 'More importantly, we've got a live one to talk to.'

'A live one? A live what?' She didn't pick up immediately. 'What do you mean?'

'Kendal police have detained a man of middle eastern appearance - and he had some very heavy weapons in his car, so he's being held under the terrorism act.'

'Weapons? In Kendal?'

'Assault rifle, handgun and ammunition. I'm meeting Max in Kendal and we're going to interview him. Do you know where the DCS is? Have you heard from her?'

By now, Helen's thoughts had lurched elsewhere. She was still processing what her husband had shared with her, but she was doing it as Helen the mother - and Debesh the father. A man with weapons, detained in the town where they lived, the town where their child went to school.

'Is he the only one?' The obvious question that a mother would ask. Then, 'What if there are others?'

Debesh picked up the fear in his wife's voice. He wanted to be with her; he wanted to set her mind at rest. Their professional world was colliding with their personal one in a way they couldn't rationalise. He tried his best.

'He's been arrested, but he's now in the hospital. He drove the wrong way out of his hotel and straight into a bin lorry. As soon as the hospital releases him and that should be soon - there's a flap about armed guards at the WGH - we'll see if he's linked in any way to our investigations. And there's no evidence of any others, the hotel said he was on his own.'

Helen relaxed slightly at this news. 'So, shall I bother driving up to Ambleside today, if nobody is going to be there?'

'I think you should. I expect the DCS will be there as she hasn't said any differently, and we'll be coming up as soon as we've seen our suspect. Or earlier, if the hospital doesn't release him today.'

As the conversation closed, Debesh hoped he'd gone some way to mollifying Helen. He knew the professional in her would be driving to Ambleside as expected, but the mother in her would feel seriously conflicted - her child was in school in the town where a gunman had just been arrested.

DCS Mordaunt, the one member of the team yet to respond, picked up the story a little later, and for a very good reason. Because it was such a perfect morning, the whole area clear, bright and still, she'd decided to get up early and go for a quick swim in nearby Loughrigg Tarn, just out of Ambleside. She'd parked close to it taking the road towards Coniston and turning right and up towards the tarn. After her swim she planned to drive down Red Bank through Grasmere village, and back to the station to begin her day's work.

She was starting to appreciate what had now become her new lifestyle. Moving into Marigold Cottage had been the catalyst. While still fully attentive to every detail of her work, she was developing a different view of the time spent between her various professional obligations.

Where previously that time had often been spent in anticipation, in planning and often in reactive mode, she was now much more relaxed. It had to be the difference between the metropolitan lifestyle - or was it the treadmill - that she'd enjoyed so far, and the entirely different way in which people in the glorious surroundings of the Lake District seemed to see the world.

One concern of hers, and the main reason why she'd been deployed to the Lakes in the first place seemed to have evaporated. There was no sign so far that any of the interested parties in this case had been involved with Captagon, the drug that had been of such serious concern to her colleagues in the Met now that the Assad regime in Syria was no more.

So it was that when she left her car to walk the few hundred yards to the tarn, she left her mobile phone in the car. It was only as the freezing water stirred her senses that she realised what she had done - something her previous incarnation would never have dreamed of doing.

Then, separation anxiety would have destroyed any sense of tranquillity. She would have been unable to allow Nature to enfold her, and her only thought would have been to get back to that phone and get connected again. (As it happens, taking her phone to the tarn would have been of no benefit - there being no signal.) But here, as she immersed herself in the energising but surprisingly cold waters of this beautiful Lakeland tarn, she simply smiled. She would enjoy her swim; she'd arranged her priorities as the new Melissa saw them and this short period of 'me time' was both welcome and well-deserved.

Of course, her new philosophical approach to life immediately took a different turn when after her swim Melissa drove down Red Bank and into Grasmere where the phone signal allowed her messages to beep at her. All three members of her team had called and each in their different way had requested some action.

Whether it was the effect of the swim, or maybe the slow burn that was modifying her approach to everything, Melissa's response was not to reproach herself, something she might have done in the past. She listened to the messages, realised that decisions had been taken with which she was broadly in agreement. They simply wanted her to rubber stamp their next steps.

What she would have chosen to do was no different from the decisions that Max, Debesh and Helen had made. Her team had worked everything out; she would discuss matters with them soon but in the meantime, she relaxed - her people were professionals.

In her first few years in the job, and on one of the many management training courses that she'd attended, the course leader mentioned an approach that she'd then embraced from the beginning of her career, and which had provided amazing benefits.

The point that so affected Melissa was summed up in a quote she applied wherever and whenever she could. 'I'm not your boss because I'm better at doing the job than you are. My role is to make you the best that you can be. You are the experts, and I'm happy to trust your expertise. I'm aiming to have a group of people around me every one of whom is better at doing their job than I could ever be.'

Melissa knew that creative thinking such as this helps the manager to avoid being flummoxed by the Peter Principle - rising in an organisation until you reach the level of your incompetence, and there you are doomed to stay. All the truly clever boss needs is access to someone who knows the answer.

Max and his team were her experts; they knew what to do and how to take the next steps. It was in that peaceful, Zen-like frame of mind that Melissa quietly made her way to the Ambleside station, perhaps a little later than she might have preferred given the circumstances, but totally free from any sense of guilt.

On her arrival, she found herself joining in what was already a lively conversation. The team was deciding the approach they should be taking now that a potential suspect had been found - at least, someone who was still alive and was worth questioning.

Debesh wasn't so sure: 'Just because he's from Dubai doesn't mean he's involved with our case.'

Helen couldn't understand why her husband, but in this context, her colleague, could feel this way. 'It's obvious, Debesh. I know I'm only the help around here,' (she smiled as she said that) 'but a Dubai national - carrying weapons which he must have obtained here in the UK, possibly in Cumbria. It's obvious he's implicated in something, and I think you should be jumping in with both feet. He's the best opportunity we've had for days to get some worthwhile information.'

Before taking up the challenge his wife had just thrown down at him, Debesh, acknowledging the presence of his boss, took a moment. 'Morning, ma'am, you've heard the news, I suppose. Do you think this guy is one of ours?'

'I certainly do, Debesh. Absolutely. He's connected to something; it's not a random event, I'm sure of that.'

'Devil's advocate, ma'am. Just checking. I'm in the minority and happy to concede. But what do we do now?'

'Max and I should go down to Kendal as soon as he's fit to be interviewed. When will that be?'

 Max perked up at the mention of his name. He'd only been partly listening to the conversation. What had disturbed him and thrown him into an almost trance-like state was the way his heart rate had risen so dramatically when Melissa entered the station. This was weird; this was wrong.

Back in the real world, Max joined in the discussion wishing to play his part and not be distracted by his juvenile response to Melissa's presence. 'Helen, contact the hospital and find out when we can interview him. I agree, ma'am,' he said, turning to Melissa and catching her eye for the first time and then continuing, 'we should go and talk to him, if only to exclude him from our investigation. And I'm with Helen on this one, Debesh. He's involved somehow, it's too much of a coincidence.'

'Happy to agree, sir and ma'am. Do we have any further intel? Is this man alone, did he stay with anyone else?'

'Good point, Debesh. Helen, another task. Check with the hotel, see if he had anyone with him, but would you also see if any other Emiratis - or similar have arrived in Cumbria recently?'

'I'll have a go. Not sure exactly how I can do this.'

'Me neither,' Max's unhelpful response, 'but I bet you'll find a way.' By finishing off with a smile, Max hoped that the patronising tone of what he'd said to Helen was reduced, but looking at her as she in turn caught the eye of Debesh, he wasn't so sure. Ho Hum! People are so sensitive nowadays. Better just crack on.

'Anything else?' Max looked to each of his colleagues. 'No? Good. So, I'll write up some notes while we wait to hear from Kendal.'

'I'll contact NCA.' This was Melissa's first real contribution to the discussion. 'Helen's right when she says there's no easy way to find out if our suspect came here alone. But maybe NCA has some access to flights, car hire and so on that we can't get. It's worth a shot.'

'Thanks, ma'am,' Helen was relieved that a burden was going to be lifted. She hated being in a position where she would struggle to find an answer. Maybe the DCS could circumvent this difficulty. 'If you're going to do that, I'll update our incident charts and bring the timeline up to date too.'

'Job's a good un,' was the best Max could contribute - his mind still elsewhere despite his trying to rein it in. And now he was going to Kendal with Melissa to interview the suspect. One car or two, he wondered.

'One car or two, Max?' Melissa was there before him. 'What'll you be doing after we get to see the suspect?'

'If we see him soon enough, I'll be coming back here, ma'am.'

'Excellent! I'll drive. Ready? And oh - Kevlar jackets. Best be careful.'

A decision like this was the default position for Melissa, a product of her Met training. Any officers going into a potentially dangerous situation were obliged to prioritise their own safety. Neither Max nor Melissa had a full idea of where this journey was going to take them, but at some point, they could be in contact with a dangerous suspect, someone who had been arrested in possession of a small armoury. Better to be prepared.

Max didn't demur. She was right. 'Five minutes, ma'am. I'll get my things together and we'll be off. Ok?' What's this with the asking her permission? He was still stumbling along. This woman was a witch. She's completely captured him. And even though he fervently wished to be captured, he was a DCI, wasn't he? She was his boss, wasn't she? Get a grip, man. Get a grip, he told himself for the umpteenth time.

No 'grip' presented itself. Max bumbled his way out of the room to freshen up - and get away from those eyes for a few moments. He searched for his Kevlar jacket, an item in his wardrobe that had arrived with all the kit that Helen had obtained for the newly refurbished Ambleside police station. He'd never worn it, and when he put it on, he was surprised at how well it fitted.

Suitably re-purposed - at least, as well as he could be, he returned to his desk, collected his laptop, mobile phone and some paperwork. As he was about to indicate to Melissa that he was now ready, Helen completed the call she'd taken while Max was out and put down the phone.

'He's still at the Kendal hospital, ma'am.'

'Brilliant timing.' Melissa was the first to respond. 'Ok, Max. Let's get to it.'

And so it was that Max and Melissa, desperately connected to each other, but for various inexplicable reasons hamstrung and failing to voice their feelings, made the awkward journey to Kendal. The hope was that they'd get to move forward with their case, but their almost silent journey left them totally unable without the words to clarify or even shed some light on the personal issues that so dominated their thoughts.

'So, how shall we play it?' Max asked his boss. 'Nick or hospital?'

Melissa was in no doubt. 'I want eyes on him from the moment Uniform picks him up. We'll follow to the hospital and then make our presence known when he arrives?'

'Why don't we go straight to Kendal nick and wait for him there?'

'Ok, if you prefer.'

'I don't 'prefer'.' Max's exasperation spilling out, not so much about the case, maybe, perhaps more because he was sitting next to the woman who now dominated his every thought.

'Context, Max, context. I want us to see if anything else is going on, if our man has any pals - I'd feel more comfortable if we had as full a picture as possible. It's not far out of our way, is it?'

'No, ma'am, it's not.' And she was right, of course - again. Max could see why the Met thought so highly of her. On every occasion she seemed to glide into the right space; she'd that ease of understanding that placed her perfectly on every occasion.

In his previous life as a pro footballer, he'd come across the same characteristic, different in behaviour, but so similar in concept. There were certain players - he was never one of them - who Max had come up against. These guys always seemed to be in the right place, and when they received the ball, they'd more time as well as that yard of extra pace to execute their flawless pass or that perfect shot. If they'd played on snow, these players would leave no footprints.

This woman was the equivalent of a premier league striker - and beautiful with it.

It was a sound idea to check and see if the recently arrested man was a lone wolf or not. If he was part of a team, they might attempt to rescue him before the police could lock him up.

'It's easy to find the hospital. It's better if we take the bypass and avoid the traffic in the town centre.'

'OK. Let's do that. How long?'

'Maybe twenty minutes, if that. We're going in the right direction - the traffic through Windermere will be lighter.'

Some ten minutes later, they passed the Merrywood hotel, the site where Janko Stanovnic had been gunned down. Normality had returned; there was no indication of the violence that had taken place there so recently. And as if to confirm that the event was firmly in the past tense, neither officer made any comment as they drove by.

They stayed largely silent through Staveley and on to the faster road as they approached the Kendal bypass. Melissa glanced to her left, and for the first time initiated a conversation. 'That monument. What is it?'

She had noticed the tall needle-like monument high on a hill overlooking the town.

'It's called the Elba monument. Something to do with Napoleon. It was put up when he was exiled to Elba, but then he escaped, and the monument became an embarrassment. Take the right here and we'll get to the hospital quicker.'

They pulled on to the bypass and Melissa sped up for a couple of miles. The conversation didn't continue. Both of them wanted it to; neither could find a way to restarting it, so it was once again under a cloud of silence that they made their way down into 'The Auld Grey Town' of Kendal, and round to the Burton Road and the Westmorland General Hospital.

Forty-five

Weighing up his options and thinking about what Dubai had left to offer him, Abdul was concerned. More than that, he was scared. As Hesham's assistant, he was always in the line of fire for something or other. As the messenger, he'd been shot so many times he was completely accepting of it. The ritual humiliation, the swearing - the odd thrown item of office furniture, all were part of the price he paid for his position, and so far it had been worth it.

Although officially he only received local wages, nothing like the fantastic salaries that the mainly western expatriates were extracting from Dubai's burgeoning economy, he now earned many times more than he could possibly have earned anywhere else.

Because on top of his meagre official salary, Hesham had continued a practice first introduced by his father. Provided he did not overindulge the freedom he'd been given (and on the horizon were signs already that these freedoms might be going to be curtailed), Abdul easily supplemented his income.

Commission on the deals made on behalf of Hesham's father was the main source, but he also received many 'gifts' from intending suppliers, and on some of the invoices he sent out there were miscellaneous items that would eventually find their way into his own bank accounts.

He was now quite a wealthy man - and he sincerely hoped to remain so. When he returned to Pakistan, he would buy a fine house and probably keep servants. His recent experiences with his new boss had brought forward that ambition, and he was actively, though quietly, planning to leave Dubai.

Investments he'd made in property back home and in gold would already provide him with an excellent retirement fund. Recently, the rulers of Dubai had decided that Bitcoin was where the future of the Emirates' economy lay post oil, and he had invested there. Once he was out from under the clutches of this seriously unpleasant new young boss, Abdul had a very positive future in prospect.

Hanging on to the dream of this future had become his primary focus. Now, nothing else mattered. For a little longer, he'd put up with the coarse, over-entitled and unbalanced young man who'd suddenly taken over his life. Hesham's father had been a crook, but he was a gentleman crook. If he had to take issue with someone, he was as ruthless as necessary, but he was politely ruthless, almost apologetic. Not so with Hesham, and Abdul, now aware that the next few minutes were going to be very unpleasant, was prepared: this messenger was about to be shot - again.

'Well? What have you found? Why could you not tell me over the phone?'

'I'm not sure you'd want me to, sir. It concerns our men - the men in the UK.'

'Well? I'm waiting.'

'The trackers on their phones: there's an anomaly on one of them. The young one, Mohammed.'

'An anomaly? What's that supposed to mean?'

'One of the team, the youngest, appears to be in a hospital, sir.'

'What happened?'

'No idea. I can't tell. I wanted you to know before I contacted anyone else. Maybe the others know something.'

'Is there anybody nearby, someone who can check up?'

'Yes, sir, one of our men stayed at a Holiday Inn in - Lancaster. That's very close, and he'll be making his way to the first rendezvous now. He can check out the situation for us - if you wish.'

'If I wish? Of course I wish, you idiot. WhatsApp him now. Find out where he is. Give him the coordinates and let's find out what's happening.'

And so he did, somewhat relieved that the battering he'd received was tame by Hesham's normal standards - no physical violence, at least not yet.

Abdul contacted the man who'd stayed in Lancaster. The man himself was confused and was waiting for an update from Dubai. So far, he'd baulked at the idea of asking as he was sure it would cause a violent response, either from Abdul or from the young man who now seemed to be running things. And that he could do without. Things were difficult enough in this strange, cold country. It was the middle of summer, but rain and wind had blown in from the west and the temperature was down to fourteen degrees.

The order was simple. He was to make his way to the Westmorland General hospital in Kendal and, without admitting to any connection to his colleague, find out what was going on. He had to speak to someone: messaging his colleague wasn't enough. Abdul was clear: 'Go to the hospital, walk around and see what you can see.'

'Is that it?'

'What do you want me to say? Use your initiative. Find out what's going on.'

'Do they have Security? Can I get into the hospital?'

'No idea!' Abdul noticed that Hesham's body language was mirroring his own. So, he was on the right track, although he guessed that his boss would at any minute grab the phone from him and scream obscenities at the man - a man who in fact, was asking exactly the right questions.

'See what you can see. If you can't find out what's going on, we'll make other plans. We can always put the mission on hold for a better time.'

Abdul shouldn't have said that. It was the trigger that Hesham needed, and he immediately lunged towards Abdul, wrenching the phone from him.

'Listen to me. Go to the hospital. Find out what has happened and get back to me. That's what you're being paid for - so earn your money.'

Utterly useless, was all that Abdul could think. Whatever was the point of that? Belittling and confusing a man, a man vital to the success of this endeavour - something already fraught with risk and needing committed and motivated professionals to carry it through. No, Hesham was showing himself up. He was inadequate and proving himself unable to lead his organisation - almost every crazy decision he took was further proof of this.

Hesham thrust the phone back into Abdul's hands. 'Get this organised - it's not that complicated, is it? Well? Is it?'

'No sir. I'll make sure he does what you say.'

'Don't bother me again until you have a solution - and you've applied it successfully.'

Whatever that meant was lost on Abdul. What did the man expect from him? He got back to his operative who was nervously waiting for some orders.

'This is what you are to do. Go to the hospital now and look for Mohammed. When you find him, let me know what's happened. If you can't talk to him, look around and see if the police or military are involved. That's the most important thing. See if anybody other than hospital staff are involved.'

'Yes, sir. I understand. I'm coming off the motorway now towards the town. The hospital is very close. I'll call you when I get there, and I'll update you.'

'Mohammed is very young. Can we trust him to keep the mission confidential?'

'I can't answer that, sir. I don't know him well. I hope so,' came the reply.

'Hope so? Do you think that our young sheikh will be happy with 'hope so'?'

'What do you want me to say? I see the sign to the hospital now, sir. Five minutes away.'

'We can't take the risk.'

'Risk? What risk? I don't understand, sir.'

'If the police are involved, we're going to have to take a decision - I know exactly how our young master will want this to go. Do you understand me? Do you have your weapons with you?'

'I do, sir.'

A commonly held opinion (is it mostly held by women?) is that a man can't keep more than one idea at a time in his mind. I'm not sure this is true, but as the import of Abdul's thinking began to crystalise in the mind of this young soldier, that theory began to hold some substance. As he realised what he might now be expected to do, he completely missed the turning at the traffic lights and had to make a rapid adjustment a few hundred yards further on.

'I think I understand, sir. Although, I'm sure Mohammed will keep quiet if he's questioned.'

'If he's in hospital, they will have found his weapons. So, it won't matter if he keeps quiet, will it? They'll arrest him and interrogate him.'

'I'm driving towards the hospital now, sir. I'll find a place to park and then I'll observe. It may be better for me to look at the exits and entrances to the hospital because then I'll know if the police are around.'

'That's a good idea, the first I've heard for some time,' Abdul replied, feeling slightly relieved. At least this man seemed to understand the situation.

'I'll wait to hear from you. Don't be too long in getting back to me. We'll decide our action when you know what is happening. Be prepared. You know what you must do,' the final peremptory remark allowing Abdul to regain his sense of authority and disconnect the call.

While Abdul may well have been satisfied with the arrangements, Hassan, the twenty-six-year-old UAE mercenary soldier had found himself in the middle of both a logistical and an ethical dilemma.

As he drove towards the hospital approaches, the logistical dilemma seemed to sort itself. He immediately saw that without having to enter the hospital, he could have sight of its two main entrances. One of these would have to be used by any police or military personnel should they decide to move Mohammed to more secure accommodation.

And Hassan noticed something else that pleased him even more. There was only one exit from the hospital. This was a driveway some two hundred yards in length that joined the main road at a T junction. It was perfect for him. He would have a far better chance of satisfying the needs of his crazy master, too. A police van or even an armoured car, should the military be involved, would have to stop at the T junction, making a perfect target for whatever he decided to do. And he could easily position himself far enough away not to be noticed.

He drove past the hospital entrance, turned his vehicle and then drove back to park up a few yards beyond it. Traffic passing by was light and he knew the way back to the motorway wouldn't involve driving through the town.

The logistical dilemma, he decided, was easy to solve, and within one minute of arriving at the hospital entrance drive, he was convinced that it would achieve nothing if he were to go walking around the hospital wards and corridors looking for Mohammed. Even if he did find his colleague, and there was no guarantee that he would, what would he say - what could he do?

However, on the ethical side, there was no mistaking the inference he'd picked up while talking to Abdul and receiving the latest tirade from his employer. Mohammed had been in a car accident, and his car was full of weapons.

This was the UK, and the UK had recently suffered greatly from various forms of Islamic terrorism, unlike the UAE which surprisingly, given its ever-increasing influence in middle eastern politics, never had. The authorities would deal with Mohammed as a terrorist; they would be looking for accomplices, for a plan, for a target, or series of targets.

Hassan would disappear until the British interrogators had done their job, found out about the team that was even now making its final plans for an attack on a target right here in Cumbria.

As these thoughts coursed through his mind, the ethical dilemma that had so troubled him faded away as simple pragmatism took over.

Mohammed was no longer of any value to the team, and therefore to his boss. The over-entitled disgrace of a man who now held Hassan's future, and the future of his family in his hands, required him to save the project by eliminating his colleague.

It had never occurred to him that he might have to kill one of his own team, and given a choice - which, of course, he knew he didn't have, Mohammed would have been the last on his list.

No, the choice was whether Hassan and his family would have a future. Reality kicked in: he knew exactly what he now had to do.

The clincher was that in the boot of his car he had a weapon that was designed to meet his needs: the Starstreak surface-to-surface missile. Abdul had included it in the deal that had seen his team so well prepared for their mission. That mission was now severely compromised - or would be if Mohammed were to be interrogated with anything like the severity that Hassan was familiar with. The British had their sense of fair play, didn't they? But in circumstances like this?

There was no alternative. He had a task to complete. He'd observe and wait and if the police or possibly some military personnel turned up, he would know what to do.

After all, when he discovered the missile was to be part of his arsenal, he'd hoped for the opportunity to use it. That old saying 'be careful what you wish for' now had a troubling resonance, but for now he would familiarise himself with the instructions that had helpfully come with the weapon. They were in Arabic too – another bonus.

Forty-six

I've just heard from Archana - she's airborne and on her way to Mumbai. I can't tell you how relieved I am. My mind has been full of mad rescue plans and derring-do nighttime journeys across the border between Oman and Dubai, the lot. 'If you can dream it, you can do it', Walt Disney is reputed to have said. He never tried to get someone out of Dubai in a hurry. I've done nothing more than dream it for days now, but finding a way to do it? Not a chance.

But now, if she gets to Mumbai and through Indian immigration, she'll make her way to Pune and to her family home. Then we can regroup - Fancy Dan talk for working out what the hell we can do now.

Our work in Dubai will have to go hang; we can't start again. A pity in one sense as it was a viable business making real profits and allowing Archana to manage my other enterprises successfully.

But with what happened to Stephanie in the BVI as an example of what could happen in Dubai, we need to refresh our thinking.

I do know what I'll be doing, though. Archana is a data genius; she can find out stuff, any stuff. Once she's safe and well - and firing up her computers once more, her main job, correction - her only job - will be to find me the name of the person who's behind all this. When I get that name, my own next assignment will allow me to bring all this to a halt. Attacking my family? Nobody does that - nobody.

Sorry about the bluster. It's how I feel, and I know it's alpha male crap and not sensible thinking. I'm too wound up. Before I can achieve my own Walt Disney moment, dreaming it so I can do it, Wojtek and I need to neutralise the threat that's affecting us here. And to tell you the truth, I've no idea how I'm going to do that. Is that man who came into the house the only one around? Are there more? How can I find out? I'm hoping Archana might help me there.

Forty-seven

'How should we do this, ma'am? Make our presence felt?' Max was driving through the roundabout just before the hospital entrance. Cars were peeling off to the left into the local retail park so their occupants could worship at the various domestic shrines to be found there, B&Q, ASDA and the rest. The stretch of road they were now on was quiet. Max slowed his vehicle while waiting for some kind of instruction.

'I'm thinking not, Max. We'll not get involved. Not yet anyway. We want to interview our man, but Uniform can do the paperwork, and we'll interview him back at the nick.'

'So why come here?'

'I mentioned context before. Just that. Let's see who comes to pick him up. I'd like to know what decisions have been made before we jump in. Also, let's get a look at our man - will he be in a wheelchair, on a stretcher? Will he walk out, and if he does, how will he look?'

While these notions weren't new to Max, he could see that his colleague automatically seemed to use a finer brush to colour her thinking, and this enhanced her decisions. She was right: any further actions on their part would take place within a context. If the military - or the security services - were on the case, Melissa and her team would be erased from the equation.

On the other hand, if those services hadn't yet got up to speed or if they hadn't yet picked up the information, there might be an opportunity for the team to find out if this man's presence had any local relevance, anything to do with them.

They both suspected that it did but so far had no concrete info. Maybe finding out a little more about the suspect by observing his behaviours before interviewing him might yield results. Maybe context was key? And if it wasn't? Well, he was now sitting next to the woman who dominated his every waking moment - a phrase that he conceded applied directly to his state of mind. She was there, sitting next to him. She was important. How to convey this hope into reality?

'I'll park up here.' She'd turned into the approach road and found a place to pull over where she could see the point at which the exit from A&E and that from the main entrance came together. All vehicles leaving the hospital had to pass by this spot, so they would know immediately if any official-looking transport, military, police or other had arrived or was departing.

'Will this do, Max?'

'Perfect ma'am.'

'What's with the ma'am?'

'What do you mean?'

'Oh, come on! We're sitting in a car together, and I know you're thinking what I'm thinking.'

'I don't wish to sound cryptic.'

'So, don't. We've got to make this work, haven't we?'

'This?'

'You and me. We've got to make this work. So don't be obtuse.' Her hand reached out and took his. He allowed her to hold him while he tried to process the last few moments. He'd no idea what to say but felt he had to contribute in some way.

As usual, he missed the beat just as a police vehicle turned the corner into the hospital approach and slowly drove past them.

'That'll be the escort.'

'You sure of that?' Max had difficulty getting those words out. On seeing the police Transit van turning into the hospital, they'd released hands and were pretending to focus on what they could see.

'We'll park that thought. OK?' Melissa had turned to him and emphasised the thought with her eyes.

Max nodded; he had no idea how to continue. All he knew was that this woman was - maybe was - realigning herself with him. There was nothing to say, it was true that almost every thought he had was focused on this event happening, but now, what could he do?

He did what he always did - even giving a note to self to bloody well stop doing it. Displacement activity as a substitute - worked every time. And luckily, he had one in the form of the police vehicle as it made its way to the hospital entrance.

'If they've come for our man, it's a good place to observe. We'll introduce ourselves when we find out where they're taking him. And that'll also let us know what level of security is involved.'

'The choice of police is the clue, I guess. I reckon it's going to be Kendal nick,' Melissa replied.

'Ten minutes away at the most, ma'am.'

'Do you want me to clock you one?'

'Sorry?'

Melissa smiled, 'The ma'am thing. But you're probably right. Work situation, professional environment.'

'Oh. Yes.' Max got his act together. 'You're right. And yes, professional and personal are different. And professionally, there are at least two officers and they're both going into the hospital.'

'Yup. They'll be our men. We'll wait for them to bring out the suspect, see what kind of state he's in, and then follow? Is that a plan?'

'Sounds good to me. Will we have the authority to interview him?'

'Unless the security services are already here, which I doubt, the answer is certainly yes. I'll make sure of it.'

Max didn't doubt that either. This woman knew what she wanted, and it would appear she made sure that she got it. Possibly that might include him.

He didn't like to think about his relationship with Melissa in those terms, so once again, displacement theory came to his rescue.

'It's not two officers, it's four - or more.' And he was right. Two more police officers exited the vehicle – this time armed with assault rifles and handguns.

One of the armed officers went through the hospital doors with a colleague while the other armed man and the fourth officer took up positions on either side of the hospital entrance. This was much to the consternation of an elderly couple who were making their way towards a waiting taxi. Hospital transport with an armed guard was something they hadn't expected.

'They're taking this seriously,' Max continued. 'Have we had any updates?'

'Not that I'm aware of. Contact Debesh, see if he knows anything.'

Max immediately contacted his colleague. 'We're here outside the hospital and an armed police unit has arrived - we think to collect our man. Have you heard anything? Do you know where they'll be taking him?'

'No, sir. Nothing. Nothing at all. I was waiting to hear from you.'

'OK. We're parked up and waiting to see what happens - and where he's going to be taken. I'll get back to you as soon as we have any further information. Cheers! Out!'

'Out? We are wearing our formal hat now, aren't we, Detective?'

'Probably the better way, ma'am,' was all he could reply.

'You're right. And - we have action!'

The two officers at the main door had taken up a position suggesting that their suspect was on his way out, moments later a young man, maybe mid to late twenties was Max's estimate, handcuffed to a uniformed officer and accompanied by his heavily armed colleague, came out of the building.

The man was walking somewhat gingerly but didn't seem to need any physical assistance. Nevertheless, as he came out of the hospital entrance, the second unarmed officer and his colleague grasped a hold of the man's upper arms as they moved towards the police vehicle.

The rear door of the Transit was already open, and before placing the man in the vehicle's cage, he was uncuffed from his escorting officer and the free handcuff attached behind his back to his other hand. The door was closed firmly as the two armed officers continued scanning the area for potential trouble.

There being none, and their quarry now safely in their vehicle, the armed officers stowed their assault rifles and let themselves into the rear passenger seats while their colleagues took their places in the front. Their respective doors closed almost simultaneously.

Most of the windows of the hospital which faced this scene were now populated by interested faces and much medical activity had come to a halt while this particular young man was being removed.

Max and Melissa watched from their vantage point. The police vehicle reversed out of the area where it had been parked and turned on to the short drive that would take it and its five occupants to the main road.

'So, we'll follow at a distance?' Max stating the obvious.

Melissa took it as the obvious too. 'Yes, if that's all right with you DCI Wordsworth.' But she said it with a smile that Max both saw and heard in her voice.

'Can I just say ma'am - Melissa, sorry! Can I just say that - I don't even know what to say. Christ! Sorry! I'd like to - I'd love to, I would.' Then, and before he put the car into gear, he turned towards Melissa and for the first time in this new understanding, he did something that he'd been hoping to do for so long, he looked deeply into her eyes.

Whatever he said next was obliterated by the explosion. The laser-guided Starstreak missile, held by Hassan and fired using the bonnet of his car for stability, had taken less than two seconds to hit its target. The police Transit vehicle and its contents were immediately destroyed; the blast blowing out many of the windows overlooking the scene, with flying glass and debris injuring many of the staff members and patients who'd been rubber-necking the proceedings.

Hassan watched horrified as the missile struck his target. Five men including his colleague Mohammed were now dying or had died in unimaginable agony - and he was responsible.

Unable to move for a few seconds as the shock of the unfolding event washed over him, he had to jolt himself back into action, and taking one last look at the hellish scene he'd created, he got back into his car to set off towards the village of Endmoor.

He would get to the motorway and loop back towards his original target. He would have a success to report to his bosses, but would he ever sleep again? He had killed before, several times, but what he'd done in the last few moments was beyond redemption - he'd deliberately murdered a friend.

For Max and Melissa who seemed to have truly connected for the first time, their moment was immediately shattered by the explosion, and for several frightening seconds after the immolation of the police van, debris continued to land both on their car and all around them.

One of their tyres was blown out by some sharp object and the driver's side window was smashed by the crash of a headlight casing, missing Melissa by inches.

Shards of glass from the side window had also shattered over Melissa. As the explosion occurred, she'd instinctively turned towards Max for comfort and he'd taken her in his arms, inadvertently shielding her face from the shattering glass.

Not so his own face. A long sliver of the shattered window grazed past his head, nicking him above the eyebrow and scraping a furrow through his scalp as it passed. Blood cascaded from the top of his skull, down his face and on to Melissa. She felt it immediately.

'What's happened to you? Let me see.'

'It's ok. I'm all right - I think. What about you? The glass. It's all over you. What the fuck has happened?'

'God knows. A bomb? Can you see the police van? Oh God, they'll all be dead.' Melissa was panicking - she knew she had to calm down.

'Can you get out of the car?'

'I think so.' Max wasn't at all sure he could. His vision was obscured by blood and as he tried to wipe it away from his head, he found himself picking out pieces of glass.

Worried that he might damage himself further, he closed the one eye that was particularly affected and gave up trying to tidy himself. He opened the passenger door - having to force it as it had been buckled by the blast, but by pushing his shoulder hard against it, he managed.

Pleasantly surprised at finding himself standing and with apparently no serious damage done, he turned his attention to Melissa. As she got out, Max saw her back was a pin cushion of glass.

'Turn around,' let me see, he commanded. 'Can you take off your coat?'

'My coat?'

'Not a request, ma'am.' Melissa had slowed to a halt, frozen as she looked around her and saw the devastated police vehicle that had had once contained five men, the immediate victims of something, but what?

'Sorry. Of course. Here, help me with the sleeve.' As Max did so, he saw that dozens of shards of glass came away from Melissa as her coat was removed.

'You've been lucky.'

'Let me see you now,' was her response.

The Kevlar lined anti-stab jackets that Melissa had insisted they both wear when leaving Ambleside had probably saved her life. Even the collar had been fortuitously turned up, as it now held a six-inch sliver of glass that could well have impaled itself in her neck.

However, she was more concerned to make sure that her man was safe. He was so much more important to her now.

At the same time the professional in her, surveying the scene and noticing how the various actors in the next part of the process were beginning to take on their roles, that professional had worked out what had happened.

'There was a car up there, wasn't there?'

'Yes,' Max replied. 'There was. A single man. We should have checked him out.' He was now feeling better on two counts. His own injuries were slight; he knew he could stop the bleeding from the gash in his skull with lint from a first aid kit, and he would do this now because on the second count, he could see that Melissa was not seriously injured. He too could start thinking about what the fuck was going on.

'It was a missile - or a rocket. God knows what, but it was fired from there. It had to be. Did you see anything, Max?'

'To be honest, I was looking at you. And by the way, good call on the Kevlar.'

Melissa clicked into real time. 'Call this in, find that car. It was a white Focus - did you get the index number?'

'No, I'll put a call out for any white Focus going south towards the motorway. I'll see if there are any traffic cams too. We might get lucky.'

He heard the sound of sirens, many of them. 'It's already been called in. I better call Ambleside. Let them know what's happened - let them know we're safe.'

'Look at this.' For the first time, Melissa had lifted her eyes from her immediate surroundings, and in particular, from the wellbeing of Max, and started to take in the effects of the strike on the police vehicle.

The Transit was still burning; she'd also heard the sound of ammunition going off, probably explaining why people were staying away from the smouldering ruins. There was nothing anyone could do to help. The vehicle was now unrecognisable, a twisted wreck of steel and smoking rubber, with the exploding fuel tank spreading debris over cars and structures in the immediate vicinity.

Beyond the destruction to the cars, the crater in the road and the debris everywhere, Melissa could see that the windows of the hospital facing the explosion had been blown out, and a number of small fires in and around the buildings were now burning.

The rescue services had begun to arrive. Five police cars were the first to show up. Max noticed that three of those cars were from the Armed Response unit. Were the dead police officers their colleagues? They had to be - they all would have known each other.

The first of the fire engines arrived and its crew set about damping down the remaining flames. They were aware of the exploding ammunition, and although its frequency had died down, they maintained as safe a distance as they could from the vehicle.

Gradually the smoke and the few remaining flames died down, and one of the firefighters, using what looked like a Perspex shield, approached the remains of the Transit.

Max and Melissa watched on with many others in and around the hospital as he searched the wreckage for signs of life. A few moments later, he turned to his colleagues and with a shake of his head signalled what all the onlookers to the scene already knew.

Max was in touch with Ambleside. 'There's been an incident here, Debesh. It's a bad one. We think it's a bomb or a missile that's gone off. A police Transit van containing our suspect and four officers has been destroyed, and there's a hell of a mess around here. I'm pretty sure the security services are going to be involved now.'

'Are you two OK?'

'We were affected by the blast, but far enough away from it, thank God. Our car is kaput, though. Can you come down and pick us up? Until then, we'll help around here, make ourselves useful. Lots of damaged vehicles, windows blown out all over. I don't yet know if there are any other casualties, but we're in the middle of a major crime scene now, so we might as well get the investigation started.'

'Are you injured, sir?' Debesh was more insistent than Max would have preferred.

'I have a small gash on my head and the DCS had the good sense to insist that we both wore our stab vests, so we are pretty much good to go.' He looked across at Melissa who nodded in affirmation.

'Sir, you'll both be in shock. You should sit tight until I come and get you. The emergency services will want to look at you and check you both out.'

'Thanks for the advice, Debesh. Duly noted.' Max closed the call.

'What did he say?' Melissa knew but wanted Max to spell it out.

'He said something about shock.'

'And?'

'He may be right - he probably is right, but just now, I feel OK. You?'

'Same. Can you make sure the glass is all gone, please?'

Max double-checked and could see no more shards of glass clinging to Melissa. 'Can you feel inside your shirt for me, just see if ...?'

'Would you not prefer to do it?' Melissa laughed as she said it. Then, 'Maybe too soon?'

'And totally inappropriate - but tempting,' was all that Max could muster.

'I think I'm fine,' Melissa continued, 'and I don't believe I'm in shock yet. Debesh was right, though, and we should keep that in mind. Ready? Let's go and show ourselves. And by the way, tonight you and I will be having a meal and some stiff drinks together, so please don't make any other plans.'

Forty-eight

'You're right, Frank. There's a connection!' I'm answering a WhatsApp audio with Archana as I try to sneak out of the bedroom without disturbing what I'm hoping is the sleeping form of Meg. I'm probably on a loser here, and there'll be some explaining to do as she has this bat-like radar that doesn't miss anything. I'll deal with that on my return, and I'm already thinking that a cup of tea might help me here - even if it is two in the morning.

The timing is a bit odd, which explains why I'm not quite up to speed yet. But it'll be morning in Pune and Archana always was an early riser.

'What am I right about, Archie?'

'I've been looking into stuff.'

'Hold on. Where are you?'

'I'm at home in Pune - I say home. You know it, it's not exactly Dubai, and Dubai is where I want to call home. Pune is not my home because ...'

'Because it isn't Dubai, I know.'

Archana had chosen Dubai over Pune, and I can sense the resentment in her voice. She doesn't want to be in Pune - she left the place years ago, and this is obviously a defeat. She's lost face - or thinks she has, with her family. You can imagine their thoughts - and she's unable and probably unwilling anyway, to explain the real reasons behind her sudden arrival.

I try to get her to a level where we can discuss her reason for calling me.

'You're safe, now. That's the point. You'll get back to Dubai - or to some other more attractive place soon - I promise.'

'I'm holding you to that.'

'Make sure you do - now tell me about this connection. A connection to what?'

'You remember you asked me about the Saudi family - the client that ...'

I stop her from elaborating the point. Even on WhatsApp with its end-to-end encryption, I'm thinking security. 'Yes, I remember. And?'

'Well, the family business was taken over by one of the sons. He's only twenty-four or five, and it appears he's a bit of a shit.'

'Archie, I still have the word 'and' hanging around.'

'Be patient. God - men! Just wait, will you? The business works out of Dubai - for obvious reasons. There's a suite of offices in Emirates Towers and his apartment is in the adjoining hotel building. His employees - the employees of his dad, the man whom you...'

'I remember, go on,' stopping her train of thought in the hope that she doesn't mention any names that a web crawler might pick up. Yes, I'm being paranoid, but in the current circumstances - and, oh, Meg has followed me downstairs to the kitchen, so this conversation has become even more difficult.

'Well, I set up my systems yesterday and when I got online, and I did some deep diving. That's the great thing about India - bandwidth.'

'Archie! Cut to the chase - please.'

Meg is putting the kettle on and pretending not to listen. Ha! I swear that those ears have grown to three times their normal size - and they are swivelling towards me. She smiles and mouths 'who?' I mouth 'Archana' back, and she returns to her tea-making while giving an expert performance of someone not listening to anything that is being said.

'I started to find out about him - this young son who's now running that family business. By the way, I understand why you were cutting me off - sorry, I'll be more discreet.'

'Thank you. I think we've to be careful, that's all.'

'I agree.' Not so Meg, apparently. She has two mugs of tea in her right hand and as she leaves that room to take them back upstairs, she gives me a wink and raises her nightie.

To Meg, I say, 'I'll be right up.'

She replies, 'Good. Don't let it get cold - and I'm not referring to the tea.' And off she goes. This is an invitation that even after being together with her all this time, my body is telling me in a most obvious way that this is an invitation I should accept. And Archana is still at her most enigmatic.

'So, what's been happening. Have you found anything out?'

'Of course, I have. I did some snooping around. A lot of it is in Punjabi and Urdu and Arabic, so kudos to Google Translate, but there's so much email and social media traffic going around about this guy.'

'How does that affect us? Let me rephrase that. Does it affect us?'

'Of course it does. It's him. He's our guy. They hate him - Abdul and all the people who work for him, they've been sharing their complaints, their gossip without - I must say - much concern for the future. When they're angry, people seem to lose all sense of - I'm sure there's an English word for it - you Brits define that kind of word. Anyway, this man is the person who sent a team after Stephanie; he's tried to get me through his contacts in the Dubai government, and all this because he's after you.'

'How the fuck do you know all this?'

'Ha! Through Abdul, the assistant, the very unhappy assistant, Abdul. And this Abdul is at the end of his tether with his new boss. He hates him, he's being asked to do things that offend him, and he's shooting his mouth off in emails and Facebook to friends of his.

'Things are so bad he's planning to sell up everything and move back home - I think he's Pakistani - and in the meantime, he's been telling anyone who cares to listen all the reasons why he hates his new boss and how he thinks everything is going to come tumbling down because of his incompetence.'

'So, what's the connection? Why is after us - and why is he coming after me now?'

'Abdul's boss found out about you - probably via Stephanie - that was awful, Max, what happened to her, it was horrific.'

'Yes, and that's why I was so concerned for you.'

'I get that,' Archana continues, 'However, he found out, and this young boss decided to show how clever he was and kill two birds with one stone - I like that expression - Cambridge English taught me that - when he set off on a plan to take over the business of one of the larger Dubai crooks, that Janko Stanovnic you asked me about before, remember?'

'I do. And he's involved?'

'Abdul says this was when he began doubting the competence of his new boss because he deliberately targeted Stanovnic by killing his sister. There was a murder somewhere near you - a young girl was strung up over a lake, or something. Do you know anything about that?'

'I heard about it, yes. Meg mentioned it to me when I got home last time. That was him?'

'Yes,' Archana is in full flow now. 'It seems Abdul was offended by the way this girl was chosen. She was used as bait to get Stanovnic out of Dubai, so that Abdul's boss could take over his businesses. But Stanovnic's are really dirty businesses, drugs, girls - the worst - and Abdul feels that he doesn't want to be associated with that kind of stuff.'

'And you got all this information how?'

'It seems genuine, Max. So many threads to it. Five or six of the men who work for the organisation seem to be a bit old school. They don't like the way things are going either and they certainly don't like their new boss.'

'Where do I come in?'

'It's obvious, but Abdul's most recent correspondence made it very clear. The new man - his name is Hesham - you need to know his name, trust me. This new boss - he's a sheikh too and he now knows what happened to his family, and who was responsible for it. Do I need to make it any clearer?'

She didn't. It was obvious. 'No, Archie. I get it. What's this about two birds?'

'Here's the thing. And I think it's this that pissed off the Abdul man. Hesham thought he was being clever. He wanted to show what a brilliant strategist he was by having Stanovnic and you taken out at the same time. But he got angry over something and decided that he's going to start his own little war instead.'

I'm very concerned now. I've already had some guy attack Meg, and someone has been in my house walking around carrying an assault rifle.

Archie hasn't finished. 'His first plan didn't work because the man he tasked wasn't up to it. He came to your house but didn't get you. And this is what's been a step too far for the Abdul guy.'

'What has?'

'His boss's demands. The orders that Abdul had to implement. When his man couldn't get to you, it seems that Hesham stamped his little foot and told his operative to go after Stanovnic and then leave immediately. He now has other plans.

'And this is it - and why Abdul and his colleagues have had so much to moan about to each other. The new plans, plans that Abdul is now responsible for, take him and their business into entirely new areas. This business never was 'pure' in any sense, but what they are being required to do now is so toxic that it's got them all thinking of how they can get out and away from it.'

'And these plans are?' I think I know where this is going, and I can't keep this developing feeling of dread from welling up inside me.

'Hesham has sent a squad to take you out. A group of mercenaries is in the UK now - this is the thing that tipped Abdul and his colleagues over the edge, they are to take you out after you've watched them slaughter - his word - slaughter your family.'

I'm lost for words - and of course any romantic feelings I had towards Meg and how we might be spending the next few minutes have also evaporated. A squad? Mercenaries?

Is this my Karma? Yes, I deserve it. Live by the sword etc. But I won't let it happen. Whatever I've done, whatever I do has been my choice. I am ace at my form of moral relativism and feel perfectly happy in justifying my actions - to myself. My business affairs have always involved difficult and unpleasant choices, and while I know that most 'normal' people might disagree with some of the choices I've made, they've not had to make them, I have. Most, if not all of the people I've dealt with have been deeply unsavoury characters, and to a certain extent, I've done the world a favour by eliminating them.

None of this is any help to Archana, nor to be honest, does it justify the things that I've done while making my living. She's likely to be the next collateral damage, should Hesham be track her down, and judging by what I'm hearing, that may well be possible. I try to haul myself out of philosophical mode.

'Brilliant work, Archie. I need to ask, though. Can anyone trace you because of it?'

'I don't think so. I flew Air India, so I doubt that this Hesham or his people will have access to my ongoing flight from Mumbai. And I didn't buy a ticket to Pune until I reached India. Also, I paid for it in cash - rupees, not dirhams.'

'You've given me a hell of a lot to think about now, my dear. I've things to do and people to see. But I want to make sure that you are ok. How are you off for money?'

'That's the least of my worries. I'm fine there, thank you. My biggest challenge is my mum, actually. She knows I've had some problems - but she thinks they're with a lover or maybe I've been fired. Whatever it is, she's comforting me all the time with food. I'm putting on so much weight - she's feeding me too much.'

'It's a great worry to have, though,' I reply. 'As long as that's all for now, I'm happy for you. And with your new friend, Abdul, can you keep me up to date with him?'

'I think so. He's online all the time. Looking for ways to get out of Dubai, too. He wants to choose the best option. I believe he keeps his passport and visa - it's not being held by his employer, and he's quite proud of that. So, he's trying to work something out, transferring his money and so on.

'He'll resign his job and then he'll leave. He's an employee, so he does have certain rights in the UAE, and can leave the country quite easily. In the meantime, he's behaving like a little old woman, complaining to anyone who cares to listen to him, so yes, I think I can keep you up to date. Why, what do you plan to do?'

'Probably fire you for sexism, to begin with. 'Little old woman' how dare you!' Archana hears the smile in my voice and laughs back. 'I should send you some of what he writes. You'd think the same.'

'You're probably right.' I'm now assessing the real threat to my family - and to myself of course. Is there anything I could do about this Hesham guy?

I ask. 'Any advice?'

'Such as?'

'Not a clue.'

'Well, that's not very helpful, is it?'

And the truth is I don't have any idea about what I should do. But I don't want to share my doubts with Archana. 'It'll depend on what's going to happen here,' I reply. 'He's sent people to the UK, so this is obviously the next hurdle. Let me think about it and I'll get back to you. Any info you pick up, please send it immediately. This is a very important time for all of us.'

'Of course. And be careful, Frank. This Hesham is now boss of a large organisation. His people might think he's a shit, and he may be, but he's a powerful shit.'

'You're right, Archie, I do know. But you're safe for now, and I've been warned, thanks to you - so I can prepare. How good are your systems?'

'I've been very pleased by how quickly I've accessed all the information I've shared with you. So, surprisingly good, I'd say.'

'If it's possible, I'd like you to try and find out a little more for me.'

'What can I help you with?'

'This Abdul is involved in organising a team to attack me, right?'

'Apparently, yes.'

'OK. Can you find out more? Can you see if it's true to begin with, and if it is, is there any evidence, names, places - anything that would allow me to get a step ahead? I'm going to get my family to safety, but if I must confront these guys, I'd rather not do it face to face.'

'I'll see what I can find - I'll get on to it now.'

'Thanks. My house is as safe as I can make it, but only from burglars. It's not a castle and this is not the Middle Ages. I don't want to have to defend a siege. I'd rather be a guerilla - you see my point?'

Archana replies, 'Of course. You don't want to get into a battle. I've known you long enough, Frank. I know the way you work.'

'Anything you can get will help me out. I'd rather go for them than wait for them to come for me.'

'Got it! I'll find out what I can and get right back as soon as...'

'Talk to you soon. Bye!'

And I've no doubt that she will. In the meantime, I need to get my act together and marshal my resources, as they say. That won't take long. I do have weapons, and I know how to use them so that's a good start, and I've made the house as safe it can be from attack - although leaving the front door ajar seems like a strategic error, not to be repeated.

I also have Wojtek - and that's about it.

Equally, I'm hopeful, though not entirely confident, that if I can find out who's looking for me I can deal with them effectively. That will depend on their level of expertise, of course, but now I know what's behind all this, I realise the seriousness of the situation.

I'll move my family away from the house to somewhere safer, so I won't have to be worrying all the time about them if the house is attacked. Where exactly, is something I need to think about. Putting them anywhere may well involve danger for those looking after them, so I'm thinking that a hotel or a resort, somewhere with organised security, might be the best choice. That's top of the list now, finding somewhere to put the family - that and finding an excuse that will stand up to Meg and her sceptical mind.

And I'm going to have to be super-vigilant - making sure that nobody catches me by surprise.

And once again, my thoughts come back to Wojtek. I must set out this stall for him too. He needs to know much more that I've told him, so he can make an informed choice. I know he volunteered his services, and he'll be very useful. But he's got a new love now, and he's a guy who helps me out from time to time, that's all. He doesn't have any skin in this game. How much should I reveal to him before I think about holding him to his promise?

Now, my mind is already racing. What to do about Meg and the kids? The problem I have with Meg is that sometimes she's simply too smart for my own good. She knows, always knows when she should be on alert: witness her recent foray downstairs while I was talking to Archana, so whatever plans I make must allow for that.

When I get back upstairs, Meg is waiting for me. She's switched on the TV and is watching some news programme. She knows, I'm sure. Well, I'm not sure what she knows, but her mind has moved away from the implied promise of a little while ago, and to be frank, so has mine.

I flop into the bed next to her - flop being the operative word - and we both prepare to take in the current cataclysmic world event, but no, it's a segment with a celeb pushing his book, Celebrity Knitting for fuck's sake! At least this means that we turn to look at each other, and this is the only motivation I need. And I go full honest with her; there's no other way as she'll see through any attempt to disguise what she's going to ask her to do.

'Something's come up, and I'm worried for you and the kids.'

'Oh, so you're going to tell me the truth now, are you?'

Told you, didn't I? There's no point in trying to fabricate something here, she's just too smart. She continues, 'It's been weird for a while, hasn't it? That incident at the spa? Whatever you and Wojtek have been up to in the basement?' The basement. So, she knows about that too? 'And you, you've been preoccupied with something, Frank. Better you let me know, eh?'

While in principle, I agree with everything that Meg has said, going 'full honest' with her might well mean that I end up by losing everything, including her. I don't think Meg knows what my main work involves, but as I've said, if she did find out, she'd leave me - she'd be off like a shot.

You realise, don't you, that she's a good woman married to a bad man? I know that, and I also know I don't deserve her, and I can't let her know everything as it would fracture our relationship beyond repair.

What I do want, and this has recently become more and more obvious to me, is that I want to redeem myself in her eyes, and also in mine. I want to give up everything that I can't admit to - especially my wet work - as soon as I can. But this new issue must be resolved first.

I'd no expectation at all that someone would come looking for me in this way; I thought I'd covered my tracks well - I worked hard enough at it after all. But now? If I do make some sort of confession, I'm still going to have to filter lots of it.

If I admit everything, neither of us will be equipped to cope with the aftermath. I decide that for better or for worse, somewhat ironic as we're talking about my marriage here, that she has to have enough information to see that getting away from the house is a good idea, but she simply can't know it all.

So, rather than confess everything and make myself hostage to fortune forever, I decide to shift the blame. I'm far enough down this track anyway, and there's no moral high ground left for me to try to preserve. 'It's come as a bit of a surprise, love. One of our business clients has taken offence and he's turned nasty.'

'Nasty enough to attack me?' It's a fair enough response.

'No darling, that wasn't him. That thing at the spa? It was an over-enthusiastic action - some chap who worked for him using his initiative. It was a mistake.'

'Maybe, but I'm still sore. Who is this client - and why haven't you called the police?' She's relentless. 'Is this person British?'

And this is the moment for me to go all in. 'No, and that's the problem. He's one of Archana's clients, not mine, he's taking it out on me because he can't find her. And that has led - by extension - to you being threatened too. So, I need to fix it.'

'By extension! Frank Blain, I'm not one of your dozy customers. I don't need a word salad from you. Why are you lying?' She turns and looks me straight in the eye, then snuggles close and says, 'Tell me what's going on. If I know, I can help, can't I?'

The temptation is overwhelming. Tell her the truth, you idiot. She'll understand. And that's the problem - she probably will understand all too well, and then I'll be completely fucked. I'll lose my wife and my family, and I'll probably lose a lot more if Archana is right, and there's a team that this Hesham guy has sent over to do me harm.

Once again, I have to continue vamping till ready, 'If I knew the detail, honestly, I'd share it with you. I'm trying to find out from Archana what made this man so angry. She's reluctant to say - even though I've promised her that whatever she's done won't affect our relationship.'

'Whatever she's done? You told her that?'

'Of course, we've worked together for a long time. I trust her.'

'And I love you, Frank. But sometimes I think you must be a fuckwit. Whatever she has done has had an angry man chasing after you -

and 'by extension' me and the kids. You've let Archana put your family at risk, and you trust her?'

I know I'm pissing against the wind, but I must defend this, so I come in a little more heavily. 'Apart from your unpleasant language - please wash your mouth out - you've got most of the picture. I don't know what's happened, yet. Until I do, and based on our long working relationship, I'm prepared to believe that whatever Archana's done has been a mistake or a misunderstanding.'

'Our family is being threatened.' Meg is dealing with me as she might with a particularly stubborn piece of mechanical equipment, pushing all the levers hoping one of them might work. 'It's obviously much more than an error of judgement, isn't it?'

I concede. 'It seems so, yes. But until I find out...'

'Until you find out? You're allowing our family to be put at risk?'

And there's the 'in'! I take the cue immediately. 'No, we've got to make you and the kids safe so I can get to the bottom of it. I've an idea of what we must - what Archana - must do, but to keep us safe while it happens, it would be a good idea if you and the kids were to get away from here for a few days - just until I know exactly what's going on - let me concentrate on sorting it.'

'But you don't know what you're sorting out.'

'I think I do - at least, Archana tells me she has a plan, but I don't want to take the risk with you and the kids - we don't want a repeat of that spa incident again, do we?' Too patronising? You think? I'm doing my best here. It's not good enough for Meg.

 'Frank - are you telling me not to trouble my pretty little ...'

'Nothing of the sort! But, if you are all here, I'll be concentrating all my energies on you, looking after you, keeping you safe. I don't think the house is well suited for that as we're isolated, and we can be seen from too many vantage points.

'What I'm suggesting is that we take the kids somewhere where you are among people, somewhere secure and safe. Only for a short time, but that would set my mind much more at rest, and I can concentrate on helping Archana. If I solve her issues, our problems will go away too.'

'Where do you have in mind?'

I play what I hope is my Ace. 'Center Parcs! It's secure, it's full of people and the kids will love it.' There's a Center Parcs about an hour away from the house, a few miles beyond Penrith, and we've been there a couple of times before. I'm thinking this is a brilliant suggestion, and I'm looking at Meg and trying to work out if she is in sync with my brilliance.

And she is. Perhaps not with the brilliance part, but she concedes that getting away with the kids might be a safe option, especially as a place like Center Parcs has its built in security. In our experience, it is so secure that even people who have bookings find it difficult to get into the place.

'Frank, you know, that seems a sensible suggestion.' I hear the words come out; they don't quite compute, but I understand that this time I have got my way.

'That's great. Let's get you all booked in - and me, I'll want to be there too.'

'I thought you...'

'Yes, but if I get this problem sorted quickly, I'll want to be with you and the kids, won't I?' I'm obviously over-egging the whatever-it is, but this is a small victory, and it will make the choices that I must make, much easier. They'll free me to move away from preparing to defend my castle and my family within it to my much-preferred mode of operations, that of the guerilla force, by far the most effective combat mode for a small army - in my case, an army of two, assuming that Wojtek is still up for it. If not, a very small army of one.

Meg agrees. And she knows it'll be an easy sell to the kids because they love Center Parcs. I also know that she's dubious about the whole affair, but frankly, that's OK with me - as long as I can get her and the kids away PDQ, I can begin to focus on my real problems. As it is, my fingers are crossed in the hope that nothing stupid happens while the family is at home.

Straight to the internet - Friday is arrival day and, although they pride themselves on their high occupancy rate, today they have a villa free for us - and it's a top of the range one. I sort all that out, payment and so on. I arrange to print off the details as I won't be going, and Meg will take the paperwork with her.

I pack a holdall too, a holdall that I won't be taking to Center Parcs - it'll be in our packing but will come back with me. Fleeces, two woolly hats, a couple of groundsheets, the sort of camping stuff that I could explain away to Meg if I need to. I'm not sure what's going to be happening, so I've gone for the boy scout option - 'Be Prepared'.

All this done at about three in the morning, so when I get back upstairs, there's even time for a couple of hours snoozing and cuddling to take the edge off things. And surprise, surprise, as I get back into bed and spoon up with Meg, I discover that there is an edge that Meg, after only a little encouragement, gently relieves. Happy days!

Later that morning, I give Wojtek a call. He picks up immediately. 'Hi, Wojtek. Are you busy? Good! Just a quick one. You know this issue we have? Yeah. I don't want to say too much over the phone, but it's kicking off, I think.'

'Are you ok?' he replies. 'You want me to come over?'

'No, I don't think so, not yet anyway, but I've received some information that's troubling me, and I wanted you to be aware.'

'Information?'

'Yes, something's developing and I need to make some plans - for me and for the family. I thought I'd let you know.'

'I'll come over, boss. If we need to do stuff, it's better we talk about it.'

'I'm not sure it's a good idea. There's a risk now that wasn't there before, and now you're building your love nest in Ambleside, I'm concerned ...'

Wojtek laughs, 'You're a crazy man, boss. Love nest - ha ha! She's great and we're very happy, but these other things are also important, are you talking about the friend that visited us?'

'I am. Although he may not be alone this time; we think he's other friends who may well want to come around - quite soon, I think.'

'Other friends - more of them?'

'So I'm told.' I want to give him more detail but I'm a bit twitchy about this conversation. 'You know what? I think it would be a good idea if we did have a chat. Shall I come over to you?'

I know how he'll reply, and I wait for it. 'No, I'll come and see you - I don't want you stealing my woman.'

I didn't see the last part coming, but Wojtek is laughing. 'I can be over in an hour or so, is that all right? I can come now if you ...'

'No, there's no rush. I need to sort the family out too. I've plans to make, and I'm not quite sure how they will work out. See you later.'

Forty-nine

Max and Melissa were released from hospital a few hours after the devastating explosion that had killed the four police officers and their suspect. The miracle was that because the target, the police Transit van, was over a hundred yards or so from the hospital itself, there were no other serious casualties.

Max had a cut in his scalp that needed butterfly stitches; Melissa, who'd not been physically injured, her Kevlar vest having performed so admirably, was suffering from shock and couldn't concentrate on anything - apart from the moment she and Max had shared immediately before the explosion. Focusing on that helped her to settle: her confidence that there was a connection that needed to be nurtured was helping her to come to terms with the aftermath of the incident itself.

The damage around the hospital was mainly limited to vehicles hit by falling debris and to windows blown in by the force of the explosion.

A dozen or so people, medical staff and patients, had received minor injuries from flying glass. They'd been observing the exodus of the young man with his police escort a little too closely and were caught when the windows shattered.

Debesh, who'd responded to Max's request, was told on his arrival that the two of them were being kept under observation and that he might need to return later.

Knowing their own vehicle had been destroyed and that they'd no means of getting back to Ambleside, Debesh, who's flat was only ten minutes' away from the hospital, went home to wait for their call. He was happy to do so as this meant some bonus time for him. He checked in with Helen who was still up in Ambleside, and he picked up his daughter Ellie from school. Together they enjoyed a long and meandering walk by the river and followed that with an ice cream treat at a local café.

When the two of them eventually did arrive home, Helen was there to meet them. She too had finished work early, there being nothing else to do but wait for Melissa and Max to get everyone up to speed. The family had tea together, and Debesh started to read a story with his little girl when the inevitable phone call came.

Debesh closed the call. 'They can leave now. They're both OK - Max has a slight head wound and they were concerned that Melissa, DCI Mordaunt, might have had shock. I'm to take them back up to Ambleside. I won't be long.'

'Why can't Uniform sort out their transport?' Helen suggested.

'You know, you're right,' Debesh replied. 'It never occurred to me. That is one brilliant suggestion. Let me clear it with the boss.'

Max was happy for Debesh not to act as chauffeur on this occasion; indeed, he suggested he would be far better off enjoying a quiet evening with his family. There was plenty of detail for them to get stuck in to but now was not the time; tomorrow was another day. Also, Max felt that the journey he was about to have with Melissa might well have a slightly different atmosphere to it, maybe one that he was not quite ready to share in a car with his closest subordinate.

Opening the door of the police vehicle as it arrived to pick them up, and gesturing to Melissa to take a seat, Max referred to the two of them as walking wounded. Melissa picked him up on that immediately saying that didn't apply to them and that they'd both been very lucky.

He and Melissa were going back to Ambleside, and now as a couple. But once again, his tin ear - that almost unwavering ability to miss the beat in such situations, had almost done it again.

That same tin ear had already blown potential relationships in the past. Nervous or ill-thought-out remarks were to blame, such as the one he'd just uttered. Circumstances like this were difficult for him; he'd never found it easy just to chat. He'd even been on courses where they talked about ice breakers and ways of initiating and maintaining conversations. He'd a mental block; this whole area was lost to him.

But now he was aware that making fatuous remarks or worse, wisecracks to fill the space in the silence would work against him, and he needed a different approach, a non - approach. He said nothing as the vehicle moved on to the Kendal by-pass and picked up speed on its way to Ambleside.

It was Melissa who broke the silence, but not by speaking. She took Max's hand in hers. Careful to be discreet, her hand staying out of the eyeline of the young PC who was driving them, she continued to face forward in her seat, her facial expression and her body language suggesting nothing more than that of a professional person being given a lift.

Max, however, was burning. Holding Melissa's hand, feeling her thigh close against his, and the implication of what might happen when they arrived at their destination had his mind screaming possibilities. He was fifteen again, his hormones whizzing, and adventures that he'd no full understanding of, looming.

They were a couple of middle-aged adults. They'd both been round the block. At least, he had. He didn't know much about Melissa's past life - yet, but he knew that a woman as attractive as she was, and more importantly as intelligent too, would have a back story.

For Melissa too, knowing that Max had escaped serious injury and that their minds and thoughts were apparently now in sync, a new landscape was now opening up.

From the moment she'd first met him, thoughts that there might be something had never been too far beneath the surface. He was irascible, seemed to be insensitive on occasions, but there was something almost magical in the way he fascinated her.

The most important factor was that he'd not come on to her. He'd never made a play, never tried to inveigle or influence her. Their one fumbling chance at taking things further when they went out for a drink together had been a disaster that they both acknowledged. It was how Max dealt with it that was so impressive, Melissa thought. No annoyance, no passive-aggressive changes in his behaviour, he'd been quite chilled about the whole thing.

Yet, and this was something she knew, and it was something more than feminine intuition, the flame still burned. Max still wanted her, and she was almost certain that she wanted him. She'd realised he'd neither the strategy nor the tactics to make it work. She would have to help him, and in the simplest way of all, she did.

'Dinner at my place?'

All Max had to say was yes. And that he managed to do without ballsing it up.

Fifty

It's about eight in the evening when I get back from dropping Meg and the kids at Center Parcs. As I'm leaving and before they've had anything to eat, the twins insist that they get straight to the pool to show us how well their swimming is coming on. I take that opportunity to make my exit, and on the way back I contact Wojtek.

'I'm sure we'd be better off not trying to deal with this matter from inside the house. What do you think?'

'I agree. Is it sitting birds?'

'Sitting ducks.'

'Right. Two of us can't defend an attack, can we?'

Got it in one. 'So, what do you suggest?' I've my own ideas, but I also want his input. He's got military experience. Mine has always been a question of needs must.

'We'd better get to the house quickly, though,' is his first response. 'Even if we're not going to stay there, we need to get weapons. Otherwise, we're fucked.'

'Have you a weapon with you now?' I'm concerned that if we do go to the house, the bad lads may already be around, and we'd be helpless.

Wojtek replies, 'I've a pistol, that's all.'

'Me too,' I respond, 'but that's better than nothing. I'm twenty minutes away. Meet you outside the Swan?' The Swan is a pub on the outskirts of Grasmere and on the road that both Wojtek and I will be using. We'll be arriving from different directions.

'See you then,' he replies. 'This could be fun, boss.'

I must admit I'm surprised that he's seeing this as fun, but I've always known how capable he is. If I were in a fight, he'd be the first person I'd want to back me up. Maybe he does enjoy the opportunity? I confess that on occasions, I've enjoyed - maybe enjoyed is not exactly the word, but I have obtained a sense of satisfaction from some of my own projects.

Given the information that Archana has found, the risk we're both taking is that the bad lads, our adversaries, are already tooled up and waiting. I've no way of knowing what the state of play is here, but now my family is safely out of their reach - I'm crossing my fingers here, of course - I can now concentrate fully on the next stage of this mission. As it's existential for us, I should concentrate on it, shouldn't I?

We have to take the risk. What I'm proposing is that we'll get quickly into the house to free up any weapons we'll need. If we can get away with them, we'll be in a much better position to handle the near future.

Wojtek meets me outside the Swan, and he parks up and gets into my G Wagon. 'Hi boss. This is a surprise. I didn't expect to be going to war.' He laughs as he says it, but I get the truth of what he's saying. I'm dragging him into danger. He came over from Poland years ago to make a better life for himself – so he could remit money to his family.

Given that it's now possibly a better idea for young English men to go over to Poland for a better life, I'm surprised not only that he's still here, but that he's up for assisting me in such a dangerous endeavour.

'I see you've got your weapon,' as he shows me it, a modern pistol, a Sig Sauer from our armoury in the cellar at home. 'Good choice, Wojtek. Mine too.' I open the glove compartment and show. The two are identical.

'We need more, boss. These won't be enough. What should we do now?'

I have my plan. It's crap as we have to do this in plain sight, but I can't think of a better one. 'We'll go down to the house now, get as many weapons as we can and get away.' I've thought this through already so I add, 'It will be safer to go in from the front as there are fewer places where a sniper can hide.'

If they have a long gun, we'll still be in trouble, but the back door would be too dangerous to use as it opens on to woodland. It's where the kids have their leaf slide, and where there are countless places nearer to the house allowing for weapons with a much shorter range to be used effectively.

Wojtek agrees. 'Fine by me. Do you have binoculars, boss?'

'I do.' I'm quite chuffed to be saying this. Bonus points for me.

'Good,' he replies. 'Then let's do it this way. We'll drive up close to the front door, then you take both guns and binoculars and take up position - that's what you say right? - take up position by the tree.'

He's referring to the large chestnut tree some five yards from our front door. It would give me excellent cover while at the same time the binoculars will give me a reasonable chance of clocking potential danger. You see what I mean about Wojtek? He's a natural. He sees things in ways that elude me.

He continues, 'I'll go to the cellar, and I'll bring up weapons. I take maybe two journeys.'

'Let's do it!' Then, to be sure, I ask again, 'Are you sure this is OK with you?'

He says, 'Start the car.'

It's only a couple of minutes' drive down to the lane that leads to my house. We observe as much as we can, carefully looking in all the vehicles on Broadgate as we make our way.

Driving up to the house, rather than go straight in, I decide to take the right fork in the lane fifty yards or so from our gates. This is a very rarely used lane, but if I were going to attack the house from the rear, I would probably use this route to drop off men and weapons.

There's no sign of anyone. The only person who normally uses this lane is Wojtek when he does his logging - oh and me, when I use my digger to dispose of bodies. Not that I've done this on a regular basis - just once. But I regret that I did such a stupid thing as it was this that's caused all the trouble.

There being no obvious signs of anyone around, we turn the car around and make our way back down the lane, this time turning up towards the house. We're both hyper-alert now, looking for any sign that someone might be waiting.

The gates read my number plate and open as we approach them, closing behind us. We pull up in front of the house and I half turn the car around, backing the rear door of the G Wagon up to the steps leading to the front door. This is the most dangerous part, as we've no real cover to use. We're visible from many angles, but as I've said, it would probably take a trained sniper with a long gun to be assured of a hit.

I make my way to the chestnut tree. Rather than stand behind it, I try to make myself as small a target as possible. I can't lie down as grass and ferns make it impossible for me to see anything, but I crouch and raise my binoculars with my left hand. I've my own gun in my right and Wojtek's pistol tucked into my belt.

I survey the field that stretches away from me over what used to be a tennis court to some trees and then the village. There's nothing to suggest danger, not even a dog walker, and that's a rare occurrence as another name for our drive, one that I've given it, is 'Dogshit Parade'.

Meanwhile, I hear Wojtek open the door and move inside. He's obviously learned his lesson from the last time as he's made sure the door closes behind him.

I wait, scanning the area for signs of anything that could worry us. A few minutes elapse while at least a part of me waits for a bullet to come my way - a most disturbing feeling, my nerve ends jangling with anticipation.

I'm startled by a sudden noise, but it's Wojtek. He opens the front door and quickly offloads a large bag - I've no idea what's in it, what he's chosen, into the back of the G Wagon.

'One more journey, boss. OK?'

'Fine, Wojtek. Make it quick, though. I'm not happy hanging around here.'

'You're loving it, boss.' It's a joke and not well received. 'Get a fucking move on - please!' My response still doesn't take the smile away from his face as he disappears once again.

Ten minutes later, we're back at the Swan and in the lay-by next to the car park. I've chosen to park there, my thinking being that if we were to sneak into some really quiet place, away from everything, we'd immediately arouse suspicion from the first car or person to pass by. Here, we're a couple of blokes having a chat - and sorting out our weaponry - 'Nothing to see here. Move along, thank you.'

I have to say that I wouldn't like to be taking us on. I've been careful to set up my armoury very well, if I say so myself. I had no real idea when I started this collection, but over the two or three years I've been working on it I've acquired some pretty powerful stuff, mostly guns - machine pistols, assault rifles, handguns and the like. Wojtek's second journey brought the ammunition, an equally important element in this equation, obviously.

Of course, my collection is not known to the authorities - it's not even known to my family. Some years ago, I did make an application to have a shotgun licence. I would have the locked cupboard and everything, but my application was rejected on the grounds that I couldn't justify having a licence. I didn't hunt and I wasn't a farmer. Apparently, the Hunter boots and the Barbours don't automatically qualify you, either.

We start to select what we think will be appropriate to secure our near future. The key to our choice of armaments is our main tactic - not to defend the house from within, but to attempt to attack any intruders from vantage points away from the house.

I'm pleased to see that Wojtek has backed up the theory with practice - two Sako TRG 22 A1 Finnish sniper rifles, each fitted with a AAC Cyclone suppressor.

I've used an earlier version of this rifle before, and it's perfect. It's lightweight, beautifully made and incredibly accurate. The suppressor is going to come in handy too, I guess, as if anything does go off soon, we don't want the whole of Grasmere jumping up and down at the sound of gunfire.

Also, we might have an additional advantage as the suppressor can reduce the flash of the gun being fired - 'every little helps', as someone once said. The weapons come tidily packed in what the manufacturer calls a Logistical Pack. It's really a natty briefcase, but it means that everything is immediately available.

My only concern is that the rifles are sniper rifles. The bolt action isn't too good in any kind of close-quarter firefight, but hey, is that going to happen? I hope not.

It's a given that we'll be using the handguns we're already carrying. Ever since the house was visited by a scary looking guy carrying a big gun, both of us have felt the need to be armed, despite the risk involved in carrying a weapon here in the UK - it is frowned upon.

We both have our Sig Sauers - I've sometimes used a Glock, but overall I prefer the Sig. Wojtek has brought four packs of ammunition for the Sigs, two packs for each of us, and one pack each for the Sakos. I haven't asked him, but I'm assuming, as I think he has, that if we have to use all this ammo, we're fucked anyway. What's going to be most important is any surprise we can take advantage of.

'So,' I ask Wojtek, 'do we have a plan?'

'We should have.' His gnomic reply states the obvious with a strong Polish accent. 'You're right not to defend house from inside, Boss. I think we should each take up position where we have good view, but not too close.'

'Agreed. Maybe one of us by the chapel, he can keep an eye on the back of the house, and deal with anyone who comes down from the woods.'

We call it the chapel, but in its life it's been a billiard room, a kids' playroom and now we use it to store stuff. I've been meaning to make more positive use of it for some time, but now I'm welcoming the fact that it offers a great vantage point - and a place where I or Wojtek can remain unseen.

It's at the back of the house about twenty yards away and looks over the lawn. The kids' leaf slide is also near, although they gave up on that madness a while ago - much to my relief, and that of Meg too - although for different reasons.

'So, the chapel. That's one of us. And the other?'

'Mmm.' Wojtek replies, his inner gnome obviously working overtime. 'What do you think about line of sight? Is that what you say?'

'Yes, ours or theirs?'

'Ours. Do we have to see each other?'

'Oh, I get you.' He's quite right to raise this. Although the chapel is a great place for one of us, keeping an eye on the front of the house is a different matter altogether as there is no obvious cover for one of us to use.

'We'll use our phones,' is his answer. 'Not ear buds but plugged in. I can be at the chapel, and you can keep an eye on the front.'

'From where?'

'I have a thought.' And he leaves it there, a gnome in overdrive, obviously.

As I've no idea at all when any of this might happen, I suggest to Wojtek that we go and have a meal somewhere. He agrees, muttering something about 'condemned men' and then pointing out that we've not thought about any kind of provisions. If we are going to stake out the house for a while, we won't be eating our ammunition, so we need something more substantial.

We decide to go straight into Ambleside and do a Tesco shop. There's also a fancy restaurant nearby that I've been meaning to take Meg but never got round to it.

Our evening becomes quite civilised as we sit down together for what turns out to be a beautifully prepared meal. We've got our vehicle parked up across the way - I chose our table carefully, so I can keep an eye on it - now that it's fully loaded with what looks like a madman's assorted picnic choices and a very handy arsenal.

Just as I'm asking to settle the bill, I receive a WhatsApp message. It's from Archana. 'Check bomb explosion nearby. Probably linked. Abdul has told the team to press on immediately.'

Bomb explosion? That girl certainly knows how to spoil a party.

Fifty One

The news of the missile explosion had reached Dubai within minutes. As he left the devastation behind him, and on his way to the motorway, Hassan had called Abdul, his immediate boss.

'I did what you asked, sir, but I had to use the missile. It was the best option as I couldn't get close enough.' This from the man now responsible for the deaths of at least five people - including one of his team.

'You used the missile?' Abdul hadn't expected that. He'd bought it only because it made the original weapons' deal sweeter. Suddenly very worried, Abdul needed to find out more so he could prepare the defence he would now need. As he began, Hesham, hearing one side of the exchange, rushed over to him and snatched the phone.

'You did what? Who is this? What did you just do?'

Hassan repeated what he had just said to Abdul. 'I fired the missile, sir. It hit the target and destroyed it.'

'A missile? What missile?'

'I was supplied with the missile along with the other weapons, sir.'

Hesham is confused. 'I didn't authorise the use of a missile. Where did you get it?'

Abdul intervenes, trying to mollify his boss as sees the signs of an impending explosion. 'It was a hand-held SAM, sir. I authorised it. I thought you'd approve. It was a free bonus and when I bought ...'

'You thought I'd approve of starting a war. Where did this happen?'

'It was outside the hospital, sir - where our man was being held. It was the only option; our man couldn't get close enough to guarantee a hit.'

Hesham's rage is just building. 'Couldn't get close enough? He's a trained sniper, isn't he?'

'Yes, sir, but his weapon doesn't have the range - it's for close quarter work. The assumption we were making was that we'd be getting close to the enemy.'

That does the opposite of calming Hesham. His rage builds and at first he takes it out on the inanimate objects quietly sitting on the nearest desk. A glass desk ornament made for Watani, a popular civic programme celebrating all that is good about the UAE, goes straight through the screen of his very expensive TV. Next, those swinging metal balls, so popular as 'executive toys' destroy a light fitting as they make their way over to the other side of the room. Not yet content with the mayhem he's creating, Hesham throws an office chair at Abdul, catching him on the shoulder. Abdul cowers behind his own desk while his boss, now completely unhinged, screams obscenities at him.

Suddenly, Hesham stops. He takes a breath and in that moment, he remembers he has a man on the line who hasn't yet been cursed out. Now he focuses on Hassan, thousands of miles away in the UK who, far from being congratulated as he expected, has evidently made his boss very angry.

'Listen to me, you fool. Remember your family is here and so far, you have done exactly the opposite of what I wanted you to do. This was meant to be a quiet mission. If I had sent a marching band to do the job, they would have created less noise than you have. The military, the police - all the security services will now be looking for you.

'These are your orders. Do exactly as I say and do nothing else. Join the two men who are waiting for you.' He snaps at Abdul, 'Can I assume that they are still available?' Abdul, still covering his head with his hands, nods a yes.

'Get to the house where our target is and dispose of him and his family immediately. Do not wait a second more. Do you understand me, you idiot? The next few hours will determine all your futures. If you fail me again, I'll have you all destroyed!'

Hesham didn't wait for a response. He closed the call and turned to his assistant who was still trying and failing to make himself invisible.

As a motivational speech, this was not exactly Henry V at Agincourt material. Hassan was now left to his own devices without any help from his boss, and Abdul had experienced the full-on anger of a man whose authority, who's right to make any demands at all was now seriously in question. The only person who felt he was still in charge was the ridiculously over-entitled young man himself, now strutting around his office, at any moment likely to pick up some object to hurl at his assistant.

'What are you going to do about this, you idiot? This is your fault. I never authorised this - you never asked permission.'

'Sir' Abdul had to try to extricate himself. 'The situation called for it. You made it very clear what had to happen. The missile was added to our weapons free of charge - I thought that you'd approve, and our man decided it was the only option.'

'Why didn't he use his rifle?'

Hesham's ignorance once again. The authorised weapons were for close combat operation. He'd expected the team to invade the house, kill its occupants and leave. He'd not thought of equipping them with anything that could guarantee a long-range hit. Hassan had been told it was vital his captured colleague be taken out. He had no option.

The Starstreak missile was perfect for the job, and it had been deployed successfully. Yet, this ignorant, incompetent young man was now putting the whole mission at risk by behaving like a spoilt child. He should have been congratulating his man, offering him assistance to complete the task. Instead, he was setting up the whole mission to fail, and Abdul knew that if it did fail, it was not

Hesham who would be blamed. He tried again.

'With respect, sir. You were insistent that this part of the mission had to end in the way that it did.'

'By using a missile? A missile When did I say - how many people were killed?'

'We think five altogether, sir. The other four were police officers.'

'This gets worse.'

'It had to be done that way. Otherwise, it would have been a disaster. The whole of the mission might have been compromised - if Mohammed had been taken into interrogation - I couldn't take the risk.'

'The person who's taking the risk is me, not you, you clown. These decisions are mine to make. Mine!'

Abdul didn't need any further prompting; the decision had been made for him. 'Final straw', 'Last chance saloon', whatever the local cultural cliché was that went through his mind at that moment, he knew he could no longer work for this man.

He'd accepted the abuse and his infantile behaviour for too long. This, he thought, was just the precursor to the eventual unravelling of Hesham and his businesses. With him in charge, there was no future, and no point in waiting any longer. Abdul's money was safe, he'd made sure of that, he always had his passport with him and his visa allowed him to travel to and from the UAE. He would do it.

'Sir. I will leave now.' He quietly walked towards the door.

'You'll go when I tell you to go!'

'I can no longer work for you.' And, standing as tall as his five foot two frame allowed him to, he moved towards the door, walking out of the room in as dignified a way as he could muster.

On reflection, it wasn't particularly dignified as he couldn't help but hunch his shoulders in anticipation of something being flung at him. However, once out of Hesham's office, but not away from his screaming and shouting, he didn't dare wait in the elevator lobby. Instead, he ran down three floors of the emergency staircase before he felt confident enough to take the elevator down to the main foyer of the Emirates Tower.

The exit strategy he now embarked on was not some random choice - his decision-making process, even in times of stress, was different from that of his mercurial boss. He'd planned his escape carefully as he knew it eventually had to happen. The signs were obvious long before this recent crisis, but he wasn't quite sure when he'd need to put the plan into action. Now was the time.

Rather than use the Metro, he jumped into one of the cabs lined up outside Emirates Tower and rushed straight back to his room in Bur Dubai. Within a few minutes he had added one or two precious items to his already prepared go bag. He then he took a second cab up to Jebel Ali - almost the full length of Dubai city - and at a cost that in his previous life he would never have contemplated. There, he boarded a bus to take him to Abu Dhabi.

His plan was to stay there with friends for a few days before taking a flight from Abu Dhabi to Lahore. He hoped this would confuse Hesham and anyone else who cared to look for him. If it worked, he could retire as a wealthy man and more importantly, he would never have to endure such humiliation and distress again.

While relaxing on the peaceful, air-conditioned two-hour bus journey to Abu Dhabi, and now in more of a reflective mood, Abdul couldn't resist taking up his iPad and telling the world that his now former boss had lost the plot and was completely out of his depth managing his organisation.

He was careful to give no indication of his own travel plans, but on his various social media platforms, he felt obliged to say that he would no longer work for a man who'd cast adrift his own men in the UK. He added that his madman of a boss had made impossibly unreasonable demands of them too.

So that they could return to their families in Dubai - his men had been ordered to attack a British man - and this is what had tipped Abdul over the edge, they were to kill the man's family too. This was to be done immediately, and without question, or the whole team and their families would pay a terrible price. Abdul told his readers - whoever they were - that he would have no part of it.

A curious by product of social media seems that people post outrageously indiscreet things, and they openly give secrets away that possibly might be better kept secret. People are watching, others are listening, and bots and web crawler apps provide made-to-measure gobbets of information for others to act upon, and not only in ways that the originator of the post might have intended.

In this instance, more important and far more relevant than any web crawler or malevolent bot, was a tiny, modest, but extremely alert young woman in Pune, India. She'd set up her own tracking systems for exactly this kind of occasion, and as soon as Abdul's resentful and angry posts began to flood his pages, Archana was on to them.

She quickly WhatsApped everything to Frank Blain, the one person in the whole world for whom this was more than gossip. This was gold-plated, get-out-of-jail-free information to him, the kind of detail that allowed the strategist in Frank to plan his next steps.

He now knew 'what' was going to happen and he had a much better idea of 'when'. What he didn't know was 'who', but Archana's timely assistance had helped. Whoever they were, they were professional. They had a mission - were highly motivated - and he now knew they and their families had been threatened, as had Frank's.

Fifty-two

Archana's messages arrive as Wojtek and I, coming to the end of our meal, are scoping out the house and discussing the various ways we might defend ourselves when attacked. There's urgency now, but it can't diminish the sense of excitement that's generated by our having to look at my house, so much a vital part of my life, in an entirely different way.

I wouldn't be having a dessert now: indeed, if Archana's messages had come a few minutes earlier, I might well have lost my appetite, and that delicious steak I'd just enjoyed might have been sent back uneaten.

Simply put, I'd never considered the house as a target, or as a position to defend. If I had, I might well have chosen to live somewhere else, as it would be impossible to defend from a determined enemy. All that money I've spent on internal security assumed that someone might try to break in.

But I was now too aware that there were other ways in which we could be attacked. The house was surrounded on almost all sides by places where people could observe - and if necessary, fire on us from a distance or mount an attack.

What I'm now forced into doing has reset my view of the house, although I still love it dearly and I'll fight to protect it and my family. Archana's messages have set the time frame; Wojtek and I will prepare as well as we can.

My question to her about how many people this Hesham guy had sent over received a disappointing reply. She mentioned a team, but a team could have any number of members, couldn't it? I wondered if there was any other way I could find out. Could we track the team somehow? Was there information anywhere that would give me an answer?

So, I try Archana again: 'This Abdul chap? Can you speak to him - or message him? Do you think he knows anything about this team?'

Her reply offers a possibility. 'He seems to chat a lot. I don't know if he restricts his conversations - I've observed them, that's all. I've never joined in on any, though.'

'Could you give it a try, Archie? He might be in a sharing mood. After all, it seems he's quite bitter about his boss.'

'I'll have a go. I'm connected to his posts. Let me see what I can do.'

Even at this time in my life - I sent my first email way back in 1996 (Pompidou Centre, Paris), so I've always had the use of it - I'm still astounded that I can chat to Archie in Pune about something going on in Dubai while I'm scoping out a possible attack on my house in Grasmere.

She gets back to me within ten minutes, 'You're a magician, Frank. I'd never thought about contacting him directly. Abdul wanted to talk - to anyone. He can't stop. I guess it's all been building up in him for so long. One of the team was killed - that explosion I mentioned. I don't know why - but it was another member of the team who was responsible. He took him out. That angered Abdul and that's why he's left Dubai.'

'So, one of the team is down?'

'Yes, the other team members are angry with their boss too - and there's bad blood with the team itself, because of that explosion. There are three of them now - there were four originally. Abdul says his boss has lost control. He threatened the team and despite what's happened, he's insisting they come for you immediately.'

More intel than I could have dreamed of. Three coming for me. We are two. The odds aren't too bad after all. I pass this info on to Wojtek as we continue our planning. All he does is smile and suggest we have a coffee.

Fifty-three

It's been a strange day for Max so far, and so he imagines, for Melissa. They've both been to work, Melissa in and out of the Ambleside office, Max, once down to Kendal to check how the clean-up at the hospital was going and to check if any further intel had been gathered. They've used their computers to share internal memos, situation reports and to keep each other, as well as Helen and Debesh, up to date with what is going on. Nothing to see here, nothing at all.

But that's not how it is. The workday is coming to an end, and with it has arrived an entirely new beginning. Max won't be driving down to Morecambe tonight, and he's pondering whether he should mention this to Debesh and Helen along with all the other stuff he's been sharing.

After enjoying their first morning coffee together in the large, comfy bed at Marigold Cottage, Max and Melissa were pleasantly unembarrassed in each other's company. Considering Max's leaden-footed excursions of the recent past, this was of some significance, and he congratulated himself on how successful the strong and silent approach had been.

He'd deliberately refrained from the wisecracks and the self-deprecation, and it seemed to have worked. He felt more at ease with himself, and of course with Melissa, than he could ever remember.

Their conversation had lasted long into the night, as had their generous, but gentle lovemaking. Both had brought them so much closer together and had allowed many of the barriers that troubled them to fade away.

Max had also learned more about Melissa's past. While she was aware of much of Max's previous romantic history, thanks to that otherwise disastrous evening in The Golden Rule, so far she'd been reticent about her own. This was not deliberate on her part; the opportunity had simply not presented itself.

She too now felt more comfortable with Max and wanted him to know more. After all, her experiences had shaped her. She was who she was because of them.

'It was a long time ending,' she began. 'A little over three years.'

'Three years ending?' Max was confused.

'I think that now, yes,' she continued. 'It was bound to end, but it took that long. It's why I've been so apprehensive since. He was a beautiful man to begin with. Lawyer - I met him on a case. I was recently promoted to sergeant, and he seemed perfect for me.

'We moved in together almost immediately. And I was all for it, Max, I really was. But then...' She faltered, not quite sure how to continue. She put her coffee mug on the bedside table and moved more closely to Max, holding on to him more tightly than he had expected.

'What happened?' Max was aware there was much more for her to say, and it was troubling her.

'He began to resent my success. From early on, I was surprised as I thought he was such a high-flyer. But no, he plateaued very quickly, and I didn't.

'It took me ages to work out what was going on; he seemed to be accepting of my career, but there were always barriers. When I woke up to it all, it was obvious - he was trying to control me.

'I understand that now, but I didn't then. I'm strong, competent and I thought I knew myself very well. It took me ages to work out what he was doing. His own success became less important to him than my failure. It was so difficult to understand, and so completely pointless too.'

'Were you married?'

'God no. The saving grace. We were going to - at the beginning, but somehow the idea of building a relationship together took second place to its politics. My interpretation, but it caused us to split. He became more interested in my failure than in his success.'

'And it took you three years to see that?'

'Don't be difficult. Everything is easier when you look back at it. It's obvious even to me now. But then? I'm supposed to be an intelligent woman. I've a great career. I've had an AC from the Met up here telling me how important I could be to their plans.'

'You didn't tell me that.'

'You knew I'd met my AC - at Sharrow Bay. I told you all, remember? But there's a lot I haven't told you. Stuff that I couldn't - still can't share.' She turned her face towards him, 'even though I want to.'

Max was trying to unpick the tightly wrapped package he'd just received. So much to question, so many routes to take. Melissa continued.

'There are matters to do with the cases - our cases - that I'm not permitted to share, I'm sure you'll understand. But I want my life - everything to do with me - to be as open as possible. I want to keep nothing from you.'

'You're a highflyer. It must be difficult for you, in a relationship, I mean,'

'Yes, it is. And it may well be for us. You've got to be prepared for that too. It's what killed off things with James and me. My career in the Met was working out well - for me. It simply didn't work out for James. It crushed him.

'Eventually, I began to see what he was doing. He was sabotaging me, actively preventing me from developing. I missed appointments - James would 'forget' to tell me. He'd make it impossible for me to go on a course as he'd suddenly become ill. He became - I used to call it beige - you know when everything is filtered so there's no colour, no life - no point.

'Whenever I suggested a new anything - a trip here, a party there, you know, the kind of things that couples do naturally - the answer was always no. Our lives together became separated - and then parallel, I know it sounds pathetic, but I just didn't see it until I saw it.'

'Saw what?'

'His behaviour, and the pattern that was developing. Our friends, my friends, oh, and my mum. I began to see he was driving a wedge between me and the people who were important to me in my life. He never had a good thing to say about anyone - then there were implied threats, offensive remarks...'

'He was grooming you. Coercive control?'

'Both. Exactly. It was.'

'You?' Max was shocked. Of all the women he'd ever met, this one was the least likely to be forced down that route.

Melissa sensed that in him. 'Yes. Me. And I know that now. He was grooming me, but I was blind to it for ages.'

'And then?'

'There was an incident The last one. That finished us. It all became clear, and I left. Ran away. Back to living with my mum.' Melissa left the incident, whatever it was, unexplained and Max didn't follow up. He was beginning to understand the coping mechanisms she'd developed. Rather like his own, he concluded, and continuing to play the 'strong and silent' card, he waited.

Melissa continued, 'They say there's a level playing field, there's no discrimination and everyone has the same chance to succeed. I'm not really moaning, Max, but with all that stuff going on in my personal life, it was a very difficult time.'

'But you're through it now, aren't you? Look at what you've achieved.'

'Yea, professionally, I'm doing well. But emotionally, I feel I was so naïve for so long - this is why I've found it so difficult with you.'

'With me?'

'Yes, with you.' She held on to him even more tightly as she said, 'From the first moment it was obvious, wasn't it? You and me? I think I'm frightened. I'm so reluctant to allow myself to go down that road again.'

'You don't have to.' He felt her flinch slightly. 'No, really. Not with me, you don't.' Max wasn't entirely sure how he should proceed, but he tried, nevertheless.

'I know. At least, I think I know. It's not meant to sound trite, but if it helps, let me at least tell you you're safe with me. I'm not that kind of guy. I've no interest - I'm probably incapable of doing it anyway, but I've no wish to control you, or prevent you from ...'

Melissa smiled. 'I know that's not you. I want you to understand, though. There's always going to be pressure, professional and personal. The question is will it be worth it?'

'I see this differently.' The conversation was leading Max to help him solve a similar dilemma of his own. His history of failure had always been there when the possibility of a new relationship loomed. It had shown itself in his preliminary skirmishes with Melissa, but she was a prize worth pursuing and he didn't want to be deflected by his past failures. He wasn't going to allow it to happen with this woman.

'This can work,' was Max's reply. 'We can - and we will make it work. OK?'

'I hope you're right. Yes, we can make it work.' Heart and head were hard at work here, and Melissa allowed the heart to win for now. She was with a man she probably - no possibly - could love; a man whom she knew could love her too.

There were questions further down the line that would have to be answered and that's where the head rather than the heart might edge ahead. But for now, for this very precious moment, she would simply enjoy being with this wonderful man.

Fifty-four

We've driven part of the way from Ambleside to Grasmere and parked up in a lay-by at the opposite side of the lake from our house. Grasmere's not one of the larger lakes, more of a tarn. The American writer Nathaniel Hawthorne described it as a 'pocket handkerchief', which I still think is a bit harsh.

We've walked a couple of hundred yards to where we can see the house looming over the vale. With my binoculars, I've a good view of it and the surrounding trees and undergrowth. We can't guarantee we'll see everything - or indeed anything, as of course, highly trained men will know how to approach a target without being seen - but we don't have many options. We've both agreed that this is better than moving up to the house in daylight.

Wojtek has decided for both of us - Polish National Service seems to have awarded him a stripe or two; he's certainly the commanding officer here. Providing we don't catch sight of any strange movement; we'll move just as it gets dark. He'll take up a position by the chapel and once again, I'm to be consigned to the front of the house.

'It makes sense, Boss. But not by the chestnut tree this time. That's too close. The best place is over by the rock, the one past the tennis court. You'll have a better view of everything.'

I'm looking through the binocs as I demur. 'If they come up the drive, I'll be too close.'

'Naa, it'll be perfect. Trust me.' And he smiles that smile again. The position he wants me to take up is about fifty yards from the house, down near a rock where the kids used to play, that is before they discovered the joys of their leaf slide.

From there, I can cover the main entrance to the house and the side that faces the lake. From the chapel, Wojtek will have a view of the rear of the house, and that's the side we think the bad lads are most likely to use.

I don't normally think of Time in any philosophical sense, but as I'm sitting at the other side of the lake and contemplating what I'm expecting to happen over the next few hours, it strikes me. Etched on the very rock where I will soon rest my weapons is a sign of just how insignificant all this chaotic activity is. What's happening to me is life and death, but only to me. The universe is rightly unconcerned.

I've been prompted into this unusual mode because of this rock, and something Meg and I found. A few years ago, we were sitting together on the rock and looking up at the house. There was moss covering the surface, and for some reason I'd peeled it away. I was amazed to find what turned out to be a set of neolithic cup rings there, carvings into the rock itself, left by prehistoric travellers, possibly on their journeys to the axe factories in the Great Langdale valley not far from here.

Archaeologists think that these cup rings were an equivalent of today's holiday snaps, a familial reminder of a particular group of people passing by that spot at a certain time and added to with new cup rings as their families increased. And we're talking 4000 years BCE here.

Now I'm going to take up a few minutes of the universe's time to settle what in cosmic terms is a petty squabble.

After a quiet, and as you've possibly gathered, a somewhat reflective hour or so, we decide it's dark enough for us to make our way to the house.

This is the moment of greatest risk, and we've argued the toss about this next step more than any other. How do we get into position? Do we park away from the house and sneak up to it - or down to it from the hill behind? Or do we brazenly drive up to it on the assumption that nobody's waiting?

If we choose the second option and drive up to the house, we're fucked if anyone is waiting for us as we'd be toast in an instant. On the bright side, however, if there's nobody there, it'll mean that we don't have to lug our stuff up - or down - to the house.

We choose the first option. It's the more tedious, but it's safer. We park about four hundred yards away and quietly make our way through a gate and on to a field that leads us up to the house. As far as we can see, there's nobody around, not a jogger or even a dog walker - and we're normally infested with them.

About halfway up to the house, we split up, Wojtek to the right and on to the rear of the house, me to the left and towards the rock which is to be my sentry position for the immediate future. Neither of us sees anyone, and just after we split, we confirm that our WhatsApps are working.

I get to my rock and look around. By now, my eyes are accustomed to the dark and I don't see any movement anywhere. Even the village, only a few hundred yards down the hill from me is silent, almost in anticipation, although I doubt very much that anyone, especially me, has even the remotest idea of what might happen.

I set out my own stall. My handgun is the Sig - my first choice, so I'm happy. I also have my Sako sniper rifle - Wojtek and I have agreed that on balance, they are the best choice we have in my armoury. (So they should be, as each cost over twelve thousand quid - plus suppressors.) We also have spare ammunition, a warm blanket, a fleece each and a thermos flask.

I connect again with Wojtek on WhatsApp, just to check. As I do, I notice that I've just placed my weapons on the cup rings that troubled me before, placing my pathetic set of manoeuvres into a context that continues to disturb me.

I'm in that reverie when Wojtek breaks it. 'Ok, Boss? You can hear me?

'Perfect - loud and clear,' I reply. We're using WhatsApp because we've good phone reception around the house and WhatsApp is reasonably secure. So, if necessary, we can use video and text, messaging each other if talking becomes impossible for whatever reason. Sounds like a plan, but as we all know, plans are just plans.

And our plan is simple. Fingers crossed that the bad lads are not already in position and waiting for us - it's that good a plan - we've taken up our positions. Although I can't see Wojtek, where we're both located gives us a view of over 90% of the area surrounding the house.

After ten minutes or so, I conclude that we've got here first. Wojtek agrees. 'Be patient, Boss. It's gonna happen soon. I can feel it.'

I wish I could feel it too, but I can't. What I'm feeling is annoyed, and this is alien to me. In my own work, I'm normally juiced, tightly wound up for the moment; my nerves so stretched I can hear everything, see everything with such clarity. Here, I thought it would be the same, but it's not. I'm not as alert as I expected to be. Maybe it was the meal? Whatever, I'm surprised and I'm having to force myself to get motivated. This is crazy. It's not a project, is it? It's not some random person I've been asked to remove. It's my family. If I'm not up for this, what the hell is the point of anything?

Fifty-five

'Are you all in position?' In his Emirates Towers office Hesham el Hashimi was also using WhatsApp. He was in direct touch with the three remaining members of his team and expecting them to carry out his very specific orders.

His now former assistant Abdul having left the scene - that departure was a work in progress that Hesham would deal with later - Hesham had decided that he would play a more active role in the mission than he'd previously intended: he would command it.

'Answer me. Are you in position now? Do you hear what I am saying? I demand that you answer me now.'

'We're in radio silence now, sir.' The reply was guarded. It was one professional talking to a non-professional, obviously, but when that non-professional was a wealthy over-privileged idiot, it begged a question or two.

'I insist that you answer me now. That is an order!' Hesham was becoming more and more frustrated. He wanted them to open the video on their phones. He wanted to see what was going on. He needed to see Frank Blain and his family as his men carried out his all-too-specific demands.

'Yes, sir, we are on our approach. Out.' The connection between Dubai and the UK was terminated.

The senior of the three remaining team members had taken that important decision because his so-called boss obviously had no idea of the potential danger he was creating for his own men. The was not a YouTube prank. People were going to die here.

He'd already lost one of his team, his death demanded by the insistence of the young man who was now putting the rest of the team at risk. He disconnected his WhatsApp and then quickly contacted his two colleagues. 'Don't take any calls from our lord and master. I've told him we're on radio silence. Keep it that way.'

Now shut off from everything that was happening in the UK, Hesham's anger exploded - and was immediately taken out on various inanimate objects that were available in the room. Abdul, who would normally have been the recipient of Hesham's excess, was no longer around, and no other member of his staff was anywhere to be seen. Hesham compounded his own misery by fruitlessly trying to get back into contact with his team, but as he couldn't reconnect, they had to continue their mission without his valuable tactical and strategic advice.

Military service is compulsory in the UAE. Had Hesham served, his input could well have been welcomed by the men he'd selected for the mission. However, this young man with his position of significant financial influence, had chosen to evade serving his nation so successfully that he hadn't the faintest idea of what he was requiring his men to do.

This was a video game to him, something with which he was very familiar. After all, he did score well on shoot-em-ups 'Shmups' - although this was his only qualification to lead his men into a possible firefight.

Reality was different. The three men were approaching the house. They'd decided to attack from the rear, descending towards the garden through the woodland that surrounded the lawn. It was an unusual choice for men trained in the deserts and wadis of the Middle East, and not without its own challenges.

Crawling through the undergrowth might have seemed a good idea in principle, but the fallen trees, the accumulation of twigs, branches and leaves - and the fact that everything was much drier than most Lake District summers expect, meant one thing: noise.

Wojtek, located by the chapel at the rear of the house and closest to the woodland, became aware that something was moving. In happier times, this would have been a deer, possibly a wayward sheep, but these were not happy times.

He'd camouflaged himself as well as he could, and his weapon was not only suppressed, but covered too so as to minimise any flash.

He trained his rifle, its telescopic sight allowing him to scope the area from where he'd heard the sound. Nothing. He waited. The sound was too close for him to safely contact Frank. He decided to wait and see.

***

Stuck by the rock, I'm starting to feel a bit chilly. Despite the fleece and my woolly hat, the temperature has now dropped. I've seen and heard nothing for ages, so I decide to check with Wojtek.

'Anything Wojtek?' No reply. 'Hello Wojtek. Can you hear me?' Again, nothing. Then some crackling, definitely crackling, but he's not responding. Is something going on?

This is my problem. I've never had any military training, and I've never been on any kind of manoeuvres that could have given me a set of 'next things to do'. I fell into my line of work entirely by accident, and although I've built up a pretty impressive CV - not that I'd want anyone to see it, of course - I've always been a singleton, a lone operator. I've always worked for myself, never had a boss, don't take orders very well, if at all, and well, you know the rest.

And Wojtek has told me to stay put. It's as near as he's ever come to giving me an order, but 'stay there, boss' was an order, wasn't it?

I'm worried now. I'll give it a little longer, try him again in a couple of minutes, although I'm very tempted to go up to the house.

***

Wojtek had been right: it wasn't a deer. From his position near the chapel wall, he could now see the man twenty yards away, perhaps a little further. His first thought was to take him out.

He saw the barrel of the man's gun; it was trained on the house, not the chapel, meaning that so far, his own position hadn't been compromised. But the others? What of them? Wojtek decided to wait; he could keep an eye on this one for a little longer. He heard Max in his earpiece.

Fucking stupid idea WhatsApping! Phones have screens. Screens light up in the dark. The signal wasn't as good as they'd hoped it would be, either. He'd have to reconnect - again. He tried; his eye taken off his target for a moment, and that's all it took for him to see another threat - one much closer to him.

While glancing down towards his phone, his peripheral vision caught sight of a second man less than ten yards away - much too close for him to think of contacting Max. He had to do something - now.

Slowly, very slowly, Wojtek moved his weapon, lining up the Sako on the nearer target and squeezing off the shot. A loud hiss, but no flash. Straight to the head and the man slumped forward. Immediately he reloaded and lined up on his second target.

The first man had heard the shot, maybe even the bolt action on Wojtek's rifle too, and broke his cover to look around. Wojtek fired a second time, catching his target somewhere in the upper body, but not stopping the man from firing back.

A bullet crashed past him, missing him by inches and ricochetting off the chapel wall. This guy was using a suppressor too; his weapon discharging with a similar hiss, but its flash lit up the sky for a second.

A second shot from Wojtek finished the job. Again, to the head: the bullet entered the forehead and smashed through his skull.

Wojtek reloaded again - this rifle was the wrong choice. He should have chosen an automatic as he needed speed. He glanced around, searching for another man. There were three, weren't there?

That was Wojtek's last thought: so banal, but sadly so correct. There was a third man. He'd come down the hill directly behind the chapel and heard the sound from Wojtek's first shot. He confirmed his position when he heard the bolt action followed by the hiss of the subsequent shot. He hardly had to move.

His weapon was automatic, an H&K, also fitted with a suppressor, and it spat its stream of bullets into Wojtek. The Pole had no chance.
***

Shit! I'm still trying to call Wojtek and now I've just seen a flash from behind the house - and there goes another. I know he told me to stay put, but is something's going on, I should be there. After all, it's my war we're fighting.

I decide to have a look. I admit I don't have any military training, but one thing I am good at is sneaking up. It's how I've made my living for the last fifteen years or so.

I ready my Sako, pushing the Sig into the waistband of my trousers. I've two more clips of ammo for each weapon and I find a pocket for those.

Making my way to the south-facing wall of the house, I catch a repetitive hissing sound, and I'm aware of maybe six - could be more - flashes. That's not a Sako. That's a semi, or maybe a fully automatic weapon being discharged. It sounds like it's coming from twenty or more yards away and round the corner from where I am. Maybe the woods - or by the chapel? If it's by the chapel, that's where Wojtek has stationed himself.

I've no choice: I must find out what's going on. I get down very low to peer around the corner and towards the lawn at the rear of my house.

The sight that greets me is one which in theory I might have wished for. A man carrying a sub-machine gun is warily walking over my lawn from the chapel. He's looking for something in the woods a few yards away. I see it too. It's a body, a man slumped forward. I can't see his head, but I do see his gun.

I can't tell what kind it is, but its barrel is pointing skywards. The man uses his own weapon to nudge the body in front of him; he's checking for a sign of life, I guess. He then moves a few yards closer to me and goes through the same ritual with a second body.

Wojtek must have killed two of them Then, fuckwit that I am, it dawns on me. This guy has killed Wojtek, and he must think he's killed me because that's the only reason he'd be walking around so carelessly.

That was the longer set of flashes I saw. He's carrying an automatic SMG, maybe a Mac or an H&K. The burst I heard must have been the one that killed Wojtek. Bastard!

If Wojtek and I had thought this through better, we wouldn't have gone for sniper rifles. The kind of close-quarter weapon that the guy has just used against Wojtek should have been our choice. My mind is racing now, and part of me is weighing up whether Wojtek was compromised because of the bolt action on his rifle. That must have slowed him down.

Meanwhile, the more alert part of me has decided my next step. No messing. I take aim at him and squeeze off one shot. It hits him in the chest and down he goes.

As he drops, he turns to where he thinks the shot has come from. He tries to raise his weapon to respond, but although he's not dead, he seems badly damaged. He is speaking, although I don't know what he is saying, He's calling to me.

Then he speaks to me in English. 'I think you win. Come over here, sir.'

Not being born yesterday, I choose not to take that journey, but I'm in a quandary as to what I should do. I have to make sure that this guy won't trouble me again, but I'm also desperate to see Wojtek. He may be lying wounded; I know he'd be focused on getting to see me were the roles reversed. But what to do? That guy has a weapon that can spray a whole magazine in seconds. He could cut me down before I get within a few yards of him.

'Throw out your weapons!' I think that would be a good start, so I try it.

No response. I repeat my request. Again, no answer. 'I said...'

'I heard you sir. I can't. I can't move. I am dying.'

His voice is soft. I can feel he's in pain, but I've no idea if this is a feint or not. I try another approach.

'Who are you working for? Who asked you to come over here to kill me?'

'Kill you?' He is surprised. 'I thought the other man ...'

'He was my friend. You were sent to kill me. I also hear you were to kill my family.'

'I did not approve of that. I am a soldier, not a murderer.' His voice is certainly weakening and I, a murderer, not a soldier, am quite familiar with that tone.

I repeat the question: 'Who gave the orders?'

'I think, sir, you know the answer. The young sheikh in Dubai, the son of the man whose family he believes you killed. It was he who ordered...'

His voice falters. 'Sir, I am in pain. I'm finished. My colleagues are dead; there is nothing I can do. He can't punish me or my men, but he will punish our families. He is sure to do that.'

He stops talking and now that I'm highly attuned to his voice and to his breathing, I can hear that he is slipping away.

I decide I do need to get closer to him. He must be out of the equation before I can get to Wojtek. I stand and take a step forward. Big mistake. The bastard lets off a volley of shots, one of which clips my shoulder, and I fall back to the ground. It's not a serious wound, but it's a complete breach of the protocol I thought we'd set up between us, and that was too close for comfort.

I don't now know how dangerous he still is. Obviously, because he missed, he was flailing as he fired, but he nearly got me.

I fire into him from my prone position. I reload and fire again, once again cursing our choice of a bolt action weapon. I see the body jolt as each shot hits. Then I wait - maybe two or three minutes: I need to be sure. Very carefully and watching for any signs of life I circle towards him, going way out to the left before approaching him from behind - my gun trained on his body all the time.

There is no movement at all. That guy won't trouble me again.

I leave him where he lies, after having removed what turns out to be an H&K, a pistol and two grenades. I look at the other two bodies. In each case, their heads have been Wojtek's target, and he's hit them full on. I leave their weapons where they lie as now, I must get to Wojtek.

The burst of flashes was the burst that killed Wojtek. He's been hit by upwards of a dozen rounds, his head, shoulders and upper body are almost unrecognisable. But it is Wojtek, my friend Wojtek, the man now lying where I should be lying. This is all because of me and my life choices, nobody else's.

And once again, I've put the people closest to me at risk. First Stephanie in BVI, then my own Meg at the leisure centre - Archana in Dubai, and now Wojtek. If I ever do get out of this mess, I'm going to make a vow of - something. I don't know what that something is, but this can't go on. If I'm to even pretend to live a normal life, I've got to dig myself out of the charnel house that has appeared around me.

***

And 'digging myself out' has turned out to be literally true. It's now just after six in the morning, and I've been working all night, trying to clear up the mess of my very own battlefield, not that I'm proud of it. Four casualties including Wojtek, genuinely one of the kindest and most thoughtful people you could ever wish to meet. Now dead, and a bloody mess because of me and my ego.

Obviously, I couldn't leave things as they were. So, this is what I've spent the last eight or so hours doing.

First, I waited to see if the battle that we'd just fought had attracted any attention. It hadn't. When I'd satisfied myself there were no more bad lads around to worry me, I looked around trying to decide how to clean up the mess. May main challenge was what to do with the four bodies that now were a prominent addition to the garden's features.

I would have appreciated having Nip with me. I could have done with the company, but he was holidaying at Center Parcs - and thinking about that gave me a reminder, I must extend Meg's stay for a few more days as I'm not going to be here.

And I never thought I'd be thanking my kids, but last night it was their leaf slide that turned out to be such a boon for me. As you know, they'd connected their sleds to a kind of pulley system allowing them to transport stuff from the house up to where they had made their camp.

Using their leaf slide made it so much easier for me to move the four bodies, one at a time, from where they had fallen up to the woodland area at the very top of the garden, a place where normally nobody ever goes. It was the same area where I'd previously buried that Saudi family - the very family that was now the cause of all my woe. There appears to be some truth in Karma.

My little tractor with its digger attachment was only about fifty yards away from the end of the leaf slide, so I used it to dig a trench and then I laid the four bodies and their weapons into it. This was not an easy job, and I was knackered by the time I'd finished.

My last task was to return to where each of the bodies had fallen and attempt to clear up as many traces, blood, body parts - particularly in Wojtek's case - as someone had emptied a whole magazine into him.

I got out the garden hose and I hosed down each of the areas, but there was so much blood. I thought of praying for rain; if I was lucky, nature could then take its course and after a few days the garden would look less like a butcher's shop at the end of a busy day. Of course, with Wojtek gone, I'd no longer any access to the super-capable multi-talented helper who could have made my problems disappear in a trice. Hope is pretty much all I had left.

I did my best to clear the mess, but I've got to say that in the light of day, and given any kind of clue, some bright spark could easily work out what had happened.

Sadly, it's equally likely that if that same bright spark were to get up to the top end of the leaf slide, the track I've made to the newly created ditch might also offer some clues.

But now I've no choice. It was a knee-jerk response, and yes, it might have been better to load the bodies into the G Wagon and find a place to dump them. I did consider that, but I think I made the right decision. After all, the bodies of that Saudi family haven't troubled anyone while they've been up there - except me and my paranoia.

But the bottom line, and the real reason why I decided to bury the bodies as quickly as I could, is that I've no time to spare. I've one last task to do and that's going to involve me being away for at least two, maybe three days.

And that means that I've got to straighten things with Meg - God knows what I'm going to do there - and I've travel arrangements to make. So, the idea of my driving around the countryside looking to fly-tip four bullet-ridden bodies lost its appeal quite quickly.

I'm stuck with the decisions I've taken and I will make them work. I've been in more difficult situations before - I haven't - but I'm adopting the power of the positive here, as it's all I've got left.

Back in the house, and after a long shower and some serious thinking, I'm clean and I'm focused. I've a small wound on my left shoulder where a bullet nicked me. It hurts, but it's not bleeding too badly, and I'm hoping it won't need medical attention. I've bandaged it pretty well, so fingers crossed.

Now, I've things to do. First, down in the cellar and into the safe room, I offload my weapons and ammunition. I wind up the computers and have a look the security footage of last night. On the positive side, the CCTV system works extremely well.

The whole event was recorded, every moment of it. Reluctantly, I decide to wipe the lot, although I'm very tempted to put all the material on to a flash drive and keep it for later. However, the nowadays rarely seen Mr Sensible in me decides that another stupid idea is not required just now, thank you, so I wipe everything.

I lock the safe room and go back upstairs as I have a bag to pack, and I need to get my act together. I open my iPad and go online and book an Emirates flight from Manchester to Dubai for tomorrow.

I'll travelling business class, meaning that a limo will collect me from here to take me to the airport. Now I'm going to get some sleep. The limo won't arrive for a few hours, and that bottle of Lagavulin on my nightstand is waiting for this very occasion. I'll work out what to tell Meg and the kids tomorrow morning. For now, before I completely fry my brain, I just want to get some sleep.

Fifty-six

Debesh was in a cheery mood as he welcomed Max. The sun was shining; Helen and he had made the trip to work using their time wisely to plan the holiday they would soon ee taking, a couple of weeks camping in France.

At the beginning of the holiday discussion some weeks ago, Debesh hadn't been at all keen on the idea. He was a city boy, and his move to what he thought of as the country was made entirely because he wanted to be with the woman who'd stolen his heart.

But Helen had been on camping holidays with her family since she was a little girl, and she dearly wanted Ellie to follow in her footsteps.

'She'll love it, Debesh - and so will you.' And that had been the theme for weeks now. Slowly, she'd drip-fed the idea to Debesh, selling its features as benefits just as if she was selling him a timeshare apartment. And, because he was a man and still in the thrall of a beautiful woman, he fell for it.

On the journey this morning they'd agreed to go ahead. Debesh was in a good mood with himself because he'd only been huffing and puffing about the camping holiday. Wherever they went would be perfect - as long as he was with his girls. Helen, Ellie and their happiness was all that mattered to him now.

So, there was extra motivation to get their cases wrapped up. There were still loose ends, but as Debesh was feeling so highly motivated, he wanted to spread a little stardust on his boss. Quite a challenge, but you never know.

'There's been lots of movement today, sir.'

'Make my day, Debesh,' Max responded in a toe-curling impression of Clint Eastwood. 'Movement of what and where?'

'We've information now that there was a team sent out from Dubai, and they may well be here in Cumbria.'

'How did you get that intel?'

'From Helen, sir.'

Helen explained - she though it would be better than having Debesh mansplaining for her. 'I contacted people who use airport and flight databases. We were looking for single men arriving in the North of England from Dubai. Our problems all seem connected to Dubai, so it made sense.

'It's not too difficult to filter departures from Dubai and arrivals in the North of England. Scotland too, as it turns out. We can trace at least four men who would fit the profile. It's not an exact science, but these men are all UAE citizens, and they arrived, two to Manchester, one to Glasgow and one to Newcastle, all on the same day.'

'More of an inexact science,' came the gruff reply. No stardust had yet landed on Max.

Debesh joined in. 'We know there are things happening here that are connected with Dubai. Stanovnic for one - and the first death, the one at Rydal caves.'

'I grant you that,' Max's still less than enthusiastic response, 'but why send a team here? Stanovnic was dealt with and there's nobody around now who's connected with him, is there?'

Helen was the first to reply. 'I think there has to be, sir. This didn't all happen without a reason, without a target. You remember our first conversations? You said that the girl's death at Rydal was a signal. We've not found out who the signal was for, have we?'

'It was for Stanovnic.'

'Mmmm. Maybe, but I'm not so sure. I think there might be something else going on.' Her voice became almost conspiratorial as she continued. 'And we've had a senior officer from the Met working with us on the case. Do you mind if I ask?' She addressed her question directly to Max, 'Has the DCS given you any information - over and above what you've already shared with us?'

If this was 'les majeste', it was done with a smile and totally without guile. And Helen was right to ask, as Max knew full well. Put like this, he could hardly deny her request.

'I've heard nothing to substantiate this, Helen, but you're right, and it makes sense. There is something else going on. Melissa, DCS Mordaunt, has said as much. I think she's shared everything she can with me. And that does beg a question. I'm sure when she receives this new information, and well done on that, by the way, she'll help us moving forward.'

Debesh intervened, 'So there is something, sir? Is that for definite?'

'We've had lots of discussions, and having a DCS up from the Met meant we haven't included the NCA in our investigations at all. She also met her AC from London too, didn't she? So, it doesn't take a genius to work out that something is afoot, but I've not kept anything material from you.'

'I wasn't suggesting you had.'

'No, I know, Debesh. But for clarification, we've all wondered why a London DCS would be sent up here. However, there is one piece of information that I've not shared, and which might turn out to be relevant.'

'Oh, go on, then, what is it?'

'It's a sin of omission - I didn't deliberately hold it back: it's to do with Stanovnic. Border Force let him through, even though there was a red flag against him.'

Silence. Both Debesh and Helen thinking this through. This was new to them, but more importantly, and although its import was beyond their respective pay grades, neither of them needed to say that if

Stanovnic had been allowed to enter the UK, maybe there was an agenda in play - and they weren't privy to it.

'So, there is something going on?' Debesh was frowning, still trying to compute what all this meant.

'Whether it's still going on, whatever 'it' is, is a moot point. The DCS is still here, as are we. So, we'd better justify our continued existence.'

Debesh pushed a little further. 'But you have a personal relationship with the DCS now, sir. Doesn't that give you any insights?'

Wordsworth looked at his DS. A good man, a truly generous man with a wonderful spirit, and he knew he was right, absolutely right.

His response: 'You and Helen have both a personal and a professional relationship. Do you tell Helen everything?'

'You know I don't - you know I can't, sir.'

'Exactly. So, let's move on with the information that we can use and leave speculation to others. By far the best way.'

The atmosphere had turned prickly with Helen and Debesh wondering why Max had withheld the information on Stanovnic, while Max was reflecting on his new relationship with Melissa. Could he really handle being intensely involved with someone who was bound by the nature of her work to keep him out of her thinking - even when they were both on the same case?

The reverie only lasted a few moments. The office telephone rang and Helen, being nearest to it, answered.

Helen turned to Max. 'It's for you, sir. A Miss Bath, Miss Marjorie Bath.'

Max turned to Debesh. 'Do we know a Miss Marjorie Bath?'

'We certainly do sir. You remember - the lady who found Stanovnic's sister at the caves?'

'Of course! Miss Bath. I do remember. I'll take the call, Helen.' He moved towards the desk, switched on his professional smile and said, 'Good morning, Miss Bath. And what can I do for you?'

Miss Marjorie Bath was the elderly lady whose original discovery of Christina Stanovnic flailing above the pool at the Rydal caves had begun this whole journey. Max now remembered how touchy she'd been about the use of her name, how she had insisted in being referred to as 'Miss Bath' and not 'Marjorie'.

Max and Debesh had spoken briefly to her at the scene - she'd insisted she wait for them to arrive, but was clearly suffering from shock, and possibly hypothermia. Max had dispatched a young WPC to take her home - promising to meet her later that day.

When Max and Debesh got to Grasmere to take her statement, both men were struck by the profound way the incident had affected her. She was very frail and in her middle seventies and coming across the sight of that young woman as her life ebbed away from her had had a dramatic effect.

As the two police officers sought and failed to take her statement - the process had to be repeated some days later - Miss Bath was almost catatonic in her responses. She was pleased that the police had kept their promise, but beyond that there was little that either Max or Debesh could glean from their conversation. The woman had been traumatised, and nothing was going to get the image of that young girl out of her mind except perhaps, time.

Now, listening to her as she spoke, Max knew that time had partially done its job. This was an entirely different person. She was alert, articulate and with, so she believed, a message of great importance.

'I'm pleased speak to you again, Detective Chief Inspector. I appreciated your kindness on that day, and I'm sorry I couldn't be more helpful.'

'It's entirely understandable, madam. You'd witnessed a traumatic event.'

'I certainly had. And I'm much better now. I did try to help the girl, and that was all I could do. I have to say that I still feel some guilt that I wasn't successful - maybe if I'd come across her twenty years ago?'

Miss Marjorie Bath was seventy-six years old and lived in one of the large houses on the Red Bank Road out of Grasmere. She'd lived alone since her mother's death over twenty years before, rattling around in her draughty old house and refusing every suggestion that she move to somewhere more comfortable - and warm.

The image of the girl had stayed lodged in her mind and it visited her every day and often during the night. The guilt associated with that image weighed heavily too. Could she have done more to help the girl? Had she tried hard enough to save her?

Despite the many assurances she had received, both from the police and from people in the village who had soon found out about the incident, Miss Bath couldn't find a way of excising those memories from her mind. And as she had nothing but time on her hands, she had plenty of that for reflection and was not happy in herself.

She'd tried to displace the memories by thinking differently, and by deliberately forcing herself to get out from her house to do some serious walking.

Her twelve-year-old Labrador bitch had always been her walking companion and despite getting on a bit herself, she still enjoyed the daily walks that she and her mistress took, mostly around Loughrigg Terrace, but sometimes over towards Easdale or Silver Howe.

It was this morning's walk that had occasioned the phone call, and Miss Bath was delighted that she got straight through to DCI Wordsworth. This was a man whom she trusted - although he obviously had a grumpy side to him - she remembered how short he had been with her when she mentioned his surname.

'I thought you should know. I don't know if it's relevant, but I was concerned enough to want to mention it to someone, to mention it to you, actually.'

Max was already on his reserve tank of patience; he still couldn't understand why people weren't more direct. He decided to move things on.

Just as he was formulating his next phrase, Melissa appeared. She was all smiles having brought coffees and Danish pastries for all from The Apple Pie, the local bakery.

'Ah, Lady Bountiful has arrived. Good morning, ma'am.' Debesh was first to avail himself. Grabbing a coffee and a pastry for himself and one for Helen, smiling and thanking Melissa at the same time, he said, 'The DCI is talking to the lady who discovered the first body - the girl at the caves.'

'Do we know why?'

'Not yet, ma'am, the boss has just picked up the phone.'

All three listened as Max tried to develop the conversation. 'I've some colleagues with me now, Miss Bath. With your permission, I'll put you on speakerphone so we can all hear you. Do you mind if I do that?'

'If you wish. I've no objection. Yes, I'm happy with that. Shall I tell you what I saw?'

Max looked around at his audience, rolled his eyes in frustration and answered, 'Yes, if you would be so kind.'

Melissa was tempted to slap him, but the old lady didn't pick up on the sarcasm, or at least, if she did, she motored straight through it.

'It was on my walk this morning. My dog and I - you've met my dog, haven't you DCI Wordsworth?'

'I have, madam. I remember her well. You were saying?'

'Well, we decided that we might take a walk up to Silver Howe as it was a pleasant morning. We set off, and I don't know if you know, but after the cattle grid, you come across a large house up to the left. There's a family living there, I've often seen them, but today there was nobody around.

'My dog, Lucy she's called, getting on - like me, I suppose.' Miss Bath allowed herself a little laugh, Max allowed his teeth to grind a little more. 'Because of her age, I don't normally put her on a lead as she never strays. She's very good that way. But today, something strange happened.'

'And what was this strange event?' Max didn't have the kind of vocabulary that could jolly on a person, get them to expand more quickly. He knew that this conversation would have been much more productive if Helen had been doing the talking, but the horses were in mid-stream.

Miss Bath continued. 'Lucy ran off - just as we were walking past the drive up to the big house, she went haring away. I've never seen her run like that since she was a puppy. I called her, but she refused to come to me. I have to tell you, Detective Chief Inspector, this behaviour surprised me, and I didn't know what to do. She's over twelve now and has never done anything like that before.'

Max's reserves of patience were now completely depleted, and he was about to become a little less understanding when he caught Melissa's eye.

The tiniest of signals from her slowed his impatience down. He took a breath and in his kindest and most polite tone he asked, 'And what did you do then, madam?'

'Well, I hope that I don't get into trouble for this but - I followed my dog. I followed her into the garden at the back of the house.'

'And did you find her?'

'Oh yes, Detective Chief Inspector. I found her. She was licking and sniffing the blood.'

Suddenly, the three listeners to Miss Bath and her meandering conversation were on full alert. 'The blood, Miss Bath? What do you mean?'

'There's a small building at the back of the house, like a little church; it's got stained glass windows and such. Just by there, Lucy found the blood. She must have smelled it from all that distance away. I was thinking it was an animal, but there's so much of it all around that it would have to be a very large animal. Maybe a deer?

'Maybe a poacher shot a deer, do you think? They must have taken it away because there's no sign of anything there. And I think someone has tried to hose the blood away because the area is very wet, and it hasn't rained for a long time, has it?'

Max was trying to get his head around what he'd just heard when Miss Bath added, 'Then Lucy found some more blood. Again, lots of it. About ten yards away - and beyond that...' Miss Bath could not help but share her confusion. Her tone of voice said it all. 'Lots of blood, but no deer anywhere.'

'Miss Bath. Where are you now?' Max's voice was businesslike and firm.

'I'm at home.'

'Have you told anyone else about this?'

'Who would I tell? I hardly speak to anyone these days. I was so pleased to get in touch with you so quickly.'

'Would you mind if I and my colleagues came to see you now? This information is very valuable, and we don't want to waste any time.'

'I suppose I would be all right. I've made no plans.'

'Excellent. We'll be with you in less than twenty minutes. Please stay where you are - and don't discuss this matter with anyone other than me? Will you do that?'

'Of course, Detective Chief Inspector. I am happy to wait - for you.'

Once again, Max and Melissa glanced at each other. This time, Melissa's eyes smiled at him. She could love this man, couldn't she?

'Debesh. You know the house she's referring to?'

'I think so, sir, yes.'

'Go straight there - take a couple of uniformed PCs too. Get Forensics up there immediately. DS Mordaunt and I will go to see Miss Bath. Maybe we'll bring her to the house, but I'll liaise with you first. OK?'

'Yes, sir, that's fine by me. We may be on to something - at last.'

A few minutes later, DCS Mordaunt and Max were in his car heading to Grasmere. Max thought this might be the appropriate occasion to ask a question he'd been formulating for too long now. 'Could this be the real reason why you're up here ma'am?'

'Again, with the ma'am? I'm not quite sure what you mean Detective Chief Inspector.'

'I'm sure you are, but if you don't want to say, that's OK with me.'

'Max,' her tone was downbeat, but serious. 'There are lots of things I want to say to you, but this isn't one of them. Just now, I'm not at all sure what it means. It could be something big; it could be connected with the cases we're following, but we don't know, do we?'

'That wasn't my point.'

Melissa was quick to respond. 'I know it's not your point. And we may well have many conversations like this. There are always going to be sensitive areas, particular types of information that I can't share, but I don't think this is one of them. I've honestly no idea at all what, if anything, this is going to mean to the investigation. So, let's go and see your lady and see what we can work out from there.'

The two police officers arrived at Miss Bath's house in silence, each of them processing their short altercation. Melissa was particularly worried. Although Max, in one of their more intimate moments, had said that he was fine with the fact that she was of senior rank to her, and he'd specifically said that it wouldn't affect their relationship, here was evidence to the contrary. And it was troubling. Melissa had been here before, and she recognised the signals.

Miss Bath was standing at her front door along with Lucy the Labrador as Max and Melissa got out of their car.

'Miss Bath. It's a pleasure to see you again. May I introduce Chief Superintendent Mordaunt of the Metropolitan police?' Max was very aware of how important the protocols were with this lady, and he was determined that she wouldn't be troubled by any awkwardness on his part.

'I'm pleased to see you again, chief inspector, but I'd hoped it would be under happier circumstances.'

Max realised that, rather like the first time they'd met, this lady was again suffering from stress. She was busily tying knots in a handkerchief and her eyes avoided any focus on either him or the DCS. She'd been very troubled by what she'd seen, and Max's original idea of taking her up to the scene that she'd described to them was immediately shelved.

'Do you remember the young WPC Melling who came home with you the last time we met? She brought you home that morning?' Max had an idea that this would work.

'Yes, a very pleasant young lady.'

'She is, and she's on duty today. Would you mind if I asked her to come here to take a statement from you? It would save you going back to the scene - we can look after everything from our end.'

Miss Bath burst into tears, and Melissa went towards her to comfort her. 'I was dreading going back up there. I didn't want to see...'

'You won't need to, Miss Bath,' Melissa began her contribution. 'DCI Wordsworth, call in the WPC and have her come over immediately.'

'Yes, ma'am.'

Miss Bath had to get it out of her system. 'There was so much blood everywhere. I've never seen anything like it, never wanted to. What do you think has happened?'

Melissa replied, 'Obviously, we can't be sure until we've examined the scene, but we're very grateful to you for drawing our attention to it.' There was a crackle on the radio and Max responded. 'WPC Melling had been deployed to the house, so she's only a few moments away.' He smiled. 'She remembers you.'

A short time later, Max and Melissa, having left Miss Bath in the capable hands of their young WPC colleague, made their way up to the house that had caused so much consternation. A PC was already stationed at the gate, and he acknowledged the arrival of his two superiors with a salute.

'Your colleague DS Datta has already arrived, sir. He's looking at the house.'

'Thanks, we'll park up and find him.'

As they got out of their car, Debesh came forward to meet them. 'Anyone in the house?' Max was thinking of a home invasion.

'I don't think so, sir. There's no reply, so I can't be sure. A couple of points, though. The house is all closed up and it's very secure. It's got strong doors and windows and there's CCTV everywhere.'

'It would be helpful if we could get into the house. Who lives there? And do we know if there is anyone at home?'

'We don't. No.' Debesh continued, 'And we're going to have some difficulty getting into the place.'

The Forensics team was arriving. Max and Melissa waited for them to offload their equipment and get suited up. Then they walked around the house, checking doors and windows just as Debesh had done. He was right: this place was a fortress. Steel doors, powerful window frames and what looked like thick toughened glass all around the ground floor as far as they could see. And Debesh was right about the CCTV too. Max counted six or seven cameras from just where he was standing. Whoever lived here took his security very seriously.

Reaching the lawn at the back of the house, the Forensics team began to fan out. Melissa noticed some blood, a small splash on the wall of the house, just by a corner. She was about to mention it when a number of calls distracted her. 'Here!' 'Over here!' 'Blood over here!' Three separate indications that something very worrying had happened.

'Don't come any closer, sir.' The command came from the white-suited forensics man a couple of yards away from Max. 'Let's not contaminate the scene.'

Forbidden to move any further towards where the Forensics team was operating, Max and Melissa returned to the front of the house.

Melissa didn't want to waste any time, 'We need to get into the house. We can't do anything practical until Forensics has finished, but if we could access this CCTV system - and incidentally, make sure that there's nobody at risk in the house...'

'We've got reasonable suspicion. We don't need a warrant, ma'am.' Debesh understood what Melissa was thinking.

Max was more circumspect. 'How do we get in? You've just said the place is like a fortress.'

'Good point. Maybe Forensics has some kit we could use?'

Max was quick to reply, 'They won't - unless you can do something magical with a swab or two? We need proper kit. The front door needs to be forced. There used to be a garage here but that's long gone. I'm thinking the fire service. Give them a call, Debesh. Everything's come to a halt for now and we've to wait until Forensics has finished, so we might as well wait for the fire service to come and join us.

'There's a pretty cafe down in the village. We'll have a coffee there - I missed out on the Danish earlier, didn't I - and when it's the right time, our duty PC can let us know. How's that for a plan?'

And so, the three police officers took their break while their colleagues from Forensics set about their task at the rear of the house undisturbed. The contribution from the fire service soon came from Ambleside. Its fire station was staffed by on call volunteer firefighters, and five of them had answered the request to take their equipment to Grasmere.

Breaking into a house was a new challenge and they were up for it. They got their Land Rover, equipped with cutting gear and all the necessary tools, up to the house in Grasmere just at the time that Max and his team's enforced coffee break was coming to its natural conclusion.

Returning up the hill to the house, Max and his colleagues saw the gardens were now the scene of intense activity. Four tents had been set up in the garden suggesting four areas demanding special attention.

Two of the Forensics team members were searching the grass and brushwood between the tents, and yellow markers had already been put down where presumably, something of interest had been discovered or noted.

Max looked towards the far end of the garden. A PC was walking down the slope from higher up in the woodland that surrounded the house. He saw his detective colleagues and called out to them. 'You might want to come up here and have a look.'

Max, having already been once bitten, called out to the nearest Forensics man, 'Is it OK if we go up to join our colleague?'

'Knock yourself out. We've enough to be getting on with. However, if there's anything up there that worries you, don't poke around. Let us know. Is that ok?'

'Absolutely. Thanks. Right. Who's going up there?'

Max was thinking about the time he'd clawed his way up and down to Rydal caves on the morning that this investigation began. He'd learned nothing from that experience: he was wearing the same shoes as he had on that day.

'Debesh, dear boy. I will opt out of this adventure - for the moment, as will the DCS. Go up and have a look, and report back to us if you think we should come up for a closer look. And that reminds me - I should have done it earlier. While you're exploring, I'll go back down to the village, and I'll buy a pair of walking boots to keep in the car. This is the second time I've been caught out like this.'

'What a good idea, Max,' Melissa showed her interest. 'I'll come with you - and maybe you and I can do some fell walking if we get to have a few days off.'

Max smiled at Debesh, 'So, that's the plan. There's a shop a couple of minutes away down in the village, so we'll be back soon. If you find anything exciting up there, give me a buzz.'

Fifty-seven

The Marhaba Meet and Greet service is the best way to avoid the long queues at Dubai airport. A friendly face, an efficient golf buggy ride and a genuine sense of welcome means that I was through immigration in less than ten minutes - and I didn't pay the two hundred and fifty quid for the elite service, either.

I'd passed through Dubai a few weeks ago without difficulty, coming from a job in the Philippines and I had a short stopover. That was the last time I'd seen Archana, and I can't deny that there was something of a squeaky bum quality to the experience this time as I presented my passport.

The young man zipped the passport through his machine and – nothing. 'Welcome to Dubai, Mr Blain,' was all he said.

The buggy took me to the taxi rank and within seconds I was in one of those super-efficient Dubai taxis chatting to the driver, a young man from Kerala who, like thousands of his counterparts, looked shop window dressed, even though he'd probably slept in a tiny bunk in a cabin along with fifty other guys.

'Capitol Hotel, please.' And off we went. The Capitol is the hotel I'd sent Archana to recently. It isn't one of the newer Dubai hotels, it's maybe twenty years old, but it's close to the airport, very comfortable, and I've allowed it to become a bit of a fixture in my life. We're all creatures of habit.

I check in; I've only brought a rucksack as I'm not expecting to stay for very long. Desperate times call - well, you know the rest, so this has to be the moment. As Macbeth says, 'If it were done when 'tis done, then 'twere well it were done quickly.' My thoughts exactly.

I know who's been causing me all this grief. I know I've put myself and my family at great risk in so many ways - Christ, I've left a crime scene I'm just praying nobody gets to see, I've had my wife and children threatened, and all this because of my own stupidity. I should never have got involved with the el Hashimi contract - there are so many things I shouldn't have done, but it's too late now.

I've started to think that I'm not getting out of this unscathed - too many variables. So, now I'm going to do the one thing I know I can do, or at least, I believe I can do, and then I'm going to work like hell to put as many pieces back together as I can.

My legitimate businesses can look after Meg and the family, I'm not sure of this, but I don't think they'll be taken away under the proceeds of crime legislation. But to be honest, I'm not sure of anything any more - except for what I am going to do now. I am sure of that: this must be done.

I've a flight back to the UK booked with Turkish Airlines for tomorrow evening. If I finish my project successfully, I should be back home in the early morning on the day before Meg and the kids return from Center Parcs.

That's reminded me to call Meg and check up with her. I get through straight away. Cabin fever. She's bored, wants to come home and I've said she just has to wait until the day after tomorrow - and I'll have a special meal prepared for their return. No pressure, then, just a normal husband doing the husband thing.

Fifty-eight

'You're going to need those new shoes, sir.' Debesh's first words as Max and Melissa arrived back at the house. 'This is big.'

Max was wearing his new footwear as he got out of the car. He hadn't gone for the full conqueror of Everest look; his were 'approach shoes' as they're called in the trade, not quite trainers, but not quite boots either. Perfect for hiking or indeed for everyday wear. Max had hit on the ideal pair almost immediately, and the child in him wanted to experience them straight away. He was about to be granted that opportunity.

'What have you found?'

'Back up that path there, sir. Beyond the garden into the woodland.' Debesh pointed to where Max could see a sort of pathway and what looked to be a series of ropes strung up for the full length of the path.

He turned to Melissa. 'Coming?' 'Of course, I am - try and stop me,' she replied. Max noticed for the first time that she was wearing the same kind of approach shoes he'd just bought. He hadn't noticed. Melissa watched it sink in. Men!

'Is there anyone up there now?'

'About half the forensics team so far, sir. They all need to be up there - it's a big find. Also, they're waiting for a cadaver dog. Shouldn't be long. It's been working at a site near Keswick earlier – and they're on their way now.'

Max couldn't wait to see what all the new fuss was about. He marched up the pathway towards where he heard the sound of concerned, professional voices, Melissa annoyingly a little ahead of him, even though he thought he'd moved at a good pace.

He addressed one of the white suited people. 'DCI Wordsworth, DCS Mordaunt. Sitrep, please.'

The white suited figure was someone who Max had worked with before. He dropped his mask and hood. 'Hello Max, we do find some interesting things together, don't we?'

'Hi Dave. And this one?'

'Well, so far we appear to have found one or two - we're not sure exactly how many - but let's say one or two freshly dug graves. See that tractor over there? That's been used - the engine's still quite warm. Down in the garden there appear to be maybe four sites where the blood spatter suggests a death or catastrophic injury. No hospitals have reported anything, so we're thinking that there could be up to four bodies buried over there.'

He pointed to an area some distance away where the surrounding soil and brushwood showed signs of recent activity. Tracks leading directly to the tractor also suggested that something significant had taken place.

'You've asked for a cadaver dog? Why not just dig them up now?'

'We will, Max,' Dave replied. 'The dog's not for here. It's for further on up there.' The forensics man pointed to another area twenty or thirty yards away. 'Same patterns, but those aren't recent. That's why we've asked for a dog. We could dig there, but if there are human remains, we've got to do it properly. I think we'll dig anyway, just to make sure, but as a first pass, we'll tick all the boxes correctly.'

Melissa wanted certainty. 'Your thoughts are that so far a number - two, three, four?' Dave interrupted, 'We think up to four, ma'am.'

She continued. 'Ok, four. It's possible that four people have recently been killed, then taken from the garden down there and buried up here.'

'It's hypothetical at the moment, ma'am, but I think, yes.'

'And who's is this house?'

'It belongs to a Frank Blain, ma'am. He's a family man, wife and two children.'

'Could the family be the victims?' Melissa was shocked to hear herself suggesting it might be a domestic matter.

'Yes, ma'am, it's possible. We won't know until we do some digging.'

'Here's what I want you to do, Dave.' Max took over. 'I want you to lift the topsoil on what you think to be these graves so that we can establish who is in them, and whether or not it's a domestic matter. Meanwhile, we're going back down to the house to get into it and see if there's anything there to trouble us.'

'That was our plan, exactly,' Dave replied.

'I'm glad that we're all in sync, then.' Max smiled. He'd worked with Dave before, and he knew the guy would do a good job, he also felt that winding people like Dave up occasionally was good for the soul.

Back down at the house, Debesh was waiting for his colleagues. The firefighters had brought their kit into the porch and one of them was working on the front door.

'How we're doing?' Max asked his colleague.

'Almost there. Not easy, though. It's solid steel in a steel frame and the locks are electronic - palm operated. The guy who owns this place didn't want anyone breaking in.'

As he was speaking, two men pushed hard on the door, and it partly opened. The firefighters congratulated themselves and stepped aside allowing Max, Melissa and Debesh to squeeze through the now open door and into the house.

Debesh was the first to cotton on, 'All these doors are the same; all electronically locked. They guy was either paranoid or ...'

'I'm going with the 'or',' said Max.

'Me too,' was Melissa's response, 'Let's get as many of these doors open ASAP.'

The firefighters were about to pack away their kit when Max called them back and explained that there was more he needed from them. As they set about opening the downstairs interior doors, Max and Melissa climbed the stairs up through the great hall and on to a minstrel's gallery. There they tried opening the locked doors on the first floor, knocking loudly on each one, but receiving no reply.

'We've got to get into these rooms.' Melissa was obviously concerned about the whereabouts of the family.

Two of the firefighters came upstairs and began to force the doors open. The indoor rooms in the house were less well fortified, and because their door frames were wood, not steel, the firefighters quickly devised a technique allowing them to force each door open.

The police officers entered each of the rooms as soon as they could but found nothing. Nobody was in the house, and there was no sign of any disturbance anywhere.

'First signs are that it wasn't a domestic matter. Look around, everything is neat and tidy. No signs of distress.' Both Max and Melissa had already drawn the same conclusion as Debesh.

'Small mercies,' was Max's only comment.

Meanwhile, the door down to the cellar had been breached. In response to that news, the two officers went downstairs to join Debesh, and a new challenge was presented to everyone.

The firefighters went down into the cellar first, as there didn't seem to be any proper lighting and there were obstacles in the way.

On their return, one of them reported back. 'I think the cellar has been deliberately left unlit - possibly to deter any exploration - maybe by children.'

'Why do you think that?' Melissa was unsure.

One of the men answered, 'Because, at the far end of the cellar, there's been a lot of work done, and I think they've installed what could be a safe room.'

'A safe room? Maybe someone is in there. Can we get into it?' Max asked.

'We can try,' said one of the firefighters. 'We don't think there's anyone in there, we've tried to make contact. It won't be easy to get in to it, though. It's a toughened steel door, stronger than the front door - and it has a steel frame too.'

'So, any suggestions?' Max was concerned at yet another hold up. By its very nature, the door to a safe room was going to pose a problem.

The man offered an idea, 'You can't force it, it's flush, so there's no leverage. I work in the garage in Ambleside, and we've an oxyacetylene torch there. Should I make a call?'

'Brilliant idea!' Max was all for it.

While waiting for the oxy torch to arrive, there was now some discussion as to whether this operation could be carried out safely. Max didn't want to waste a moment, and waiting for a properly equipped team to come from Lancaster or Workington - even Sellafield was suggested, didn't wash with him.

'It needs doing now,' he insisted. 'Can we do it now using that kit?'

'Yeah. I can do it,' the garage mechanic offered. 'I've worked with oxy torches on the rigs. I'm a qualified welder; I know how to use the kit safely. But, I'll have to work alone. There'll be a risk of fire and I'll be generating fumes too. I'll use my own breathing apparatus, so it should work, and our radios will keep us in contact.'

While waiting for the garage mechanic cum firefighter cum welder to begin his assault on the safe room, Max and Debesh made their way back up the hill and towards the area where the forensics team was now focused.

'This doesn't get any easier,' Max remarked to his colleague as he realised how unfit he was.

'Good exercise, though.' Debesh replied. 'It'll help you with that fell walking you're going to be doing in your new boots.'

Before Max had a chance for a rejoinder, Dave, the forensics man interrupted the banter.

'Four bodies in there; three of them appear to be Asian at a guess. At least, they're dark or sallow skinned, and there's one white guy. Dead from gunshot wounds. To be honest, it's a messy sight. Their weapons are there too.'

'Weapons as well? Weird, but thanks, Dave,' replied Max. 'Now what?'

'We'll dig them up now and get them to a mortuary for the post-mortem examinations. Also, while we're up here, we'll have a look at what could be at least one other grave. The cadaver dog was very excited: there's definitely something we should look at.'

'Let me know if you find anything where the dog was interested. Debesh and I'll come back up - but we need to see what's happening down at the house now.'

'Will do. Take it easy - lovely shoes, though. Are they new?'

'A pleasure talking to you, Dave. See you later.'

'What, no sharp riposte, sir?' Debesh enquired.

'Noted for a later occasion, Debesh. I'll let a few build up; I'm sure you know what they say about revenge?'

'Certainly do, sir.'

The brief interlude where both men gently contemplated the

possible forms that any such revenge might take was broken when a crackly voice informed everyone listening that the door into the cellar room was now open.

'Perfect timing,' said Max. 'Let's find out what's been going on.'

Arriving at the front door of the house, they met the mechanic who'd obviously completed his task. He was filthy, and as he took off his mask his face was unnaturally white against a very definite black background.

'Give it a few minutes for the fumes to clear, then it's all yours,' the hero of the moment suggested. 'Looks like it'll be worth the wait, too.'

As the firefighters were packing away their kit and tools, yet another job well done by the on-call crew, Max took a moment to thank them. He added that he'd open a tab for them tonight at the Golden Rule so they could enjoy a thank you drink. The fire station was next to the police offices that Max and the team used, and therefore very close to the pub, so the offer was gratefully accepted.

'Nice touch, Max,' Melissa said, approvingly.

The firefighters left. And, although they'd put in a hard shift forcing opening upwards of a dozen security doors as part of their special assignment, it was now only mid-afternoon, and many of them would now be going back to their day jobs in the village. On call firefighters in Cumbria need to live or work no more than five minutes away from the fire station.

After a further fifteen minutes or so of waiting, Max's patience had worn too thin. 'Come on,' he said, 'let's have a look at what's down there.'

Each armed with a flashlight, the three officers made their way down into the cellar, and eventually into the room that had posed such a challenge.

All three were amazed by what they saw. This wasn't just a safe room; it was more like a command centre.

The first thing they couldn't help but notice was the array on a wall of four large video monitors. These monitors seemed to be on a permanent sweep of the whole property.

Two monitors were concentrated indoors, and two on the gardens and surroundings to the property. Max noted the cameras were motion sensitive, as the comings and goings of the various personnel on this case tripped a camera whenever they came into view.

His first thought was to see if they could get CCTV evidence of what had gone on. 'Does this system record?'

Melissa had been looking at a cabinet next to one of the computers. 'It does. There's a collection of video cards here. We can see exactly what's been going on.'

'Ma'am, are you familiar with this kind of system? Would you know if it's been recording over the last twenty-four hours?' Max was looking for an easy answer and he hoped that he may just have found it.

Melissa looked at the computer layout on the desk in front of her. Yes, she was familiar with it. 'There's a card in now, so it should be recording.'

'Can you play it back?'

'I can try.' She sat in the high-backed office chair that allowed her access to everything, and after a few moments said, 'There's no password on it, so let's have a look.'

She wound the system back a few minutes and pressed Play. Images appeared on the screen. 'Yes, it's recording.'

'Can you rewind to the beginning of the card?'

'It doesn't quite work like that, but I know what you mean,' came the reply. Melissa was quite enjoying chatting to the technophobe. 'I'll start at the beginning of the card.'

She began to play the card that was currently in the machine: nothing came on the screen. 'But it has been recording, I'm sure of that,' said Melissa.

'Fast forward it. Let's see if there is anything at all on the card,' suggested Debesh. 'We might get some idea of what's been happening.'

'It's been in for three days. Look at the date at the top of the screen,' Melissa continued to fast forward the card until it should have been showing the last twenty-four hours, but nothing appeared.

While Max and Melissa were concentrating on the CCTV setup, Debesh had a looked carefully around the room. He opened a large cupboard. Inside was what seemed to be the product of a survivalist's shopping list. Tins of everything, bottles of water, blankets, towels, what appeared to be jump suits, even kids' games. Somebody was planning for a long stay in that room.

Another, larger cupboard caught his eye. It had an electronic lock on it, but the door had been left slightly open. He was astounded by what he saw.

'Sir, look at this.'

A testy response. 'Wait, Debesh.'

'No sir, you must see this.'

Max turned his head - and realised why Debesh had been so insistent. He was looking at an array of weapons, maybe twenty assorted rifles, pistols, what appeared to be grenades - and boxes and boxes of ammunition. Debesh noticed there were gaps where some of the weapons were missing.

'Have you ever seen anything ...?' was all he could say before

Melissa called his attention back.

'We've got something!'

'Hold that thought, Debesh.' said Max. 'Come and look at this first.'

Images had begun to appear on the screen. 'Stop there - please,' said Max to his superior. 'Let's see that in in real time now.' The clock on the monitor showed 0620. 'That's today, this morning.'

The four monitors came online. One of them showed a man going into the master bedroom of the house and getting into bed. Melissa fast forwarded again until the man moved as he woke up - went to the bathroom, the monitors perhaps providing too much information at that point, and he then went downstairs.

'That'll be the owner, Frank Blain.'

'But where's his family?' asked Max.

This was puzzling as by now they knew the family hadn't been involved in the horrific violence of the night before.

'He's definitely alone - and look, he's on a mission,' added Debesh, as all three officers saw the man grab a rucksack, check one or two things and then make his way downstairs.

Another monitor showed a car arriving and turning round near the front door. The man opened the front door, went outside and got into the car, which then left the house and went back down the hill.

'Can we get the index number?' asked Max. 'Let's find out who picked him up. That must be Frank Blain, mustn't it?'

Melissa agreed. 'Yes, and I think he's wiped the cards for the last day or so and then reset the system.' She continued, 'I'd love to know where he's going. And here's the index number of the car.' She noted it and handed a slip of paper to Debesh.

'Give this number to Helen, please. Get her to cast her spells. Mr Blain may have wiped the event, but he's not covered his tracks, has he? What was he thinking? And oh, while you're talking to Helen, Debesh, please get her to send a bunch of flowers to Miss Bath. She's been more help to us than she could ever have imagined.'

'Anything else that we can usefully do now?' asked Debesh.

'I don't think so. Forensics will want to own this place for at least a day or two. And we've got to work out what to do with Mr Blain when we find him - if he comes back. We should also be looking for his wife and family. Let's get back to Ambleside and sort out some paperwork, as there's going to be a lot of it.'

A curious atmosphere now began to develop back at the Ambleside station. Melissa was certainly on edge, and Max was surprised when after an hour or so, she said she was leaving and would see them all in the morning.

A short time later, she was back at Marigold Cottage, trying but failing to relax. She deliberately hadn't arranged anything with Max.

It was a special moment in the case and many decisions about next steps were about to be taken.

Melissa felt she'd had a difficult day both professionally and personally. She was feeling stressed and had lots to be stressed about.

And that stress was mostly about Max. She'd let herself get emotionally involved. No bad thing, as she both liked and respected him, and she'd given herself time and space before she'd allowed the relationship to begin. Now though? Wonderful man though she felt him to be, she'd recently picked up signs similar to those she'd recognised in other relationships.

Some men, maybe it was all men, found it challenging to get on with women who were superior to them in some way. In her case it was because of her rank, but she'd noticed it in other women with regard to their talent, and of course, many beautiful or sexually attractive women always had other issues to contend with. Now she wasn't at all sure that things would work out between her and Max, and she was troubled.

On another level, the professional one, she knew they were now making real progress in their various cases, and one aspect of her own mission had worked out very well.

Partly to displace her thoughts about Max, she called her Assistant Commissioner in London to bring him up to date. 'There's a lot going on, sir, and it's not a Captagon issue, I'm pleased to say.'

'Well, that's relief.' This was great news for the AC. 'When Stanovnic liquidated his assets in Dubai, all the signs were that he was going down the Captagon route. There are huge profits to be made with the manufacture and distribution of that drug, and the fall of Syria created a huge gap in the market. We were seriously worried he was going to be targeting the UK. We've since found out that the market has gone in another direction, and you've just confirmed that,'

'Where's this new market, sir?'

'Someone's started up in India and it looks like the target market is Pakistan - and Afghanistan, possibly other 'Stans'. We think it's Stanovnic's money, but someone else has access to it. We know it's not Stanovnic, obviously, but we've an idea who it might be.'

Melissa was interested, 'You know who the new person is?'

'Yes, I think we do. Stanovnic had an Indian accountant, a chap name of Kranti, I believe. He's access to lots of money now, but as I've said, his focus is on Pakistan and the wider region. Of course, this could be political - and I don't know whether it's from malicious intent or simply for profit, but this Kranti is not as clever as Stanovnic was. We're keeping a close watch on him now, and working with our colleagues in the UAE, we feel we've a good chance of nipping this new project in the bud.

'You'd be very useful if you fancied the role, by the way. There's a lot of money going into the production and distribution of this drug - all new money as far as we can see, So, I'm delighted that, for now anyway, we don't have to worry about it coming here.' There was a pause, 'Can I ask, would you be interested in taking on this new role?'

'I can't say just now, sir, but maybe, yes.' She realised where her mind was now and repeated, 'Yes, maybe. But there's a stack of stuff going on here. Today we discovered some bodies. We think they relate to Stanovnic too, as there's now a Dubai connection with them. I'll send you a report later this evening. I do want to stay here until this thing has bottomed out - if that's OK with you.'

'Of course. So, bodies?'

'Yes, sir. Four so far, but Forensics tell us that there might be some more from a previous incident. They've all been found on the same plot of land, sir, all in a garden belonging to a guy who lives locally, in Grasmere. And here's the thing, sir. There's a connection. He's just flown out to Dubai.'

'Has he, by God? Who is this man? Do we know of him?'

'His name is Blain, Frank Blain. He's some kind of management consultant and seems legitimate. No criminal record, but so much has been going on at his house that we're sure he's connected with our case.'

'How do you know he's going to Dubai?'

'He's helped us there. He's set up a very comprehensive - and expensive security system. Before he left, he wiped all the CCTV stuff for the period that really interested us, but the system started up again this morning, and it recorded him being picked up by a car. We tracked its index number, and it turns out it was a limo pickup from Manchester airport. He's on a flight to Dubai now - business class, hence the limo pick up.'

'Business class. Lovely for some,' the AC remarked.

'Yes, sir.' Melissa smiled. So, the cuts were affecting the Met too. 'We'll wait for him to return and then we'll have a word. He's got a lot of explaining to do.'

'He's not just done a runner?'

'We're thinking he hasn't, sir. Hoping, I should say. He's booked a return flight and a limo - and he's only planning to be away for one day. It's a risk, but we don't think that detaining him in Dubai is the answer. That could cause even more problems, especially if Blain has a connection with Stanovnic. We'll keep an eye on him, we'll follow any electronic transactions he makes and if we have to, we'll inform the Dubai authorities - if for example, he tries to fly to another country. But we discussed this and feel it's worthwhile taking the risk that he plans to return. From what we do know of him he seems to be a committed family man.'

'And where are they, the family? '

'Cards on the table – we're not sure, but they haven't left the country, we do know that.'

'There's a lot going on, so I understand why you want see this through to a conclusion.'

'Thanks for seeing it from my point of view, sir. The team has done a great job here. I'd hate to leave before it's all tied up. If that is OK with you?'

'Yes, of course, Melissa. That's fine with me. You know I trust your judgement. And then?'

A short pause, but Melissa had decided. She knew what she would be doing next: it was inevitable. Yes, the Lakes was a beautiful area, and yes, Max was a man worth investing time in. But in reality, the signs were already there. 'And then,' she replied, 'I'll think of your offer and probably accept it. In any event, I will be returning to the Met. After all sir, that's where my future is.'

Fifty-nine

I've as many of my ducks in a row as I know about and so I call Archana. 'Still in Pune? Is everything OK?'

'Yes and yes,' she replied. 'Although I'm bored rigid. Are you in Dubai now?'

'I am. I'm in the Capitol. Trying to settle. Have you done that research?'

'Certainly have. I was waiting to hear from you. Shall I send it over?'

'Please do. I need to look at it before I decide.'

'Frank!' I immediately sense a note of concern in her voice. 'Are you sure? Can't you let things go? Hesham's so incompetent and he's making such a mess. He's losing control anyway. And you're taking a huge risk.'

Logic again. I find logical people so difficult to deal with because they're so often right, aren't they? 'I can't, Archie. He killed Stephanie, and he's made it impossible for you to work in Dubai, he's attacked my family and a couple of days ago he sent a team of men to attack my house. Do you honestly think I'm going to let that go?'

But she won't give up, and as the information she's promised comes on to my iPad, I can still hear her as she mother hens me. She means well and she has a point. But I'm not particularly well known for my sensible decision making any more, am I?

My whole world is unravelling, and I see it as clearly as anyone. I'm thinking of what I'm going to say to Meg and the kids when they return home. I'll have to ban them from using the garden - at least until it rains. And what if while I've been away, someone's discovered what's been going on in the garden? Archana's just said that el Hashimi's out of control; he's incompetent. He's got nothing on me. My carefully curated double persona has been shredded by the man I'm now going to deal with.

Yes, it's a stupid idea. But it will bring an end to the chaos that has become my life - won't it?

I look at the information that Archana has prepared for me.

Hesham el Hashimi is now the de facto head of the massive family organisation that controls much of the seedier side of Dubai's burgeoning dark economy. He lives and works out of the Emirates Tower building on Sheikh Zayed Road. Emirates Towers consists of two buildings; Hesham has offices in one of the towers and lives in an apartment in the other, that being the four-hundred-bedroom Jumeirah Emirates Towers hotel.

His suite of rooms is on the forty second floor of the hotel and is five or six doors away from the hotel's impressive group of four glass elevators. These elevators enhance the extraordinary views of the huge atrium that stretches almost the full height of the building.

I see that Archana has been very clever and has had her friend Rima observe Hesham for me. Rima often uses hotel coffee shops for her business; she likes the buzz of people around her as she sits there with her laptop making deals.

She spent a few days in Starbucks in the lobby of the hotel and reported back the good news that Hesham is a creature of habit. He works regular hours, and he rarely seems to do much more than take the elevator from his apartment down to the lobby of the hotel and then walk across to the other tower where he takes another elevator up to his office.

He starts work at eight in the morning without fail, and at around six in the evening, he finishes for the day and returns to his apartment.

Also, he seems to live alone, although Rima mentioned that he sometimes has female company brought to visit him. Other than that, he doesn't seem to socialise.

I look at Archana's information and to make sure, I read it again. I've decided what to do. First decision: it will be at his apartment; there'll be too many people around him in his office.

What should I wear? I My first thought is Arab dress. If I wear the kandura and a ghutra, the white robe and the white headscarf that most Emirati men wear, I won't stand out. However, I've decided against it. I'm too fair skinned for one thing, and for another, I don't speak enough Arabic to carry myself off as a local. Pity though, as I'd be hiding in plain sight. Instead, I'm thinking of a baseball hat - and I've brought a wig so I can at least attempt to confuse any CCTV systems that might be tracking me.

I see that Archana's sent me the plans of the Emirates Towers buildings, and I see where the emergency exits, stairways and service elevators are located.

And this is what I've decided. Tomorrow morning, I'll take breakfast in Hesham's hotel, and at some point, I'll take the elevator up to his floor. There, I'll wait for him, hoping that he really is a creature of habit, and he won't disappoint me.

***

Here's hoping! I checked out of the Capitol at six thirty and came straight over here. I hardly slept a wink, mainly because my shoulder hurts from the bullet that nicked me. I've put some mercurochrome on it - you can buy that here - and a plaster. However, the time difference, the stress and the knowledge why I'm here in Dubai, all conspired to tempt me to drink myself to sleep, but that temptation I avoided.

It's almost seven thirty now, and I've had my eggs benedict and two coffees in the Starbucks outlet here at the Emirates Tower hotel.

I've got my baseball hat on and I'm wearing my wig. My wig is a long ponytail, slotted through the little gap in my cap. Quite natty, but not me at all. I've not received any suspicious looks from anyone, so

I'm hoping I'll blend in. I propose to lose the disguise as soon as I've finished.

I've Just confirmed my flight with Turkish Airlines for later today, so fingers crossed.

Ten minutes to eight. I walk across the hotel lobby to where the four glass-fronted elevators are busily earning their keep. Each seems to be in constant use. One opens in front of me, and I get into it joining two other men. I press floor forty-four and stand towards the back of the elevator, enjoying the view as the elevator leaps up towards the apex of the atrium.

It doesn't stop until floor thirty-eight, and the two men get out, leaving me alone for the last six floors of my journey.

Coming out of the elevator on floor forty-four, I rehearse my moves. I know that these floors of the hotel are similarly laid out, so I plan what I propose to do and walk through it. Then, I retrace my steps from the journey I've taken, walking past the elevators and on to the emergency staircase at the other side of the hotel. I use that staircase to descend to floor forty-two.

It is now four minutes to eight. I hope my man is on time or I am goosed.

I come out on to the balcony corridor that connects all the rooms, giving guests an imposing view of the atrium stretched out above them and down to the lobby far below. Now I stroll back towards the elevators, hoping, dreaming, wishing as hard as I can that Hesham el Hashimi will come out of his apartment now.

I look around. I am the only person walking towards the elevators. There's nobody else moving on this floor.

I'm maybe ten yards from the elevators when I hear a door slam shut ahead of me, and someone appears maybe twenty yards away. Perfect. That's my man and my man is on time.

I continue to walk, passing the elevators to my right. Now I'm maybe five yards away from him. He glances at me but does not compute; he's quite animated and dealing with something on his phone.

The job itself is easy. As we are about to walk past each other, I grip his robe - just where the lapels would be had he been wearing a suit - and I heave.

He's over the balcony wall in a second, and as I continue my journey to the emergency stairs, I hear the first of the screams coming up from the lobby.

My shoulder erupts in a searing pain that nearly has me fainting. You know when in a movie - sorry, in a film - when they say, 'It's only a flesh wound'? All I can say is that whoever wrote that line was writing hypothetically. It bloody hurts, I can tell you. At least, my flesh wound does, and the action of throwing the Hesham guy over the balcony has done nothing to calm it down.

I continue my walk to the emergency stairs. I lose the wig in a garbage chute as I'm passing, but I keep my cap.

I quickly walk down three or four floors noticing the CCTV cameras in the stairwell that will obviously be recording my every move. I try to make things as difficult as I can by shielding my face, but I know that if I have been clocked, I'm going to have problems getting away from here.

Back into the public corridors at floor thirty-five, I see the elevators are still working. I've no other option - no Plan B for this, not even a Plan A. I'll have to busk it as neither Archana nor I could come up with an alternative escape route. Maybe a helicopter from the rooftop? Fat chance. No, I must move now as the hotel will be locked down soon, and I've got to get out before that happens.

Three other people join me in the elevator at floor thirty-two. We descend in silence, although as we begin to get to the lower floors it becomes obvious that something is happening below. We don't stop again and as I exit the elevator, a large crowd is gathering around the body that has smashed through a coffee table and brought a sudden end to someone's business meeting. The chaos is evident, and as the quality of Security in most of Dubai's hotels is poor, nobody knows what to do.

Many of the security personnel in Dubai's hotels are recruited from the same countries and the same demographic that provides the country with its taxi drivers and construction workers. They are mostly third world guest workers from India, Bangladesh and Pakistan, although a few Russians are beginning to make their presence felt too. A security job is maybe a rung up in the hierarchy, but dealing with this kind of incident will be very challenging for them.

I walk through the crowd, quietly making my way to the main entrance. Many people are leaving, some rubberneckers coming into the hotel too - news travels fast. But I'm not stopped, and a few seconds later I hear someone ordering the main doors to be shut - they are locking everything down.

I reverse my baseball cap, and I switch to carrying my rucksack on the front not the back. My final ingenious attempt at disguise is to put on my Raybans as I flag down a cab to take me to the airport.

Sixty

Early morning the next day and Max, Melissa, Debesh and Helen have all arrived at Ambleside police station. Each has a tale to tell as information has been flooding in from many sources.

Helen began, 'Ma'am, as you know, the owner of the house in Grasmere has flown to Dubai. I've followed this up; he has a return flight booked with Turkish Airlines which is due to arrive in Manchester at 0730 tomorrow morning.'

'Great news! That's a relief too. I thought we might have lost him.'

'So, whatever has taken him to Dubai can be accomplished quickly,' continued Helen.

'That's troubling, don't you think?' Debesh, like the other three, was wondering why anyone would take a return flight to Dubai lasting only twenty-four hours.

Melissa nodded in agreement. 'We need to find out why he went. Anything else, Helen?'

'Some background on Frank Blain, ma'am. He has a family: a son from his wife's previous marriage and twin girls. They all go to private schools as day students. The family lives quietly and nobody seems to have a bad word to say about them.'

'How many people know what's happened in his garden?' Max was wondering if somebody who knew Blain might have tipped him off about the police activity.

Debesh answered, 'Obviously, the whole village knows something has been going on, but the house is isolated, and we've closed it and its approaches. I don't think anyone can see what we've been doing in the woods, but we can't be sure. No-one's put up a drone, so far.'

'And what has been happening in the woods, Debesh?' Melissa asked.

'Well, ma'am, lots. Our Mr Blain, if it is Mr Blain, has been very busy. He keeps a tractor with a digger attachment and logging equipment, saws, axes and so on in a shed up in the woods. We believe he's used the digger to bury four bodies - probably yesterday, or maybe the night before. These victims all died from gunshot wounds, and blood and tissue matching has established where each of them died.'

Debesh continues, 'And it all happened in the garden. Each of the areas of the garden that has blood traces, corresponds to one of the bodies. Oh, and all the men were all buried with their weapons too.'

Max made his first contribution, 'The Forensics guy, Dave, he said that three of the men were probably Arab - middle eastern anyway, and one of them was white. Is that so?'

'Yes, sir,' It was Helen who flipped over a page of her notes. 'And we know the identity of one of them. He's Wojtek Badura, Polish, he's lived in the area for many years. He worked as an odd job man - and has a girlfriend in Ambleside.'

'And how do we know that?'

'His wallet, sir. That and the fact he's been reported missing by his girlfriend.'

The chief superintendent intervened. 'So, one of the dead was a local man? What was he doing?'

Again Helen. 'The preliminary results of the weapons' analysis show he was killed by automatic fire from one or more of the assault rifles. These were carried by the three, are we going to call them 'Arab' assailants? His own weapon was a kind of sniper rifle, bolt action, quite unsuitable for that kind of firefight...'

'How did you know that?' Debesh was interested to know where his wife's extensive knowledge of firearms was coming from.

Helen continued, 'I was told.' She smiled at her husband. 'I had no idea. But it seems he was fighting against the three others.'

'Was Blain not there?' asked Max.

'He possibly was. We're waiting for some DNA results to come back. Excuse me one moment.' Helen checked something on her computer and resumed, 'Sorry about that - they've not sent them yet.'

'What would the DNA show?'

'Forensics found another patch of blood that didn't correspond with anything else at the scene. It was on a wall at the corner of the house, not much, but it was recent, and it suggests that someone else was there.'

'I saw that patch of blood on the wall,' Melissa said. 'I was going to mention it, but one of the forensics guys shooed us away.' She looked at Max. 'Remember?'

'Yes, I do. And the DNA?'

Helen continued, 'When your friend Dave the forensics guy said that patch of blood didn't match anything else they'd found, he called us hoping to speak to you. I took the call, and I suggested he might do a DNA comparison with Mr Blain. It seemed obvious to me, sir.'

'I bet it's Blain,' Melissa interjected. 'Well done, Helen. Clever thinking. Anything else?'

'Oh yes, lots. I hope you don't mind. I could email all of this out to you if you wished.'

'Yes, of course,' replied Melissa, 'I do want you to copy us, but while we're all here, let's take advantage of the moment.'

'Maybe a coffee?' suggested Max.

'Good idea,' Melissa agreed. Yes, we'll take a short coffee break. Max, pop out to the Apple Pie for us, would you? I think we all deserve a Danish to celebrate.'

Debesh made sure that he didn't catch Max's eye as his boss, almost sheepishly, made his way out of the building.

'That's democracy,' whispered Melissa as she smiled at her two remaining colleagues.

'It's something - not quite sure what,' was all that Debesh could offer.

A few minutes later, the small committee reconvened, and Helen was the first to speak. 'We have the DNA results now. And they do show a match for Frank Blain.'

'Thanks, Helen,' replied Melissa, once again fully in control of this meeting. 'That clarifies things, doesn't it? It seems that Blain and his Polish pal had a stand-off with three foreign attackers. Four men died, and Frank Blain was left to clear up the mess. Obviously, he had something in Dubai that needed his urgent attention - we don't yet know what that is - so he took the risk leaving such a mess behind, but not before he'd tried to hide the bodies of the four dead men. Is that about it?'

'Yes, ma'am,' Debesh replied. Max said nothing - was that petulance, wondered Melissa?

It wasn't petulance; Max had been listening. He asked, 'And the other possible graves? What's happened there?'

'I hadn't forgotten, Max,' said Melissa. There's frost in the air, thought Debesh. 'One thing at a time. Helen, do you have any information on the other possible graves?'

'Yes, ma'am. Not everything. Things are a bit more complicated here, but here's what we have so far. Forensics was right - it was another grave site. They've recovered four bodies there too, but these bodies were buried at least one, maybe two years ago. And they believe it's a family.'

'Cause of death?' Max asked.

'They can't be definite yet as the bodies have largely decomposed.' Helen wasn't enjoying this part of the discussion - the details had made her want to retch. 'However, evidence from one of the bodies shows it was killed by a single shot to the forehead. Forensics suggests that may be the method used for them all, but they're not certain yet.'

'Their ethnicity?' asked Max.

'Again, not yet clear, sir, Helen replied. 'They'll get back to us as soon as they know. They're confident that they can answer all our questions; they need a little more time.'

'Thanks, Helen. Great job.' Melissa was very impressed by the togetherness of Debesh's young wife. She reminded her of someone not too far from this very conversation.

'Yes, well done, Helen,' added Max. 'Thanks for all this. I think we've got a case. You deserved your Danish.' And he smiled.

'Next steps?' Debesh was keen to move things forward.

It was Melissa who answered. 'I need to contextualise this for you a little.' She looked at her colleagues, three people whom she had come to respect, and one who she was almost in love with. Now was the time to come clean.

'I was parachuted in to work with you because of the Stanovnic situation. You know the 'what'. What you haven't been told is the 'why'. Sorry, Max, I couldn't share ...'

'Perfectly OK, ma'am. I understand.' Max tried to get the tone of his response right but just failed. He could see his relationship with this woman sinking under the waves as she spoke. She was totally in command, uber-professional and very scary.

'I was here to assist you with the murders, of course, and I've been truly impressed by the way you - by the way we've worked together.

'The bit I've kept quiet was the Captagon stuff. That was my primary reason for being here.'

'And what the hell is Captagon?' Max was beginning to get a touch of petulance. First the Danish pastries, now a big secret?

'I've heard of Captagon,' said Debesh. 'It's a drug, isn't it? Like Oxy or Fentanyl maybe?'

'Yes,' replied Melissa, 'cheap and easy to manufacture and it's huge all over the Middle East. The Syrian government manufactured it and made billions. But with the fall of Assad, lots of its production facilities - and its markets - have come up for grabs. We were very concerned at this happening at the same time that Stanovnic liquidated his Dubai assets and came to Europe.

'The Met has a watching brief for this kind of activity, and it was in my portfolio. That's primarily why I was sent up here. We thought that Europe - and the UK - would be the new marketplace. We were very worried.'

'And now?' Max wanted this bottoming out. He didn't yet know whether he should take offence.

'Stanovnic was in a feud with someone else in Dubai. We think we know who. And that's why the girl, his sister, was killed.'

'You thought he was going to start up some kind of operation with this drug, did you?' Debesh wanted more clarification.

'At first, yes. Then it became obvious that Stanovnic had no such intention. In fact, we've information that things are developing away from here - and apparently using Stanovnic's money too, now he can't use it himself.'

'How?' Max was now perplexed.

'Simple. Stanovnic's businesses had an accountant, and that accountant has maintained some access to his money - not all of it, but enough for him to use as seed capital for his new business.

Instead of spending it on nightingales' tongues and beautiful women, he's decided to develop his own drugs empire. We don't think he's bright enough and he's probably not ruthless enough, either. So, for now we don't see it as a threat to us here in the UK.'

'Is this Blain involved?'

'Not with the drugs side, but we're now sure that he's the other part of the feud. We've information that one of Stanovnic's business rivals, a young man who's recently inherited a huge family enterprise - drugs, women, trafficking - all good stuff, had his nose put out of joint somehow by Blain. He set Stanovnic up - got him to come here to the Lakes. We thought it was for drug-related reasons, but it was to achieve a different objective. And it seems to have worked - in part. Stanovnic is no more.'

Max wanted more information. 'And this Dubai based man?'

'I'm not a betting person,' replied Melissa, but I'm prepared to bet that he's the reason why Blain is now in Dubai.'

All three of Melissa's colleagues pondered on what they had just heard.

'What are we going to do now, ma'am?' Debesh was the importunate one.

'That's the easy part. As you know, we're all assuming that Blain will return to the UK. The signs are that he will and unless he's been warned, and he may well have been, we'll lift him when he arrives back. Then the law will take its course. I'm certain we've got our man - thanks to you - and if we make the proper case, I doubt if he'll ever see the outside of the prison estate again.'

'What do we need to do now?' Debesh asked.

'As things have gone the way they have, we need to see if Blain returns to the UK. If he doesn't, then Interpol will take over and track him down. We're keeping an eye on his movements. For obvious reasons, we're trying to keep the Dubai authorities out of the picture, but we've a trace on his passport.

'If he does return, your job here will continue. It's still your case. All the evidence collection and everything Blain has done here in the Lakes will be yours – I'll see to that.

'The NCA and Interpol will probably take over the larger investigation as there is much about Blain that we can't find from here: his international activity, his overseas contacts - perhaps what he really does for a living. It's a can of worms and it'll probably have to be opened by someone other than you.

'The bottom line though, is that I'll be leaving here soon, and I wanted you all to know so that there is no misunderstanding. You've been a fabulous team to work with, and you've achieved great things. I'll be leaving later tomorrow - I've an important set of meetings coming up in London. I have to say I'll miss you all, there's no doubt about that. And Debesh, I'll have to leave Marigold

Cottage too, and that I'll really miss. So, can we please get our paperwork up to date now - while await the return of Frank Blain?'

Some long minutes later, the mushroom cloud from the bomb that had exploded in Max Wordsworth's head still hadn't cleared. He sat at his desk in a trance.

Debesh and Helen sensing this walked stiff legged around him for a while but eventually had to make their excuse to leave as the atmosphere in the room became unbearable. Debesh suggested that he and Helen pop over to the owners of Marigold Cottage and share the news with them. That was a good idea, agreed Melissa, thanking them again and suggesting they finish early as they'd both been very busy over the last few days.

They couldn't get out of the office fast enough. Both knew what was happening but had nothing to offer that would help Max and Melissa deal with their endgame. Apparently, that relationship was over.

Once Helen and Debesh had left, Melissa wasted no time. 'I'm sorry, Max, but I know you'll understand.'

'So, it wasn't?'

'I thought it was, I really did. I've come closer to you than I've come to anyone for years. I know I could love you, Max.'

'Then what are you saying?'

'My work - and my life - is in the Met, not here.'

'If I can learn to love the Lakes, you could give it a try.' Max tried to inject a little humour, but as usual, the tin ear effect clouded things.

'Max, I do love the Lakes. It is a wonderful place, and as I've said, I could love you, I'm sure of that. But honestly? It would never work, would it?'

'We could try.'

'I'm in line for an Assistant Commissioner post. It's simply too important for me. I can't take the risk, I'm sorry. I couldn't live up here. Could you live in London?'

With flawless logic, she'd played the trump card. Of course, Max couldn't live in London, he hated the thought of the place. Yet he was assuming that Melissa would up sticks and rush to join him. He'd given no thought to what she might do if she did, where they might live - he'd presumed, and that was the mistake.

Melissa didn't have to explain that the little signs of resentment she'd picked up from him recently were what had scuppered things for her. She'd been there before and had no intention of returning.

She knew she could love him; she'd given herself to him, shared her bed with him, but the undercurrent was always there. He might not have sensed it, but she certainly did.

'So, do we just pretend nothing happened?'

Melissa hated the 'It's not you, it's me' thing - especially when it was him. But she had to follow the route to the end - Max deserved it - she should have been stronger.

'Lots happened, Max. There've been beautiful moments, and I still think you're a wonderful man, but I must go back to the Met, back to London. I'm happy for our relationship to continue; I don't want to lose you. But if I stay up here, I will. I know that.'

'What do you suggest?'

'Honestly? I've no idea. Let's see how it goes. If we are as tight as I thought we could be, it will work out. Maybe I'll develop too - and perhaps I'll take more of a risk. But now, I'm not ready for that, and I'm sorry for hurting you.'

Max was having a 'helicopter experience': he was now outside his body, hovering over it and listening to this woman as she gently eased him out of her life. She was doing a great job.

On his way back to Morecambe that night, Max ordered his Indian take away meal for one: she was right, this was hurting, but as he more than anyone else knew, Time heals all wounds. 'Let's hope that's true,' he said to himself as at this moment, there was nobody to listen to him.

Melissa looked around Marigold Cottage for the last time. It had been a magical experience for her, and she'd almost been carried away into the sunset by a knight in tarnished armour. But she knew she was making the right choice.

Her future was not in the beautiful seductive valleys of the Lake District. Her future was somewhere else - somewhere where she would control all her choices. It had almost been a fairy tale, just not quite.

Epilogue

I've been diagnosed as a psychopath. And it's official. That's a gift I didn't expect to receive, but over the last few months I've learned so much about myself, most of which I would have preferred stayed out of sight.

And now the divorce! Meg hasn't been to see me since my sentencing, and I received the letter from her solicitors today. Given my present circumstances, she wants an immediate divorce - and she's demanding full custody of the children.

Of course, I won't oppose it. I want her and the kids to get on with their lives as I won't be helping very much with their upbringing. To be frank, I don't think I'll miss the kids all that much, but Meg - I did - I do love her.

'When sorrows come, they come not in single spies, but in battalions.' The boy Hamlet was right. When everything came out into the open, I obviously couldn't defend much of what I'd got up to, but it's fair to say the last few months have surprised me by how quickly everything unravelled.

Today's breaking news is that I'm wanted in Dubai for Hesham's murder. They've also discovered that I apparently murdered his family and buried them in my garden, so they'll want me back in Dubai for that too.

They have capital punishment in Dubai - the firing squad, so that's got me thinking. I think that means I won't be extradited as the British government doesn't extradite accused criminals to countries where they might be executed. But could they come to some kind of arrangement?

I hope I don't end up in Dubai; their prison system seems worse than ours, although you can get your sentence reduced by half if you manage to memorise the Koran in Arabic. That would be a tough ask for me. Oh, and apparently, the Saudis are interested in me too as the family of four they found in my garden was originally from Riyadh.

Some clever cubicle monkeys got to work and found my correspondence with Stephanie and Archana. Other contracts of mine came up too; some with other clients I'd forgotten about. That meant I was charged with six extra murders - I knew they were mine - but, and I think this is outrageous, there were five more that were nothing to do with me.

When I flew back into Manchester, and after the embarrassment of having four police officers board my plane to arrest me, I was held in Belmarsh prison in London - because I was apparently a terrorist! How stupid is that? I'm not a terrorist; I'm a man who made a living from doing unpleasant work, I'll give you that, but my 'victims' were all evil creatures. I was performing a service - I really was.

I wasn't even held in a cell for the first week. I went straight to the prison hospital as my shoulder needed a minor operation to clean the wound. Obviously, my cloak of invincibility hadn't worked because that minor 'flesh wound' I received during the gunfight had become badly infected.

And naturally when it came to my trial, I pleaded Not Guilty to everything. That didn't wash with the jury - and it certainly didn't impress Meg. She'd come to see me regularly before the trial, and she was fully on my side to begin with, happy to believe my version of events as she always did - or so I thought.

But the thing about Meg is that she's so straight up, so honest, that when the evidence began to pile up, she stopped coming to see me and eventually sent a message via her solicitor that she would never see me again.

And now I'm in a hospital. It's a special hospital but again, this came as a surprise. The verdict was manslaughter due to diminished responsibility: another insult. I was set up for about ten full life sentences apparently, but my barrister suddenly decided to go down the medical route. My legal team asked me, of course, and I said OK - not because I expected it to happen, but blow me, I was diagnosed as a psychopath. The nerve.

 The Judge granted an Indefinite Hospital Order. I'm obviously concerned about the indefinite bit, which I think is a bit harsh, but on the plus side, I don't have to spend it in a real prison.

I'm a hospital patient now, not a criminal. And I'm very well treated. I have my own room, not a cell. It does have bars on the windows, but apart from that, it's very pleasant.

You do have to choose your friends carefully here. There are a lot of seriously strange people around, so I keep my distance. My plan is to settle in and then take advantage of all there is to offer. I was thinking of doing a degree. That's possible, but there are loads of other courses available. There's also a brilliant library, and I've a TV in my room.

My counsellors say that I must work towards coming to terms with my actions. They've congratulated me on my being a good dad, although I imagine the bar is set pretty low here, so I'm not taking that too seriously. They also say that I've been a good husband, and that I ran my businesses very efficiently.

They are not happy about the wet work. Not the job itself, although of course they disapprove; they are uncomfortable about my attitude towards it. I've been as honest as I can with them. To me, it was just work: it didn't bother me.

And that's the problem - or the 'challenge' as my psychiatrist has put it. He talks about a 'disconnect' between the way I was able separate my domestic life and my work as a management consultant, from all the murders - his term. They were simply contracts to me, and for reasons that I can't fathom, that concerns them.

Apparently, until I'm able acknowledge that side of my personality in a way that is satisfactory - to them, I'll be staying here, and that, it would seem, might take some time.

THE END

TONY HUNT

As a management consultant for almost thirty years, Tony Hunt delivered over two thousand presentations in over thirty countries. His many business seminars now continue to sell well on the internet.

He and his wife Wendy live in a house once owned by Beatrix Potter, their five children now making their own way.

Tony writes short stories, plays and novels, and has also narrated the work of many writers for Amazon Audible.

Short Stories

      Geordie Boy

      ForGiving

Plays

      Happy Endings

      Dark Charity

Books available on

      www.amazon.com

Business Videos

      Presentation Skills

      Time Management

      Everybody Sells

      Leadership Excellence

      Brilliant Customer Service

      Brilliant Change Management

Videos available on

      www.ukwebinars.com

      www.udemy.com

      www.lecturio.com

      FB TonyHuntsBooksandVideos

Printed in Dunstable, United Kingdom